Sage
Along the Way

A Novel

By
Cassandra Miller
Author of *Toasting Cora*

To Nancy,
From your very
kind sister,
(and me) —
Cheers,
Cassandra

Chelsea K Publications
Mukilteo, WA
Copyright © Cassandra Miller, 2015
All rights reserved.
ISBN 978-0-9755721-1-5

Acknowledgements

Many thanks to my dear friend Amy West, who provided a glimpse into
the world of a talented hair stylist.
To my editor Jackie King, who took on this arduous task
in the midst of her own sorrow. Thank you for your grace,
gentle guidance and clarity of vision.
To all my grandchildren, present and future. May you grow up in a more
enlightened world. And if that is not possible,
may you all strive to make it so.
And to my amazing husband Rob, who has expanded my world into
unimaginable dimensions and fulfilled dreams
I had never dared to dream. I love you.

Cover designed by N.K. Fox

This book is dedicated to my own personal Cora, Mabel Booth.
She embraced me as her own and loved me fiercely,
without agenda or expectations.
Missing you, Mabel, today and always.

The first problem for all of us, men and women, is not to learn, but to unlearn.

~Gloria Steinem

**History, despite its wrenching pain, cannot be unlived, but if faced with courage,
need not be lived again.**

~Maya Angelou

CHAPTER ONE

Standing in line at my local Starbucks, I pondered my many choices for morning fortification and tried not to listen to the conversation behind me. "She has such a wonderful personality," the not-quite-elderly woman was saying. "You'd love her, I just know it. Won't you let me introduce you to her?"

"Mom, I know you mean well, but I'm just not ready to meet anyone yet, let alone the nice girl at your dentist's office. How can you possibly know enough about her to think that we'd have anything in common?"

I smiled. The poor man, having a living, breathing stereotype for a mother. Obviously he had no idea how lucky he was.

"Well, I know that she's about the right age, maybe a little younger than you, and cute, very cute, and…"

"And she has a wonderful personality, I know. Tell me, have you shared this little plan of yours with her?"

"Just enough to find out she's single and willing to meet someone."

My turn to order: "Double tall nonfat latté, please."

Meddling Mom lowered her voice slightly. "Listen to that. Coffee's so complicated now. But that's a girl who knows what she wants."

"Mom, please."

If I'd had the courage, I would have turned around and smiled at her, given her a little encouragement so she would know that someone appreciated her observations. But my brain was foggy in the pre-coffee hours, and I would no doubt have emitted misleading signals. Amazing how a nice coffee buzz—not trembling-hands-intense, but just this side of jittery—cleared the cobwebs and made me feel suddenly clever and articulate. As I moved over to the pickup counter, carefully not glancing behind me, I wondered what it would be like to have a wonderful personality, *sans* caffeine.

I've encountered such people: women who glide effortlessly from one conversation to another at a party, delighting everyone with their witty little anecdotes that fit each topic perfectly. Women who tread just this side of cynical, earning such descriptions as Urbane and Well Read. Women who are remembered as more beautiful than they really are. How did one acquire such a winning demeanor?

"Double tall nonfat latté!" the barista called as she placed my order on the counter.

"Thank you," I said. I always said thank you and I always left a generous tip. I wanted to be thought of as a good customer. My face may have been forgettable and I may not have had a personality to speak of before my morning java, but at least I could safely say the coffee vendors didn't dread my presence.

Glancing at my watch, I smiled. Ahead of schedule. So, I chose a corner table for two to share a few precious moments with my newspaper and latté.

I sipped and read the bad news, savoring the smell of coffee, truly one of the greatest pleasures in life. Well, my life anyway.

Looking up, my eyes met those of a woman who could only be the smothering mother. She smiled at me. She waved. Her son stared at his shoes. I returned her smile, then escaped into the latest developments in the Middle East.

"She's awfully, cute, Sam. Why don't you go talk to her?"

"Mom, I told you, I'm not ready. Now can we please just drink our coffee?"

Cute. Now I was the cute one? Was everyone cute in her eyes? I peered as discreetly as possible over the top of my paper. Actually, Sam was fairly cute himself: fortyish, sandy hair, pale eyes. But clearly he wasn't interested in me; it was only his mother who appreciated my charms. Allowing myself one more peek, I saw Sam himself looking my way; before I could pretend to look at something on the table, he caught me looking back. Caffeine had begun flowing through my veins, and I summoned its power now, for courage. Lowering the paper just enough for Sam to see the rest of my face, I smiled. He did the same—nice smile!—and as I was about to pretend to read again, he mouthed the word "Sorry."

I shook my head, waving off his apology. His mother only wanted him to be happily attached. She wanted love for her son. Nothing wrong with that, really, though I was sure her methods could be a bit maddening.

Sam looked at his watch. "Mom, we really need to leave if we're going to get you to the doctor's office on time."

"Oh pshaw." She actually said 'pshaw.' "The way they keep me waiting? I don't mind being a little late." And, to my horror, she very decisively stood up and walked to my table.

"Mom!" Sam called in vain.

"Hello, dear. My name is Molly Logan, and that squirming man back there is my son, Sam. You have such a lovely smile, I just had to say good morning and introduce myself. I hope I'm not intruding." And Molly Logan sat down at my table.

"Not at all." I hoped I sounded sincere. "I'm Sage Whitaker."

"Sage. How unusual! I like unusual names, but my husband was set on either Samuel, which was tolerable, or Barbara, a name I cannot abide. Thank heavens I didn't have a girl! Now, down to business. Age has taken away all traces of shyness, if there ever were any, and probably a few of my manners as well. So, I'm just going to tell you why I've accosted you this way. My son's marriage officially ended several months ago. He has a thirteen-year-old daughter. She's a very good girl, though a bit spoiled. Sam needs to start dating again, and he just doesn't quite know how. He thinks I'm meddlesome and interfering, but he'll thank me if I find the perfect woman for him. By the way, I never liked his wife, not from the minute I laid eyes on her. But you I have a good feeling about. Now, are you single?"

"I am, but to be honest, I'm not dating at the moment."

"Hmm. Broken heart, right? Thought you'd met Mr. Right and he turned into Mr. Hyde? You poor thing. Did he abuse you? There's so much of that going around these days. What's wrong with the men in our society? How have we bred this generation of monsters? Of course, now they say it was always happening but people ignored it, hushed it up. Who knows? Anyway, just because you met one mean old apple doesn't mean the whole bushel should be tossed out."

My chest felt tight, the air heavy. Who was this woman? How could she know so much? All I wanted was to get away from her, fast.

"Actually, I enjoy it. Being alone, I mean," I said, trying to sound dismissive.

"Nonsense. You know, honey, life is so short. You hear it all the time, but honestly, you're young and strong and suddenly one day you look in the mirror and see a very old stranger. Everyone knows it will happen, but no one really believes it until it does. And getting old is the best-case scenario, it's not guaranteed. You might not make it that long. You never know when a train is pulling away from the station and chugging full steam ahead to run you down. Do you really want to die alone?"

"Mrs. Logan..."

"Molly, please. Mrs. Logan was what my mother-in-law insisted I call her until the day she died. I'm Molly."

I sighed, relaxing a little. "Molly. I understand that your intentions are good, but I don't think I'll sign up for your matchmaking services today. I'm sorry, but I have to run now or I'll be late for work. But I do promise I'll stay away from trains today."

"Run, run, run, that's all you poor young people do. Here," she said, rummaging through her enormous purse. She brought out a pen, then took the napkin from under my coffee cup and scribbled on it. "This is Sam's name and number. Call him when you change your mind. He's a very nice man. Not an abusive bone in his body, you can trust me on that," she whispered loudly.

I stuffed the napkin in my coat pocket. "Thank you. It was nice to meet you, Molly."

"You too, dear." She held her hand out to shake mine. Hers felt cool, the skin thin and fragile, spotted wildly purple; her hands looked so much older than her face.

I smiled, squeezing her hand gently. "I hope I see you again sometime," I said, and I meant it. Breathing a little easier, I looked back at her and waved before pushing through the exit door. Sitting alone at the table Molly had abandoned, Sam stared at the floor, shaking his head.

In my car, I wondered about Molly. Had she somehow actually sensed something about Colin's abuse? Was it written on my face? *No*, I told myself, *she's just heard the statistics somewhere and drew a possible conclusion. If she makes the same assumption about all the women she encounters, she'll be right*—I'd read this just recently—*more than a quarter of the time. It was simply the luck of the draw that I was the one she asked.*

Then, in spite of myself, I thought about Sam. What had happened to his marriage? Was he, too, a victim of some form of abuse? Molly had never liked his ex-wife: why? Was Molly difficult to please? Or, was the ex-wife truly a horrible human being who neglected her child and took her perfect husband completely for granted? Did *she* have a wonderful personality?

I thought about Sam's face: very pleasant smile, nice eyes; they were green, I thought, or maybe light blue like his mother's. Hmm.

Pulling into my customary parking spot, I shook the thought away before it fully formed. All thoughts of Sam and Molly were hereby banished. Sam and Molly? Where had I heard that combination before? Had I met a couple with those names somewhere?

I walked to my desk, still trying to place the elusive couple, but the question was blown out of my mind by a sour wind. Waiting for me, taped to the phone on my desk, was a message from everyone's least favorite client, the aptly named Mrs. Crow. She had belonged to everyone at one time or another, bounced from one caseworker to the next in a vain attempt to find a workable fit. But Mrs. Crow just could not, would not fit, she would not fit one little bit. (I recited that twisted little Seussian rhyme to myself each time Mrs. Crow resurfaced.) Now, the newest team member was always given the territory in which Mrs. Crow resided: a cruel initiation ritual borne of necessity. Few people could stand dealing with the woman for more than a few months at a time.

My work history, a series of meaningless clerical jobs, had left me feeling devoid of worth. What was I contributing to the world, I'd ask the mirror each morning before trotting off for my day of filing and typing letters. So, I begged for a loan from my brother and returned to college. I'd started with only about a year's worth of credits. Going back was hard, working all day, attending class and studying at night. It took five long years, but I finally graduated. Social work degree in hand, I dutifully—and ecstatically—applied to my nearest social services office.

There I met Althea Markham, the manager of the division. She was plainly skeptical of my naïve, earnest desire to help the poor and wretched, but the department was perpetually understaffed. Against her better judgment, I'm sure, she hired me on the spot.

Althea was a great boss: kind, fair, but tough when she had to be. She was a beautiful, ageless African-American woman who dressed in a seemingly endless array of animal print skirts and tunics. Her jewelry was similarly exotic—chunky pieces that I loved but could never get away with. On Althea, they looked perfect.

I was so thrilled and grateful to be on Althea's team that I promised, rather melodramatically, to make her proud. She was amused; even I could see that, but neither of us acknowledged it. I was too happy. I was a Social Worker at last, specializing in serving the needs of elderly and disabled adults. From the frying pan, I had run headlong into the fire.

It had never occurred to me that there might be unappreciative or even belligerent clients; I was there to help, after all. I had imagined only sweet, cookie baking, wise but financially unfortunate ladies who would greet me with a hug and thank me tearfully for the miracles I would bring to their lives. And, to be honest, there were a couple of those wonderful women in the messy mix of my caseload. Of course I had little time to devote to them because so much of it was dedicated to addressing the complaints of Mrs. Crow and her ilk.

I knew that Mrs. Crow's first name was Elma, but I would never dare use the name in her presence. In bright red block letters across the front page of her very thick file, the first unfortunate soul who had worked with her had written the warning: DO NOT CALL HER ELMA!!!! The consequent horrors of doing so must have been excruciating. So, I'd never made that mistake. Oh, but there were so many other traps to fall into, so many ways to rouse her boundless ire.

Mrs. Crow loved to abuse her state-subsidized home care assistants. Mrs. Crow's assistants, in fact, were replaced much more frequently than were her rotating caseworkers. Mona, the homecare assistants' supervisor, would oblige each employee's refusal to return to Elma's home—sometimes after a month, sometimes a week. Often, the poor assistant lasted only one visit. Then, because Elma Crow was such a problematic client, Mona was obliged to accompany the newest sacrifice into the lion's lair.

There, in the presence of Elma's new assistant, Mona would patiently explain the rules to Elma yet again: there was no outside work. No lawn mowing, no outside window washing. No planting of spring bulbs, no weeding in the garden. Her helper was not to stand on chairs, ladders or stools to clean light fixtures or ceilings. No lifting of heavy objects.

"Doesn't everyone turn the mattress each time they change the sheets?" Mrs. Crow would scream each time. "Doesn't everyone move the refrigerator to sweep the kitchen floor? What kind of place are you running?"

Mona would ignore her objections and continue: the assistant may take you to the store and to medical appointments, but not to the local bar for a few cocktails, much as that might improve the situation—at least temporarily—for all concerned.

When the rule review was over once again and Mona had emerged, slightly battle-scarred, she would call me with an update. Here she was again, before I had time to dial Mrs. Crow's number—a number I had memorized but always looked up anyway just to buy myself a few

more moments to prepare—"Sage, you've got to help me. Elma…"—
while we would never speak the forbidden name in front of the woman,
we took an admittedly perverse pleasure in using it *ad nauseum* with
each other—"is totally abusing her homecare assistant again. She's even
calling it a maid service now. Can we at least reduce her allotted hours?"

"If only she didn't need transportation. That's the only thing she
needs that's considered personal care. Without that she wouldn't qualify
for services at all."

Mona sighed. "If only. But since her stroke she really does need
to be driven to her medical appointments."

Now I sighed. "Let's do another joint visit. I guess it's time to
give her the Stern Warning chat again. I can go over all her tasks and see
if I can at least cut back on her hours a little. How many people has she
gone through lately?"

"She's on her fourth this month! I've finally relented, Sage. I've
actually started sending her my absolute best worker. I hate to do that,
punish my employees for being good, but if anyone can make this
woman happy it will be Michelle."

"Michelle Coulter? She's great! I've never heard anything
negative about her. Poor Michelle, she's too sweet to be thrown to such
a nasty wolf. Are you giving her a bonus or something?"

"No, I can't. But I'm making cookies for her. Yeah, let's do the
visit. Do you want to set it up, or should I?"

"How about if you set it up as a routine visit, and we'll ambush
her. What do you think?"

"Perfect. Thank you, Sage. I'll call to let you know when the
queen has granted an interview."

"Okey dokey."

That was how it worked: I conducted a visit to a new client's
home to determine eligibility for a variety of services, some of which
involved help with household chores and transportation. I would grant
permission for whatever services were needed, then turn them over to
another agency to implement and oversee the services on a daily basis.
Calling me in to help with the Elma situation was calling in the big guns,
at least in theory.

In truth, I had no real power. Problem clients would pretty much
have to commit a felony to be kicked out of the program. Government-
run programs do not want to be sued by an elderly woman or her family,

no matter how evil she may be. If she qualified for services, she received them: till death do us part.

Fourteen months on the job as a professional helper had cured me of the need to help. I longed for the money-grubbing private sector once again. The grass really had been greener over there, or so it seemed now.

I wrote in my planner under today's date: *Spoke with Mona about meeting with EC. She'll call.*

Turning to my to-do list, I was about to dive in when the phone rang again. Panic set in, and I began my silent chant: *Don't be Elma, don't be Elma, don't be...* "Community Support Services, this is Sage, may I help you?" I was hopeful it wasn't the Dreaded One; she usually didn't let me finish my Cheerful Greeting.

"Hello?" someone asked.

"Yes, this is Sage. May I help you?"

"Oh, Sage. It's Ruth, honey. How are you?"

I exhaled, well... sighed with unqualified relief, actually. "Hi, Ruth. It's so nice to hear from you. How are things going?"

It was one of my sweet little cookie bakers. She was very sweet indeed, very small, and made very good cookies which she insisted I eat straight out of the oven during my visits, and take a few with me for later. Of course I always objected at first, mildly, but Ruth would have been devastated if I'd ever actually resisted her attempts to fatten me up.

"Oh, I'm fine. I just can't remember when you're coming to see me. I think I forgot to write it down, and my memory isn't what it used to be. I'm so sorry to bother you."

"It's no bother at all. Let me just look at my schedule." I paused, shuffling papers on my desk. "Ruth? It looks like we're not due for a visit until next month." I knew this without really looking at my schedule, because I had just seen her three days earlier.

"That long?" She was disappointed. So was I. When services were going smoothly and there were no new health issues, I wasn't really supposed to see clients so often. But every month I made up a reason to visit Ruth so that we could share stories, drink coffee and eat cookies together; that's what I told myself, but really it was to see her eyes light up when she saw me at the door and feel her soft, warm hug good-bye.

Those moments reminded me that I did occasionally make a difference.

"Yeah, next month. On the fifth. Unless something's changed?"

"No, no, everything's the same."

"How is your homecare worker doing?"

"Who?"

"Trina. How is she working out?"

"Oh, Trina! She's just wonderful. That girl works so hard, I have to twist her arm to get her to sit down and take a break. Are you the one who sends her to me?"

"No, not really. Her supervisor is Mona."

"Oh. Mona's a nice girl, too. You know them both?"

"Well, I've met Trina a couple of times. Remember, I'm the one who comes out and asks about all the things you need her for. I'm the one who can increase your time with her if you need more help."

"That's right. I'm sorry, honey. My memory just isn't what it used to be, you know."

"That's okay, Ruth. Neither is mine. But I'll remember to come visit you next month."

"How nice. I'll bake cookies."

"Thanks, Ruth. I'm so glad you called. See you on the fifth."

After we said good-bye, I stared at the phone, an instrument I had come to despise, except when it brought such gentle voices as Ruth's into my little world. I no longer wanted to be a social worker, it was true, but this job had taught me one important lesson. I now knew what kind of old person I wanted to be.

When the phone rang again, my skin tingled: a precursor to crawling. The clock on my desk read 8:44. I had been on duty for fourteen minutes and had not yet returned Elma's call. I was sure beyond reason, beyond hope that Elma Crow's voice would be the next one I'd hear.

Squaring my shoulders, I prepared for the role of Tough Service-Authorizing Social Worker. I took a deep breath and picked up the receiver.

"Community Support Services, this is..."

"Ha! You *are* there! Don't you ever return your calls?"

"Hello, Mrs. Crow. What can I do for you?"

My co-workers, hearing the name, stood up and peered over the walls of their cubicles.

Elma snickered. "You're pathetic. You make me sick. What you can do for me is tell that goddamn Mona to get the hell off my back.

'Oh, I'm sending you my best worker, Mrs. Crow.' Sniveling little worm. Best worker my foot. Rich little princess, more like it. Thinks she's doing us poor folks a favor. Thinks she's better than us. Big ol' diamond on her finger. Well, I don't want a housekeeper who's just going to be off on her Hawaiian honeymoon in a month. Don't you people have anyone who can do a decent day's work AND stick around for a while?"

Since I do appreciate the ability to hear, I was now holding the phone away from my ear; Queen Elma was still very audible. When she paused I responded, "Well, I have only heard good things about Michelle's work from other clients, Mrs. Crow."

"Most people are afraid to stand up for themselves. Not me!" You can say that again. "I'm not stupid, you know. That Michelle is getting married. You think a Little Miss Rich Britches like that is going to keep working once she's married? Not on your life."

"Are you saying that you'd like to keep her if she decides to stay on?" I happened to know Michelle Coulter was indeed planning on keeping her job; Little Miss Rich Britches couldn't afford to quit working.

Elma was momentarily speechless. "I didn't say that," she sputtered at last.

"So you have complaints about her work?"

"None of those girls work the way I would! But you won't let them! All those rules… never heard of such nonsense. Crap, I tell you, it's just a bunch of crap!"

"But within the crappy rules, Michelle does a good job?"

"Don't know yet, do I? She's only been here a couple of times."

Yeah, and you don't know yet whether you can bully her into doing more than she should. There was no getting around it. I was going to have to set up the meeting myself.

"Mrs. Crow, Mona called me this morning. She's very concerned about the number of helpers you've dismissed this month."

"Concerned? I'm concerned, that's who's concerned."

"We'd like to meet with you to talk about it. What would be a good day for you this week?"

"This week? It's Thursday!"

"That's right. So, would you prefer today or tomorrow?"

"Fine! Tomorrow."

"Morning or afternoon?"

"Morning, just like every other goddamn time you've been here. I'm in too much pain by the afternoon."

"All right. How about nine o'clock?" I crossed my fingers, thinking: *That way I can sleep in a bit and go directly from home— with a stop for coffee on the way of course.*

"I don't care."

"Okay. See you at nine tomorrow."

Once again, after hanging up, I watched the phone warily, treacherous beast that it was. My fellow social workers shrank back into their assigned spaces, all looking slightly relieved that I had survived Mrs. Crow's squawking, and, I'm sure, that it was no longer their turn to deal with her.

My shoulders drooped. Tough Social Worker was an exhausting persona. Rising from my state-authorized wheeled office chair, I went to check on the status of the community coffee pot. If I poured the last dredge for myself, I would be obliged to make a new pot. Ideally, there would be enough for at least two full cups, and I would be off the hook. I knew I shouldn't think that way; I should whistle a happy tune while preparing fresh coffee for my wonderful co-SW's, but after a conversation with Elma I just wasn't feeling so altruistic.

I was in luck: half a pot! Pouring coffee into my designated office cup—the one with the pink *You're Special!* inscription—I thought again about Molly and Sam. Why was that pair of names so familiar?

And it came to me at last: the movie *Ghost.* Patrick Swayze and Demi Moore were Sam and Molly! He had been a hard-working ghost, trying to prevent Molly's death, thus ensuring their permanent separation. And here was another Molly, a Mother Molly, trying desperately to hook her son up with a woman, thus diminishing her own role in his life. Interesting. Too bad I would never know how their story ends.

Full cup in hand, I went back to my desk to call Mona about tomorrow's meeting.

I looked forward to two events in my workday: my visit to Starbucks in the morning, and my afternoon phone call from my brother. Reliable as Seattle rain, Jamieson never failed to brighten my otherwise miserable day.

His call usually came between 3:30 and 4:00; he wanted to make sure I'd have time to tidy my desk and return last minute phone calls, and still dash out of the office at 4:30 on the dot. He knew I had become a clock-watcher.

Today I was impatient for Jamie's voice. He'd been distant lately, preoccupied, and I was beginning to worry. My watch read 4:10; he was late, today of all days. In spite of his many warnings not to, I seriously considered calling him at work. But his appointments might be running late today. A favorite client might want something new and exciting done to her hair. And the management at the salon frowned on incoming personal calls. No, I'd just have to wait until he could take a break and call me.

I picked up the phone on the first ring and skipped most of my usual greeting. "This is Sage," I said hopefully.

"Hey, Sagey, how's your day, doll?"

"Ohmygod it's great to hear your voice."

"Having a rough one, honey?"

"You have no idea. How about you?"

"It's been marvelous. My three favorite clients came in. One for a trim and two for special occasion run-throughs. All on the same day, can you imagine? So of course I'm running late, since I had to pay special attention to them. But it was so much fun. Sorry you're having a bad time, doll. Why don't you come down after work? You're due for a cut. It'll make you feel better."

"Sibling discount?" That was code for 'free.'

Jamie lowered his voice to a stage whisper. "Sherry the terrible is here today. I'll have to get you to pay, then I'll pay you back."

I considered this. If I paid up front, that was cash out of my pocket I didn't really have, and the salon charged a premium for Jamie's haircuts. He would then have to pay me back out of his own funds. Altogether an unsatisfactory arrangement. "How about you come over tonight and cut my hair at my place?"

He sighed deeply. Jamie hated performing his magic anywhere but at his station at the salon, where all his tools were laid out in a certain order and the lighting was right. Lighting was a very big deal for Jamie. "I have a better idea. How about we get together for dinner and a bottle of wine, my treat, and save the cut for another night?"

"Really? You and Jake don't have plans tonight?"

Another sigh. "Okay. Don't freak out, Sage, but Jake and I are no more."

"What? When did that happen?"

"Oh, I don't know. A couple of weeks ago? Six months, maybe? Who knows when these things actually die?"

"Why didn't you say anything?"

"I didn't want you to worry or think you have to take care of me."

"Too late. You're my baby brother. I'll always feel that way. What went wrong?"

"He just wasn't the one, sweetheart. We had some fun, and now it's done. Ooh, I should write a song!"

"When did he move out?"

"That was the two weeks ago part of it. We knew it was over a long time before that."

"I knew something was wrong! You've been so swishy lately. You're only swishy when you're upset. I should have asked. I'm sorry."

"Oh, Sagey, I'm all right. Please don't fuss. Listen, I have to run. We'll talk more tonight. Let's meet at that little bistro by your office. I can't get out of here before 7:00. Can you wait until 7:30?"

"Sure, I'll go get coffee and read."

"You have a serious caffeine problem, Sage. See you at 7:30."

An excuse to sit alone in my favorite Starbucks, read a trashy novel and sip my aromatic personality potion while anticipating dinner with my beautiful baby brother? Life simply didn't get any better than that, at least not at the moment.

Utterly drained from my day of giving, I ordered my latté robotically. But I waited patiently and thanked the barista sincerely when she handed me the warm, frothy elixir of life.

I sat, glancing occasionally at the more interesting faces passing by, leaping in and out of the world of my paperback: a world in which all heroines were brilliant and beautiful, all evil-doers ugly. Wouldn't it be nice if the truly evil were so recognizable? If all physical ugliness were reserved for those most deserving of such a burden?

Jamie was blessed in so many ways. Gorgeous from the day he was born, his hair thick and nearly black, his eyes bright blue. Cornflower blue, I've heard them called. I remember staring at Jamie's face in wonder, even when he was an infant. I would look in the mirror and wonder, "Was I adopted?"

But I know I wasn't. Jamie looked like our mother, who was quite a beauty herself. And I looked just like pictures I'd seen of our father's sisters when they were young, cursed with a slight pudginess I couldn't seem to exercise away, skin that was once a perfect breeding ground for pimples and now bore the scars and blotches to prove it, a nose that was ever so slightly too big for my face, eyes that were somewhere between nondescript blue and unremarkable green. I had nice legs, though, everyone said so, and my hair, a few shades lighter than Jamie's, was long and thick, with just a little curl. People said they envied me my legs and my hair. I envied them everything else.

Sipping and reading, reading and sipping, I felt a little joy, a little energy, a little hope blooming throughout my veins. Jamie was single again. I was truly sad for him, sorry for his loss, but in the blackest, most selfish corner of my heart I was thrilled that he would be more available to me.

Another warm sip. I smiled. I loved my baby brother so much it frightened me sometimes. It always amazed me when seemingly bright people screamed about the evils of homosexuality; people who would picket to fight against gay people being given the same basic human rights that everyone else takes for granted. They believed that people like Jamie had chosen a wicked path and that God would punish them. Sanctioning such an immoral "lifestyle" would itself be wrong in God's eyes, they would say. But when my five-year-old brother looked up at me with those Jamie-colored eyes and told me that he wanted to marry Mr. Watkins the mailman, I knew he was different. Different, but perfect. This was not a choice made by a sinful person. This was simply how *he* was made.

On Gay Pride Day once, I was on my way to meet Jamie downtown for the parade when I walked past an angry-looking man holding a religious-themed sign. I said, "God made my brother gay. Does God make mistakes?"

The man turned toward me, purple-faced and, I swear, spitting with every word he said, "YOUR BROTHER IS DAMNED, MISSY, AND SO ARE YOU IF YOU DO NOTHING TO STOP HIM."

Smiling sweetly, I said, "You are a hateful and ignorant man, sir, and you do not speak for my God."

Walking away, I trembled a little as I always did after such an encounter. Scary Man continued to scream after me. "I SPEAK FOR THE ONLY GOD THERE IS. I SPEAK FOR THE ALPHA AND THE OMEGA, FOR THE FATHER, THE SON AND THE HOLY SPIRIT. YOUR BROTHER WILL ROT IN HELL FOR HIS SINS!"

I kept walking, and finally he gave up, presumably to continue his dutiful picketing. The sign he carried, bearing it like a cross, read *Remember Sodom. If you pray, you won't be gay.*

I shuddered now, remembering the look of searing, sneering hatred on the man's face. Hatred for someone he had never met. Tears of frustration and anger had made my eyes red and puffy by the time I'd caught up with Jamie that day.

"What is it?" he'd asked.

"Nothing worthy of your time," I'd responded, and quickly changed the subject. My brother was the most moral person I knew. Yes, he broke some of his boss' rules, but always for the benefit of others (mainly mine). Jamie was at heart honest, kind, and compassionate. He was so empathetic he nearly lost himself sometimes, picking up on the pain of others like a radio receiver. If I had shared the story of the picketer with Jamie, he would have told me to stop wasting my energy on a lost cause, and he actually would have felt sorry for the man.

Even Dad, I thought. I winced, as another memory intruded: Jamie, cowering, Dad, monstrous, belt in hand, whipping it down over and over as I cried and begged him to stop. "Please, Dad, you'll kill him! Please stop hurting him!" His face as he knocked me away, red and twisted with hate. So much hate. *I have to save Jamie,* I thought, and it was my only thought as I leaped onto my father's back and yanked the belt out of his hand. "Run, Jamie!" I yelled, and he went to the door. He stood there, hesitating, and finally said, "I'm sorry, Daddy. Please don't hurt Sagey," before he ran at last, out the door and down the street to my friend Chloe's house, where her mother, Mary, would stand guard.

My father smashed me into a wall, knocking me off his back. I remember him moving in slowly then, moving toward me with seemingly nothing more in mind than to hurt me, to shut me up, to make me obey. I could smell his sweat and his beer as he closed in on me and I knew I would never be able to get away. In my memory it's all in slow motion, but I know it didn't really happen that way. I know he really only hesitated a moment before the beating began.

At some point I woke up on the floor and tried not to move, in case he was still there. Finally, I whispered, "Daddy?"

I heard nothing, so I started to get up. Everything hurt, but I managed to get to my feet. I looked in the hall mirror. My eyes were puffy and there was a huge bruise on one cheek. My head ached, but I seemed to be in one piece. And Jamie was safe.

The coast was clear to the front door, but he was still in the house, I could hear him somewhere—the bathroom? The kitchen? I had to move quickly and quietly. But as I closed the door behind me, I heard the sound that signaled the end of my father's tirade…the sobbing. His anger had subsided for the night and he was crying himself to sleep in his favorite chair. I knew he wouldn't come after us. I limped down the sidewalk toward Chloe's house and Mary was already running in my direction, on her way to save me. She scooped me up in her arms, even though I was nearly ten at the time.

"You are not going back to that house," she said as she cleaned my wounds.

But Jamie, his arms and legs covered with red welts, said, "We have to go back. We're all he has. Besides, he might hurt you, Mary, if we stay." He cried then, for me, for himself, but for our father, too.

Now I glanced at my watch and gathered my belongings. I tossed my empty cup into the garbage and waved at the barista on my way out. "Thank you!" I said airily, and went to meet my brother.

~3~

"Tell me about Jake," I said, after we'd hugged and sat down.

Jamie sighed, rolling his eyes to the ceiling. "I don't know, honey. I guess we just knew we wouldn't live happily ever after, so we decided to let each other go. You know, so we can both keep looking for the fairy tale, so to speak."

"That's very grown up of both of you. Jake really just ended it with you that way? So gracefully?"

"Sure he did. Why? Is that hard for you to believe?"

"Well, yeah, a little. He never really seemed that—well, mature, I guess."

"Uh huh. Well, you may have a point. But after he cheated on me three times—and got caught each time—he really felt we should handle things maturely."

"Oh, Jamie. I'm sorry. But I am so mad at you! Why didn't you tell me?"

"I know I should have. I think I just needed some time alone to lick my wounds. Is that wrong?"

I squeezed his hand. "No, I guess not. I just want you to remember that I'm here for you, okay?"

"I know you are, sweetheart. To a fault, I'd say. How long has it been since you went on a date?"

"You're deflecting."

"So be it. You're deflect-worthy. How long? Come on, 'fess up."

I mumbled something he couldn't hear.

"Huh? What was that?"

"I don't know! Six weeks maybe."

"Too long. Do you want me to fix you up?"

"No! The last time was a disaster."

"Brent? He was nice!"

"He was gay!"

"He was curious about women. He was probably a closet heterosexual."

"He spent the whole night crying about his last boyfriend."

"Okay, it was a mistake. But I do have straight friends."

"No thanks. I'm sure I'll find someone eventually."

"Do it soon, sweetheart. You need to find a decent guy. Me, I'm diving right back into the dating pool."

"Any hot prospects?"

"No. It's so depressing. Did you ever notice that when you're attached, you see someone and think, 'ooh, definite sparks there, wonder what he's like?' Well, those someones just go on their merry little ways and then suddenly you're free as a bird and you have no idea how to find them again! It's so sad. 'The people that you never get to love…'"

"Is that from a movie?"

"No, silly, it's a song. Rupert Holmes. You know, the guy who wrote The Piña Colada Song!"

"Pretty obscure, Jamieson."

"My point is, when you're available, you don't seem to have those 'wow!' moments. Must be one of Murphy's Laws, don't you think? But you'll have no trouble, once you start actually looking. You're gorgeous these days, sis!"

"Liar. We both know who got the pretty genes. My guess is you won't be single a full month before Mr. Right comes along."

"From your lips, Sage…"

"Hey, I want to tell you about this guy I saw this morning at Starbucks."

"Was he cute?"

"Very. He was with his mother. She was cute, too. She was trying to find a woman for him. They were behind me in line, and I overheard their whole conversation. First, she tried to talk him into a set up with a woman who works in her dentist's office, then she zeroed in on me."

"You?"

"Yes! She actually sat at my table and asked all about me. Told me how wonderful her son is, and that he's getting over a divorce. He has a daughter."

"Are you going to go out with him?"

"No! He told her he's not ready. But he did smile at me."

"Bingo! Mixed messages. You need to attack now, while you can."

"He was just being nice. He didn't give me his number, his mother did."

"She gave you his number? Jump on it, doll!"

"No, Jamie. If he's not ready, it's not the right time. My point was that he's got this great mom who wants him to be happy. It was just nice to see."

"Yeah, I know. I always envy people who have really great parents. But at least I have you."

"I like to think there really are these amazing families out there, happy, loving, supportive of each other. Why are some people born into families like that and others...well, you know."

"You can't wonder about those things, Sage, it will make you crazy. Some people's lives are easier than others, that's all. Everyone has problems, but some are worse than others. You just can't be defeated by hardship. You have to be strong enough to overcome it, otherwise you spend your life wallowing. How can that be healthy? Besides, we have a fabulous family now."

"I know, I know. I'm not wallowing, I just thought it was a nice little encounter with a really sweet mom and her son."

"What were their names?"

"Molly and Sam."

"Like in *Ghost!*"

"I knew you'd get that right away. Took me half the morning."

"Molly. What a neat name for an older woman. It sounds so young and hip. Anyway, maybe you should keep going to Starbucks, honey. Maybe next time it will be Lily and her son Eddie. Or Lucy and Little Ricky. Hmm. Maybe I've been watching too much classic TV lately."

"Maybe. How about Juliet and Romeo Junior? And there will have been no divorce, and he'll be ripe and ready to waltz down the aisle. Will you give me away?"

"Only if you return the favor. Oh, I can't wait to be Uncle Jamie. 'Uncle Jamie would you read me a story? Uncle Jamie, would you tie my shoe? Uncle Jamie, would you help me pick out a prom dress?'"

"You'd be a wonderful uncle."

"I *will* be a wonderful uncle. It's going to happen, sweetheart. You're only thirty-seven. You still have time."

"That clock is getting really loud, though, and there's no daddy in sight. I don't know, maybe it's just not meant to be."

"There are endless possibilities for your life, Sage. Don't close any doors just yet."

"Maybe I should think about in-vitro."

"I know a lot of guys who'd be proud to be your donor. But it's really expensive, and there's no guarantee."

"True. I'd prefer to do it the old-fashioned way, but it's nice to have another option if I get desperate."

"Just don't be desperate yet. I'll let you know when it's time for desperation."

"Thanks, I'll count on it. So where are you going to look for your next guy?"

"Through friends, I suppose. Not fix-ups, exactly, just opportunities. Dinner parties, clubbing, you know. You and Chloe should join us one night. What do you say?"

"I'd like that. It's been a while since I've been able to drag her away from Professor Predator for a girls' night out. It would be good for her."

"Sagey, you can't call him that anymore. They've been together for sixteen years."

"So? She was a child—and his student—when they met!"

"She was twenty-one, and they didn't date until the class ended."

"And he was thirty–five and in a position of authority."

"He wasn't married, didn't leave small children behind or anything like that. They love each other. Sometimes it's that simple. I'm not crazy about the guy, but he seems to be devoted to Chloe."

"And they're still not married, I might add. Chloe always wanted children, but because Dr. Despot doesn't, they're not having any. No wedding, either. I just think Chloe could do better, that's all."

"All this coming from the undisputed relationship expert of the world, of course."

"That's not fair."

"You're right, doll, it's not fair at all. And you're not being fair either. Chloe seems very…well, at least content with Paul, from what I've seen anyway, and I'm sure she would be thrilled if you'd give him a chance. Hasn't he earned it by now?"

I scowled at the table. I knew he was probably right; he usually was. The truth, at least in part, was that I couldn't bear to see Chloe so settled and domestic. I'd wanted her to be single with me. Secretly, deep in my damaged heart, I'd entertained fantasies that we'd simultaneously meet the perfect men, get married in a double ceremony and have children at roughly the same time, so that they would grow up together as we had. Alas, this was apparently not to be.

When Chloe fell in love with Professor Paul Dailey, I thought it was a temporary glitch. Now, sixteen years later, here I was still waiting for the glitch to get lost. Instead, they had become more inseparable, traveling to Europe and South America, and adding onto their lovely home overlooking Lake Washington. Nearly a perfect picture of domestic bliss; nearly, because Chloe had truly, desperately wanted to be a mother.

Paul felt it was immoral to bring more children into a world already bulging at the seams. "Studies show that this planet could comfortably feed and support one billion people. Our population has now surpassed that number by seven times, and no one seems to have noticed," he was fond of saying. Chloe would gaze wistfully past him when he pontificated on the subject, but she felt badly for her fellow Earthlings who could not feed themselves and so she reluctantly agreed they would not add to the problem.

I, on the other hand, was teetering on despair that I would never be able to add to the surplus of earthbound humans, and felt sad for Chloe's diminishing opportunity to do the same.

Occasionally, I tried to argue with Paul. "But surely you'd agree that you and Chloe would be able to feed a child just fine. Don't you think we need a generation of responsibly raised and nutritiously fed children? Those children will grow up to be in a position to nurture the planet and make it better for others. You owe it to the world to bring up a child who will help improve the situation. You know Chloe would be an amazing mother."

Each time I presented this airtight logic, he would look at Chloe, nod, and say, "Yes, she would be a wonderful mother. But it would have to be with a different partner. I will not be part of the problem."

"What about adoption? You could help solve the problem by adopting a child from a poor country." I asked this once, and once only.

His response? "I don't want traumatized children. They might never overcome their difficult beginnings. They might become delinquent."

"I hate him," I mumbled now.

"Well, there's an intelligent response," Jamie countered.

"I can't help it. Chloe seems, I don't know. Just low grade sad all the time. It's been worse lately. Something's wrong, I know it."

"You know it, or you're hoping for it?"

"Both! Neither. I don't know. Let's order. I'm grouchy when I'm hungry."

"Really? I hadn't noticed."

"Don't be mad at me. I love you."

"I'm not mad." He sighed. "But I think you need more than food. You need a man. At least for an hour or two."

I nodded. "I know. I think I'm going through withdrawal."

"Me too. Let's eat, and then we'll share something decadent."

"Drown our sorrows in chocolate?"

"Chocolate is a poor substitute for sex, but it will do in a pinch.

~4~

"Ted! Teddy, where are you?"

Usually, my big orange cat greeted me at the door, but tonight I was late and so he was hiding, punishing me.

"Come on, Teddy, don't be mad. Come out, come out wherever you are!"

From the darkest corner of my bedroom I heard the loud thud that meant he had jumped to the floor, probably from my dresser, and was making his way toward the door.

There he was now, sitting down and curling his tail around his body, squinting at the light.

"Hey, Ted. Sorry I'm late." He stood again as I approached, waiting for me to scoop him up, all fourteen pounds of him. I lifted him and he began to purr as he moved into his favorite position, facing backwards over my shoulder. I shared the events of my day with him, then put him on the floor and opened a can of his food.

He lapped up his dinner loudly as I walked into my tiny living room, grabbed the remote control and flipped on the TV for a little network news before hitting the sack.

Teddy was a tiny, fragile thing when I found him in the alley behind my apartment building one Saturday afternoon. I was taking the trash out to the dumpster and there he was.

Fluffy and orangey-gold with oversized paws, he looked like a miniature grizzly bear to me—hence the name. Dutifully, I tried to find his rightful owner; but whoever had lost—or worse, abandoned him—wasn't owning up. It was possible he'd been part of a feral litter, but there was no sign of Mama Cat or any siblings. So I became Keeper of the Teddy. I'd never been so grateful for a chance encounter in my life. Teddy was, other than Chloe and Jamie, the best friend I'd ever had.

Talk about personality! Teddy's sense of humor astounded me; who could forget, for instance, the time he left a saliva-soaked, furry toy mouse in my shoe? Then there was the playful way he danced around my legs whenever I walked into the kitchen. Somehow, he always forgave me when I tripped over him and nearly fell on my face.

Of course what I loved most about Teddy was his love for me. He saw past all that was unremarkable about me and adored me without reservation. We gazed into each other's eyes and I knew how it felt to be loved down to my core.

When he finished eating he joined me on the sofa. We sat, side-by-side, watching the well-groomed newscasters read their well-written copy about all the bad things that had happened today. Absently, I put my hand on Teddy's back and he arched it in response, looked over at me and moved to my lap, purring once again.

"That's my boy," I murmured. "Good boy, Teddy."

He leaned his body against me, tucking his head under my chin. At times like this I could feel his devotion radiating outward; this creature held me in goddess-like esteem.

True, he wasn't the greatest protection in the world. Each time Colin had knocked me around, Teddy dashed for the farthest corner under my bed to wait out the storm. But afterward, when Colin was gone, Teddy always showed concern for my condition, lying beside me, studying my face when I moaned or cried.

Colin had blown into my life like a foul wind, stirring up my tidy little existence in a way that had at first seemed exciting. In the end of course I could see only the chaos he had created.

I had allowed three beatings before banishing Colin for good. The first time, he was fairly drunk. Later, he insisted that was the only reason it had happened. At the time it was actually happening his reasons had been, in order: my stupidity, my pudgy body, my poor posture and of course my infidelity (because a guy had asked me to dance in a bar that night).

Somehow he managed to convince me that it was all because of the booze. He didn't usually drink so much, he said. He had some problems with anger because of his shitty childhood—something we had in common—and so he promised to steer clear of alcohol altogether.

The second time, he was stone cold sober.

We'd planned to meet at a restaurant for dinner, and I had made the mistake of taking one last phone call before leaving work. Colin hated waiting for anything, least of all me. He was furious when I arrived twenty minutes late— twenty-two, he said, checking his watch as I walked in—and the conversation never progressed beyond my rudeness, my lack of consideration for his feelings, my self-centeredness and my over-inflated sense of self-importance.

Finally, I'd had enough. "Thanks for dinner, Colin, it was lovely," I said, and walked out of the restaurant.

On my way home, I saw his car in my rear-view mirror. Naïvely, I thought he was following me home to apologize and to ensure my safety. He pulled up behind me as I parked in my assigned spot, as he always did whenever he spent the night. I got out of my car and locked it, and Colin seemed very calm when he emerged from his own car and approached me.

"Thanks for seeing me home, but I really would like some time alone tonight," I said.

His jaw clenched and that frightened me a little, but still he was calm, even gentle when he took my arm. "I'll walk you upstairs," he said.

As soon as I'd unlocked and opened my door, he pushed me into my apartment and locked the door behind me.

That beating left me with a broken rib—from falling onto the coffee table—along with a fat lip and one black eye.

Still, when three-dozen yellow roses arrived at the office the next day, complete with a handwritten note—on a card featuring a hopeful-looking cartoon man crawling out of a doghouse—I knew I would give him one more chance. After all, I told myself, he's had a lot on his mind lately, and I *had* kept him waiting nearly half an hour. I should have been quicker to apologize, instead of being frazzled and too caught up in my own day.

That's what I told myself. I told my co-workers that I'd fallen down a flight of stairs, and that my wonderful boyfriend had sent the flowers to make me feel better.

Teddy, of course, knew the truth, and so did Jamie. "I'm going to kill the son-of-a-bitch!" he said.

"No, you're not. He is so sorry, Jamie, really. He loves me."

"This kind of love you don't need, doll. You've become lovers with your father. You know that, don't you?"

"Stop that! Colin is nothing like Dad. Yes, he's got a temper, but he can also be kind and gentle, too. He loves animals!" In fact, Colin had *told* me he loved animals, and then completely ignored Teddy when in his presence.

"Sagey," he said, shaking his head. "You don't deserve to be beaten. You think you do, but you deserve only good things. When are you going to believe that?"

My face throbbed with pain, but I squeezed his hand and said the words that countless other abused women have uttered: "You just don't know him the way I do. He loves me, I know he does."

It was a stormy Friday the night Colin hit me for the last time. Work had been particularly grueling that week; at least four different clients had found reasons to yell at me several times each day. That Friday especially, the telephone had been relentless, presenting problem after problem requiring immediate solutions. When it rang yet again at precisely 4:30, I stared at it until it stopped.

Colin met me at my apartment. He'd said he had a big night planned for us, and he was obviously excited when he arrived at my door, flowers in hand. My bruises had all but disappeared, but now he kissed my eye and apologized for the hundredth time. I smiled and hugged him, but I was distracted and he could tell.

"What's wrong?" he asked, very concerned.

"Nothing. I've just had a really rough week, and today was the worst of the worst. I'm exhausted. Can we stay here, order a pizza or something and watch a movie? We can snuggle on the couch."

"Stay in? But I've made all these plans, Sage. I've made reservations. Just go splash your face, freshen your makeup and get dressed up. You'll be fine."

Getting gussied up for a big night out was the last thing I wanted to do that night. I couldn't even imagine having the energy to pick out something to wear. I knew it was important to Colin, but I truly wanted only to curl up in front of the TV and do nothing all night. Surely he would understand. Whatever surprise he had cooked up for me would be much more enjoyable on a different night.

"I'm sorry, honey, I really don't want to go out tonight. I'm weary to my marrow. Let's crawl into our little cocoon here and shut out the rest of the world for the next twenty-four hours or so; what do you say?" I nudged him playfully, grinning in what I hoped was a suggestive way.

He exploded.

He punched my stomach hard; I doubled over and I felt the back of his hand hit my face. Falling onto the coffee table right onto my sore rib, I screamed, begging him to stop, but he probably couldn't even hear me over his own voice.

It was a furious stream of vile, unthinkable names he spat at me. Words so cruel they hurt as much as the blows landing on my body, even as I tried to stand up.

When I rolled from the coffee table to the floor, he started kicking me. I curled into the fetal position, trying to protect the rib that had just been re-injured; this seemed to anger him further, and he kicked my back.

At some point I must have blacked out. When I became aware again he was on top of me, pressing down on all my wounds. Sneering and spitting into my face, chanting his vile vitriol in rhythmic breaths, he raped me.

I was horrified by what was happening, but felt somehow disconnected from it at the same time. His face was so ugly, contorted with rage and yet still smiling a little, enjoying this obscene victory.

Closing my eyes, other images appeared. Other faces, looking at me just like that. Dim memories flashed through my mind in bits and pieces, like a slide show that wasn't working quite right. Somehow, those flashes were more terrifying than Colin. I opened my eyes again, back to the here and now. Back to the devil I knew.

When it was over Colin stood up and zipped his pants. "Why do you make me hurt you?" he screamed. "I hate you for making me do this!" On his way out, he slammed the door so hard a picture fell off my wall.

I tried to stand up and fell to my knees. I crawled, literally crawled to the door, reached up and locked it. I don't know why, really. Colin had a key of his own.

Crazily, I called for Teddy, but he had already appeared at my bedroom door, his tail puffed up and lashing wildly, his eyes wide. I reached for him and called his name, sobbing, just wanting to touch something soft and warm. Cradling him like a baby, I rocked and cried until I simply couldn't anymore.

Then I took inventory. My underwear were gone, my skirt torn. I could see red fingerprints on my legs. My entire body throbbed, my kidneys ached. Still clinging to Teddy with one hand, I stood slowly, using a chair to brace myself with the other. Not quite as shaky now, I looked around. The coffee table was broken in the middle, the wood top forming a v on its base. Glass, broken into odd, jagged shapes, lay where the picture had landed.

Slowly, I walked to the bathroom, flipped on the light and looked at the rest of the damage.

One eye—the other one this time—was swelling already, as were my lips and cheeks. My face was going to be a mess, that was for sure. But I began to worry that he might have really hurt me badly this time, internally.

And then it slowly began to sink in. Colin had beaten me again. He had raped me; my mind replayed the horrible things he had said to me as he'd used my body that way, in an act of rage, of hatred. Of punishment and power.

How could he do this to me? How could he hurt me like this?

As I weighed my options, those fractured images kept returning to me. And I knew that if I were ever going to call the police it would have to be now, while the evidence was fresh and while my apartment and I could be photographed in this state. I would be taken to the hospital; they would use a rape kit to extract DNA from my body. I shuddered, hearing a doctor's voice talking me through it, seeing a police officer looking at me, judging me.

Later, with Colin's eyes on me, I would have to testify in court. My motivation would be questioned, my character analyzed. Colin would deny everything. He would say I'd staged everything for revenge or something. *Mr. Prescott is an upstanding member of the community, Your Honor. He's from a prominent family and has a thriving law practice. This woman admits to having a consensual sexual relationship with him, and now she's crying rape? There was no forcible entry that night, she let him in. The bruises and wounds in these pictures could have been the result of an encounter with a different lover—or someone Ms. Whitaker hired for that matter.*

Yes. The 'woman scorned' defense.

Or, he would find a way to "prove" he wasn't there at the time it happened. He would come up with an airtight alibi. He could do that. It would be easy. It happened all the time.

My heart was pounding now. I was cold, freezing, right to my bones, but I was sweating. I tried to push these thoughts away, tried to talk myself into doing what I knew to be the right thing—trying to get Colin off the streets.

But even if he were found guilty, how much time would he serve? Two years? Less? And then, well he'd be really angry, wouldn't he?

Knowing I was probably making a mistake, I put Teddy down, walked to the kitchen, took my clothes off and threw them in the garbage. Suddenly violently ill, I ran for the bathroom and vomited into the toilet. I brushed my teeth. Then I stepped into the shower and scrubbed all traces of Colin away.

I stayed in there for a long time, letting the hot water run over my aching body. And a thought came, a whisper that I didn't understand: *Why did this happen...again?* More flashes: a field, a letterman's jacket. "NO!" I screamed. And once more, I forced myself to focus on Colin. By the time I crawled under the covers, he was all I could think about.

The next day, I asked the maintenance guy at my building to change the lock on my door and install a deadbolt. About the lock I said, "I heard on the news there's a rapist in the area. This will make me feel safer. Thank you, Marty." To explain my face, I told him I'd walked into a wall. "Clumsy me," I said.

"No problem, Sage," he said, never taking his eyes off his task. But as he was leaving, he turned back to me. "If that wall ever comes back here, he won't get past me."

I hesitated, then nodded and closed the door.

An x-ray confirmed that Colin had re-broken my injured rib, plus one on the other side. Elsewhere there was a lot of deep bruising, but no permanent damage. My doctor scowled at me, but tacitly agreed to buy my lame story about my ongoing clumsiness.

Three days after the attack, Colin sent flowers again to apologize "for my outburst," his note read. Those damned yellow roses. He called me at the office, as he had the other times, to see if I'd received them and to make up.

When I heard his voice I started shaking. "Hey, sweetheart," he said. "Listen, I am so sorry about...everything.

I know I don't deserve it, but please give me another chance. I was just so disappointed because I'd made all these wonderful plans for you. I'd made reservations, prepaid for a limo. I had gifts waiting for you. To show you how much I love you. So please let me make it up to you. Sage? Are you there, honey?"

My stomach lurched. "Colin, I can't see you anymore."

Hanging up, I could hear his voice. He was asking: "Why?"

Jamie was furious about the beating, but he calmed down quickly when I told him I'd cut Colin loose.

"Okay, sweetie, but be careful. Men like that kill women every day. I don't think you should be alone for a while."

"It's okay. I've changed my locks."

"That's fine for when you're at home, but what about going out? He could follow you home and overpower you before you even get inside.

"Yep. He sure could."

"Come stay with me for a month or so, Sagey. Give him a little time to get used to the idea that you're out of his life."

"Okay, but Teddy has to come too. I know Jake's not crazy about cats."

"He's allergic, but I'll talk him into it."

"We're a package deal, Jamieson."

"I understand. I'll make it happen."

And so Teddy and I stayed with Jamie and Jake for three weeks, until I couldn't stand hearing Jake sneeze anymore, and it had been two full weeks since Colin had called any of my numbers.

I never told Jamie about the rape.

Chloe invited me over for lunch while I was still staying with Jamie, saw my bruises and started yelling. "You have got to call the police and press charges against that son-of-a-bitch!"

"I'm not calling the cops."

"Why not?"

I looked into her eyes and she saw it all. She held me and I sobbed as we rocked back and forth, back and forth, her voice so soothing and calm. "It's not your fault, Sage, not your fault at all," she murmured, stroking my hair and rubbing my sore back.

"Why does he hate me so much? What did I do? Will anyone ever love me? Am I too ugly to be loved?"

"Ssh, ssh, it's okay. He doesn't hate you, he hates himself. You've done nothing wrong. You're beautiful, inside and out. Someone will see that and love you forever, I promise you."

I looked at her then, taking in the details of her: the wild red curls going off in every direction, the line of freckles dissecting her nose. "I'm so scared, Chloe."

"I know you are, Sage. But you won't be scared forever. You could still call the police. I'd be with you through the whole thing."

"I can't. I know he shouldn't get away with this, but I just can't face the court appearances, the insinuations, and having to see Colin—no, I just can't do it, Chloe. If I damaged his reputation or actually cost him his career—I really think he'd kill me."

She stroked my hair and rocked with me again. "Okay, Sage. It's all right."

Right about the time I went back home, Colin surfaced again, calling me at work every other day to beg for "one more chance." The last time I turned him down, he began to yell at me: "You ungrateful cow. Do you know how many women would kill to go out with me?"

I felt sick, thinking of those other women. But I took a deep breath and said, "Then go out with them, Colin." I hung up the phone. In spite of myself, I thought, not for the first time, that maybe I really had been the problem. Maybe he wouldn't have a reason to beat anyone else.

That night I had Jamie follow me home. I was a little shaken, but not really surprised when I saw the yellow blooms waiting for me in front of my door. But after that night, Colin suddenly went silent.

At Chloe's insistence, I joined a rape survivors' support group. It was helpful to hear other people's stories; eventually I found the courage to tell my own. Gradually, I eased back into my routine and, as Chloe had predicted, stopped being afraid every minute of every day.

And now here I was, almost a year later, sitting on the couch with Teddy, feeling safe and relaxed and enjoying a little quiet time, just the two of us. He looked up at me, squinting and purring, and I touched his soft, warm back.

The knock on the door made us both jump.

~5~

Teddy stood up on the sofa and watched as I tiptoed to the door. It was after ten; no one came to visit that late unannounced, not even Jamie. And we'd parted company a mere hour ago. Who could this be?

I was so sure it was Colin's face I'd see through the peephole that I started shaking before I even reached the door. Closing one eye, I peered through. *No. Not Colin,* my mind registered. But it couldn't be the person it appeared to be, so I looked away for a moment, then tried again.

It couldn't be, but it was. This apparition before me did not feel any less dangerous than Colin's appearance would have. He looked older, but there was no doubt who this was knocking on my door. *How? How did he find me?* I stood with my back to the door, trying to will him away.

He knocked again.

"Go away!"

"Sage, please open the door."

"I have nothing to say to you!"

"Please. I just want to talk to you."

I looked again. "How did you find me?"

"It wasn't easy. Please, Sage, let me come in."

"Listen to me, you son-of-a-bitch. I am going to count to three. If you're not gone, I will call the police."

"Sage, I am here to tell you something. It's important."

"I said, get the hell out of here!"

"It's Grandma Jamieson. She passed away."

Tears stung my eyes and I fought them back. I would not cry in this man's presence; I would show no emotion. I didn't know how this news had reached him first. It was so unfair! Grandma Jamieson, a.k.a. Grandma Lucy, was my mother's mother. Yet here was my father, delivering the news of her death, as if it were any of his business. I wanted to know why.

I reached for the baseball bat I now kept in a corner by the door, breathed in deeply a couple of times, and let him in.

He nodded and walked past me, looking around. He stopped by the kitchen table. Teddy watched him intently, as did I. With the bat, I motioned for him to sit, then pulled out a chair for myself.

"Look, I know you don't think much of me, and to be honest I don't blame you. But you have nothing to be afraid of, Sage. I just wanted you to hear about this from me. From family."

"We're not family."

"That's not a choice you can make."

I opened my mouth to tell him to go to hell, that he had no idea what defined a family, but he held his hand up to silence me. I flinched, and he sighed.

I was still furious, but now the news began to sink in. Grandma Lucy, the sanest member of the family except for Jamie, was gone. We'd kept in touch, but she lived in Idaho, and I just hadn't found the time to get out there, not for years.

We wrote often, though, and called on holidays and birthdays. I'd wondered why she hadn't answered my last letter.

Last letter. That hit me hard now; all the lasts that I hadn't recognized as such while they were happening. The last time I would ever hear her voice—that was two months ago, on January 12th, my birthday. Her last words to me: "Come out and see me this summer, would you honey? You and Jamie? I'd so love to see you two. Think about it, all right? I love you, Sage, sweetie."

"I'll try, I promise. Bye, Grandma Lucy. I'll talk to you soon," I'd said, as I always had.

"When?" I asked now. Such a cliché, to ask when someone had died, as if it really made a difference. But I just needed to know when she had officially left me.

"Yesterday morning. Her neighbor called me. I'm guessing I was the first Whitaker in Lucy's address book. Maybe our last name was the only information the neighbor had."

Alphabetical order: Craig came before Jamie and Sage. That was a reasonable explanation.

"Maybe, but you're not her family, Jamie and I are."

"I know. I'm sorry. She left everything to you and Jamie, so I guess it falls to you to go out there and take care of her house and belongings. Can you do that?"

Briefly, I wondered if Jamie could get away long enough to help me. It was a trip I'd prefer to take with him.

"Yes. Of course I'll do it. I'd do anything for her. *She* was always good to us."

"Sage, are you going to hate me forever?"

"I hope so."

"I want you to know that I've changed, Sage. I quit drinking; I've been sober three years now."

"Congratulations."

"I've met someone. I'm getting married."

"Bully for you."

"You don't think you could ever forgive me?"

"Uh, let's see. Forgive you for what exactly? For torturing us on a daily basis? For abusing our mother until she ran away? Or for just being a low life that had no business being a father?"

And the son-of-a-bitch looked me straight in the eye and said, "For all of it. It's been a hard road, Sage, but I've finally forgiven myself."

"How nice for you. Now I'd like you to leave."

"First, let me give you my number."

"I don't want it."

"I'm leaving it anyway." He took a business card from his wallet and wrote a number on the back, then slipped it under the daffodil-filled vase on the table.

At the door, he stopped and spoke again. "I hope to hear from you sometime, Sage. I'll always love you. And I'm sorry for everything. Sorrier than you'll ever know. It would mean a lot to me if you were at the wedding."

Without looking up I asked, "How did she die?"

"Pancreatic cancer. I don't know when she was diagnosed. Well, good-bye, Sage."

I didn't move until I heard the door open and close. Then I pushed away from the table, walked to the door and locked it. I leaned the bat back into its corner and stared at it a moment before I turned around.

Back on the table I could see the business card; my heart pounded as I crept toward it, watching it warily as I would any dangerous thing. Up close, I saw my father's writing: *Call anytime. Dad: 555-2120.* I flipped it over. *Craig Whitaker, Freelance Photographer.*

So. New career, new life. What had he told his ladylove about his children, I wondered. How much did she know about the man she planned to marry?

Teddy appeared at my feet, then followed me back to the sofa. Plopping down, I sighed. Grandma Lucy was gone, and my father knew where I lived.

Bad news all around. *Should I call Jamie, tell him tonight?*

No, I decided. This news could wait until morning.

~6~

I slept restlessly that night; sometime toward morning Teddy left in disgust and headed for the more peaceful sofa. My dreams were brief but frightening; images of monsters lurking outside my door lingered after I finally gave up on sleep altogether and shuffled into the bathroom.

Because I'd scheduled the meeting with Elma Crow and Mona for 9 A.M., I would have an extra half hour to play with. Elma did not live far from my apartment—not that she would ever know that—or my local Starbucks. I decided that was where I would spend my extra time. I would order an extra big latté, sit and read in glorious, coffee-scented solitude.

"Good morning! Venti nonfat latté, please," I requested pleasantly.

The barista repeated my order while writing it on the huge cup that would hold my delicious, foamy morning fix. I paid, complete with generous tip, and turned toward the waiting area by the magical espresso machines.

I watched the milk being steamed in its metal pitcher, a thermometer clicked in place to ensure the perfect temperature. Meanwhile, little glass cups collected the liquid ambrosia so vital to my daily existence.

Engrossed as I was in the ritual and alchemy of coffee preparation, I didn't sense the approach of an intruder. In fact, Meddling Molly Logan actually had to touch me to get my attention.

"Sage, darling it *is* you. When you didn't respond, I thought I might have the wrong person."

Startled, and still without my coffee, my brain searched for her name.

"Venti nonfat latté," the barista said, sliding it across the counter.

"Thank you," I said, before turning back to my unexpected complication.

But before I even took my first sip, it came to me. "Molly! Nice to see you again."

Before she could respond, a young girl appeared beside her. Long-limbed and lean, arms folded on her chest, she looked utterly bored. But her face was sweet: light brown eyes and matching freckles on her nose. Her hair was extraordinarily straight, probably the result of painstaking ironing in front of the bathroom mirror this morning; it too was light brown.

"Grandma, I have to go," she said, dangerously close to whining.

Molly smiled. "Sage, this is my granddaughter, Savannah. Sam's daughter, the one I told you about."

"Nice to meet you, Savannah. You have a lovely name." I held out my hand to shake hers, thinking she might appreciate such an adult gesture.

Until then, she had barely looked at me, but now she rose to the challenge, stepped forward and shook my hand, firm and strong. She didn't smile, but she looked straight into my eyes.

"Thanks," she mumbled. And then, back to her mission: "Grandma, really. I'm going to be late for school."

"Oh, so what if you are. The state our school system is in, I can't imagine you'll miss much. But, if you insist, let's go. So nice to see you, Sage. I hope I run into you again, when I'm not on duty. Sam had to go out of town, you see. He doesn't like me to drive much, but the school's not far. And of course I had to stop and get Savannah a hot chocolate for the road."

"Ooh, sounds good," I said, a bit too enthusiastically.

"It's all right, but they put whipped cream on it, and I didn't want any," said Savannah, tossing her perfectly straight hair. "Come on, Grandma!"

"All right, all right. Have a wonderful day, Sage. *Arrivaderci!*"

I watched them leave. At the door, Savannah turned around and, almost carefully, waved good-bye. I smiled.

It was nice to see Molly again, and I'd enjoyed meeting Savannah, but I was grateful that the interruption in my sacred bonus time alone was only a brief one. I sat at a table and opened my book.

But, try as I might, solitude was something I could not enjoy that morning. Thoughts of my father kept intruding: big as life, sitting at my kitchen table. After reading the same line in my book six times, the words still had no meaning for me. His words were the only ones I could hear. *Bastard!* I thought, slamming my book shut.

So I sat, sipping my latté and thinking about our exchange the night before. I looked at my watch: still fifteen minutes before I had to leave. Sighing, I dug out my cell phone from my purse and called my brother.

"Good morning, Sage. How're you?"

"I've been better. Brace yourself, Jamieson. I have bad news. Grandma Lucy died."

"Oh, no. Sagey, let me call you right back, okay? I'm going to pull over."

In the time that it took Jamie to pull off the road, he'd also pulled himself together. Amazing, how he could do that.

I stared at the phone until he called me back. "Hey. Are you okay?" I asked, knowing he was.

"Yeah. Such a sweet lady. I'm going to miss her. But she lived a good long life, on her terms. That's something to feel good about."

"I know."

"Are *you* okay? How did you find out?"

"Yeah. That's the kicker, actually. It was Dad, Jamie. He came to my apartment last night. I saw him."

Silence, so deep and thick I could almost hear it. "Jamie?"

"How did he find you?"

"I don't know."

"What did he say?"

"He told me about Grandma Lucy. You and I are the only beneficiaries. We need to go out there and clean out her house, put it up for sale or whatever we decide to do with it. We'll need to meet with her lawyer, I guess."

"That's it? After all these years he showed up, dropped this bad news on you and left?"

"Not quite. He *apologized*, Jamie. Said he's a different person, he quit drinking, he's getting married. He's a photographer now."

Silence again.

Finally, I heard him clear his throat. "What did you say?"

"I told him to get lost. He left me his business card with all his phone numbers. He invited me to the wedding."

"Well, I hope he's not terrorizing his fiancée."

"Are you all right, Jamie?"

"Yes, Sage, I'm really okay. He can't hurt us anymore. I honestly hope he's happy."

After we said good-bye, I thought about what Jamie had said. Was it really true? Had we come to a time and place when our father's actions, past or present, would no longer sting? If so, when had that happened?

The truth was, for me at least, I wasn't sure I would ever be able to forgive him, and that in itself hurt. That man, the father I remembered, was cruel beyond comprehension, beyond booze. There was no way to justify his abuse.

Of all the memories I'd longed to erase over the years, the moment I learned of my mother's death still topped the list. It's not as if she ever would have been crowned Mother of the Year. She did leave us, after all. For a while, I'd entertained a secret fantasy that she would appear one day and spirit us away to some enchanted place where we would never be beaten again.

Then she, and all such childish dreams, died.

As on every other day, Jamie and I had rushed home from school and through our chores. I had cleaned up the breakfast dishes and put a roast in the oven—at eleven years old I was responsible for the evening entrée—and we had raced up the stairs to play in my room so that we wouldn't have to face our father until the last possible moment. Each day, we would pause when we heard him arrive, listening carefully, like rabbits sniffing the air, gauging the danger of another animal's presence.

Dad was never in a good mood when he got home from work, or ever, but there were always clues as to the intensity of his distress: how loudly his metal lunch box landed on the kitchen counter, how many bottle caps per hour clattered across the table. This day, something was clearly more wrong than usual.

He was quiet. Deadly quiet, like he always was before a particularly bad beating.

We heard his soft footsteps on the stairs and I reached for Jamie, instinctively putting him behind me. My bedroom door creaked open and our father stood in the doorway, huge and smelling of whisky. I knew the difference between whisky and beer. Beer wasn't good, but whisky always meant trouble. His eyes found us cowering in the corner, and he pointed at us, swaying slightly.

His voice was low, almost a whisper. "I got somethin' to tell you. Your stinking whore of a mother's dead. Killed herself with her drugs. Well, good riddance to so much trash. Now you know what happens to that kind. So straighten up and fly right. Especially you, little Mommy's boy, little pussy."

He spat out those last words as he lunged for Jamie. With all my strength I pushed him away. "Leave him alone, you goddamn bully!" I screamed. I had never cursed in his presence, wouldn't have dared, but I knew how dangerous he was in that moment. I had to divert his attention somehow; I had to protect my brother.

Shaking, I stared him down, one arm held back toward Jamie, a signal for him to freeze behind me. "It's your fault she died!" I continued. "You made her leave us!" I thought he would probably kill me that night, and I worried what that would mean for Jamie, but I couldn't seem to stop myself. My only thought was to get him to hurt me instead. How better to accomplish that than to tell the truth? But he just looked at me with those wild, rolling red eyes and tilted his head sideways.

He lowered his voice to that terrible whisper again. "Your mother never wanted you. She cried when she found out she was pregnant. She *wanted* to leave you." He bent down, putting his face close to mine. "She hated you. *You're* the reason she left, not me."

Straightening back up, he swayed again. Then he cleared his throat and walked to the door. We flinched when he turned around again. "Don't bother coming downstairs tonight. No dinner for you ungrateful brats."

As he clomped down the stairs, quiet no more, we heard him stumble. *Please fall down, please just die,* I wished silently, eyes closed tight, fingers crossed. But we heard him continue walking down, safely, to the floor below.

I ran to the door, closed it, ran back to Jamie. Clinging to each other, we tumbled to the floor in a heap, rocking and crying as softly as possible.

I felt the weight of it on my chest: the cold, awful truth. Our mother was gone forever. We would have to look for hope somewhere else.

Pulling into the visitor parking lot at the mobile home park where Elma Crow lived, I took a deep breath. I parked and turned the car off. I would wait there, in my car, until Mona arrived. I would not enter Elma's lair alone.

~7~

The meeting with Mrs. Crow began pretty much as they always did. Mona and I laid down the law—again—and Elma scoffed and rolled her eyes at the ceiling, never moving from her Naugahyde throne.

Today, however, there was one new twist.

This time, while Mona was again explaining the rules of her services, Elma suddenly turned her head toward me. Looking straight into my eyes she said, "I came from money, you know. I didn't always live like this. I know what it's like to have nice things. Well, maybe I don't have much anymore, but by God what I have can be well cared for. Doesn't anyone understand what that means?"

Because she seemed to be talking to me, I answered, trying not to break out of my character of Tough Social Worker. "Mrs. Crow," I said for the hundredth time, "we are not here to provide maid services. We are here to provide basic household and transportation services with the aim of enabling you to remain in your home as long as possible."

"Yeah, I've heard that speech somewhere before. I guess you and I just have different ideas of 'basic.' I'm sure glad I didn't have kids. Your generation seems to be nothing but a bunch of lazy, ungrateful brats. You think the world owes you. Here's some news, Tootsie: *you* owe your *parents* for everything they gave you. You should work your fanny off every single day of your life. That's the only way you really earn what you get. Sitting there on your high horse telling me what I can and can't do—you call that work? You're worthless. You do nothing but make people miserable."

I sat, watching her mouth move, hearing her poisonous words, and suddenly it was hard to breathe. I felt as if I were sinking into deep, dark water. My heart pounded, I began to perspire, and I was absolutely, to my very bones, terrified of Mrs. Crow.

Somehow I stood up, trying desperately not to tremble. "I'm sorry, I have to go. I'll call you later, Mona."

I ran to my car as if a monster were chasing me. As I sat behind the steering wheel, my entire body shook and it took several tries to get the key into the ignition. In my rearview mirror I saw Mona running outside, trying to wave me back, but I pretended I didn't see her. My only thought was to get away.

Knowing I shouldn't be driving in this state, I pulled out of the trailer park and drove around the block. There I found myself on a quiet street lined with modest but well-tended homes. I parked in front of one, turned my car off and started taking deep breaths, trying to regain control.

What had just happened? It was as if something, or someone, had grabbed hold of my heart and squeezed. But it was more than that. I was frightened, afraid for my safety, as I hadn't been since—

—since I was a child in my father's house. It was a paralyzing fear, the absolute terror of a helpless child. Even during Colin's attacks, my mind had been busy, watching for opportunities to escape or fight back, sifting through lists of options. I hadn't panicked, not like this.

And, as my breathing slowed and my heart approached its normal rhythm, the events of the morning became very clear. *That was a panic attack.* I replayed Elma Crow's words: *lazy, ungrateful brats.* "You owe your parents for everything they gave you," she had said.

There was no mystery here. My father had shown up last night to drop some bad news—as if his very presence wasn't enough—and today The Client From Hell had spat a few of his favorite sentiments at me. My reaction was perfectly understandable. Normal, even, under the circumstances.

Everything they gave you.

What had my parents given me? I thought about it, trying to be objective. Life: yes, they had created me, and I was grateful to be alive. They had also produced Jamie, their *pièce de résistance*. For that I was eternally indebted to them. And my father had given us shelter and food, the latter of which he routinely withheld as punishment. And unfortunately, what we most needed shelter from was him.

I had several fractured but vivid recollections of being with my mother: sitting in her lap and listening to her read a book. Bath time— warm, bubbly water and my mother's soothing voice. I remembered her smell, her long silky hair, the warmth of her body as she gathered me in her arms. I remembered making her laugh once—I watched in awe as she threw her head back in pure joy; her dangly earrings sparkled and swayed like pendulums. I had no idea what I'd said that made her so happy.

I remembered moments when her energy knew no bounds. She would dance, twirling in circles, hands above her head. Or she would paint for hours—standing at her easel, swaying between brushstrokes, her hair wild, sweat trickling down her back. When I approached her during those sessions she would say, "Oh, Sage, darling! Look at you! You're so beautiful! You see this painting? It has to be as gorgeous as you are, so I have to work very hard, do you understand? Please get your own lunch today, sweetheart, cereal or something, all right? Mommy needs to work!"

Even clearer were the memories on the flipside. The times when my mother would suddenly cry for no reason. When she would stay in bed for days wanting only darkness.

And the worst ones of all: the screaming, the dishes breaking, the name-calling. The horrible sound when my father's fist made contact with my mother's face. I remember the heaviness of the air as he beat her, my mother's sobs when it was all over, when he was gone somewhere and she was recovering. There were times when I actually played a morbid little guessing game with myself, trying to predict how and where she would be hurt that time. Would he slap her or punch her? Would he leave bruises? Would she bleed?

The last memory I have of my mother was when she said good-bye. Kneeling down, she pulled me close. Her face, wet with tears, was inches from mine when she whispered, "Don't worry, Sage, my love. I will be back for you and Jamie. Someday I'll be a famous artist and we'll live in a mansion and you and Jamie will have nannies and we'll travel the world together! Life will be grand! That's a promise, Sage, never forget what I said."

And I never did. I held her promises close and blew them up into the grandest of illusions, until the day my father delivered the news of her death. Then I knew. There would be no fairy tale ending for any of us.

Last night, my father had once again brought news of death, and today for a brief moment I'd thought I was about to die myself.

Sitting in my car outside a stranger's home, I nodded, understanding why I'd been compelled to run from Elma Crow. Demons, yet unconquered, had chosen an opportune moment to haunt me again. To announce their presence. *Surprise! We're still here! What are you going to do about it?*

Memories of my father's angry face came to me. And his hands–
–hot, red hands connecting with my cheeks, squeezing my shoulders and
shaking me, throwing me like a rag doll against the wall, while I yelled
to my brother, "Run, Jamie! Now, run away now!"

It all came rushing back and I cried in my car, leaning over the
steering wheel, until I looked into the rearview mirror and saw Mona's
Toyota pulling up behind me.

~8~

Mona made me leave my car where it was. "Let's go get a cup of
coffee and then I promise I'll bring you right back to get it."

Coffee did sound good, so off we went to the closest Starbucks.
"Sit down. I'll order," she said.

I told her what I wanted and tried to give her money, but she
refused. "You can buy next time."

"At least let me get the tip."

"Next time."

No one was in line, so within minutes Mona was back with our
coffee, warm and comforting in my hands.

"Okay, so are you going to tell me what the hell that was about?"

Weary beyond words now, I sighed. "It's a long story."

"You don't have to tell me, Sage. But that looked to me like a
full–fledged anxiety attack, and you're the most together person I
know."

"What?" *Me? Together?*

"You can handle anything, even Elma Crow. So what was
different about today? And why were you crying in your car?"

I shook my head. "I'm really tired. I got some bad news last
night. My grandmother died."

"Oh, Sage, I'm so sorry. Were you close?"

"Yes. Well, in spirit, anyway. We didn't see each other as often
as we would have liked. Anyway, my brother and I are going to have to
go take care of her things, and I'm not looking forward to it. I guess I
just couldn't handle Elma's rant today. I'm really sorry I left you there,
Mona. It won't happen again."

"I'm not worried about that. I'm worried about you. You just don't seem like yourself. Maybe you should see a doctor, get a little help through this tough time."

I shook my head. "No, I'm fine. It was just bad timing for a visit with the Evil One."

I convinced Mona I was okay, and she drove me back to my car; I smiled and waved good-bye, feeling like a complete fraud.

Despite the double shot of espresso running through my veins, I felt as though I could sleep for a year. I thought of my father's face again, this time soft and concerned. I saw him sitting at my kitchen table, speaking in quiet apologies, telling me how much he'd changed.

But my father had spoken of Jamie only in passing, only to say he too was a beneficiary of Grandma Lucy's will. He'd asked me to come to his wedding, but hadn't included Jamie in the invitation. No, apparently his son still wasn't good enough, even for the new improved Craig Whitaker.

"Bastard," I said out loud. But it didn't seem like enough. "Fucking bastard!" I yelled. There. That was better.

I started my car and pulled away from the pleasant little anonymous house.

In the office, I sat at my desk listening to my voice mail. There was already a message from Mona, "just checking in," numerous others from dissatisfied clients, and of course one from Ruth, wondering again when she could expect my visit.

Thankfully, Elma Crow had so far been silent since our meeting.

After returning several clients' calls, I spoke briefly with Mona, assuring her that I was all right. We were saying good-bye when I looked up to see Rachel peering into my cubicle, smiling.

Hanging up the phone, I returned her smile. "Hi!"

I did not know her well, but Rachel was intriguing, to say the least. She'd been a social worker for years now, and she still loved it. Many attempts had been made to promote her, but she didn't want to be moved to management. She preferred working more directly with clients, she'd explained.

Rumor had it that Rachel was married to a successful attorney, so she was working here strictly by choice. She was also unbelievably gorgeous, tall and willowy with the most amazing huge brown eyes I'd ever seen. Pictures of her twin sons adorned her desk, themselves genetic miracles. She had it all, and yet she chose to continue down this maddening path. I had often wanted to ask her, "Why, why, why?" but as I said, I didn't know her well and felt I couldn't really question her sanity aloud.

"Hi, Sage. Want to get a cup of coffee?"

"Oh, twist my arm." I took the mug from my desk and followed her to the staff kitchen.

I was in awe, watching her move. She was one of those women: the gliders. Words like poised, self-assured, stunning—words that were used to describe women like Princess Grace and Audrey Hepburn—easily applied to Rachel. I couldn't help but wonder what it would be like to inhabit her skin, just for one day.

We poured and sat across from each other at a small white table. She smiled again. The woman positively glowed. "So how are you doing, Sage? I've been meaning to ask, but, well we're all busy, obviously."

"I'm fine. It's not quite…"

"What?"

"It's not really what I was expecting."

"Ah. People are a little more demanding than you thought they'd be?"

"Uh, *yeah*. I can't believe how many angry, bitter people there are."

Rachel smiled again. "I know what you mean. It makes me wonder what their stories are. How did they get to be who they are now? Because you know they didn't start out that way."

"But that's no excuse. A lot of people had lousy childhoods or tragedies in their lives, but they don't all go around trying to make life miserable for everyone else."

"You're absolutely right. Hardship is not an excuse for treating people badly. But it is an explanation. Everyone faces tragedy, illness, the death of someone they love. People are abused as children, or as adults. So many terrible things happen. But we all have a choice: do I let the bad things in my life destroy my character, or do I hold on to my integrity and create my own joy? Too many people don't think about it consciously, and so the choice is made for them. They react to life's struggles and feel victimized, instead of choosing a healthier response. I really admire people who survive horrible things, truly traumatic events, and are still able to see the good in people, the beauty in the world. The others, the nasty ones? I just feel sorry for them."

She was younger than me, I was certain of it, and yet Rachel seemed so wise. Was she human? I was beginning to have my doubts.

"I know I should feel sorry for them, and I do on a certain level I suppose. But mostly I just dread dealing with them." I smiled. "You love this job, don't you Rachel?"

"Yes, I do. I look forward to it every day. Since I had the babies, I only work part-time, but I just can't give it up completely. Althea's been really flexible, thank goodness." She sipped her coffee, then looked me in the eye. "You *don't* love this job, do you Sage?"

"No, I really don't. I thought I would. I wanted to. I owe my brother thousands of dollars for the crummy degree I needed so I could get hired for this crummy job, and now I hate it and I'm stuck. I feel so stupid, so useless. Sorry. I have no idea why I'm spewing like this."

"That's okay. You're not stuck. Your degree will help you no matter where you end up. But trust me on this, Sage. Don't stay in a job that you hate. It will eat away at you until you become one of those automatons out there that are just putting in time until they can retire. Or, you might become one of those nasty, bitter people we were just talking about.

"There's something I've been wondering, Sage. I saw the bruises and the black eyes. I heard your excuses. But someone was abusing you for a while, right? Your boyfriend?"

I started to deny it, to ask what on earth had given her that idea, but her face was so concerned, so kind, I couldn't come up with any words at all. Finally, I nodded.

"Yeah, I thought so. Listen, you don't have to talk about it. I just understand that you've been hurt pretty badly. But I also see that you're a good person, kind and funny and sweet. You didn't let an abusive relationship change all the good things about you. So don't let a job eat away at you either. Yes, I love this work, but it's clear that it's not for everyone. It's just not right for you. You need to find something that fits, that's all. Like a good pair of shoes."

"You think I'm a terrible social worker."

"Not at all. I think you're a good social worker. I just think social work isn't good for you. You know, my brother married a woman who used to be an accountant. She was really good with numbers, but she hated the work. She decided to follow her heart and start over with a whole new career singing commercial jingles, of all things. It was scary for her to make such a huge change, but she did it and she's never regretted it. She would have had big regrets if she'd been an accountant her whole life. And it all happened the way it was supposed to, because she has a little girl now, and with her new career she can choose her own hours and limit her time away from home. See what I mean?"

I put my coffee cup down on the table and looked at Rachel. Saw her perfect features, her flawless skin, those enormous chocolate eyes. Damn, I really wanted to hate this woman, but unfortunately she was just way too nice. *Bet her brother has beautiful eyes, too. Hmmm.* I shook my head, trying to focus.

"I do see what you mean, Rachel. But I thought I was following my dream when I became a social worker. How many dreams is one person allowed? Especially when I went into debt to pursue this one."

"I don't think there's a limit on dreams per person. But you do only get one life—at least as Sage Whitaker."

"Well, one can only hope."

Rachel reached out and touched my hand, laughing. "I like you, Sage. And I just hate to see you feeling stuck in a job that doesn't bring you joy. You were so enthusiastic when you started, and now, what, a little over a year later? I see you looking so unhappy and it makes me sad for you."

"I appreciate that, I do. It's just—I've never been a very joyful person anyway. I don't know if I can be."

Rachel's face darkened then, and she actually held my hand. "I'm so sorry. I can't imagine not feeling joy in my life. Hey. If you ever want to talk, I'd love to listen. Anytime, okay?"

Now I was starting to hate seeing the concern in her eyes; I wanted to take it all back. "Oh, no, I didn't mean my life is joyless. There's a lot about my life that makes me happy. My brother is so incredibly good to me, for one thing. He's truly the best person I know; he's amazing."

And just like that, Rachel was glowing again. "What's his name?"

"It's Jamie. Jamieson, actually. It was my mother's maiden name."

"Is he younger than you?"

"Yeah, three years."

"Do you have any other siblings?"

"Nope. Just the two of us."

"Is he married?"

I always hesitated when answering this question. Until recently, it would have been illegal for Jamie to marry someone he truly loved, and usually when someone asked that question, they were asking if he was married to a woman. I could just say no, he's single, which would be true right now, but it would not be the whole story. The whole story wasn't exactly this semi-stranger's business, of course, but long ago I decided never to be uncomfortable with anything about Jamie, and part of that promise meant saying the truth out loud. Jamie wasn't in the closet; why should I be?

"He's gay."

"Oh! That's…"

"And he's single."

"Oh!" she said again. Then, leaning forward, she said, "Can I ask you something?"

"Sure."

"How long have you known?"

So many ways to answer this question. "He came out officially when he was in high school."

"Did you suspect before he told you?"

I laughed. "I knew my brother was gay before I knew what being gay meant. I mean, I knew that he was different, that he was attracted to boys instead of girls. I didn't understand at first. I didn't know there were variations like that. It seemed kind of funny, that my brother liked boys the way I did. But I never thought there was something wrong with him because of it."

"What *did* you think?"

"Honestly? I worshipped my brother, still do really, and I just thought that liking boys made him even more special."

"Was it hard for your parents to accept?"

You have no idea. "My mother died when we were very young."

"Oh, I'm so sorry, Sage. I didn't know."

I knew what the next question would be, and I felt my throat closing.

"What about your dad?" Yep, there it was.

I had a prepared speech for these occasions, and I found it usually ended the conversation. Without making eye contact, I recited: "We're not close to our father. We went to live with a friend when we were eight and eleven."

This time, to my surprise, my performance elicited a very different response. I glanced up to see Rachel's eyes filling with tears; she stood up and walked around the table, then leaned down and put her arms around my shoulders. "I'm sorry, Sage, for everything you've been through. You're not telling me a lot, but I can see that you've had a very rough time. How wonderful that you and your brother have stayed so close."

I froze, feeling like I couldn't breathe. There weren't a lot of people who showed this kind of affection to me, and Rachel barely knew me.

She slid back onto her chair, dabbing at her eyes with a tissue from the box on the counter. "I'm sorry. I shouldn't have just hugged you like that. I'm afraid I've made you uncomfortable."

"No, not at all," I lied.

"It's just that I'm so close to my family. I used to take it for granted that parents were always loving and kind, that everyone loved spending time with their families. But this work has taught me that a lot of people have been treated cruelly. Now that I'm a mother, it hits me hard sometimes.

"Was your father abusive, Sage?"

I nearly gasped. Was I really so transparent? "I can't, uh, this is not a good time. I need to get back to work. Thanks for the coffee break."

"I'm sorry. I've overstepped. I thought it was a possibility because you were so vague about your father, and because you moved away from him so young…"

"No, I just, I can't…"

We were standing now, and I was trying to leave. Rachel touched my arm, gently turning me to face her again. "Sage, I have a friend who is an amazing therapist. If you ever decide that you need to talk to someone, I'd be happy to give you her name."

"Thanks, but I don't—I couldn't." I turned away again, toward the door. Rachel meant well, I knew, and I didn't mean to brush her off. I turned back to her once more. "But, hey, if you have any unmarried brothers, let me know. I'm sure Jamie and I would both like to meet them."

She smiled her winning smile again, but the softness stayed around her eyes. "Sorry. Ben is my only brother, and he is ecstatically married. Although, I did think he might be gay at one time. Took him a while to find the right woman, so he kind of gave up for a while."

I relaxed. Now I could ask Rachel a few questions. "Would it have been hard for you if he had been? Gay, I mean."

She tilted her head, thinking. "At first, maybe. I'd never entertained the idea before. But when I suspected he might be, I actually kind of hoped he was gay. I thought it would be fun to have a gay brother. Is that silly?"

"I don't know. I mean, part of me still thinks it would be nice if Jamie woke up straight one day. I worry about all the hate crimes, for one thing. And if he got married and had babies I could be Auntie Sage. But you know, he could still have a family. In some ways, I love that he's gay. I can talk to him about anything, and apart from menstrual cramps, he really understands. Men can be so foreign, but Jamie and I have always spoken the same language. Hey—next time he comes by the office, I'll have him come up so you can meet him."

"I'd like that. Sage? I really am sorry. I didn't mean to be nosy or push you past where you wanted to go. Forgive me?"

"Of course. Don't give it a second thought."

"Thanks. Hey—are you going to that communication training on Monday?"

I'd completely forgotten about that. I'd signed up ages ago; the title was something like Communicating Effectively with Difficult People. At least it was a full day out of the office and away from the phone. "Yes, I am. I'll see you there?"

"That will be great. Let's sit together, okay?" Rachel said.

"Sure. Thanks."

I looked back into the kitchen once more before going back to my desk. Why had I never noticed the tissues on the counter before? Did Althea just expect us to fall apart periodically? I couldn't remember another office I'd worked in where tissues were a permanent fixture in the lunchroom. A cost effective, impersonal acknowledgement of our day-to-day difficulties, I supposed. I shuddered.

"Are you okay?" Rachel asked, joining me at the door.

"Yeah, fine." Maybe she was right about me. Maybe I had no business working here at all.

Jamie didn't call that afternoon; I waited even beyond 4:30 trying to will the phone to ring, but it remained stubbornly silent, fickle beast that it was.

When I got home, I called his cell phone. He didn't pick up, so I left a message. "Jamie, please call me. I miss you, and we have to plan our trip to Coeur D'Alene. Just call me when you can, okay?"

I hung up, and Teddy jumped into my lap. "Hey, Ted. How're you doing, huh?" He purred softly. Moving my hands through his soft orange fur, I smiled. Teddy had a way of clearing my mind of clutter. His life was pretty simple; he ate when he felt hungry, napped when he was sleepy and when he needed attention, he demanded it. Pulling him close, I felt his warmth, marveled at his concentration as he kneaded my leg. He was a great friend, but right now I longed for someone to talk to who could respond objectively. While it was pleasant to be viewed as a deity simply because I could open a can, such adulation did not always make for useful input.

No, I needed to talk to someone who knew me. Really knew me. That meant one of three people: Jamie, who was incommunicado at the moment, Mary, Chloe's mother, or Chloe herself.

I dialed Chloe's number, hoping she wasn't out with Pretentious Paul, PhD, her significant-other-but-not-husband.

When we were growing up, Chloe had daydreamed about her wedding in minute detail. "You'll be my maid-of-honor, Sage, so your dress will be special. We'll be outside on a perfect summer day, and there will be pink peonies and white roses everywhere. I'll have a long train and a sparkling tiara in my hair. Like a princess. And my husband will cry when he sees how beautiful I am. And you'll fall in love with his brother or friend or whoever his best man is, and we'll buy houses right next door to each other and our daughters will grow up together and be best friends just like us."

Cynical even at twelve, I would counter with, "And then when your husband beats you up and screams at you, your kids will run to my house. My husband will be passed out by then, so we'll be safe."

She would look at me sadly. "It's not going to be like that, Sagey. Not all men are like your father."

"How do you know?" A cruel question, since Chloe's father left before Chloe was born.

But Chloe chose to ignore my meanness. "Mom says so. She says some men are kind and gentle, but that women don't need them to be complete. She says it's just nice to have them around sometimes. But I want to get married to a nice man who will love our kids and not run away. Jamie would be a good daddy, wouldn't he?"

This I couldn't argue with, but I still couldn't buy into Chloe's little fantasy world. Now I worried that my jaded view of the institution of marriage had influenced Chloe more than I realized at the time, because she allowed herself to fall prey to Dr. Paul 'Breeding is Immoral' Dailey.

Once in a while her desire to become a mother flared up like a painful rash creeping over her body and then Chloe would spend entire days sobbing. Occasionally, she even entertained the idea of leaving Paul, but he always managed to calm her down and convince her, at least temporarily, that bringing more children into this terribly corrupt and contaminated world would be selfish and irresponsible.

I hated Pompous Paul. Yes, the world needed a lot of improvement, no doubt about it, but I held stubbornly to the idea that, more than anything else, the world needed more mothers like Chloe.

"Hello?" Hooray, she was home!

"Chloe, please tell me it's a good time to talk."

"Sure, honey, it's fine. What's going on?"

"I saw my father."

Chloe gasped. "Where? When?"

"Last night. He came to my apartment."

"How did he find you? You're not listed!"

"I asked. He just said it took some effort."

"What did he want?"

"To tell me that Grandma Lucy died."

"Oh, no, Sage! I'm so sorry."

"Jamie and I have to go to Coeur D'Alene to sort through her things, sell her house and all that. But get this: my dad told me he's sober, he's changed, he's getting married, and he wants me in his life. I told Jamie all about it, and he seemed fine, but now he's not answering his phone and that's not like him."

"He probably just needs time to process it all."

"I suppose. Chloe, I think I had a panic attack today. I was meeting with a nasty client. She started yelling at me about how ungrateful my generation is for all the sacrifices our hard-working parents made for us, and suddenly I couldn't breathe. I was terrified! I thought I would die right there if I didn't run away."

"What did you do?"

"I ran away."

"Oh, Sage. Are you all right?"

"Yeah. I don't know. I'm kind of a mess, actually."

"That's understandable. How long has it been?"

"Since I've seen my father?" I thought about it. "It was that last time he came to your place, after we moved in with you and your mom. I never saw him after that."

The night we learned of our mother's death, we'd run to Mary and Chloe's house. I'd wanted to stay, but Jamie finally convinced me to go back; he thought our father might change, not be so angry now that our mother was gone. But I knew then that I had to save Jamie, and that eventually I would remove him—and myself—permanently from our father's home. After the inevitable next beating, Jamie was finally convinced as well.

So I watched and waited for an opportunity. One night, after Dad had passed out in his chair, TV blaring, I found an old suitcase under our father's bed and packed it with as many of our belongings as I could carry. Slowly, carefully, Jamie, the suitcase and I slipped down the stairs, behind the snoring chair, and out the door. When our feet touched the sidewalk we ran, holding hands, as fast as we could. "Don't look back, Jamie," I panted.

Mary said nothing when we arrived at her door. She simply let us in, opened her arms and held us close.

Several days passed before Dad showed up at Mary's door. I could see his face through the three small windows in the wooden door; I watched as his features stretched and twisted, moving from one to another of the wavy glass rectangles.

Gasping, I ran to Jamie, stepping in front of him, ready to die for him, for Chloe, for anyone else this monster might hurt. Chloe came close and held my hand. "Mom!" she called.

Mary looked at us before she went to the door. "It's all right. Stay there." She opened the door, blocking our view with her body. "What do you want, Craig?"

"Lucy told me they're here."

"Yes, they're here."

"So you're keeping them, then?"

"Yes."

"Have you called anyone about it?"

"No. But if you fight me on this, I will call the police, social services, the newspaper, anyone and everyone I need to."

There was a moment of terrifying silence.

"Fine. Take 'em. But don't expect any money from me. You'll get nothin', you hear me? Here." Mary took something heavy from him. "It's the rest of their clothes, and all the schoolbooks I could find. I think it's everything."

"Fine."

"Tell Sage she can keep the suitcase she stole."

"I will. Anything else?"

"Just—just that I'm leaving. I'm packing up and moving out. Don't know where, just somewhere else."

"All right, then. Good-bye, Craig."

"And Mary?" His voice sounded strange then, almost kind. "Tell 'em I did the best I could. Tell 'em that, would you?"

Mary, the bravest woman in the world, looked right at my father and said, "No, Craig. I'll never lie to them like that. They've given you many opportunities to straighten up and be the father they need and deserve. But that father disappeared a long time ago and never showed his face again. How many times have I begged you to get help, to stop hurting your children? Your *babies*, Craig. Georgia's babies. I begged, I offered my help…"

"You threatened to kill me," we heard him say.

"I tried to keep them so many times, but they *chose* to go back home to you. They kept hoping for a miracle. They felt *responsible* for you. Well, not any more. They've had enough. And so have I. And if you ever try to hurt them again, in any way, I will kill you, Craig. Don't doubt that for one minute. From now on, all communication with Sage and Jamie will go through Lucy or me. Is that clear?"

"Crystal. But I won't be in touch. They're your kids now."

"Fine with me. You know, I hope you can save yourself before it's too late. I hope you truly come to understand what you've become. Now you'd better leave." He hesitated, and Mary stood there watching him until I finally heard his footsteps move away from the door and down the front walk. Mary brought in what he'd given her—clothes in a plastic laundry basket, and a bag filled with books—then closed and locked the door. I dragged a chair to the door and stood on it, watching my father walk down the block, willing him to disappear.

As far as I knew, he had never come to Mary's house again.

"Wow. I'd forgotten all that," Chloe said now. "God, Sage, he was a scary man. And now he wants you to what, see him? Spend Christmas with him?"

"I don't know." Suddenly I was bone-tired. "You know what, though? I think I'm done with all this for the day. Can I meet you tomorrow? Lunch or coffee or something?"

"Sure, sweetie. I'll call you in the morning, all right?"

"Thanks, Chloe. I'm just, I can't..."

"I know, Sage. Go have a good long cry, and then get some sleep. I'll talk to you in the morning."

And to my surprise I *was* crying, before I even said good-bye.

~10~

Saturday morning I woke to see sunlight streaming through my bedroom window. I knew I'd slept in, because Teddy had already left me behind.

My eyes hurt, my nose was stuffy and my lips were rough and dry from breathing through my mouth all night. I had followed Chloe's directions and had myself a good cry, all right. I'd sobbed all the way to sleep.

I squinted at the clock: almost 9:30! I *never* slept this late. Wondering if I'd missed a phone call, I rolled out of bed and shuffled into the living room to check for messages. Sure enough, there was Chloe's voice. She'd called half an hour earlier.

"Good morning, Sage. I hope you're feeling better. I'm available if you still want to get together for lunch. Call me!"

I'd forgotten about extending that invitation, but lunch with Chloe sounded wonderful. I just had to try to reach Jamie first.

He answered after the first ring of his cell phone. "Hi, Sagey," he said. Clearly he was much more wide-awake than I at the moment.

"You didn't call me yesterday. I couldn't reach you!"

"I know, doll. Sorry. Something really weird came up."

"Yeah? How weird?"

"Well, a new client came in yesterday. I'd never seen her before, but she asked for me."

"Someone famous?" Jamie had, on occasion, cut some very well-known hair.

"No. Sage, it was Dad's fiancée."

"What? How did she…?"

"Apparently Dad has put some effort into finding both of us. She told me that he wanted to come see me, but given our difficult past, and your reaction to his visit, she convinced him to let her approach me first. They invited me to the wedding."

"Well. Seems to be a common theme. What was she like?"

"She was striking, actually. Southern. Very genteel. Soft-spoken. Tall, slender, quite attractive. Thick hair, natural looking color. She said that she never knew the man we'd grown up with, that he'd changed his life by the time she met him. She said she couldn't imagine him being mean to anyone. *Her* Craigy wouldn't hurt a fly, darlin'!

"Then came the punch line. 'Of course we don't believe that homosexuality is normal or natural, Jamie. We believe it's an abomination. It's against God's plan, don't you see that? But we hate the sin, not the sinner. You just need Jesus in your life, sweetheart. Your father hurt you when you were young and that makes you want to be loved by men, don't you see? He knows he's to blame for your sinful lifestyle, and he wants to make amends.' How about that?"

I was stunned. Our father had always punished Jamie for his differences, but because we'd moved in with Mary when we were so young, Jamie had never actually come out to him. We had never said the words out loud. But he'd known, he'd always known. How could he not? Even so, it was a shock to hear of his fiancée speaking about it so openly. "What in the world did you say to her, Jamie?"

"I laughed! I couldn't help it. Laughed in her face, as if she were joking. I said, Honey, don't you realize that the man beat me *because* I was gay? Because I was already gay at three and five and seven years old, and he knew it? 'Oh, no, Jamie, that just isn't true. Little boys can't be homosexual. It isn't possible.' Wanna bet, sweetheart? I asked her. How do you suppose he knew that I'm gay, when he hasn't seen me since I was eight?"

"How did she respond to that?"

"She told me that he 'kept tabs' on us through the years. Stayed in touch with Grandma Lucy. Even so, can you see Grandma saying, 'Oh, by the way, Jamie has a new boyfriend'?"

"No way. Maybe he flat out asked her. She would have been honest. But the bottom line is that he always knew, just like I did. You know what I wonder? I'd like to know just exactly how he described his 'meanness' to his southern belle."

"It turns out that they met at church, Sage. Our Daddy's done found religion and he wants to reform me. Well, I gave Wendy a lovely cut and blow dry, said 'Very nice to meet you,' and sent her on her way."

"Wendy, huh?"

"Soon to be Wendy Whitaker."

"Well isn't that precious."

"Hey, they can be as religious as they want to be, as long as they don't hurt anyone."

"Right. Like trying to reform all you poor misguided homosexuals doesn't hurt anyone?"

"It doesn't hurt me. It's laughable, really. It just means that having a relationship with my father is still as impossible as it ever was."

"Bastard. How dare they think they have the right…"

"Ssh. Sage, it's all right. Let it go. They are entitled to their moronic, uninformed, ignorance-based opinions. We all are. He's just found yet another way to keep us out of his life. Pity him, don't hate him. At least he doesn't seem to be violent anymore. I didn't see any bruises on Wendy, and she truly seems fond of him."

"Thank God for small favors, I suppose. You're a better person than I am, Jamieson. But why didn't you call me yesterday and tell me what happened?"

"I just needed some time to process, doll."

"You needed some time alone without all my venom, right? I'm sorry."

"Don't be. You're my little tigress, my most dangerous protector. I *like* knowing that I can always count on that. You just need to learn how to do it for yourself."

"Yeah, I know. Hey. Want to have lunch with Chloe and me today?"

"Just us girls? Wouldn't miss it."

After Jamie and I said good-bye, I called Chloe; then I made myself some coffee and stepped onto my balcony. My little balcony barely held one chair and a tiny table, but there was a flowerbox on the railing, and I kept it full of red and purple petunias.

Best of all, my mini-veranda faced a greenbelt area full of cedar and hemlock trees and their residents. On any given day I could stand there with my morning coffee and watch a pair of squirrels chasing each other, leaping from branch to branch and spiraling down tree trunks. Or chickadees flitting and chirping; jays might squawk at each other from the tallest branches, and once in a while, a woodpecker might actually peck wood for me.

Now I stood watching, waiting to see who would appear in this daily opera.

Bees zigged and zagged along their erratic flight paths. Two butterflies twirled around each other, then separated and flew on to their individual destinies. And finally, my favorite character of all entered the scene.

A hummingbird, his throat so red it nearly glowed, buzzed into view. I backed into my chair slowly, silently, and my hummingbird (as I had come to think of him) darted toward the flowers. I could hear his wings, almost a purr, revving up slightly, rhythmically, as his long, slender beak dipped into each blossom.

When his breakfast was over (at least at this stop), the tiny bird hovered over the flowers, looking in my direction. He always did that; I liked to think he was thanking me, but he was probably just watching for signs of danger, for any possible threat I might pose.

As I got ready to meet Chloe and Jamie that day, I couldn't get that hummingbird out of my mind.

"Chloe, you're stunning," Jamie gushed as he greeted her. It's what he always said when he saw Chloe, and in response her face always turned crimson. "You just *have* to let me do your hair someday."

"Jamie, not even you could tame this mess." She giggled.

"*Au contraire,* I could make it sleek and sexy, I swear. Promise me you'll come see me, sweetheart. For a special occasion or something."

"I'll think about it." She turned to me then, and her hug lasted a bit longer than usual. "How you doin', sweetie?"

"I'm fine. Much better now that this guy has resurfaced," I said, pointing at Jamie.

We sat, talked, looked at menus and decided on lunch. Jamie shared the story of his encounter with our future stepmother, and we all laughed at the absurdity of life.

When our food arrived, we shared bites from each entrée, as families do.

After lunch, we lingered over coffee until finally Jamie said, "Well, I'm off to work. Lovely to see you both."

"You're working?"

While Jamie and Jake were together, Jamie had changed his work schedule so that they could spend their weekends together. It was a big sacrifice; Saturday had always been Jamie's busiest—and most lucrative—workday.

"Yeah, it was hard to keep saying no to Saturday clients, so now I'm taking on a few. I'll probably end up with full days on Saturdays and take another day off during the week."

"That makes sense, I suppose," I said. "We'll just have to spend Sundays together."

"Of course." He leaned down and kissed first my forehead, then Chloe's. "See you soon, ladies."

He started to leave, and I remembered with a start the main reason I'd wanted to see him in the first place. "Jamie!"

He turned quickly, hearing the urgency in my voice.

"We have to plan our trip to Coeur d'Alene!"

Waving my words away he said, "I'll call you, Sagey," and the door closed behind him.

I frowned at Chloe. "I really have to pin him down about this trip."

"That's going to be a hard trip. Lucy left everything to you two?"

"Everything. The house and everything in it, plus whatever else she had. I really don't know anything about her financial situation or even what the house is worth. It's big, but it's old, and I know nothing about the market in that area. Guess I can go online and research it a bit."

Through the window, we saw Jamie pause on the sidewalk. From the inside pocket of his jacket, he took out his sunglasses and, in one fluid, ultra-cool motion, put them on his face.

I watched Chloe watching Jamie, her chin resting on her hand. "He is beautiful, isn't he?" she said as he walked away, waving at us one more time.

"Yes, he is. Inside and out."

"Sometimes I'm still that little girl who wants to marry him, you know."

"I know. I'm sorry."

"Hmm? Oh, no, don't be. He's like a brother to me now. But what beautiful children he would have made."

"He still could, you never know."

"You know what I mean. He would have given *me* beautiful children."

"Feeling some baby fever today, Chloe?"

"Yeah. It's been bad lately. I don't know why." She sipped her coffee. "Of course it doesn't help that Paul is probably having an affair."

"What? Chloe! You buried the lead! What's going on?"

She took a deep breath and let it out slowly before she spoke. "Paul has a very young, very attractive new assistant. When she first started, he talked about her constantly: 'Nicole is so ambitious and bright. Nicole has such an interesting style. Nicole is such a fast learner, I only have to tell her something once and she's got it down cold. Nicole's memory is amazing.' After a while, it was Nicki: 'Nicki's a dancer, you know, that's why she's in such fabulous shape. Nicki's so well read for someone her age. She understands all my references. It's incredible!' Blah, blah, blah.

"But then, and this is the most frightening thing of all, he stopped talking about her completely. Never mentions her. Ever. So yesterday I asked about her: 'How is Nicki doing these days? Is she all settled into the routine?' Sage, he was working at his desk, in the office at home. And he froze. He didn't look up, he just stopped moving for a few seconds. Then he continued doing whatever he was doing, opening mail, I guess, and said, 'She's doing very well. Best assistant I've ever had.' He didn't elaborate or tell me some little anecdote, or describe any of her perfect attributes. He's screwing her, I just know it."

It did sound damning, all of it. But I'd always known he was a rat bastard, which is ten times worse than being either a rat or a bastard. I reached across the table and squeezed Chloe's hand.

She sniffed. "I lie in bed at night, usually alone since he's working late so often now, and I think about everything I've given up for him. And I think about what I looked like when *I* was his little protégé. About how naïve I was. How I'd hang on his every word, swallow my own opinions because he was so brilliant, he *had* to be right about everything! Sage, I gave up all my dreams for him, and he let me. Forced me to, really, with a thousand ultimatums and now he's fallen in love with someone else. I wonder how long it will be before he breaks the news to me."

She was crying openly now, dabbing at her eyes with a tissue she'd fished out of her purse.

I was so angry I couldn't see straight. My face was so hot I thought it might actually be steaming, and all I wanted to do was hurt Paul, badly.

"You're not really going to wait for him to dump you, are you? You have to confront him! You have to stand up for yourself, tell him he can have his little Tiffany!"

"Nicki."

"Whatever. Tell him you're sure she's much closer to his emotional age. Better yet, tell him she must be fulfilling his dormant need to raise a child. Tell him that you deserve so much better, and that you are thrilled to have come to your senses and can't wait to end his tyrannical domination over your life!"

She nodded, looking at the table. "I can't afford the house, I'll have to move out. God, I'm such a cliché. Fall in love with an older man, give him the best years of your life, then have it all turn to shit, right before your eyes, as he falls in love with a younger, younger woman. I'm pathetic."

"Bite your tongue. There is nothing pathetic about you. Paul is the pathetic one. In fact, that's his new name: Paul the Pathetic. Pathetic

Paul. He can't sustain a real relationship based on mutual respect and equality. No, his relationships are with women young enough to be his daughters, which he refuses to have because that would mean he'd actually have to grow up."

"I wasn't young enough to be his daughter."

"He's fifteen years older than you. Technically, he could have been your father."

"I suppose you're right. God, Sage, I feel like such a fool."

"Well you're not. You're a good, kind, loving woman who fell in love with the wrong guy. It happens."

"But I've wasted so much time."

"Hey, listen." I took a deep breath, trying to slow my heart rate a bit. "You've learned a lot. You've traveled the world. It wasn't a waste. It's just time to move on. Right?"

"I guess so."

"Okay. So let's go get your stuff. You can stay with me until you find your own place."

"Now? Today?"

"Why wait?" I jumped out of my chair and threw on my jacket.

Chloe stared at me. "You really hate him, don't you?"

I sat back down, looking right in her eyes. "He never deserved you. Someone out there does, but it's not Paul."

"Do you think there's even a chance that I'm wrong? That's he's not having an affair?"

I thought about it, trying to be objective. "If he's not, he wants to. From what you've said, Chloe, he has a serious crush on this girl. What's the difference whether or not they've actually had sex?"

"No difference, really. You're right. But Sage? You're going to have to let me be sad about this for a while. And I need to talk to him before I leave. Please…" She held a hand up, silencing my objections. "I have to do this my way. I'm going home now, and I'll call you when it's time."

My shoulders drooped with disappointment—I wanted her out of there NOW—but I nodded. "Okay. Call anytime, I don't care if it's three in the morning, just call and I'll be over there. Promise?"

"I promise."

"Chloe, you're going to be okay."

"So will you, Sage."

The call came at midnight, and Chloe was calm as slack tide. "It's all true," she said. "They're in love, but she won't sleep with him until he's through with me. He's just a big old coward; he says he hasn't been able to bring himself to tell me. The poor girl has been waiting for months! Is it all right if I come over now?"

"Of course! But don't you want me to come get you, help you load some stuff into the car?"

"No, that can wait. I just really need to get out of here. I'll be there in half an hour. Thank you, Sage."

Damn. I was all riled up and ready for a confrontation. I wanted to blast Paul with a dose of venom so potent it would stop his heart, if he had one. I couldn't remember being so angry, so filled with fury. I picked up a cushion from my sofa and screamed into it, then threw it across the room. It landed on the floor with a soft, ineffective thud.

"Prrt?" Teddy asked, walking in from the bedroom where he'd been waiting for me.

"It's okay, Ted. I'm just a little crazy, that's all." He padded over and jumped onto my lap. I heard his purr revving up as I sat back, giving him more room. He had no idea what the problem was and he didn't care, as long as I was there with comfort and a predictable feeding schedule. Settling in now, I couldn't help but smile at his utter contentment, his uncomplicated happiness as he rubbed his neck against my hand. He leaned against my body, drooling with joy, and I stroked him gently. I began to calm down, and together, we waited for Chloe.

~12~

"Are pets allowed?" Chloe asked her prospective landlord.

It was Sunday, the day after Chloe's late night departure from Paul, and we had been looking at apartments all day. This one seemed the most promising: a clean, two-bedroom corner unit in a lovely little brick walk up. Across the street, facing the living room window, was a park with walking trails. The rent was reasonable for the area, and best of all it was only a ten-minute drive to my place.

"Small dogs and cats are allowed, with a non-refundable deposit."

"How much?" Chloe and I asked together.

"A hundred and fifty per pet. There is a limit of two pets." The landlord stood in the doorway watching us, holding a clipboard.

I wondered if Chloe was stalling. She didn't have any pets, at least not yet. Paul had been against that, too. He wanted no ties, nothing to worry about leaving behind when they traveled.

"How soon could I move in?" she asked at last.

"It's almost ready. We've painted already, obviously; now we just have to replace the carpet. But we have to check your references anyway. Here's the application. You can fill it out now if you like. If everything checks out you can move in next weekend. It will take a couple of days to process the paper work, and then we'll need first and last month's rent, the damage deposit, and the pet deposit. Come on down to the office and we'll get things rolling." He twirled and led the way to the staircase.

Chloe and I looked at each other. "Gay," I mouthed to her. She responded with a 'thumbs up' signal.

Chloe filled out the application and left it with Gay Landlord— his name was actually Alan, we learned—and we set off to find the nearest Starbucks.

"So what's this about pets?" I asked.

"I think I need a cat."

"I agree! Can I go with you to pick one out?"

She laughed. "Of course. I need an expert opinion."

"I'm no expert. Teddy found me."

"And he's given you massive cat knowledge. Besides I couldn't deny you the joy of looking at kittens."

"Oh, thank you, thank you! Look! There's a Starbucks right there by the park! It's a sign!"

Chloe laughed again. "Come on, my treat."

When our drinks were ready we sat outside. It was a bit chilly, but we hoped the sun would peek through the thin clouds.

"So, are you really as together as you seem?" I asked her.

"No. I'm actually a bit of a basket case. But I can look ahead to a time when I *will* be together. I can envision it." Chloe's voice broke a little; she was close to tears.

"I'm sorry. I shouldn't have said anything."

"No, it's okay. It just comes in waves, you know?"

"Yeah. But Chloe, he's so not worth it."

"Not him. It's all that time I spent on him. All those years. That's what I'm grieving. I'll never get that time back. And I have to go over there. He's going to pay for my new apartment. Just the move-in expenses; I'm not going to ask him to pay my rent every month. But I'll be damned if I'm going in the hole to move on with my life. He owes me that much, don't you think?"

"Damn right! He's got tenure, he can afford it."

"Oh, trust me, he can afford it. He's got all kinds of assets: real estate, stocks, a huge inheritance from a great aunt who died two years ago. I could sue him for a bundle. We had a long-term, common law marriage. I am legally entitled to half of everything."

Somehow, I couldn't imagine Chloe actually doing that.

"Well, you're certainly entitled to some compensation for sixteen years."

She shook her head. "I don't want his money. He always made it clear that it belonged to him, not us. I just want enough to make a fresh start. But I will threaten to take more if he doesn't want to cooperate. No, I can support myself just fine once I get back on my feet. I don't need him."

"You sure don't. Are you going to teach?" Teaching had always been Chloe's intention; she had earned her degree, had even gone through her student teaching requirement, but Paul had begged her not to work when they moved in together, saying that he wanted them to spend every available minute together. Meaning of course that she would wait around until he was available. So she took care of the house, the garden, and Paul, each year feeling ever so slightly more like a maid than a partner; another revelation she'd saved for today.

Chloe shrugged. "I hope so. I'll have to figure out how to get a valid certificate. I've stayed in touch with friends from college who are teaching now; maybe they can help.

"I still can't believe it, Sage. Why didn't I ever listen to you?"

I shrugged. "You were in love. Why didn't I listen to you about Colin?"

I saw her shudder. She picked up her coffee and held it with both hands. "Good point. Speaking of whom," Chloe said, "have you heard from him again?"

"No, not since those flowers mysteriously appeared at my door. He hasn't even called. No messages, nothing."

"Thank goodness. I really thought he might kill you, Sage."

Now I shuddered. "You and me both. But I'm through with all that. No more abuse for me. One red flag and I'm outta there."

"Well, you'd have to actually date someone to be able to spot a flag, red or otherwise."

"Yeah, yeah, I know. I've got perfect strangers telling me to start dating again, not to mention Jamie. *Et tu*, Chloe?"

"It's time, that's all. You need to get back on that horse."

"I've dated! A little."

"Rarely, and you haven't seen anyone more than once. You've barely dipped your toe in the pool."

"Will you listen to me when I tell you the same thing?"

"Maybe. It's hard to imagine right now."

"I know, sweetie. Men are selfish, emotionally and/or physically abusive pigs."

"Except for Jamie."

"Except for Jamie and other nice gay men," I agreed. Suddenly, a disturbing idea occurred to me. I gasped. "Jake cheated on Jamie, Chloe. Repeatedly. Do you think that gay men are pigs to each other?"

"I don't know. I hope not. Are lesbians pigs to each other?"

"Depressing thought. You'd think women would at least be decent to each other."

Chloe sighed. "You'd think. I guess it makes sense that some gay people are good to each other and some aren't. If only we were gay. We'd treat each other so well."

"I know. If only. Hey—have you called your mom yet?"

She shook her head. "I'm dreading it."

"Why? You've got the greatest mom in the world!"

"I know, and she'll try very hard not to say 'I told you so.' She'll bite her tongue in half avoiding those words, but I'll hear them between the lines anyway. She never liked him; she always agreed with you that he'd exploited me. But you know, I was with Paul for sixteen mostly happy years. At what point is a relationship successful? Just because it ultimately ended doesn't mean it was a total waste of time, does it?"

I scowled at the table. Tough questions. Yes, Paul was a cad who was now repeating the same offense that had brought Chloe into his life to begin with. But surely he had loved her somewhere along the way. I looked at her. "You seem stuck on this whole idea of wasted time. We talked about this. It wasn't such a bad way to spend sixteen years of your life, was it? You guys were happy for a long time. You're right, it was a successful relationship. He just lost his mind and blew it in the end, that's all. He's afraid of his own mortality and he's fallen into that weird trap, thinking that if a young woman loves him he'll never be old. Your mom will understand all that."

"You think so?"

"Of course." It was strange, but suddenly I couldn't for the life of me remember why I'd been so angry with Paul. For hurting Chloe, obviously, but maybe it had been a little out of proportion? I had wanted to hurt *him,* scream at him, tear him into tiny little pieces. I'd been disappointed that I wouldn't be able to confront him, felt deprived of my opportunity to verbally eviscerate him. Why? I shook my head, dismissing the question. "Call your mom. She'll be hurt if you wait too long."

To say that I'd been idolizing Mary Delaney my entire life would be an understatement. Chloe's mother represented to me all that was right and good in the world. As a young, single mother she had struggled with a fledgling, home-based business before it was fashionable, designing, making and selling jewelry, art, baked treats and canned goods from her garden. Somehow she'd always managed to pay her mortgage and put food on the table.

When Jamie and I moved in, it must have put an enormous strain on an already precarious situation, but Mary never complained or admitted to any hardship. She'd told me many times that she never entertained the idea of alerting the authorities or sending us to foster homes. Grandma Lucy offered to take us, but she could see that we were happy with Mary and settled into our school; plus, no one could bear the thought of Jamie and me moving so far from Chloe.

Mary grew flowers in her yard, lush and vibrant, carefully planted for blooms in every season. She often coaxed me outside and pointed out the stars of the moment: crocuses, hyacinths, daffodils and narcissus, peonies and irises. And her favorites, salvia and fuchsias, which she loved because they attracted hummingbirds. Mary adored hummingbirds, and always hung feeders in addition to planting their blossoms of choice, "to make sure they feel welcome."

Soon after Jamie and I began living with Mary, she pointed out the first hummingbird I'd ever seen. Somehow, I'd always just missed seeing them. I was beginning to think they didn't really exist when she tried once more to point one out. "Look! See, between those two trees!"

She'd knelt down beside me and pointed. "He's going to the red feeder, do you see him?"

And I did. I saw it hover, dip, and drink Mary's homemade nectar.

"That one's called Anna's Hummingbird," she whispered.

"Who's Anna?" I wanted to know. "Why is it hers?"

"I think they were named for a duchess named Anna. But Sage, isn't he beautiful? They fly like fairies, don't you think?"

As we watched, another one buzzed over to the feeder, too, and the two tiny birds flared their tails and darted toward each other.

"Oh! They're fighting over the feeder," Mary said.

"Why? Isn't there enough food?"

"Yes, sweetheart, there's plenty. I make sure it never runs out. And they eat from many flowers, too. It's just that they both think it's their food, and they're not very good at sharing."

Anna's Hummingbird won that round, and the other, a Rufous according to Mary, zipped off to parts unknown. Moments later, Anna's disappeared too.

My shoulders drooped.

"Don't worry, Sage. They'll be back." Mary straightened up, putting a hand on my hair.

"It's not that," I said. "Why can't they share? Why do they have to fight? What if they hurt each other?"

Mary squatted in front of me, looking right into my face—the face that was still bruised from the last beating by my father. "Honey, those little birds won't hurt each other. You saw, they never even touched. They just try to scare each other away, that's all. It's their instinct. All they know is that they have to eat. They know if they don't eat, they won't survive. That's all they think about, all day." She smiled. "If they could talk, all they'd say is, 'I'm hungry, I'm hungry, I'm hungry. Time to eat, time to eat, time to eat.' Until their babies come along. Then they'd say, 'Got to eat, got to feed the babies, got to eat, got to feed the babies.' So when another bird comes along, they think, 'He's taking my food!' and they try to scare it away."

I listened carefully to everything she said. "Do you understand, Sage?" she asked.

Slowly, I nodded. "They're just trying to survive. They have to fight. I understand."

Mary looked at me a long time before she drew me into her arms and held me tight.

I had always loved Mary, but at that moment something cemented between us. From then on, I utterly belonged to her.

"I guess you're right," Chloe said now. She brought out her cell phone and dialed. I watched as she waited for her mother's voice. "Mom? Hi. How are you? That's good."

Mary always said she was doing great, feeling fabulous, enjoying the limited celebrity her businesses had brought her. Life was always wonderful—and getting even better—from Mary's perspective.

Chloe listened attentively and as always said, "That's really good, Mom. I'm so happy for you! Uh, Mom? Listen, I have some news." Another pause. "Paul and I have split up. Yeah. Well, it was sudden for me, too. I'm staying with Sage for a week or so until my new place is ready. Thanks, I appreciate it, but Sage's place is really convenient. Yeah, I'm having coffee with her right now. Tonight? Hold on." She lowered the phone and whispered to me, "She's inviting us to dinner tonight. What do you think?"

"Absolutely!" I said, but added as an afterthought: "If you want to."

Chloe smiled at my enthusiasm and told her mother, "We'll be there. What time?"

Mary Delaney was one of those fortunate women who actually grew more beautiful with age. Angles that had looked a little sharp on her young face had softened with time so that now she looked nothing short of perfect, at least in my eyes.

Her hair was a darker red than Chloe's; it was auburn, a word I loved. She still wore it long, pulled back into a thick, wavy ponytail.

Mary had often described herself as a painfully thin, gawky teenager and young adult, and now a little extra weight had given her some curves. She rarely wore pants—she said that skirts were just more comfortable. So she wore them most often: cotton prints with a sweater or t-shirt, and sandals or clogs, or no shoes at all. Her toes were adorned with even more silver rings than her fingers, her toenails always painted bright colors.

Her jewelry business was still going strong—so strong that she had long ago moved to a larger home and converted an attached garage into her very own studio—and she always wore some of her latest creations. Today, a long silver chain hung around her neck; suspended from the chain was an enormous cat, crafted from silver and black onyx, sitting with its tail wrapped around its sleek body, its eyes knowing slits.

The earrings were mismatched: a mouse and a bird. Mary loved to infuse humor into her work.

Now, standing on her front porch, she greeted us, her arms wide open, encircling us both. "My girls!" Oh the joy of being called a girl at thirty-seven!

After the triple embrace, Mary turned her full attention to her daughter, holding Chloe's face in her hands. "You are going to be just fine, my darling, I promise you that. You will come to treasure this turning point; you'll thank the gods above, I promise you!"

"Thanks, Mama," Chloe whispered.

"These are for you!" I exclaimed, holding out the flowers I'd insisted we buy on the way.

"Thank you, Sage. You're so good with flowers, would you arrange them for me?"

"Of course." She led us into the house and reached up to a high cupboard, retrieving a large green vase. "Scissors?" I asked, and she brought them to me. I set about my work—flower arranging was something I took very seriously—and Mary turned back to her daughter.

"I made something for you just last week," she said, leading Chloe into her studio. "My sub-conscious must have known something was happening."

I dropped my scissors and followed, eager to see Mary's latest creation.

Mary's studio was devoted to her many artistic endeavors. Clay sculptures in various stages of completion lay on two long wooden tables. At the far end of the room stood an easel holding a canvas that we couldn't see—but we were never allowed to look at unfinished paintings anyway.

There was one painting on the wall. I recognized it from the old house. I'd always assumed it was one of Mary's and I loved its bright rows of colors. At the top was a green horizon and hint of blue sky. Fields of Flowers, Mary had said it was called. It had hung above the fireplace the entire time Jamie and I lived in that house. But now I noticed it wasn't signed in the corner as Mary usually did, with her first name only. I couldn't see any signature or initials anywhere on the painting. I made a mental note to ask about it later.

Below the painting stood a huge oval table with a smooth, green marble top, covered with pieces of silver, agate, onyx and a rainbow of quartz, along with the worn leather bag that held her tools: Mary's jewelry station.

From the center of the marble surface, Mary lifted a necklace. It was a pendant hanging from a black silk cord; she held it out to her daughter. Chloe held it up to the light. "Mom, it's so beautiful!"

Mary always used natural stones, but I wasn't sure what this was. It was reddish orange in color, perfect for Chloe, and carved into the shape of an open hand, palm up, complete with a long, healthy lifeline. Impulsively, I touched the cool, smooth surface.

"It's carnelian," Mary said. "It's supposed to help you break out of ruts, begin new things, become more centered. I don't know why, the stone just called to me. It whispered your name, Chloe."

"Thank you," Chloe whispered back.

"Here," I said. I took it from her and she held her hair up while I fastened the necklace at the base of her neck. "It's beautiful, Mary."

Chloe looked down and touched it again. "New beginnings." She reached out and touched her mother's hand.

"Let's go open some wine, what do you say, my darlings?" Mary said, leading the way back toward the kitchen.

I went back to work on the flowers, trimming and cutting, putting them together exactly as I'd imagined, then threw away the scraps and presented the bouquet to Mary. "Oh, Sage, they're so beautiful. You really have a gift."

She put the vase in the middle of the table, then got to work at the stove, cooking up some snacks for us while she chatted and hummed.

Finally, she joined Chloe and me around the table; we drank wine and ate the sautéed mushrooms Mary herself had harvested on a hike the day before. We watched the ever-present hummingbirds, dipping their slender beaks into the feeders hanging from the eaves outside the kitchen window. We laughed at old stories and new, laughed at silly things, laughed just because it felt so wonderful to be together again. It had been too long.

"And how is Jamie?" Mary asked.

"He's great. Just broke up with Jake, but he's doing really well," I said.

"Gorgeous as ever," Chloe said.

"It's so easy and so very sad to fall in love with someone who can't love you back," Mary said, gazing over our heads. "Gay men, especially. They can be so…. Well, so woman-like, I suppose. Sensitive, compassionate. Kind. Straight men seem to think they have to plow through the world, bulldozing, defeating whatever comes their way. Conquering. You know, the Alexander the Great syndrome. They feel they have to conquer women, too. Why is that? If only they realized that we make really great partners."

"Maybe there's hope for the next generation," Chloe said.

"There's always hope, honey. There's hope for all of us if we stay open to the possibilities," Mary said. She stretched across the table and squeezed our hands. "Have faith, my darlings. The universe is unfolding as it should."

I had never completely bought into the idea of Fate, or God, or The Force, or anything that may have some kind of control or plan in our chaotic existence on this chaotic little planet. But Mary couldn't have possibly looked at life any other way, and sometimes, like now, in her presence I could almost catch a glimpse of that peaceful, benevolent cosmos she lived in. "I'll drink to that," I said, lifting my glass.

Then Grandma Lucy floated through my mind, and I wondered if she was up there among the stars now, watching over me. How wonderful it would be to have a guardian angel like her. I decided to share the news of her death with Mary, hoping to hear such a hopeful theory. "Mary, I have some bad news. Lucy died."

"Oh, sweetheart, I'm so sorry. I hope she didn't suffer."

"I don't really know. She had cancer."

"Now tell her how you found out," Chloe said.

Mary looked back at me, already knowing. "You spoke with your father?"

I nodded, looking at the table. "He showed up at my apartment."

Mary took a deep breath. "Was he sober?"

"Yes. He says he has been for years now."

"Well what do you know. I really didn't believe he'd ever stop drinking."

"Oh, yeah, he's reformed all right," Chloe said. "He's getting married, he's all Born Again. Tell her about his fiancée."

"Did you meet her?" Mary asked.

"No, Jamie did. She called the salon for an appointment with him, showed up and introduced herself. Basically, she told him that she and our father hope that someday, with Jesus' help, Jamie will be cured of his sinful homosexual lifestyle," I said.

"She didn't."

"Yep. You know the drill: 'We hate the sin, not the sinner.' She even went so far as to share her theory of the reason for Jamie's gayness. It's because of our father's cruelty, you see. Jamie is looking for a surrogate father. Interesting, wouldn't you say?"

I could almost see the steam coming from Mary's face. She flushed bright red, but her voice stayed calm. "How did Jamie respond?"

"Oh, basically a 'thanks for trying to save my eternal soul from damnation, but no thanks' kind of thing."

"That man has the patience of Job. I would have dragged her out by her freshly cut hair," Chloe said.

"Well, Jamie is no caveman," Mary murmured; she sipped her wine. "Do you have to go to Coeur D'Alene, Sage?"

"Yeah. Jamie and I have to go clean out Lucy's house and put it up for sale. She left it all to the two of us."

"It's such a beautiful area. You two had some peaceful summers there with Lucy. You should make a vacation of it."

"I'd like to. I just need to pin Jamie down on a time to go. He's been a little evasive."

"He'll get there, honey. He just needs to process things his own way. This was a lot to deal with: your grandma's death and having contact with your father, all at once. How are you doing with all that, Sage?"

"I'm fine," I said.

"All evidence to the contrary," Chloe grumbled. "She had a panic attack!"

"You did?" Mary asked, her eyes suddenly huge. "Under what circumstances?"

I sighed, glaring at Chloe. "With a really nasty client. She went on and on about how ungrateful my generation is, how we need to genuflect in our parents' presence. Suddenly I couldn't breathe. My heart was pounding, I broke into a cold sweat, and I was convinced I would die unless I got very far away from that horrible woman."

"Sweetheart! What did you do?"

"I drove away—just a short distance—parked and waited until I calmed down. But I've been fine ever since, so don't worry about me."

"I'll try not to. Sage, honey, have you ever thought about seeing a therapist?"

This again? "No. I don't see the point. Sitting with a stranger and talking about things I'd rather not think about? How could that possibly be a good thing?"

"You might be surprised." Mary smiled. "There's something very powerful about having your pain acknowledged by another human being in a safe environment. If you change your mind, let me know. I have a number of friends who are therapists, and I'm sure one of them would be a good fit for you. Promise me you'll think about it? Especially if you experience any more episodes."

"Promise," I mumbled.

"Good. On that note," Mary said, standing up slowly, "I will get busy and whip up our main course. We need something tasty to go with this wine. But first, let's raise these glasses to Lucy Jamieson, one of the sweetest, most unselfish people I've ever known. Lucy, you'll be missed. May your spirit guide and protect us. To Lucy!"

"To Lucy," Chloe and I echoed.

"Need any help with dinner, Mom?" Chloe asked.

Mary put us to work chopping vegetables for a salad. All traces of my father were gone now; the spirit of Grandma Lucy prevailed, and soon we were all laughing again.

~13~

Monday morning I woke with the dread that had come to define that day of the week for me. But then I remembered: I was going to a training today. I'd be out of the office, away from that evil phone.

I'd set up my coffee pot the night before, timing it to finish brewing just as my alarm went off. Now, standing on my balcony, warming my hands on my favorite mug, I heard Chloe stir on the sofa.

"There's fresh coffee!" I called in through the screen.

She mumbled something that sounded like gratitude, and a few minutes later she joined me. Her hair was a crazy jumble, and her eyes weren't completely open. It was so good to have her here. I grinned. "Okay, tonight you get the bed," I told her.

Somehow I'd never gotten around to upgrading the twin bed Mary had donated to me when I moved out of her house, and from the first night Chloe had arrived she'd insisted that the sofa would be just fine. I'd thought about buying a bigger bed many times over the years, but my tiny little cocoon felt safe somehow, even though it was too small even to share comfortably with Teddy, but we managed somehow.

"No, the sofa is fine. I wouldn't have been able to sleep last night no matter where I was," Chloe said.

"Even so, it's your turn for the bed tonight. I mean it," I said, trying to sound firm. "What's your plan for today?"

She sighed. "I'm going to go see Paul and try to negotiate a deal. Then I'll pay the deposits on the apartment and maybe do a little shopping for furniture, towels, dishes and all that stuff. Later on, I'm going to call my friend Shelley to ask her advice about how to get back into teaching. Then I'll probably collapse and have a mini-breakdown. How about you?"

"Well, I'm going to an all-day training to learn how to communicate better with evil, nasty people. Funny, I'd rather practice speaking with nice people. There are still nice people out there, right?"

"There will be, because I'm going to be an amazing teacher and mold all those impressionable little minds so that someday they all become wonderful, compassionate people."

"Brilliant plan, Chloe! Catch them while they're young! Why didn't I think of that? Why did I decide to help people on the other end of the life cycle? That was stupid!"

"It seemed like a good idea at the time, right? Listen, you've just had some bad days lately. It will get better. Things will feel more balanced. There are wonderful, kind people out there, trust me."

"I know. It's just that the rotten ones are so *loud*." I thought about Elma Crow's voice and shivered. "I need more coffee."

I gave myself plenty of time to get to the office building where the training was being held. It was an unfamiliar address, and I was afraid I might get lost. (It had been known to happen on occasion.) But, lo and behold, I drove straight there and had a little time on my hands before I had to go inside, so I very dutifully checked my work voice mail.

Hooray! There was only one message, and it was from a pleasant client at that: Susan, a forty year old with Multiple Sclerosis. She used a wheelchair most of the time now, but she had a great attitude and a loving family (hmm, could there be a connection between those things?) and she still remained as active as possible. Her message was simple: "Hi, Sage, it's Susan. I know we're scheduled for a visit this week, and I wrote down the day and time, but I've lost the note. When you get a chance, would you give me a call to remind me? Thanks!"

I could feel the tension ease when the computerized voice told me that was the end of my messages. Things were going so well, I decided to call the receptionist and ask her to check my inbox for new clients.

"Hey, Erin, it's Sage."

"Hi, Sage. How are you?" Erin was probably all of twenty-four, petite and perky. The girl couldn't help it; she was simply a happy person. Perfect to field calls from not-so-happy clients. "You're gone all day, right?'

"Right, I'm at a training. I just thought I'd check in and see if there are any intakes for me."

"Okay, just a sec… Sage? There are two for you."

Two more people to add to my caseload, and, right now, before they had faces or voices or personalities of any sort, they were perfect.

"Thanks, Erin. Would you read them to me?"

One was an eighty-two year old man with the improbably generic name of John Smith, a widower living alone in a small apartment, just needing a little help with housework and transportation. He sounded wonderful.

The other was a woman, seventy, still living in her own home. Her name—her name was very familiar somehow: Molly Logan. Molly—*Oh my God!* Could it be the same Molly Logan?

"Uh, would you give me those phone numbers? I'll call and set up the initial visits."

"Wow. You're dedicated, aren't you?" Erin commented before dictating the numbers.

As soon as I'd exchanged good-byes with Erin, ("Have a great day, Sage!"), I called the number for Molly Logan, and a sleepy voice answered, "Hello?"

"Hello, is this Mrs. Logan?"

"It's Molly. Who is this?"

"Uh, my name is Sage…"

"Sage, darling! How wonderful to hear from you! It was so fabulous running into you with my granddaughter the other day. Have you decided to call my son, is that why you're calling, for a little encouragement?"

Yep, definitely the same one. "No, actually, I'm calling on business. I work with social services, and I've been assigned to your case. So, I need to make an appointment to come see you and figure out what kind of help you need."

Silence.

"Molly?"

"Well. The Lord does work in mysterious ways, don't you think, sweetheart? This is kismet, that's what it is! You're the case manager they said would call?"

"Yes, I am, and I just need to come see you to get your services started."

"You know, it was Sam who looked into this whole thing. I really don't think I need any help. But you come see me just the same. We'll have coffee and chat. Do you need my address?"

"No, I have it. Are you busy tomorrow morning? About ten or so?"

"Tomorrow morning is perfect. I'll see you then. What a lovely surprise!"

A lovely, albeit strange surprise. It seemed Molly and Sam would continue to be minor characters in my life after all, at least for a while.

I wrote the appointment down in my all-in-one planner/purse— so far I'd resisted getting an electronic version—then called my other new client. I recorded that appointment as well, zipped my planner closed and headed for the classroom. The planner I chose to use was not perfect. It was big, holding an entire yearlong calendar. It had a built in wallet, with room for cash, coins and credit cards, but really had no place to store other items I would normally carry in a purse. My cell phone could be tucked inside the planner section, but anything else made it too bulky to zip closed. My key chain hung from the loop where the strap attached, and I tended to tuck a lipstick in my pocket, when I remembered one at all. But I liked the ritual of actually writing down my appointments, and I wasn't ready to give that up.

Rachel was already there, Starbucks cup in hand; she waved me over. "Hey! Good morning, Sage. How was your weekend?"

"It was pretty good, actually. How was yours?"

"Wonderful, thanks. Well, this should be interesting."

"I hope so."

"Oh! Before I forget, I wanted to ask if you want to have lunch one day soon."

"Sure." I'd hung my planner/purse on the back of my chair, so I grabbed it and opened it up on the table in front of me to check my appointments for the week. "Are you free Wednesday?"

"That would be great. I work until noon Wednesday, so I'll just go to lunch with you before I go home. Perfect!"

"Great!" I wrote Lunch w/Rachel on the square for Wednesday at noon.

The instructor took her place at the front of the room; everyone stopped talking at once, then giggled a little at the sudden silence.

"Hi everyone," she said. "I'm Linda MacAvoy, and I'm here today to talk about talking. To communicate about communicating. Hopefully I'll present the information in a clear, concise and interesting way, which is basically the aim of all communication. But putting forth your ideas clearly, concisely and in a way that will encourage the listener to take in your message fully and accurately, becomes an even bigger challenge when that person is angry, upset, or simply unwilling to listen."

As Linda MacAvoy spoke, I noticed the door open. Through it walked the most striking woman I had ever seen. She must have been over six feet tall, and she carried herself like royalty. Her skin was the color of my morning latté, her face smooth and chiseled to perfection. Her hair had been pulled away from that perfect face and tucked into a small knot at the top of her long neck. She wore a deep red suit. I stared. I couldn't help it.

She was walking toward our table. Oh my God. I was going to be sitting with Rachel and this exotic queen. No question who the lady-in-waiting was here.

Linda paused just half a beat as she noticed the latecomer and walked over to give her the materials for the class. I honestly wondered why no one had gasped when she entered the room.

The tables were placed such that there was only room for two people on each side. Her Highness sat opposite me, angled so that she could watch Linda. Her perfect profile was in my line of vision.

Now I nearly did gasp, realizing that my huge, ungainly planner/purse was still on the tiny table along with the handouts and notepaper. Quickly, I zipped it up and hung it back on my chair, then turned my attention back to Linda.

Throughout the morning, I tried not to stare at my new sovereign. She was so exquisitely beautiful it almost hurt to look at her. I was sitting with two women who could be walking down a red carpet in couture gowns. I knew it was silly, but a part of me wanted to hide my face, to disappear. Surely my flaws had never been quite so screamingly obvious before.

Rachel and I spent our lunch break together, and when we came back to the room, our companion had chosen a different table to share for the rest of the day. She was behind me now, but every once in a while I still peeked at her, just a little.

When Linda ended her lecture, we all clapped and thanked her. Rachel and I gathered up our papers, and I tossed my giant planner/purse over my shoulder.

Suddenly, without warning, The Queen was towering over me. She had crossed the room to speak directly to ME. I was terrified and thrilled at the same time. I smiled up at her. She did not smile down upon me.

"What's your name?" she demanded.

"It's Sage Whitaker. Nice to…"

"What do you do?"

"Uh, I'm a social worker."

"You are. In what capacity?"

"I work with elderly and disabled adults." I was confused, but felt oddly compelled to answer her questions.

"Hmmpf. Well, I came over here to tell you that you need to watch your actions. Body language and behavior communicate much more than you realize."

"What do—what did—how…"

"When I came in and sat at your table, you closed your purse and removed it."

Ohmygod. *It's okay,* I told myself. *It's a simple misunderstanding.* "Oh, no, no, no. I was just moving it to give you more space. It was a cramped area, and I…"

"You moved your purse away from me. That was a very racist gesture, and you need to be more aware in the future. I'm fine, I can take care of myself, I'm a very strong person. I'm going to be taking the bar exam very soon. But someone else might be devastated by such a gesture, so I wanted to address it."

I glanced at Linda MacAvoy, who was busily tucking papers into her briefcase. Was this a demonstration for the class? Was it a joke? I looked at Rachel, who was watching from a distance, looking concerned.

I decided to use my newly honed communication skills. "I am very sorry if what I did made you feel uncomfortable. I would like to explain. My purse, which is also my planner, was hanging on my chair. I put it on the table so that my co-worker and I could coordinate a meeting. When you joined us at the table, I moved it back to my chair so that we would all have more room."

"I'm going to be an attorney. I'm a smart woman. I know about these things. And I'm telling you that what you did was make an extremely racist overture, and you need to change your behavior in the future."

Now I was angry. She wouldn't even listen! My face was hot and I was dangerously close to tears. No, I would not bow down to this merciless queen. I did not deserve this tirade.

Or did I? Was she just responding to something intrinsically ugly inside me? Could she see through me?

She was still standing there, arms crossed over her chest, bending down slightly, closer to my face. I looked to Rachel again, and she started walking toward us.

I had to escape, but this woman seemed to be waiting for me to say something. "Well," I said, with as much sarcasm and smugness as I could muster, "I'm sure you'll make a really good lawyer." What? That was the best I could do?

Rachel steered me away and walked with me to my car. "Are you okay? What was that all about?"

"She thinks I'm a racist! She *called* me a racist! Loud enough for other people to hear it! She wouldn't listen to me! She hated me! She kept sneering at me! Rachel, why do people pick on me? Is the word VICTIM tattooed on my forehead? Is that how people know they can just abuse me and push me around and get in my face for NOTHING and treat me like absolute shit?"

"Ssh, Sage, it's okay. Take a deep breath, all right?"

Rachel put her arm around me and actually kissed my cheek. "There is nothing wrong with you. I know you've been through a lot, and I know that must be why you reacted this way to what that awful woman said."

"How would you react?"

"Well, what exactly did she say?"

"That moving my purse away from her was an act of racism."

"But you know it wasn't. You know you were trying to be considerate. She came in late! She didn't know you were just moving it back to where it was in the first place."

"I know! I tried to tell her that but she wouldn't listen!"

"Well, then, I would have told her that if she walks into a situation late she shouldn't assume she has all the information. And I would have said that attacking a perfect stranger for such an innocuous thing is obviously not going to make the world a better place. In fact, I think I will tell her that!"

I watched as Rachel turned back toward the building. "No! Rachel, don't go back!"

"Why? That woman thinks she has the right to pick on innocent people. That's absurd, and she needs to know that." She kept walking.

And it came: creeping over me, almost a living thing, that panic. I tried to get my breathing under control. I tried to call for Rachel, but she was too far away to hear my gasps. All I could think was: Don't go, don't go, don't go. Going back was DANGEROUS. Going back could kill you.

I managed to open my car and sit in the driver's seat. There I waited, trying to breathe more deeply, to calm my mind until it finally began to work. My heart slowed a bit. I found a napkin in the glove compartment and dabbed at my eyes. Then I got back out of my car and looked for Rachel.

She was in front of the entrance to the building, talking to the Giant, gesturing wildly. Rachel was nearly as tall, and now she pointed in the woman's face. And—could this really be happening?—the woman held her own hands up, seemingly in surrender.

Finally, the red suit went in one direction and Rachel started back toward me. The panic attack had been a quick one; I hoped nothing of it remained on my face.

Rachel grinned at me. "Well, like most bullies, she was a coward at heart," she said. "Sage, are you all right? You're so flushed."

I took a deep breath. "I'm fine. What did she say?"

"Well, at first she said, 'Excuse me, I was just trying to educate your friend.' I said, 'But unfortunately you were completely wrong and way out of line, and you refused to listen to reason. I was *there*, by the way. Her purse was on the chair until I asked her to lunch. She put the purse on the table to check her schedule. The instructor started speaking, which distracted her from putting it back. Then you arrived, LATE, I might add, and she returned the purse to its original, out of the way location. I watched her do it! She was trying to be considerate, to welcome you to our table. That's all there was to it!' Then she caved. 'Well, it seems I was mistaken,' she said. 'Please apologize to your friend.' I said that I'd tell you what she said, but she really should apologize herself."

"Did you really?"

"Yeah, but she said she had to go study for the bar exam."

"Thank you, Rachel. You hardly know me, and you stood up for me."

"You're welcome. I just hate bullies. You have to stand up to them, that's all. You can't let someone like that make you doubt yourself. She's statuesque and has a strong presence, and I'm sure she's used to being noticed and admired, but that doesn't mean she has the right to push other people around. Right?"

"I guess. Thanks again."

"You're very welcome. I'll see you tomorrow, Sage."

I watched her walk away. She turned once and waved at me. It occurred to me that there were people who would have paid to watch the scene I'd just witnessed. *Tonight, on ESPN! Battle of the Beauties! Watch as a gorgeous brunette social worker gets into a heated debate with a stunning African-American attorney! Who will communicate more clearly? Who will dazzle with her logic? Whose legs are longer?*

On the way home, I again marveled at Rachel's spontaneous decision to confront my attacker. It reminded me of something Mary would do. Or something I would do, if Jamie or Chloe were the ones being bullied.

So why couldn't I do it for myself?

~14~

Molly Logan lived in a modest rambler with a lovely flowerbed cut in half by the front walk. Spring tulips were in full bloom now; someone (Sam?) had cut off the faded hyacinths and daffodils. I could see what little was left of their stems, just a couple of inches above the soil. The tulips were beautiful, in red, yellow and bright purple, bowing in the breeze like well-trained butlers.

She opened the door before I could knock, and threw her arms around me as if we were the closest of friends, reunited after years of separation.

"Come into the kitchen, Sage. I have coffee for you. I know you like coffee. Sit down, sweetheart!"

I sat at her kitchen table, putting my briefcase on the floor beside my chair. "Thank you, Molly." It felt strange, sitting in this woman's kitchen, being welcomed as if we actually knew each other.

She brought my coffee over in a large, flowered mug. There was a sugar bowl on the table and Molly slid it over to me across the vinyl tablecloth. "Do you take cream? I have heavy cream and half and half. What would you prefer?"

"Half and half is fine, thanks."

Flitting from drawer to fridge to the table, she reminded me of a bird: fragile, but moving in quick, sure, instinctive steps. Finally, she joined me at the table with her own coffee, steaming in a cup that read World's Greatest Grandma.

"Now, tell me all about this job of yours. What are you here to offer me?" she asked.

There was my cue. I shifted into automatic, the speech I had memorized months ago, complete with pregnant pauses and compassionate tones. I slid the neat folder out of my briefcase that held the ten-page intake form for my assessment of Molly's needs.

And just as it had happened so many times before, I saw my new client's eyes glaze over as she stopped listening to my meaningless words.

In the earliest days of my new career, I had actually paid attention to those cues, stopped myself, rephrased and asked questions to ensure that I was being understood. But after a while, I found myself just going through the motions, knowing I would eventually have to explain the program all over again to my poor confused client. I would feel ashamed of my laziness, my lack of enthusiasm, of having clients sign papers that made little sense to them. It felt manipulative, wrong in fact, but truthfully I was weary to the bone of answering the same questions over and over.

Now Molly's eyes met mine. "I'm sorry, dear, I always drift off when someone speaks legalese. Please go on."

I smiled. If she could be fully present, so could I. "You know what? I hate *speaking* legalese. Here's the deal. I'll go through a list of tasks, and you tell me how well you're able to perform each one without any help. At the end of it all, I calculate how many hours of help you'll get each month. Does that make sense?"

"You bet. Fire away."

"Okay. How about housework? This place looks great, Molly. Do you do all the cleaning?"

"Well, no, I don't. These days it just wears me out. I was in a car accident a few years ago and my right leg has never been the same. It just hurts sometimes, with very little provocation. So I dust and keep the kitchen clean, but Sam cleans my bathroom so I don't have to kneel down or scrub too hard, and he vacuums for me and makes my bed."

"All right. Laundry?"

"I still do all my own laundry," Molly said, obviously pleased with herself. "And I fold it and put it all away, except for putting clean sheets on the bed. Sam does that."

"What kind of help do you need with transportation? Medical appointments? Grocery shopping?"

"I still drive, but only during the day, and only short distances. But if I'm having some kind of test done at the doctor's office, sometimes I get a little shaky. So Sam would rather take me on those days. It's usually just once every couple of months or so."

"Okay. Molly, how are you doing with your bathing? Are you pretty comfortable getting in and out of the tub by yourself?"

"More comfortable than I'd be with someone else there!" She laughed and sipped her coffee.

"I understand, but really—are you shaky then, too?"

Suddenly her smile was gone, and she nodded. "Sometimes it's pretty tough, Sage. There are days when this body just doesn't want to cooperate with me. Don't get old if you can help it, doll."

"Well, as they say, it beats the alternative."

"Ha! Good point."

"So if I sent you someone who could just hold your arm to steady you a little bit as you get in and out of the tub, how would that be?"

"The same person every time?"

"It might be someone different once in a while, if your regular person was sick or something, but yes, you'd have one person coming to you most of the time."

"So I'd get to know her. It would be a girl, right?"

"Absolutely."

"Okay. I suppose I could deal with that."

Every once in a while it really hit me, how hard it must be to accept this kind of help. There was nothing horribly wrong with Molly, she was just getting a little frail. So she was beginning to lose a little independence here and there; she understood that it was for her safety, her health, her well-being, and yet—

—and yet each step downward was a loss to grieve. There would never come a time when Molly woke up suddenly twenty years younger, able to take care of herself completely. This was the beginning of the end of her life, and she knew it. That's why there were tears in her eyes as I finished my assessment, and informed her that she was entitled to sixteen hours per month, to be divided up according to whatever schedule would work best for her and for the assistant who would be assigned to her.

"The supervisor for these services is a woman named Mona. She's really nice, and she'll be out to see you, too. Then she'll figure out the best person to send to you and get it all started. Do you have any questions?"

Molly dabbed at her eyes with a tissue I had given her—I carried them in my briefcase—and smiled. "I'm sorry. I just don't know what's wrong with me. Here you are, telling me I'm going to get some help around here. That will ease the burden on Sam—that's a good thing! And I'm blubbering like an idiot."

She sighed, her eyes closed tight. Then those eyes opened and looked directly into mine. "I do have one little question, though. Have you changed your mind about calling Sam? No, listen to me, Sage. He's a wonderful man, and he's so lonely. He needs help with Savannah, and..."

"Molly, I know nothing about kids. I've never been a parent, and besides I'm really not ready for a relationship."

"You would be ready for the right one. Look, I know I'm a pushy old woman, but I've wasted a lot of time in my life, so I know a little something about that. Why not just ask the man out for coffee? What could possibly be wrong with making a new friend?"

I had no answer for her. Worse, I found myself agreeing to call Sam! Sitting behind the wheel of my car, I stared at the number Molly had written down for me again, ("Just in case you've misplaced it," she'd said) and wondered what the hell had just happened.

~15~

Red and yellow tulips, a gift to myself, bowed from a vase at the center of my kitchen table. I sat, alternately staring at the flowers and the slip of paper bearing Sam's phone number. Yet again, I debated with myself. Chloe had been off running errands and dealing with Paul until late in the evening, and so I had passed three nights alone this way since meeting with Molly. I was growing weary of both sides of the argument.

I promised Molly I'd call her perfect son, and at that moment I'd really wanted to call him. What's the harm, after all, in an innocent cup of coffee or lunch with a new acquaintance? It's healthy to meet new people, no matter their gender. If there's a spark, we could take it further, but it would be perfectly fine simply to make a new friend, too. So stop being such a coward, such a **drama queen**, *for god's sake and just call him!*

But—and there's always a but, isn't there?—this is how it starts. Sam and I meet for coffee, then lunch, then dinner. He seems wonderful and I fall in love with him. Somehow I forge a relationship with his daughter.

(Forge—funny word to describe an undertaking so completely foreign to my experience. I would have to "forge" a role as surrogate mother. And I would be a total fake and Savannah would know it immediately and hate me forever! Okay, calm down. No forging will be done today.)

And ultimately Sam will turn into some kind of monster and everything will fall apart and I'll never see Savannah again. She will rebel, angry with her father for pushing me away after we'd bonded so completely; she'll become a runaway, living on the street and selling her body for drug money.

That's it. I can't call.

But I have to. Come on, Sage, be rational for once in your life. Aaaaagh!

I picked up the phone, dialed his number quickly before I could change my mind again, and began pacing. *He probably won't be home, and I'll have to leave a message, and he won't know who I am and never call me ba—*

"Hello?" Nice telephone voice.

"Hi. Uh, Sam?"

"Yes, this is Sam. Who's calling?"

"You probably don't remember me, but my name is Sage. We sort of met through your mother at Starbucks one morning?"

He laughed. "I sort of meet a lot of women through my mother, but yeah, I remember you. Mom said you're her new caseworker, is that true?"

"Yeah, small world, huh? And I actually ran into her one other time, when your daughter was with her. Savannah, right? She's beautiful."

"Thanks. Yeah, I think she's pretty amazing, but that's my job, right? Mom said you were going to call me, but I didn't think you really would. I hope she didn't bully you too badly."

"No, not at all. Well, maybe a little. Somehow I promised her I'd call you, and I really hate to break my promises."

"That's admirable."

"Thanks. Uh, so I was just thinking maybe we could appease her by meeting for coffee sometime." *Good. I'm not begging a stranger for a date, I'm offering a way to satisfy his mother's demands, no strings in sight.*

"Coffee would be nice. At Starbucks it sounded like you and I are in the same boat. Recently single and not looking for a relationship?"

"Exactly. But I could always use another friend."

"Who couldn't? Okay, let's meet for coffee. My treat. It's the least I can do after you endured Molly's Matchmaking Services."

"Deal."

"How about this Saturday, 11 o'clock, same Starbucks?"

"I'll be there."

"Good. Okay, Sage. Nice talking to you. See you Saturday."

"See you then. Bye."

I hung the phone back on the wall and sat heavily, suddenly exhausted. *So, friendship it is.* He had made that clear. I had told both Sam and myself that making a new friend would be just fine. Did I mean it?

Yes, of course I did. But, a tiny little part of me also wanted Sam to fall madly in love with me at second sight, propose right then and there and carry me off to live in a castle with his sweet and lovely daughter, Princess Savannah.

Sighing, I lifted myself off my chair and walked to the fridge, looking for some kind of nourishment. Teddy, always hopeful when I was in the kitchen, joined me as I pushed things aside, looking for some perfect forgotten item in the back. "Are you hungry too, Ted?"

"Prrrt?" he responded.

I found some takeout fried rice; it smelled okay, so I warmed it up in the microwave, then opened a can of cat food for Teddy. "Here you go, buddy," I said, plopping it down in front of him. He immediately dipped his nose into the can, his tail stretched out in a straight line behind him.

Eating my rice right out of the carton, I watched Teddy go through his post-meal bath ritual. He closed his eyes, licked a paw and brought it up, over an ear, down his face and back to his mouth where he licked it again. So efficient. When he deemed his face clean, he slid down to the floor to work on his back, twisting his neck around at an impossible angle. Cats must have been the inspiration for yoga. No other creature could possibly enjoy stretching so much.

Once again, after eating marginally nutritious food and before contemplating which TV shows to watch, I resolved to join a gym, take a yoga class, do something active each day. Starting tomorrow.

In the meantime, I stretched out on my sofa, beckoning Teddy to join me, which he did eagerly, and I clicked on the TV, hoping that Chloe would come home soon.

Coffee on Saturday, two days from now. In spite of myself, I hoped this meeting would change my life.

~16~

Sam rose awkwardly when he spotted me walking toward him. Even more awkwardly, he shook my hand. "Uh, nice to see you again. How are you?" he asked as we sat down.

"I'm fine, how are you?"

"Good, I'm good."

I eyed the coffee sitting in front of him. We both started talking at once.

"I think I'll…"

"What would you li…"

In spite of Sam's generous offer to buy my coffee, I figured going Dutch was fine for a first date, on the outside chance that was really what it was. "I'll just go get some coffee," I said. "I'll be right back."

There was a long line, so I wasn't quite right back, but soon enough I was sitting across from this very pleasant-looking man drinking a yummy warm beverage. There were worse ways to spend a Saturday.

"So, where's Savannah today?"

"She's with her mom. Every other weekend."

"Ah. Does she get along with her mom all right?"

"Yeah, they're fine together. It's just that I was always the stay-home parent until we split up, so Gwen agreed it made sense for me to be home base for Savannah."

"Did your mom really hate your ex from day one?"

"No, actually, that's selective memory on her part. Mom liked Gwen to begin with, but when our marriage started crumbling of course she wanted to blame someone and she felt she had to side with me. The breakup wasn't anyone's fault, really. We just… weren't right for each other. I couldn't… be… the kind of husband… she deserved."

Oh. My. God. Granted, I truly felt I was a little more perceptive than most people in this arena, but this was so damn obvious it was sad.

"So, how long have you known you're gay?"

For the first time since I sat down, Sam actually looked at my face. He opened and closed his mouth several times. When his shoulders sagged in defeat I was suddenly sorry for my bluntness.

"I'm sorry I was so blunt."

"How did you…"

"Have you not come out yet?"

"Well, maybe I've put one toe outside. I have friends who know. My ex-wife, of course. But my mom knows nothing, obviously. My boss, co-workers, my daughter, they're all in the dark. How did you know?"

I shrugged. "My brother is gay. He's got a lot of friends who tried to pass for a long time, lived a double life. A couple still do. I can spot it a mile away. I hope I didn't spook you."

"No, no, it's fine. It's actually a relief not having to pretend."

"So when do you plan on sticking, oh, say a whole foot out of that stifling little closet?"

"I don't know. God, it's so scary. What was it like for your brother?"

"He was never really *in* the closet. It's just that as we grew up, one day we finally had a word for it. But no one ever thought Jamie would marry a cute little cheerleader and live happily ever after."

Sam turned purple. "God, was Gwen a cheerleader?" I asked.

"Uh huh. *Everyone* expected me to do that, so that's what I did. I played football at U Dub."

"You were a Husky?"

"Yeah, went to the Rose Bowl and everything. Gwen was indeed a cheerleader, a really good one. She's very cute and very sweet."

"The all American couple."

"Exactly."

"How long were you married before she figured it out?"

"She knew there was something wrong almost immediately. Our sex life, well let's just say it wasn't great."

"The poor woman. She had this hot husband and couldn't figure out why he didn't want her."

"Well, I don't know about the hot part, but yeah, that's pretty much how it went. I tried to make her happy, I really did."

"But you're gay."

"Exactly."

"Did you think it was wrong, unnatural, all that stuff?"

"Yeah, I guess. The guys I played football with—wow, all the gay bashing that went on. It was like being gay meant you weren't even human."

"So you felt you had to live a lie."

"I thought I could change."

"Surprise, you couldn't! That's so sad, Sam. For all of you. You have to tell Savannah! There's no telling what she's picked up on. She may have really strange and horrible ideas about what broke up your marriage. The truth will be better than whatever she's thinking, trust me."

"Maybe. I've been considering it. I just want to do it the right way. Whatever that is."

"And how is Gwen doing?"

"Really great. She's dating a nice guy. They're talking about moving in together. And I think she's almost forgiven me."

"Good for her."

"Funny thing is, she's never been homophobic. She's always had gay friends. But she never even guessed that I might be."

"She was too close. She loved you. It was easier for her to think there was something wrong with her. But I'll bet deep down somewhere she knew."

"I suppose."

"So are you dating a really great guy too?"

He laughed. "Not right now. It's tough having a relationship from halfway inside a closet, you know?"

"I can imagine. Hey. You want to go for a walk?"

We walked around for hours that day, had lunch together, drank several coffees from several Starbucks, and found that we had a lot in common. He'd even had an abusive boyfriend once!

"It was awful, Sage. How could I tell anyone about the abuse, let alone call the police about it, when I wasn't supposed to be dating men? I thought about saying he'd mugged me, but then how would I know who he was? I didn't think I'd be able to lie like that anyway, so the bastard got away with it. I actually told everyone that I'd fallen down a flight of stairs, can you believe it?"

"Yeah, actually I can. It's not too much easier to report abuse when *everyone* knows you date men, believe me."

Sam was so easy to talk to. I told him about my horrible job I'd once wanted so badly, and about my terrible childhood, and even about Grandma Lucy's death.

"Well maybe you can use your inheritance to figure out what you really want to be when you grow up," he suggested.

"Maybe. I have no idea how much I'll end up getting, but maybe it will be enough to pay Jamie back and buy some time to find something else. That's a nice thought."

We ended up having dinner together that night, and when he walked me back to my car I gave him a big hug. "You know what? I was so disappointed that you only wanted to be friends."

"You were?"

"Yeah, you're a cutie! But now? I'm so glad we're friends!"

"So am I. Next time maybe we'll do something with Savannah, okay?"

"I'd love to. Good-night, Sam!"

I tucked my toes into my favorite slippers that night and sat on the sofa, sipping cocoa. It had been such a long time since I'd spent a day with someone whose company I so thoroughly enjoyed. Of course I wasn't stupid enough to fall in love with a gay man, but I definitely wanted him to be part of my life.

Hmm. Wouldn't it be nice if...

I smiled, hatching my little plot.

I kept smiling as I rinsed out my cup. Still smiling, I called Teddy and headed for bed.

~17~

"Come on, Jamie, we've got to get this over with."

I had waited six days—six!—before calling Jamie. He'd been neglecting me horribly: no daily phone calls to look forward to, no dinners, and my hair needed cutting badly. In short, I'd had no Jamie fixes at all. And I knew why he'd been avoiding me.

"Oh, Sagey, can't you go without me?"

"No. Absolutely not. This is your responsibility too."

"I know, but business is so crazy right now, I just can't get away."

"Bullshit. It's always crazy, and you can always get away."

"Sherry will can my ass without hesitation."

"Not for taking a vacation to settle your dead grandmother's affairs! How long has it been since you've taken a day off?"

He mumbled.

"What?"

"I don't want to go, Sage."

There it was, finally. The truth.

"Why?"

"I don't want to see that empty house. I don't want to remember being there with Grandma Lucy. I don't want to bump into people who remember seeing me as a child and have to listen to, 'Oh, I can't believe you're all grown up!' Please, Sage, spare me all of it. You're the big sister, aren't you supposed to protect me? No, no, ignore that. I know that's not fair. You've done more than your share of protecting me. Honestly, I really don't know why I dread it so much, I just do."

"Well, I think you should face your fear. I can't do this by myself, Jamie. There's too much work to do. We need to take a week, maybe two, clear out the whole house and put it on the market. We need to have it appraised—I have no idea what it would be worth, do you?"

"No clue. You can have all the money if you do all the work," he offered.

"Jamie, no. Please. You have to come with me. I need another pair of hands, another brain. Someone to ask, 'what do you think?' when we're sifting through Grandma Lucy's stuff and deciding what to keep and what to toss. You need to be there to claim what you want, I can't do that for you."

"Oh, all right. All right! How soon do you want to go?"

"As soon as possible. I'm going to take two weeks off. Can you?"

"Two weeks! No. No way. If I don't work I don't get paid, Sage."

"Jamie, I know what your bank account looks like. This is the rainy day you've been saving for! Come on. This way we can take our time. We can get everything done all in one trip. And we can enjoy ourselves a little. Swim in the lake. Soak up some sun. What do you say?"

"It's still spring, it won't be very warm. And the lake will be freezing."

"Jamie, I really need this break. And I need you! Please?"

"Okay, Sage. Only for you. But you owe me big, you hear me?"

"Great! Fabulous! Thank you! Oh and I think I know how I can repay you."

"Really?"

"I met a guy."

"Praise the Lord!"

"He's gay."

"Uh oh."

"And he's wonderful! He was married, played it straight for a while until he couldn't anymore. He has a daughter, Savannah."

"Beautiful name."

"Beautiful little girl. I've seen her. Anyway, his name is Sam."

"Sam as in Sam and Molly the meddling mother?"

"The very same Sam."

"Sage, obviously Molly thinks Sam is straight."

"Well…"

"No way, Sage. You will not fix me up with a closet queer. Been there, done that too many times to count. Not going there again."

"But he's so ready, Jamie. He just needs one final push…"

"Find yourself another pusher. Once he's come out into the real world, if he's still interested, have him call me."

"But Jamie, he's so…"

"No, Sage. You don't understand. It's just so painful to be 'The Reason.' Everyone blames you. 'Our wonderful son/brother/cousin/whatever would never have become gay if he hadn't met you, Son-of-Satan-and-all-that's-evil.' I'm telling you, even if this guy is perfect in every other way, it wouldn't be worth it. Let him get through that door all on his own, then we'll see. So you've become friends with this guy?"

"Yeah. It was actually supposed to be a date, but I knew right away that he's gay."

"He's still dating women?"

"No! Only to appease his mother."

"Sage, I realize that you tend to miss great big red flags, but hello! Prospective love interest dating my sister? That's what I would call crimson."

"Even so, he made it clear right up front that we would just be friends. But all that aside, if he does come out soon, you'll consider a fix up?"

"Possibly. Keep me posted." He paused, and I silently cheered at this tiny ray of hope. "Wait a minute. This wouldn't be vicarious involvement, would it?"

"Huh?"

"You have a crush on this guy, don't you?"

"No! He's gay!"

"But you didn't know that when you went out with him! Oh, it's all becoming clear now. You like him, so you want me to date him so you can still see him. That's not healthy, Sagey."

"No, it's not like that."

"No?"

"Not really. He's just a great guy and we really clicked. As friends. I mean, we talked for hours and hours, and we laughed and had a really great time. So I figured, if he clicked with me that well, there's no telling what kind of sparks he'd have with you! And yes, he's afraid to tell his mom the truth, but I know her, too, and she's really cool. I'm sure she's going to be fine with it."

"You're sure, are you? You know, there are some nice people out there who are extremely misguided. You can't always tell how someone will react to the news that her son lusts after men."

"True enough, I guess. Oh, speaking of nice people: Chloe and I had dinner with Mary. She says hi."

"I miss her. I'm really going to have to get over there one of these days."

"Maybe we can see her before we leave. Look at your schedule and let me know when you want to take the time off."

"Will do. In the meantime, come on down to the salon today. Sherry's gone all day, so your sibling discount will be honored. And my 5 o'clock spot is open."

"Hooray! See you right after work. Bye!"

I closed my eyes as Jamie expertly massaged my head before rinsing out the very expensive shampoo he always used. Having someone else wash your hair is an amazing experience. I suppose it takes us back to our childhoods, back to a time when being dependent somehow felt safe and comfortable.

I treasured all my bath time memories from before my mother left. I remembered sitting in a tub of warm water, eyes closed, her gentle hands lathering up some drugstore shampoo on my head. "Chin up, Sage honey," she'd say. "Chin up, baby. Don't let that soap get in your eyes." And, chin up, eyes still closed tight, I would always smile.

"Doll, your hair is a mess. Aren't you using that conditioner I gave you?"

"I ran out. It's not like I can afford it myself."

"Tsk tsk. You can afford it with my discount! I'll get you some more, but you really have to use it. Just let me know when you run out. Promise me!"

"I promise."

"At least I'll be able to cut off all those nasty split ends today. I think we should go a little shorter than usual."

"But…"

"Trust me, Sage. It's for the best."

I whimpered. Just a little.

But I needn't have worried. When Jamie was finished snipping and styling, my hair looked gorgeous: shoulder length, but with shorter layers, giving it a great shape. He even gave me a sassy little flip. I felt pretty!

"You're gorgeous, sis. Look at you!"

"Let's go out to dinner, Jamie. I can't waste this look!"

"Sorry, sweetheart. I have a date."

"A date? An important one?"

"A first date. We'll see."

"Save your heart for Sam. I'm telling you, he may be the one."

"Hmm. I must say, I prefer this romantic side of you to the cynic you were starting to become. Just let me know when he's taken the plunge."

"Wish I could just throw him off the dock."

"Sage, don't interfere. I'm serious. He has to do this at his own pace. But I suppose a little encouragement can't hurt, right?"

"Absolutely! A little encouragement can make all the difference!"

We walked out together, and Jamie locked up the shop. "Thanks for my haircut. I love it."

"You look great, doll." He kissed my cheek. "Where are you parked?"

"Just up the street." I could see Jamie's Prius a few feet down the hill. "Have fun, baby brother. But not too much fun."

"See you soon." He started to walk away, and so did I, in the opposite direction.

I spun around. "Hey! I almost forgot! Chloe's having a housewarming party this weekend and you have to come! Saturday at seven. She'll call you with directions!"

"Wouldn't miss it! See you there!"

I waved, turned back toward my car and hiked up the hill. I heard Jamie's car approaching; he blew me a kiss as he passed me by, on his way to what would no doubt be a fun and exciting evening. I, on the other hand, would just have to enjoy my great hair alone in my apartment. Maybe I'd order pizza!

Poor neglected Teddy greeted me at the door when I arrived home that night. Weaving in and out, around and around my legs, he made it difficult to walk; finally I dropped my purse and briefcase and scooped him up. "Did you miss me, Ted?"

He purred his response. "Sure, you sweet talker. I know you really just love me because I feed you, right?" He rubbed his face against mine, purring even louder.

After I dumped the cat food into his dish, Teddy completely forgot me and set to work gobbling up his dinner. So I picked up the phone to see if there were any messages. Surprise! The staccato dial tone signaled that at least one human being had dialed my number while I was out. Things were looking up.

I called the number to retrieve my voice mail. "Hi, Sage, it's Sam. I was just thinking about you and wondering if you might want to get together later in the week. I'll spring for coffee—any size you want. I miss my new buddy! Also, I wanted you to know that I, well I did it. I had The Talk with Savannah. She responded pretty well, I think. Anyway, I'd love to debrief with you. So give me a call when you get a chance. Thanks, Sage."

"End of new messages," the robotic voice advised.

Oh, but that was a good one. *He did it!* Now I just had to convince him to tell his mother so true love could take its course.

And then: a sudden inspiration. Chloe's party! I would invite Sam! Jamie would be there, they'd meet, and BOOM! Instant fireworks. Everything else would take care of itself.

Once upon a time I had a really great memory. I had noticed it slipping a little in recent years, but somehow I'd already memorized Sam's number. So I called him right then and there, before he could make other plans for Saturday.

But it was a young girl's voice I heard first. "Hi, is this Savannah?" I asked. Dumb question.

"Yes, who's speaking please?" Nice manners.

"My name is Sage. I'm a friend of your dad's and your grandma's."

"Oh. Yeah. I met you at Starbucks, right?"

"That's right. You remember!"

"Yeah, we were late that morning. Uh, do you want to talk to my dad?"

"Yes please. It was nice…"

"DAD! IT'S FOR YOU!"

I heard Sam's voice. "Who is it?"

"It's that girl who knows Grandma. Paige or something. Obviously she's not your *girlfriend* or anything."

"Hello?"

"Hi Sam."

"Oh, *Sage*," he said. "Hi, girlfriend." I could hear the smile in his voice.

"Got your message. Good work! How's it going?"

"Oh, I think there might be a little confusion, maybe even a little anger going on here, but it's okay. We'll muddle through."

"Muddle is a funny word. Do you know that when you press mint leaves to bring out the flavor in a mojito, that's called muddling?"

"Did not know that. Mmm. Mojitos are yummy. Anyway, want to get together this week?"

"For free coffee? Of course. But I have another proposal, too. Are you free on Saturday? If not, you have to cancel whatever plans you have."

"I have no Saturday plans. What's up?"

"My friend Chloe is having a little housewarming party. She just left her low-life boyfriend and moved into a really cute apartment. So you'll get to meet all my favorite people all at once!"

"Sounds like fun. Should I bring Savannah?"

I started to say, "Sure!" but I heard her in the background: "No, Dad. Alyssa invited me for a sleepover this weekend, remember?"

I could almost hear her eyes rolling.

"I think Savannah has another obligation," Sam said.

"Okay, then. Adults only. It'll be fun. You can be my date! Will you pick me up and everything?"

"With bells on. Should I bring a gift for your friend?"

"How sweet! But I'll take care of that. Just be here by six-thirty."

"You got it. In the meantime, how about coffee after work tomorrow?"

"You read my mind. Meet you at our place. Is five okay for you?"

"Five-thirty would be better. See you then?"

"You betcha. Have a good night, Sam."

He sighed. "I'll try. You too."

I took a book to Starbucks after work, knowing I'd have a half hour wait until Sam showed up. I could have stayed late at work, there was plenty to do, but I stayed true to my clockwatching ways and sprang from my chair as usual at 4:30 sharp.

So I sipped my latté—I couldn't wait—and read my latest trashy novel, thrilled to be finished with work for the day and waiting for my new friend.

The plot thickened, galloping very obviously toward a gratuitous sex scene, and I put my cup on the table, getting ready to thoroughly enjoy my book's steamy seamy-ness. Of course, I half expected an interruption, so when I felt someone staring my way, I wasn't really surprised.

Reluctantly, I looked up. What was going on? Was Sam early? No, no Sam in sight. But someone was looking at me, someone familiar. Who was that guy?

And it came to me. It was Marty, the handyman from my apartment building. I waved and smiled. He was always nice to me, and he'd been so kind about the whole Colin thing. Protective, even.

He walked over. "Hi, Sage. Haven't seen you in a while. How're you doing?"

"Good thanks, how are you, Marty?"

"I'm fine. Busy, but that's good too, I guess."

Reluctantly, I closed my book. "What's keeping you so busy?"

"I've been going to school at night for a while now. I went to college right after high school, but I dropped out early. I finally figured out that I should get a degree if I want to have a better life. End of this quarter, I'll have my business degree."

"I'm impressed!" I was, too, and a bit surprised. "Congratulations!"

"Well, you did it, didn't you? Decided on a different career and went back to school?"

"Yeah. Be careful what you wish for."

He laughed. "Uh, mind if I join you?"

"No, not at all. I'm just killing time, waiting for a friend."

He sat across from me. "You must be pretty busy, too. Haven't seen you around much lately."

"I guess I have been going out a little more. I'm feeling more like my old self, I guess." I looked down at my hands. It had always been a little embarrassing that Marty knew more about Colin than I would have liked. It was an unspoken understanding between us, and this was the closest I'd ever come to acknowledging it openly.

Marty nodded. "That's good. I'm glad. Hey—that guy ever come around again?"

"A couple of times. But the last time he just left flowers at my door, no note or anything, and I've never heard from him again. It surprised me, really, because I thought he'd never give up. Maybe he's just found a new victim." I shuddered at the thought.

"I'm glad he's not bothering you anymore."

"Thanks. That makes two of us. So, once you graduate, will you be abandoning me to my leaky pipes and temperamental garbage disposal?"

"Not right away. I'm actually hoping to go into business for myself. Not sure what kind exactly, but something small. Something I can build up. I really want to be my own boss. I know that small business owners are really tied down, but I'm willing to make that sacrifice to have something of my own, you know?"

"I think that's great, Marty. Good luck. But don't you dare leave without saying good-bye."

"Never. I'd never do that, Sage."

Was it my imagination, my unconsummated reading session, or was there something in Marty's eyes I hadn't noticed before? Was there really something intense about the way he was looking at me? I thought so, and suddenly I didn't know how to act or what to say. I was unnerved, and my face burned as I tried not to look at him.

"Uh, that's good," I mumbled. "Oh! Here's my friend!" I leaped to my feet. "Hi, Sam!" I kissed his cheek. Silently, I blessed him for his timing. "Sam, this is Marty."

"Hi, Marty. Nice to meet you," Sam said, reaching out to shake Marty's hand.

"Uh, yeah, you too," said Marty, much less enthusiastically. Again, I wondered: was this my imagination? "Listen, I'm gonna take off. It was great to see you, Sage. Hope I see you again soon."

Sam and I both watched Marty walk away from the table and out the glass door, heading toward whatever he was heading toward.

"Who is that?" Sam asked, sitting down. "Is *he* gay?"

"I don't think so," I said. "He's cute, huh?"

"Is he ever! How do you know him?"

"He's the maintenance guy at my building. He's nice. Guess I never really noticed how handsome he is." It was true. I hadn't noticed: those soulful dark eyes, thick hair, broad shoulders…wow! Marty was hot! "How could I have not noticed before?"

"No idea."

"He made me blush."

Sam raised his eyebrows.

"It's true! He looked at me in this smoldering way, and my face just burned! Then my brain totally disconnected from my mouth! I couldn't speak, I couldn't even look at him!"

"Sounds like he likes you, Sage. I was hoping he mumbled unintelligibly because he was interested in me, but he thought I was your date! That's why he left so fast. You should do something to encourage him."

"I'm not ready to date, remember?"

"Uh huh."

"Really, I'm not."

"He made you blush, Sage. You might be ready."

"I'm ready for more coffee. Your treat, right?"

"Absolutely. Double tall latté, right?"

"Yes, please. Nonfat!"

I watched Sam walk to the counter, but I was still seeing Marty's face when he said that he'd never leave without saying good-bye to me. He'd said it twice, staring at me with those eyes.

Never.

It hadn't been long since I'd been invited to a party at Chloe's home, but it was a different home then, and the partygoers had been mostly Paul's friends, a group of fairly snooty and pretentious self-proclaimed intellectuals. Tonight's party would be worlds away from that. I was actually excited about it, and I even caught myself primping a little. So what if my date was gay; I might as well look nice anyway, for myself if no one else.

Chloe had been barreling forward with her new life, settling into her apartment, buying artwork and furniture. Paul's guilty conscience had apparently been very lucrative for her. She hadn't revealed the actual number, but she had dropped a couple of cryptic hints: she could now take her time finding just the right teaching position, she didn't have to scrimp on furnishings, and she kept urging me to go shopping with her. "I'll give you a total makeover, Sage! New wardrobe, the whole shebang."

I hadn't taken her up on the kind offer, not yet anyway. "Maybe when I get back from Idaho," I'd said.

I did go kitty shopping with her, though. We had found an animal shelter close by and went in to find Chloe's new friend.

Seeing cats in cages always breaks my heart. Choosing only one would be difficult for me, and it turned out to be the same for Chloe. Initially she'd wanted a kitten, but she started having second thoughts immediately when she saw how many adult cats were waiting for new homes.

Each cat had a story, written up on a little card hanging from its cage. 'Clancy is a four year old neutered male. Owner moved overseas, couldn't take him along. He is a very loving cat that would do well in a home with children.' 'Sunny is a seven year old spayed female whose owners moved away and left her behind. Neighbor found her and brought her to shelter.'

Another read: 'Lauren is sweet, a true lap cat in need of a lot of attention. Rescued from home with too many cats.'

So many sad tales, so many animals in need. "How can I possibly choose?" Chloe said.

"You'll know your kitty when you see him," I said.

A few cages later, I was proven right. 'Luna is approximately two years old. She was brought in with a litter of kittens. Owner had abandoned them. Her kittens have been adopted. Luna would adapt well to any environment. Very loving cat. She has been spayed.'

I watched Chloe read about Luna, then lean down until they were face to face; it was clearly love at first sight. Luna was a very dark tortoiseshell, with flecks of brown and even orange seeming to shine through her mostly black fur. Her eyes, as she stared straight into Chloe's face, were wide and bright gold. They stared for a moment or two, and then Luna stood up and walked as close to Chloe as she could. She made no sound, but reached a paw through the bars of the cage. Chloe reached out and touched it.

"So, Luna's the one, huh?" I asked.

"She needs me," Chloe said, nodding.

When the shelter employee lifted Luna from her cage and placed her in Chloe's arms, Luna immediately started purring. She curled up and tucked her head under Chloe's chin as if they'd been together forever.

I'd gone to Chloe's apartment to help get Luna settled into her new environment and watched as she'd sniffed into every corner, exploring and checking for unknown dangers. Now I was eager to see her again, after she'd had a chance to acclimate a bit.

Sam arrived a bit late—my directions were apparently a tad confusing—but I was having a bad clothes day anyway. One of those days when nothing seemed to fit right, look right, go with the right jewelry or shoes or whatever. I answered the door in my robe. "I need help!" were my words of greeting.

"I'll try. What's up?"

"I'll model, you say yes or no."

"Oh, just because I'm gay I'm automatically a fashion expert?"

"Please, Sam. I just need a pair of objective eyes."

"All right. Model away."

First I appeared in a little short-sleeved, v-neck dress. "Well?"

"It's fine."

"Honestly."

"I don't like that shade of blue on you. It's too dark."

"I knew it! Okay! Be right back."

Next outfit: black pants, pale pink sweater.

He smiled. "I like that much more. The boots are great, and that pink is really good on you."

"Okay, but there's one more you have to see."

Last try: jeans (with my boots), and a low-cut top with long floppy sleeves and a lace collar.

"Yes! That's the one! Burgundy looks great on you! The boots have the perfect heels for the jeans. Casual, but not too casual. You look wonderful!"

"Thanks. See? You are good at this! Now it's just choosing the right earrings, and we're ready to go."

"Hey, thanks for inviting me," Sam called after me as I raced back into my bedroom.

"Thanks for coming! Introduce yourself to Teddy! I think he's on the sofa."

But Teddy, hearing his name, promptly jumped down. I could hear the plop.

"I think he's going to introduce himself," Sam said.

"Don't be offended if he runs away from you. Since Colin, he's been a little leery of men."

Fastening my second earring, I walked back out to the living room and stopped cold. Sam was kneeling, and Ted was happily head-butting his knee.

"Well! Never mind," I said. "Teddy, have you made a new friend?" But I doubt he could have heard me over the sound of his own purr.

I knew some of the people at Chloe's party, but there were a lot of faces I didn't recognize. Had Chloe really made so many friends along the way that were not connected to me at all? The thought bothered me a little; I introduced Sam to those I did know as we made our way toward the corner where Chloe stood. Joy of joys, she was talking to Jamie!

"Here are two of my favorite people in the whole world! Chloe, Jamie, meet my new friend Sam."

Jamie shot me a quick, searing look, but then he looked at Sam. I witnessed the exact moment when the sparks, fireworks, rockets and other assorted flammable items flew.

"Nice to meet you, Sam," Chloe said, and she shook his hand.

"Oh, you too, Chloe. Happy housewarming," Sam said, trying hard to look away from Jamie.

I had to work hard to keep from laughing when my brother tried to speak. "So nice to meet you, Sam, uh, Sage has mentioned you several times, haven't you, Sage? Uh, you have a mother, right, I mean, of course you have a mother, but Sage knows your mother, that's what I meant, and your daughter, too, beautiful name, Savannah, right? And." He shook his head as if he were trying to unscramble the words inside, "I'm Jamieson Whitaker. Jamie."

"Very nice to meet you, Jamie. I understand you're a hair stylist? I, uh, I wonder, what do you think I should do with this mop of mine?"

And they were off to another corner to discuss Sam's hair and pretend they didn't notice what was happening between them.

"Wow," Chloe said. "Love at first sight, do you think?"

"No doubt about it. I knew they were right for each other, I just knew it!"

"Whoa, slow down there, Hoss. It might just be a bad case of lust."

"No, really, I have a good feeling about them. Sam is so sweet, and cute—look at them together!"

Chloe nodded, watching them. "Mmm hmm. They are yummy. Okay, so they're obviously attracted to each other, but that doesn't mean it's happily ever after time."

"It might be."

"I suppose it could happen." Chloe sighed.

"Here!" I gave her the huge gift bag I'd carried in.

"Thank you, Sage!" She pulled out the little gifts I'd gathered for her: a bottle of wine, some wine glasses, a crystal suncatcher for her window, and some cat toys for Luna.

"Where is Luna? How's she doing with all the people here?"

"She's hiding under my bed, poor little thing. She's been adjusting well, but I think this party is just total sensory overload for her."

"I'm going to go find her and say hi."

In Chloe's bedroom, I closed the door and got down on the floor. Under the bed I could see Luna's huge gold eyes staring back at me. "Hey, sweetheart, it's all right," I said in my most soothing voice. I kept talking to her, cooing reassuringly until finally she crept, low to the ground, right to me. I showed her my hand, which she sniffed, and then she allowed me to pet her. Before long, she was sitting on my lap, happy as she could be.

"Good girl," I murmured.

Slowly, the door opened and Chloe peeked in. She laughed. "You always did have a way with cats."

"We understand each other. We're loners but we still need love."

"Well now that you've made her feel loved, come on out and join the party."

"Okay. Luna, I have to go now. You be a good girl, and this party will be over in a few hours." I put her on the bed, and she circled a bit before plopping down for a nap.

Walking past Sam and Jamie I heard my brother say: "Sure, I'd love to! But let me cook for you. Do you like northern Italian?"

I grinned at them, turned, and bumped into Chloe's friend Shelley. "Oh! Sorry!"

She flashed an amazing smile at me, all perfectly straight pearly whites and uncanny bone structure. Shelley was definitely one of those women with great personalities and an aura of self-confidence and composure that always seemed so alien to me. Maybe *she* was an alien!

"Hello, Sage! So wonderful to see you again! Isn't it great news about Chloe returning to teaching?"

"Yes. The world needs more teachers like Chloe."

"Amen." Shelley motioned with a long, graceful arm. "Great party, isn't it?"

"Yes, it sure is."

"Chloe tells me that you're a social worker now. I think that's wonderful, that you're out there helping people every day."

"That's the idea."

"Well, you're looking lovely, Sage. That color really brings out the highlights in your hair."

"Thank you, Shelley. You look fabulous as always."

She laughed, showing me those perfect teeth again. "You're so sweet! We should really get together sometime, you know, for lunch or something."

She really sounded sincere. How did she do that?

"That would be great." I hoped I sounded sincere, too.

"Hey. If you haven't made your way into the kitchen yet, you should get in there before the food is gone. I think Chloe's mother cooked, and it's all really wonderful."

"Thanks, Shelley. I'll do that." I walked away, aiming for the kitchen, trying to look as graceful as wispy Shelley, knowing I was failing miserably.

Thankfully, Shelley's information had been accurate; Mary stood in the small kitchen, pulling cookie sheets out of the oven. When she saw me, she put the sheets on the stove, pulled off her oven mitts and reached out. "Sage, sweetheart!" We embraced, and I gratefully breathed in Mary's aroma: a combination of spice, vanilla and something indefinably Mary.

"Stop cooking! You're missing the party," I told her.

"I'm almost done. Just have to put these cheese puffs on a platter."

"Let me help."

We worked quickly, arranging the hot little pastries in a fetching little spiral on the platter. "Perfect!" Mary said. She carried the platter to the table, then turned to motion me over. "Sage!" she whispered loudly. "Who is that striking young man with Jamie?"

"That's my friend Sam, isn't he cute? He's been passing as straight. Even got married and had a daughter."

"No kidding? He's not still married, I hope!"

"No, no. Divorced. He's finally come out to his daughter, but not a whole lot of other people in his life. Anyway, I had a feeling they'd hit it off."

"You were right. Neither one is even aware that there are other people here."

We watched for a moment or two. Jamie and Sam were cozy, all right. Heads close together, each fascinated by every word out of the other's mouth. "They're positively riveted," I said.

Mary turned to face me. "Tell me, Sage, how are you? No more episodes?"

"Uh, well..."

"Sage?"

"Just one other time. I had kind of a nasty run-in with a complete stranger. She accused me of being a racist!"

"Why in the world..."

"It's a long story. But afterward I had a little problem breathing, just for a few minutes. It wasn't as bad as the first time. I'm sure I'm fine now."

"I hope so, darlin'. But I'm concerned. A second attack in not much time might be a bad sign. I really think you should see someone. Your doctor for starters. Promise me you'll make an appointment? Please?"

I hated going to the doctor. But this was Mary, and I couldn't refuse her anything. "Okay. I promise." Mary put her arm around me and I leaned into her.

Chloe spotted us from across the room and walked over. Standing on the other side of her mother, she clapped loudly. "Everyone, attention please. I have an announcement." Suddenly, all eyes were on us; the silence was deafening until Chloe spoke again. "This beautiful woman here is my mother, and she is responsible for all the delicious food you've been enjoying!"

Chloe started clapping, and everyone else joined in. Trying to look as casual as possible, I moved out from under Mary's arm and away from her spotlight. Clapping and smiling, I walked backward until I was in Chloe's bedroom once again.

I closed the door, taking the noise level down a few decibels. Luna had disappeared. I was pretty sure where I'd find her, and sure enough there she was, back under the bed, cowering in a corner.

"I know just how you feel, sweetheart." This party was indeed worlds away from one Paul would throw; even so, many people were strangers to me, and, as my current line of work had taught me, strangers were exhausting. Sitting on the floor with my back against the bed, I waited for Luna to join me.

~19~

I had finally succeeded in getting Jamie to plan and execute our trip to Coeur d'Alene. We were leaving in just a couple of weeks, so now I was busy preparing: getting caught up at work, deciding what to pack. And, I decided to keep my promise to Mary and make a doctor's appointment at last.

"Hello, Sage, it's been a while."

"Hi, Dr. Rousseau," I said as she shook my hand.

"So what's going on? My assistant said something about panic attacks?"

"Yeah, it's happened a couple of times recently, after some stressful events. But I thought I should come in and get checked out."

"Of course. Your blood pressure is a little high, not out of the normal range, but higher than it was last time I saw you. What kind of stress have you been under? Is it your job?"

"Sometimes my job is stressful, yes. But the major things were just one time events. And those things made my job more stressful, just temporarily. So I really think I'm okay now."

"Any changes in your diet lately?"

"No, not really."

"How much coffee or other caffeinated beverages do you typically drink in a day?"

"Uh…as in how many shots of espresso?"

"Sure."

"Usually four in a day. Or six. Sometimes seven. And then I'll have a cup or two of coffee at work."

"My goodness! Doesn't it keep you awake at night?"

"No, it doesn't bother me at all."

"Well, it might be bothering you in other ways. It could be contributing to your anxiety."

"What?"

"I'd like you to cut down on your caffeine intake. Don't quit cold turkey; that would probably give you a massive headache at this point. Try to keep it to two shots per day. And no extra coffee at work, no caffeinated sodas. Deal? Just to see if it helps to lower your anxiety level and get your blood pressure down a bit."

"I guess so." One double latté a day, or two singles? Now my biggest pleasure in life had to be restricted? Well, maybe it would help me lose a little weight. It would certainly be less expensive! I could do this, and it would be good for me, I told myself.

The next morning, I had one single shot latté. Then I drank one more in the early afternoon. The morning after that, I woke up with the worst headache I'd ever experienced. I couldn't move. I felt nauseous. I made coffee and drank half a pot before I started to feel better. So much for moderation.

So the day we left for Coeur d'Alene, I stopped for a triple shot on the way to pick up Jamie.

Now I was sipping my beloved coffee as he tossed his suitcase in my trunk. I was getting excited that we were nearly on our way at last, when Jamie made a very unwelcome announcement.

"Sagey, I just have to make one quick stop before we head out of town."

"What do you mean, we have to make a stop?" I whined. "What stop? Where? Why?"

"It's just my volunteer work. The salon has been really busy this past week and I made a promise to stop and see a client today. It's not too far out of the way and I'll make it quick."

"Volunteer work?"

"I've told you this, Sage. I volunteer for a hospice program. I visit patients in their homes, bring them groceries, pick up their meds, whatever they need."

A dim light flicked on in a deep recess of my brain. Seemed like I did remember something about that, but Jamie never really talked about it, he'd just mentioned it a couple of times. I knew it had to be important to him, so I reluctantly agreed to the detour. "But then we're on our way, right?"

"Right."

He pulled up in front of a dingy old apartment building in a dingy old part of town. "You want to come in? You'd like Bobby and Noel, they're nice guys."

"Sure, okay." My only thought was that if I went with him, I could give him meaningful looks to get him to hurry up.

There was a buzzer panel outside the front door, and Jamie pushed the button corresponding to Bobby and Noel's apartment. "Jamieson?" a static-y voice asked.

"Yeah, it's me. I've brought company, too."

"That's nice. Come on up."

There was a loud humming sound, and Jamie opened the door. I followed him up the stairs to the third floor, then down the dim hallway to apartment 312. The door opened as we arrived, and a tall, wiry man appeared. He wore a faded University of Washington t-shirt over his jeans. He seemed diminished, somehow. Defeated.

"You look tired, Noel. How's he doing?" my brother asked in a low voice.

"He had a rough night, but he seems to be a little better today. Gotta hang on to those good days, you know."

He looked at me with red eyes. "I'm Noel."

"Oh, I'm sorry. This is my sister, Sage," Jamie said.

"Nice to meet you, Sister Sage." He shook my hand. His fingers were long and slender, just like the rest of him.

"You too," I said.

Inside the apartment, the lights were low, the curtains drawn. Dishes were piled high in the sink and on the kitchen table. The furniture was old and drab, the beige carpet stained yellow in several spots. In the corner of the living room sat another man—Bobby, I presumed—in an upright recliner, covered with several blankets so that all we could see were his face and his arms, which he'd placed in front of him, his fingers laced together.

Bobby's face no longer looked human. I couldn't understand how someone could be so thin and still be alive. His skin, nearly translucent, stretched tight over his skull; his eyes had retreated deep into their sockets. His arms had atrophied to sticks.

And then it finally clicked. *Hospice,* Jamie had said. I knew the term well; I'd set up such services for a few clients. Clients who were in the last stages of life. By definition—and to qualify for help—they would be alive six months or less. Occasionally it didn't work out that way, but the patient usually obliged.

Being in the presence of imminent death was something I still hadn't gotten used to. I wasn't sure it was even possible to get used to it. And yet, here was my brother, regularly choosing to visit death.

Breathe, I told myself. *Put on your best social worker persona.* Smiling, I crossed the room and gently shook Bobby's limp hand. "Hi, Bobby. I'm Sage, Jamie's sister. He's told me so much about you. It's nice to finally meet you."

He smiled a ghastly smile and nodded. "You too. Jamie's mentioned you a time or two as well." He turned his head to look at Jamie—no small feat, apparently—and grinned again.

"Noel says you've been having some trouble sleeping?" Jamie asked.

"Not too much. Just a bad night now and then."

"Have you eaten anything today?"

"Yes, Mother. I had a couple of scrambled eggs with my morphine this morning."

"Good boy." Jamie smiled. "Is there anything I can do for you today?"

"No, we're okay today. Noel's mom is coming over later to give him a break."

Noel called out from the kitchen. "Not to give me a break, to see you!"

Bobby rolled his eyes and smiled. "Right. To see me, of course. I'm very popular today. So what are you up to, Jamieson?"

"Oh, my sister and I are heading out of town. We have a family matter to take care of so we're turning it into a little vacation."

"Where?"

"Northern Idaho. Coeur d'Alene. Ever been there?"

"Sad to say I haven't. I hear it's beautiful."

"It is. The lake is big and blue, surrounded by green hills and beautiful homes. The town is quaint—a few antique stores and lots of art. I did some research, and there are some very well reviewed restaurants there now, too. And I'm hoping I can rent a boat and explore the lake one day. Maybe go kayaking."

"Sounds like heaven. Just watch out for all those Right Thinking Conservatives, Jamieson. You might get lynched. Or at least be forced to wear a pink star," Bobby said.

Jamie smiled at him again, but the smile never quite reached his eyes. He reached out and touched Bobby's hand. "We'll be back in a couple of weeks. I'll see you then."

Bobby's smile never left his face, even as a tear rolled slowly down his cheek. "Hope so," he whispered. "Damn. I'm sorry. Good-byes are tough these days."

"It was really nice to meet you, Bobby," I said. I wanted to say something profound, something memorable, but that common, trite string of syllables was all I could manage. *I'm an automaton,* I thought. But I meant it. Here was this nice man disappearing from life, moving ever more quickly toward his death and leaving us all behind, and I *was* grateful for this one moment, my only opportunity to be listed among those he'd encountered during his brief stay on the planet. I just had no idea whatsoever how to communicate all that to him.

So I too reached out and touched Bobby's hand; I squeezed it gently, thinking I truly could break those bones. They were so close to the surface. So unprotected.

Bobby lifted his face to look at me. "Don't look so sad, sweetheart," he said. "It's just a virus. I don't feel picked on by the universe. I was just really unlucky. And fairly stupid." He smiled his scary smile one more time. "But I did some serious living, let me tell you."

Pulling away from the curb, I struggled with my emotions. Of course, Jamie noticed. "You okay?" Jamie asked.

I nodded, but immediately said, "No! I'm not!"

Jamie smiled. "It's okay, Sage. Death is part of life. Bobby has accepted his situation. He's at peace."

"Yeah. Is Noel at peace?"

He looked away from me, out the window. "No. It's a lot tougher to be the one left behind."

"Is Noel HIV positive?"

"Yes."

"So next you'll be going through all this with him? God, Jamie, how do you do it?"

"I do it because they need help. I'm just part of the team. There are nurses that come in and bathe Bobby and treat his bedsores, monitor his meds, change his bed. I just run errands and give Noel a break sometimes. I give them haircuts too, do some cleaning and a little cooking. When—IF—Noel gets sick it'll be a lot tougher because he'll be living alone. His mom is great though; I'm sure she'll get a lot more involved then. But that might be a long time from now. Or never. Look at Magic Johnson."

"He's an anomaly, isn't he?"

"The drugs are getting better. People are living a lot longer now."

"Have you been tested lately?"

"Yes, of course. Still negative. And I'm careful, Sage. Hey—did you know that the fastest growing infected group in this country is heterosexual women? You need to be careful too."

"Yeah. First I'd actually have to have a sex life. Oh, Jamie. It's just so sad. How old is he?"

"I know. It's pretty hard to judge, the way he looks now. But he's four years younger than Noel."

"No way!"

"Yep. He's thirty-two."

"Wow." I drove silently for a while, thinking. I merged onto I-90, heading east.

"What?" Jamie asked, seeing me shake my head.

"I just can't believe that there are people who actually believe AIDS is some sort of punishment by God for homosexuality."

Jamie shrugged. "I think it's funny."

"Funny? What the hell is funny about it?"

"Think about it: what demographic has the lowest incidence of HIV?"

"I don't know. Nuns?"

"I mean aside from people who are completely celibate. It's lesbians! So if AIDS is evidence that God hates gay men, then by the same logic we can assume He loves gay women! See how silly it is?"

I had to smile. "Lesbians are the chosen ones! Maybe I should convert."

"Convert?"

"Sorry! It was a joke! Might be a good idea, though, with the luck I've had with men. You on the other hand seem to be doing quite well, thanks to me. How *is* Sam?"

He grinned.

I poked his arm. "Don't be coy, come on, tell me! How many dates?"

"Four. Okay, he's pretty great, I have to say."

"He thinks you're pretty terrific, too."

"He talked to you? What did he say?"

"Only that you're gorgeous, sweet, kind, pretty much perfect."

"Really?"

"Uh huh. Really. So go ahead and say it: 'You were right, big sister, I should have listened to you all along.' I knew you and Sam would be good for each other."

"Yeah, but I'm still really concerned about his closet status. I'm so far beyond hiding and keeping secrets."

"But he's making progress."

"I know. And I know I can't rush him, he's got to be ready, et cetera, et cetera. You know something, though, Sage? We are just starting this thing, and I actually thought about postponing this trip because I'm going to miss him so badly. Crazy, huh?"

"You're falling for him, aren't you?" He blushed in response. "Oh my God! You are!"

"I really didn't think it was possible to feel like this again so soon, but I think this one has a lot of potential."

"Yeah, well, are you ready to be a stepfather?"

"I'm not rushing into things that fast, Sage."

"Uh huh. Whatever you say."

~20~

There's nothing like a six-hour car trip to get siblings all caught up on each other's lives, not that Jamie and I weren't already pretty up to date. But there were recent work experiences to share, and sooner or later I got around to mentioning my conversation with Rachel the Super Social Worker.

"So she thinks I should do something else."

"What do *you* think? Are you that unhappy?"

"Well, let me see: I hate going to work, I ruin my weekends dreading Monday morning, I cringe whenever my phone rings, and, oh yeah, my evil-bitch-from-hell client gave me a panic attack. Yeah, I think I'm pretty miserable. I'm so sorry, Jamie. I promise I'm still good for the loan; I just make a really lousy social worker. I guess I didn't understand what the job would actually be like."

"I'm not worried about the money. What did you say about a panic attack?"

Oops. I hadn't intended on telling him about that. "Just a figure of speech."

"Sage, you're a terrible liar. Come on, out with it."

"It was nothing. I was meeting with this horrible woman and suddenly I couldn't breathe. I felt like I had to get out of there or I'd die. Pretty stupid, huh? It was the day after Dad's surprise visit, so I was just a little stressed, that's all."

"Oh, doll. Why didn't you tell me when it happened?"

"I don't know. I feel like such a failure."

"Sage. You are not a failure, you just haven't found your calling yet, that's all. Other than matchmaking of course. You're apparently quite gifted in that arena."

"Maybe I'll inherit enough from Grandma Lucy to pay you back and pursue another career. What do you think?"

"Pretty likely, if her house is in good shape. I was doing some research online, and northern Idaho is booming right now. With no mortgage to pay off, we should make a bunch of money—and who knows what other assets she had lying around."

"Thanks for doing the research. I meant to help with that. Anyway, *she* was an asset. I can't believe she's really gone. Everyone always says that, but I really can't. There's a piece of my brain that won't let her go."

"I know. I miss her too."

We drove on, oohing and aahing over the gorgeous scenery through the Cascade Mountains, and even the arid plains and well-irrigated crops of eastern Washington. "Look at all the sagebrush, Sage! It's so sagey!" Jamie said, as he had many times before; the hills were covered with the stuff, tufts of powdery green scattered everywhere, all the way down to the Columbia River gorge. And then the trees gradually got bigger again, turning to ponderosa pines as we approached Spokane.

We stopped a couple of times for food and bathroom breaks, grateful to stretch our legs. We cheered as we passed the Welcome to Idaho sign; we were almost there.

Finally, finally, we entered the city limits of Coeur d'Alene and found ourselves driving down Sherman Avenue, the street that runs east/west from the highway to the shores of Lake Coeur d'Alene.

It was a strange feeling, driving into town. Before our mother left, we used to come here as a family every summer, at least for a few days. I didn't remember those visits very well, and Jamie couldn't remember them at all. And then, after our mother's departure, Jamie and I had spent three entire summers here with Grandma Lucy: two before we left our father's house and one after. I thought about the two times our father brought us here, both on the day after school was let out for the year. I'd imagined he couldn't wait to have the house to himself for all those weeks. Who would he scream at, I had wondered, when he was drunk and alone? Would he hit the walls or break dishes? Or would he be completely different? Would he be happy while we were gone?

Jamie and I had often asked each other these questions, but we could only guess at the answers. All we knew at the time was that we were leaving the war zone for a while. The bonus was spending time with the best grandma in the world, the universe as far as we were concerned.

After our final summer with Grandma Lucy, we had never come back. We had always thought we would, but somehow a trip never got planned. Grandma Lucy came to Seattle a few times over the years to see us, but mostly we had kept in touch by phone.

Pulling up in front of Grandma Lucy's house, it was hard to believe she wouldn't be answering the door.

Now I was transported back to my childhood. I could almost hear her voice as we pushed the car doors closed and headed up the front walk, could almost see her stepping out onto the porch, arms held wide:

"Baby dolls!" she would cry. "Look how big and beautiful you are!" She would kiss us all over our faces, laughing with eyes full of tears. Jamie and I would cling to her desperately.

But she didn't appear on the porch today, of course. Today there was only an envelope taped to the door. Across its face, in neat, fussy script read: To Sage and Jamieson Whitaker. Inside, a note in the same writing: *Please come next door (503) for your grandmother's house keys.* It was signed *Love, Rose.* We didn't know Rose; she must have moved in since we'd been there. The intimacy of the sign-off felt strange; Jamie and I acknowledged our discomfort with a scowl, but then he shrugged. "I'm sure she loved *Lucy*, and it's just extended to us by default, that's all."

"Yeah, I guess so."

We headed to Rose's house, which was similar to Grandma Lucy's but smaller. Fewer steps led to the porch, and the screen door boasted a large cursive R. I pushed the doorbell and we could hear it, one of those eight tone rings that seemed to ask and answer its own question in some secret, musical language.

Rose opened the door, and when she spoke it seemed she had adopted her doorbell's dialect; I had never heard such a singsong greeting, unless you count Glinda, the Good Witch. "Well you must be Sage and Jamieson. How lovely to meet you! Please, do come in, I'm thrilled to pieces to have you here, just to pieces!"

She wore a red, white and blue pantsuit with a sailor collar and big red stars down the length of her pants that stopped abruptly at her ankles. Over the pantsuit she wore a white apron covered in embroidery— red roses, of course.

Rose was low to the ground and wide, and her hair, shoulder length and carefully flipped in unmoving waves, had been dyed dark brown long enough ago that several shades of gray had crept back into its roots. But her smile seemed genuine enough.

She motioned to her living room and we obeyed silently, settling on her doily-adorned sofa. Sprays of plastic roses sprang from several vases around the perimeter of the room. Something smelled musty, old. Rose sat facing us in an overstuffed chair with a—you guessed it—floral print. "Lucy was a fine woman, just as sweet a soul as I ever knew. She never stopped talking about you two, neither. Brilliant and beautiful, she said that about you both, all the time. We got to be real close, Lucy and me, and so I feel like I know you quite a little bit already!"

"How long have you lived here, Rose?" Jamie asked.

"Hmm. I'd say near on ten years. Your grandma came to see me the first day I moved in. Brought me some of her famous banana bread as a welcome gift. Wasn't that sweet of her? She sure missed you two. She always said, 'Never live in regrets, Rose. You'll drown for sure.' And her biggest regret was letting you two stay with your dad as long as you did."

Surely I hadn't heard correctly. "Pardon me?" I asked.

"Oh, yes. She wanted to get you out of his house so bad, honey. She knew he was terrible to you kids. She would have fought for you, too, if your friend's mama hadn't stepped in. Lucy had already talked to a lawyer."

I cleared my throat, which had suddenly become as dry as dust. "But why—why did you call our father when she died? It was you, wasn't it?"

"Yes, it was me. I didn't know if I should, I really didn't. But Lucy herself had planned on talking to your daddy. She just didn't get to it. She knew you all didn't have much contact with him, if any, and she thought someone should find out if he'd changed. Well, people can change, with the good Lord's help, and so I thought I should fulfill Lucy's wish and call him myself. And it seems he has changed. Found Jesus, a new lady, and wants to make amends to his children. Well amen, I said! Miracles do happen, I swear they do. So I've been dying to know: how was your reunion with your daddy?"

I sat, gaping at this strange little woman. Dimly, I heard Jamie's voice: "Rose, I think maybe you just don't know the whole story. It's all very complicated. We just don't feel it's possible to have a relationship with our father. We're very glad he's stopped drinking and that he's happy, but we just can't be part of his life, for many reasons. I'm sure you understand. Now if you don't mind, could we get our grandmother's house keys? We've had a long drive today and we'd like to get settled in."

Rose's eyes shifted between Jamie and me, as I sat with my mouth still unhinged and Jamie stood, holding his hand out to take the keys. "Oh!" she said. "Oh, I hope I haven't done something wrong. I thought I was helping. I thought I was giving you kids the best surprise in the world!"

Closing my mouth at last, I stood beside Jamie. Shock subsided, making way for the wave of pure anger that washed over me now. I could feel it, icy and hot at the same time. My hands shook; I wanted to scream or cry or hit someone, hard, preferably this lunatic Popeye in drag.

Jamie shot me a look I could read very well: *Don't say it, Sage, she meant well, she didn't know.* I knew he was right, but I didn't care one iota. I wanted to hurt this awful woman. I wanted to educate her, to blow her Jesus-lovin' mind.

"You thought you were helping? Is that really what I heard you say?"

Jamie put his hand in front of me, trying to hold me back, but Rose nodded feebly, and I moved in for the kill.

"HOW DARE YOU, YOU IGNORANT BITCH! OUR FATHER IS A FUCKING MONSTER, YOU KNOW THAT? HE BEAT US UNCONSCIOUS ON A REGULAR BASIS. HE TRIED TO KILL MY BROTHER, MORE TIMES THAN I CAN REMEMBER! I WAS A LITTLE GIRL, AND I HAD TO FIGHT OFF A GROWN MAN TO PROTECT MY BROTHER!"

Rose cowered before my eyes, flinching at every word I spat in her direction, but I didn't care. I wanted to pound her into the ground with my anger. "EVERY SINGLE DAY OUR FATHER TOLD US WE WERE WORTHLESS, STUPID, PIECES OF SHIT." I leaned down, my face inches from hers. "You made it possible for that man to find us, to invade our lives, to just appear on my doorstep. You just decided he deserved to see us, the kids he brutalized for so long." I snarled at her. "What exactly do *we* deserve? You talk it over with God and let us know, will you do that, Rose? Now give us our grandmother's goddamn keys."

Throughout my tirade I had heard Jamie calling my name, but nothing could have diverted my attention once my attack was underway. Now he stood beside me, watching his shoes. Rose turned and walked out of the room and returned shortly, holding out a pudgy hand. She was shaking as I took Grandma Lucy's keys from her, but I refused to meet Rose's eyes.

I walked out of the house without a backward glance. Jamie hesitated only half a beat before he followed, but before the door closed behind him we heard Rose calling out, her voice thick with tears and shock and shame: "I didn't know, I didn't understand. Please…"

But she didn't follow us.

Pacing like a cat whose prey had narrowly escaped her grasp, I still wanted to throw something, to scream, to pound my fist into someone. My head throbbed and I knew I was dangerously close to tears myself. I walked from room to room and back again in Grandma Lucy's house, angry that she was gone, angry that her idiot neighbor had so carelessly committed this heinous crime.

Jamie, on the other hand, had gone very quiet and still. Sitting on the sofa in the living room, he looked up each time I walked through, but he didn't speak until my sixth pass.

"Sage?"

His voice stopped me cold. "What?" I snapped.

He patted the cushion beside him. "Come on. Come sit with me."

"I don't want to sit. I want to kill that stupid bitch."

"No, you don't. Come on."

I stared at him, at his calm face, his kind blue eyes. "How could she do that? It's no wonder people aren't safe, you know. You try to hide, to stay away from bad people, and some ignorant, thoughtless person like Rose over there just points them right back in your direction! What if he hadn't quit drinking? What if he'd come looking for us for a whole different reason? What if he'd turned into some kind of avenging Christian soldier and wanted to hurt you? It would have been her fault!"

"No, it would have been his fault, but she would have made it easier for him. And I'm sure she would have felt even worse than she feels now. But it didn't happen that way. Come here, Sage."

"No, I don't want to sit down. I want…"

"What? A different father? A different childhood? Me too." He stood up and started inching toward me as though I were a bomb to be diffused.

"Oh, shit, Jamie," was all I could come up with before he finally reached me. My brother held me tight and I sobbed, for Grandma Lucy, for the nosy but generally innocent woman I had abused next door, for the whole damn mess.

Neither of us was ready to face sorting through Grandma Lucy's things, and we weren't meeting with her lawyer until Monday. So, after I washed my face and reapplied make-up, we spent the rest of the day wandering through downtown Coeur d'Alene.

Shops and restaurants lined Sherman Avenue in the downtown core. We walked along, window-shopping, until I spotted a coffee shop. Jamie groaned. "Can't you wait until dinner?"

"We're going to be here for two weeks, Jamie. I have to find the best latté in town, don't I? This is research! Besides, I'm cold."

It was still spring, so the tourists hadn't invaded yet. None of the shops we'd passed seemed very busy, and now there was no line waiting to order coffee. I asked for my double tall—and there was a bit of a question as to what constituted a "tall" drink. (Toto, we're not in Seattle anymore.) Smiling sweetly as always, saying please and thank you as always, I received my precious coffee and took the first sip before we left the shop. "Mmm. This is really good coffee, Jamieson. You should try it!"

"No, doll. It'll keep me up all night. You enjoy it, though."

We walked just to walk, and within minutes we found ourselves approaching the lake. Across the parking lot next to the Coeur d'Alene Resort, we came upon Tubbs Hill, where Grandma Lucy used to take us hiking on a two-mile loop on a hill above the lake.

"Look!" I pointed at the sign.

"Look at you, suddenly all nostalgic. You hated that walk, Sage."

"No, I just hated that we had to get up so early." Our grandmother loved the wee hours of the morning, just after sunrise when the air was still cool and the crowds hadn't crawled out of bed yet. "I guess it really was the best time to hike."

"Want to hike it tomorrow?"

"Sure!" With a fresh supply of caffeine running through my veins, it seemed like a great idea. "But only if we stop for coffee on the way."

"Of course, Sage."

We found a nice restaurant for dinner, and toasted Grandma Lucy with a wine that only Jamie could afford. Back in her house, we debated briefly about which bedrooms to use. Ultimately, we shared the same guest room we always had, curling up in the identical twin beds our grandmother had always reserved exclusively for us.

Neither of us mentioned Rose or my tantrum the rest of the night.

~21~

I woke up first, oddly enough, and looked over at my brother's bed. There he was, face down, feet sticking over the end. "Hey," I murmured. "Still wanna hike Tubbs Hill?" But my eyes simply would not stay open yet, so I drifted back toward sleep, hoping he hadn't heard me.

"Hmm? Oh! Yeah! Let's go!"

There he went, bounding out of bed, pulling sweatpants on over his boxers, lacing up his sneakers. That was Jamie in the morning: as if someone had just flipped a switch. No wonder he didn't need caffeine. "Come on, Sage, let's go!"

"All right, but you promised coffee."

"Yeah, yeah, I know." He ripped the blankets off me and offered me his hand.

I took it, and let him pull me to my feet. I'd slept in sweats and a tee shirt. "I can just go in these, right?"

He wrinkled his nose at me. "If you must. But you'll need a light jacket. Shoes and socks would be good, too."

In the bathroom, I pulled my hair into a ponytail and brushed my teeth, then cleared out for Jamie.

"Coffee, coffee, coffee," I chanted as he brushed past me. "What? It's my new mantra."

"That stuff's gonna kill you, Sage."

"Not today. Today it's going to save me."

And soon it was in my hand, warm, aromatic and delicious. "I praise you, o coffee gods," I said, breathing in that wondrous scent.

It was chilly, but beautiful: clear blue sky, the lake cool glass. We walked down to the dock silently, just looking around. A few ducks paddled closer to us, hoping for food. Off in the distance, a fish jumped and splashed back into water. "Oh, a poor effort from the American team. I give it a 6.5," I said, trying to sound British.

"Zat vas a belly flop und unvorzhy of a competitor at zis level. I geeve eet a foor." Jamie did an amazing Hitler impression.

"Very harsh marks from the German judge. Let's see what happens with the next athlete." We waited for another fish to jump, but when my coffee was gone and none had appeared, I was ready to hike. "Yes, once again the German judge has scared off all the other competitors. On to the next event. Tally ho!"

"Acht liebe. Wie giets?"

We turned and walked the length of the dock, up the stairs and to the entrance of the Tubbs Hill trail. Jamie took my coffee cup, tossed it into a nearby garbage can, and we were on our way.

The trail wound in and out of sunshine, the lake peeking in and out of sight below us. I remembered Grandma Lucy and her walking stick, how she would pause every now and then and tell us the name of a plant, or point out a chipmunk or bird. She always wore a ridiculous hat—she had many to choose from—and, nearly always, shorts.

"The old girl would have loved this," Jamie said.

"I know. Hey, slow down. Trying to kill me?"

"No, sugar plum, I'm trying to get my heart rate up into my target zone."

"I didn't realize we were working out. I thought we were just walking."

"Oh. I'm sorry. I'll go for a run later, by myself. We can take it easy," he said, patting me on the head, "if it's too strenuous for you."

"Okay, I guess we're working out. Eat my dust!"

We power-walked the loop in less than an hour. Jamie wanted to walk it one more time, but I was panting and sweaty and ready for a shower.

"Race you to the house, then," Jamie said. Another challenge, but this time I didn't bite.

"You go ahead and run back, Mr. Universe. I'm going to walk, maybe get another coffee."

He frowned, but said, "Okay then. I'll see you back there."

When my coffee was ready, I headed for the door of the shop, but before I reached it the bell on the door announced another coffee shop patron. I thought I must have simply heard wrong when the new arrival called my name.

"Sage, is that you? Sage Whitaker?"

I looked up into a face I had once known. A face from another life.

"My God, it *is* you!" the face exclaimed.

I was fifteen the last time Jamie and I visited Grandma Lucy for the summer. Fifteen, sullen, angry and a total pain in the ass, I'm sure, which was why Mary had been in touch with Grandma Lucy, and which was why Grandma had offered to take us again. That summer I met other sullen, angry kids. Some were locals, some temporary, like me.

This face, now looming above mine, belonged to none other than local boy Donny Weston.

Donny was a year older than me, and at the time we met he had beautiful, wild blond hair and golden brown eyes. His dad had a boat, and the Weston family taught me to water-ski. Jamie, too, of course, but he was a natural and I thought I'd never get up on those damn skis. When I did, Donny cheered from the back of the boat.

I lost my virginity to Donny that summer. It was painful and awful, but he held me close afterward while I cried. "I'm sorry," he whispered. I had wondered: sorry it hurt? Sorry it happened? I never asked, never said anything. Just clung to him and sobbed.

Now here he was, and he remembered me. I would not have picked him out in a crowd. Gone were those golden tresses. His head had been buzzed nearly bald, in fact, but I could see there hadn't been a lot of hair left to remove. Those eyes, though—they were still that warm, pale brown.

"Donny?"

"Yes! I look different, I know, but you haven't changed a bit!"

"Liar."

"Listen, I'm really sorry about your grandmother. She was a great lady."

My face suddenly felt hot, so I looked away and took a sip of my coffee. "Uh, were you getting coffee?"

"Yeah, I love this stuff. But I'm not in a hurry. Do you have time to talk for a bit?"

Why is it you always bump into people you haven't seen in ages at a time when you'd rather not be seen? Here I was, sans make-up, wearing frumpy clothes that now smelled like stale sweat, hair pulled back, thus fully exposing my unadorned face. Yet, he had already seen all that, and still asked me to stay.

"I—I'm not exactly presentable right now. I was just…"

"I'm sorry. Did you just go for a run or something?"

"Something like that. But…" Wow. He really looked disappointed that I might not stay. "But hey, as long as you understand I am not looking or smelling my best, I'd love to stay for a few minutes."

He grinned. I waited while he got his coffee, and we sat at a little table in the corner.

I asked the usual questions. Donny cleared his throat. "Well, as you know I'm an attorney," he began. As I know? How would I know that? But I let him continue. He said that his practice was based here in Coeur d'Alene, but that he had clients all over northern Idaho. He represented a lot of local businesses, nothing huge, but financially he was "doing okay," whatever that meant.

"What do you do, Sage?"

"Mostly wish I were doing okay. I'm a social worker, I hate my job, I hate most of the people I'm supposed to be helping. Blah blah blah. But I'm here for a couple of weeks with my brother to go through my grandmother's house and put it up for sale. I guess she left everything to us. I'm thinking that maybe I can use my inheritance to make a career change."

"Good thinking. But we can talk about your inheritance when we meet tomorrow."

"What?"

"I'm your grandmother's attorney. I thought you knew that."

"Uh..." Hell no, I didn't know that. I'd gotten a letter in the mail asking me to contact the legal offices of—there were three names listed, what were they? I hadn't paid much attention, just handed it to Jamie and begged him to make the appointment. "My brother made the appointment. He didn't mention the name." Or had he? Had he said, 'Donald something?'

"Your grandmother was so kind. She actually called when she read my graduation announcement in the paper, and told me she wanted to be my first client. She said, 'I want a feisty young guy who's sharp and up on all the new tax laws.' So I took her on, and I kept her even when I moved into corporate law. There wasn't a whole lot to do for her, updates on the will mainly, and I just couldn't give her up."

"She liked you, I remember. Funny she never mentioned you after—after that summer."

"Well, she never stopped talking about you. I saw a new picture of you every time she came in."

"Oh no. Pictures?"

"Uh huh. I always kind of had the feeling she was trying to play matchmaker."

I winced. "I'm sorry. I hope she didn't make you uncomfortable."

"Not at all. I enjoyed her very much. And it was nice to keep track of you all these years." He leaned forward. "Sage, listen. There's something I've always wanted to say. I feel I owe you an apology."

"What on earth for?"

"That summer, I should have… I mean I shouldn't have… I had no business… Hmm. This is harder than I thought it would be. Okay, I'm just going to say it. I knew you were… troubled. It was clear you were desperately unhappy. I could have stopped before things went too far. I could have made sure you were really ready. I should have at least written or called and made sure you were okay when you went back home. Instead, I was just a typical teenage guy thinking with my hormones. I was just so thrilled and excited by you that I, well I didn't think at all. I just let it all happen. I thought about you after you left, a lot actually, but I was a coward and didn't even try to reach you. I hope you were all right. I hope I didn't add to your pain."

Two creatures stirred inside me. One knew that I should be appreciating this outpouring of caring concern from the stranger before me. The other? Well, I recognized her from Rose's house the night before. *How dare you,* she wanted to scream, *how dare you think you know anything about me? How dare you presume to know what I wanted or needed when I was fifteen years old? How dare you think about me for twenty-two years? Stay out of my goddamn business!*

"Sage? Are you all right?"

I wanted to hit him, to throw my coffee in his face. But my other half fought back hard. *What is wrong with you? This is a nice man, saying nice things. Tell him you appreciate it. Tell him he didn't hurt you, that his tenderness was a revelation to you. That no one else's arms have ever felt quite so safe.*

In the end there was a simpering kind of truce, the kind where no one wins. I could not look at Donny as I rose from the table and mumbled something about having to meet Jamie. I could hear him behind me, the clatter of his chair as he stood up, the sound of his voice calling my name. Then there was the bell on the door closing behind me.

I ran a block and stopped, leaning against a store window, trying to catch my breath. But the longer I stood, the harder it was to breathe. I gasped, trying to get air into my lungs. My chest hurt, my heart pounded hard. I could not breathe, and yet I was crying. Tears poured down my face; I was shocked to feel them. Wiping them away, I could feel my heart beginning to slow down at last. My breathing was shallow but manageable.

I walked toward Grandma Lucy's, head down, hiding my face. I had left my coffee on the table I'd shared with Donny, and I longed for it now. It would have felt good in my hand.

"Why didn't you tell me Grandma's lawyer was Donny Weston?" I demanded, storming into the house.

Jamie peeked at me from around the corner. He was in the kitchen; I could smell the breakfast he was making for us.

"What are you talking about? I did tell you. Donald Weston. I'm sure I mentioned it." He almost disappeared again, back to the task at hand, but something clicked and he looked at me again. "Wait a minute. Donny? *The* Donny? Same guy?"

"Yes. That Donny. I saw him at the coffee shop, and he apologized for de-flowering me."

"What?"

"He said I was a troubled kid and he basically took advantage of me."

"Wow. How insightful. Sounds like he's trying to make amends for something he's not proud of."

"Jamie! He was presumptuous as hell! How did he know I was troubled? I didn't tell anyone about anything! How dare he assume I was this vulnerable little girl who didn't know what she was doing? I knew exactly what I was doing!"

"Of course you did, Sage. You were fifteen, away from home, angry, rebellious and reckless. You thought you'd never see this guy again. You drank, smoked pot and got laid. All part of your plan for the summer."

"So? Was that so different from other kids my age?"

"You were different."

"I didn't want to be."

"I know. Do you want cheese on your scrambled eggs?"

"No. Yes. Yes, definitely. Thanks for getting food."

"You're welcome."

"Jamie, I had another one. A panic attack. I ran away from Donny and my chest hurt and I couldn't breathe."

He stopped then, put down the spatula and came to me, held me close. "Oh, Sagey. I'm sorry. Are you okay?"

"No, I'm a freakin' basket case. What is wrong with me?"

"Not a thing, Sagey. Not a blessed thing."

~22~

Jamie had to work hard to convince me to go with him to Donny's office for our appointment. I didn't think I could ever look at that kind, earnest face again.

"Sage, *he* didn't know you had a panic attack, did he?"

"No, he just knew I was strange and moody and that I ran off for no apparent reason."

"So tell him you had a stomach ache, or that you suddenly realized you were late for something. Apologize to him for your rudeness. You might even tell him that you've had a couple of panic attacks lately. I'm sure he'd understand. But I want you at this meeting. You need to hear it all first- hand. No whining. You're coming.

"And then—Sage just listen for a minute—we need to find you a shrink. You have to start dealing with these panic attacks. I'm serious!"

"No, Jamie, I can't, I just can't!"

"Yes, you can. The hardest part is making the first appointment. I'll help you find someone good."

"I don't see the point in dredging up all that old crap. How can that make me better?"

"Well, let's see: you were functioning pretty well, apart from some very destructive choices in men that almost got you killed, and then Daddy Dearest pops into town and you start having panic attacks out of the blue. Hmm. Connection, you think?"

"So?"

"So what you're doing isn't working so well. Try something new. Anything! If you have another suggestion, I'm open."

"I'll exercise more, get into really good shape. Eat better so my mind is sharper."

"And talk to someone who might be able to help. Please, Sage."

"I'll think about it, all right? But obviously we have to wait until we go home. It's all about building a relationship, right? So I can't very well start therapy here and then leave in a couple of weeks, right?"

"True, but we can start looking for someone, even have an appointment lined up for you when we get back."

"No, Jamie. I want to have some fun while we're here. I don't want to think about any of that until we leave. But I promise I'll start looking for a shrink as soon as we get back."

"One more panic attack and we start looking right away. Agreed?"

I nodded, and shook the hand my brother extended, sealing the contract.

We walked to Donny's office, it was so close to the house. I imagined Grandma Lucy walking the same route when she went to see him. She would leave early and walk slowly, stopping here to watch a squirrel bounce on a tree limb, there to smile at a neighbor's child. A pleasant walk to see her lawyer, to prepare for her death. I shuddered.

"Cold?" Jamie asked.

"A little," I answered, rubbing my arms convincingly.

Donny's office had once been someone's home, a cute little house with a big front porch like Grandma's. Now, under the four-digit house number, a plaque read McDermott, Shanahan and Weston, Attorneys at Law, in brass lettering.

"Deep breath, Sage," Jamie whispered. "Okay?"

I nodded, and Jamie opened the door.

The secretary was pretty, with short blond hair and huge blue eyes. Immediately I assumed she was Donny's lover, of course, why wouldn't she be, and I hated her. She flashed a perfect white smile at us and told us to go right in, he was expecting us.

Smiling back, I told myself not to be so petty, so black-hearted. But I said nothing, allowing Jamie to thank her instead.

Donny's office looked exactly as it should: stately without pretension, the shelves behind his desk filled with books from which he presumably gleaned valuable loopholes and precedents. He rose from his leather chair as we entered the room and greeted us warmly, then motioned for us to sit.

Our business must have presented few challenges for him, but Donny had prepared well for our meeting, handing Jamie and me each a copy of the report detailing Grandma Lucy's estate.

Estate. That was the word that kept floating through my mind as we went through the report, page by page. Donny was doing his best to describe each of our grandmother's assets clearly and concisely, but I couldn't seem to focus on his words or the figures on the pages I pretended to read along with. Finally, one simple sentence brought me back to the moment like a cold splash to the face.

"So, with all the assets and property, each of you will be receiving approximately two million."

I looked at Jamie. He was nodding, looking at the report on his lap. I looked at Donny. He didn't seem to be joking.

"Do you have a question, Sage?" he asked.

"Uh…" It came out as a dry gasp. I swallowed. "Please say that again?"

"Two million dollars each, give or take, depending on the sale price of the house. This figure is based on current stock values and a recent appraisal of the house. Lucy had an insurance policy specifically earmarked to pay the inheritance tax upon her death, so that you two wouldn't have to worry about that. Obviously it's entirely up to you whether to keep the house, stocks or any of her other assets, or sell and reinvest the money as you see fit. I strongly encourage you both to find a financial expert to advise you on those matters."

Donny sat back in his chair. "Your grandmother was very careful with her money. She received two different inheritances during her lifetime: one from her parents and one from your grandfather's family. But she lived very frugally, and this is the result."

Suddenly I was grieving for Grandma Lucy all over again. I thought of all the things she could have done with that money. The places she could have seen, the adventures she missed out on. She would have enjoyed traveling, loved the excitement of discovery, and she could have gone anywhere in the world she wanted. Instead, she lived a small, quiet life while growing this pile of money for us.

My heart filled with love and sorrow and, finally, gratitude. One word came to mind: free. I was free to pursue a new career, even take some time off, go back to school if I needed to.

Donny continued. "As you can see in the report, she left all of her assets in the form of two trusts, one for each of you, with everything divided equally between you. Lucy's investment portfolio is pretty extensive. It's all yours, right now. The only other beneficiary is her neighbor, Rose, who is receiving a few pieces of Lucy's jewelry. That's on the back page of your report. It's a string of pearls, a ruby brooch and a diamond dinner ring. Lucy told me where to find them, but you could give them to Rose if you like."

"That would be fine," Jamie said without looking at me.

"All right. So, please go over the report very carefully. I realize this could be a little overwhelming. Please feel free to call any time if you have questions.

"There's one more issue. Lucy prepaid all of her final arrangements. She specified that her remains be cremated. That has been done. You just need to pick up her ashes—they are in an urn at the Jenkins Funeral Home. That's the one just a couple of blocks from her house."

"Yeah, I remember seeing it," Jamie said.

"Lucy didn't want a funeral or memorial service of any kind. She said that whatever you decide to do with her ashes is just fine. She told me to tell you, 'Remember, kids, that is not where I am, so don't fuss about the silly urn.' " Donny smiled.

"That sounds like her," Jamie said.

"She really was a great lady. She'll be missed. I guess that's something we can all hope for. To be missed when we're gone, I mean," Donny said.

He stood, so we stood, and Jamie shook Donny's hand. "Thank you," Jamie said, and walked out of the office.

I started to do the same, and Donny cleared his throat. "Uh, Sage?"

I faced him.

"I was sorry you had to run off so fast yesterday. I really enjoyed talking with you."

"Oh. Yeah. Me too. Sorry about that."

"Look, I'm sorry, I know you have a lot to absorb right now. But I was wondering if you might let me buy you dinner one night while you're here."

"Oh. I." There were no other words in my brain.

"I know this is lousy timing, but I couldn't just let you walk out of here. Please, Sage. Just dinner, what do you say?"

Through the open door, I looked at Jamie, who had turned to face me. He nodded, then mouthed the words *Say yes.*

Donny, standing behind his desk, missed Jamie's little mime performance. I looked back at him.

"Yes, Donny, I'd love to have dinner with you," I said, not meaning it one bit. But I trusted Jamie's impulses more than my own. And, I told myself, if I started acting normal maybe someday I'd actually feel normal.

Jamie also convinced me to take the bequeathed jewelry to Rose by myself. "It's the perfect opportunity to apologize," he said.

"But…"

"I know, I know. She overstepped. She erred. She misjudged and committed a misdeed. In her mind, she was helping. She'll probably never do anything like that again. But she still didn't deserve what she got from you, Sage. You could have explained things in a quiet and respectful way."

"I know. And I am sorry about the way I spoke to her."

"Then tell her that."

"Fine."

"Good girl."

Just like it said on the last page of the report, the specified trinkets sat in the top velvet lined drawer of Grandma Lucy's jewelry box. They were not pieces I would ever wear, but they were pretty, and clearly valuable.

Rose was very grateful, for the jewelry, and for my apology. So grateful that she shed a few tears, dabbing at her eyes with a rose-embroidered handkerchief. She insisted on making a pot of coffee, and so we sat at her kitchen table and chatted while watching and smelling it brew. Out came the matching sugar bowl and cream pitcher, which held not cream, not milk, but a non-dairy imitation cream flavored powder. Even so, the coffee tasted pretty good.

I expected to be bored or annoyed by Rose, but before I knew it I found myself enjoying her, especially her stories of Grandma Lucy.

"I'll never forget the day I moved into this house. My husband had died just three months earlier, you see, and I had to find a smaller place. I just couldn't keep up the big old house we'd raised our kids in. Oh, truth be told I couldn't stand being there without him. So I was sad and tired and scared, but right after the movers left, your grandma came to my door with that fresh banana bread, cookies and a thermos of cold lemonade. I was feeling mighty blue, but her smile just brightened me right up. Generous, that's what she was, through and through.

"She knitted booties for those little babies that are born addicted to drugs? And not only that, she went to the hospital and held those babies. I went with her once, but my nerves just couldn't take it. Those poor little babies just cry and cry like it's the end of the world. Most of them are all alone, you know, being sent into foster care. I s'pose some end up okay and some don't. Life is one big roll of the dice I guess. Lucy said she felt pretty lucky and she wanted some of that luck to rub off on those helpless little babies."

"I hope it did."

"I hope so too, honey. You know, I had a feeling you and I'd get along fine. We just got off on the wrong foot, that's all. Your brother too. What a handsome boy he is. I'll bet he's got to beat the girls off with a stick."

I hesitated, just half a beat, but I answered quite honestly. "Yep, all the time."

"Well my Norman wasn't a big looker or anything, but I loved that man from the first minute we met. There was just a kindness around his eyes, a gentleness. He was sweet, my Norman. And the greatest father you ever saw. Ask my kids. Especially Norma Jean, my baby. She was a daddy's girl from the day she was born. When she was sick with a fever? She could cry all day long, but when Daddy walked through the door at the end of the day she just settled right down, giggled and cooed in his arms. I acted like it drove me crazy, but I really loved seeing them like that, just staring into each other's eyes. The whole world disappeared when they were together."

Much as I told myself it shouldn't, it still bothered me to hear about all those perfect fathers people so loved to describe. Just a roll of the genetic dice determined whether you got Robert Young or the boogeyman himself.

"How many kids do you have, Rose?"

"I have three, honey. Norma Jean is about your age, I think. Richie is about to turn forty, and Leslie is forty-two. My goodness, time flies."

"Do they live around here?"

"Norma does. She and her husband live in a nice little house on the lake. Richie lives in Spokane, so he's not too far away and Leslie is down in Boise. They're all doing pretty well for themselves. I'm real proud of all of them, but Norma's the one who really came through for us when my husband was sick, and now she checks on me all the time. She's a sweet girl. She loved your grandma, too, o' course. Everyone did. I hope you get to meet my Norma Jean before you leave. I know you're going to be real busy, but maybe you'll get another chance to come over and visit. And honey, if there's anything I can help you with, you just let me know, all right?"

"Thank you, Rose."

"Well you're so welcome. And we'll just never talk about your daddy again, don't you worry. I know how to keep my lips zipped."

Rose made the motion of zipping her mouth closed, locking it and throwing away the key.

"I appreciate that. I do have one question, though."

"What is it, honey?"

"My father said it was difficult to track me down. How hard could it have been when you gave him the information?"

"Well, I did make him work for it. I asked him a lot of questions, and if he hadn't had the right answers I would have just hung right up on him, you can be sure of that. I didn't know the details, honey, just that he was a drunkard, and a mean one at that. When he told me that he'd made a promise to himself and to God to stay sober and be a good Christian, well I suppose I just took pity on him. He begged me for your address, Sage. He said—now let me get this right—that part of his recovery was to make amends to all the people he'd done wrong. I admired that, I truly did. So I gave him the address Lucy had for you. Lucy had told me that she hadn't gotten Jamie's new address after the last time he moved, so I gave your father the name of Jamie's beauty shop. Anyway, I guess some things you just can't forgive. Hurting your very own children the way he did—let's just say I understand why you can't give him another chance, honey."

Rose was so straightforward and simple, an open book you could read in one sitting. Suddenly I felt protective of her; impulsively, I hugged her tight.

"Oh!" she said, patting my back. "Oh, you sweet thing."

I pulled away and looked at Grandma Lucy's jewelry, still lying on the kitchen table where Rose had deposited it in a sparkly little pile. I could remember Grandma Lucy wearing each piece: the pearls with a pink silk blouse, the ruby brooch on her wool coat at Christmas time, the ring on a middle finger because she'd lost weight and couldn't keep it on her "proper ring finger" as she called it.

Now they belonged to Rose. Now *her* grandchildren would someday cherish memories of her wearing them. "Enjoy the jewelry, Rose," I said. "Think of my grandmother when you wear it."

She smiled, and I waited for her chirping voice again. "Well you know I will, Sage honey. You come back and see me again, won't you?"

I liked Rose. I liked the bells in her voice. I wished I could take back all the vile things I'd spat at her before. She seemed too precious, too innocent to hear such ugliness.

Walking back to the house next door, I wondered how a person could reach adulthood and remain so untainted. I also wondered why Grandma Lucy had not revealed Jamie's sexual orientation to Rose. Had Grandma Lucy been secretly ashamed?

No, I decided. *Rose wouldn't understand. Grandma was protecting her.*

A sad thought. So sad, that anyone would need to be protected from the truth about such a wonderful person. Sighing deeply, I walked back into my grandmother's home.

~23~

The next day Jamie and I picked up Grandma Lucy's ashes at the funeral home. We were greeted and ushered in by the funeral director, who expressed his finely polished heartfelt sympathy at our grandmother's passing. We signed papers and in exchange were given a dark bronze urn. Then we were outside again, squinting in the sun.

Jamie held the urn in his arms. "This is it? This is all that's left of a human being after living a whole, long life? Strange, isn't it?"

Tears came then, too quickly to be stopped. I crumpled onto the steps of the funeral home. "She's really gone, Jamieson. We'll never see her again! I should have called her more often! I should have come to visit her. We were just a few measly hours away! What kept us from driving here? I missed her! I wanted to see her! Why didn't I?"

"Oh, Sage. Life distracts us, that's all. We always think we'll have more time. Grandma Lucy understood that. Come on. Let's get her home."

That night I dreamed of Grandma Lucy for the first time since her death. She sat on the edge of my bed and stroked my hair. "Darling Sage. What a beautiful woman you've become."

"Grandma! I knew you weren't dead."

"Sage, don't blame yourself. Please, honey, it's not your fault."

And then she was gone. I called her name, but she didn't appear again.

I woke up crying. What wasn't my fault? That Grandma Lucy was dead? That I was an emotional wreck? Three hours would pass before I fell asleep again.

By morning the dream was far from my thoughts. My dinner with Donny was tonight and I was frantic. I spent the day trying to come up with a reason to cancel. I paced. I worried about every possible scenario. What if it goes really badly? My emotional state was fragile enough. How would I handle a rejection right now? Even worse, what if it went well? He lived here, in Idaho! How could I get involved with someone who lived in Idaho?

Then, late in the day, I really panicked. I hadn't been expecting to go on a date in Coeur d'Alene; now I realized that none of my clothes were acceptable.

"Why did I say yes? I have nothing to wear. Nothing!"

"Here, let me look," Jamie said, in that soothing 'my poor neurotic sister needs my help' voice. "Wear your black sweater and nice jeans."

"I don't have the right shoes!"

"Okay. Let's look at the shoes first. What did you bring?"

"Flip flops, tennis shoes and my red flats."

"Hmm. Not ideal, but we have no time to shop. Definitely the red. The black sweater works. The red shoes will be just an eye-catching pop of color. Perfect! Problem solved. Now get ready."

I modeled the complete ensemble, and Jamie applauded while I twirled. When the doorbell rang I raced into the bathroom to splash on a little cologne.

Checking my makeup in the mirror, I ran my fingertips over my face. At thirty, I'd been wrinkle-free. *They'll appear slowly,* I'd thought. My belief had been that I'd hardly notice the aging process, that it would happen naturally, so gradually that it wouldn't feel cruel. The truth was that those lines seemed to appear in groups, and fast. Overnight, even. Aging may indeed be natural, but it pounces on you just the same.

Now I looked myself over. Yep, thirty-seven all right. Every year it seemed that just as I began to grow accustomed to my age in theory, it landed on my face in fact.

Tilting my head, I examined my neck and jaw line. Still all right. No second chin, no jowls, no turkey neck. I could hear Jamie and Donny chatting in the living room now. One more glance…wait. What the hell?

A long, curly black hair was sticking right out of my neck. I touched it, stretched it out to its full length.

My face flushed magenta. I had suddenly become old! My hormones were shriveling up along with my unused ovaries and leaving me an old hag with stray hairs in strange places. Soon I would be wearing a scarf to protect my perm, tying it under my fuzzy chin! Warts would no doubt be springing up on my nose shortly, and my withered hands would discolor with countless age spots. How did this happen?

Tweezers. Without tweezers, this date would not take place. Frantically, I searched my makeup bag, knowing I didn't bring any. Grandma Lucy's medicine cabinet? No tweezers. She probably never grew old lady fur. Why was I so cursed?

"Uh, Jamie, could you come in here just a minute?"

"Where? The bathroom?"

"Yes, please."

I'd opened the door a crack and he peeked through. "What are you doing? Donny's waiting," he whispered.

"Do you have a pair of tweezers?"

"You don't have time to pluck your eyebrows, Sage. Besides, they look fine."

"Not my eyebrows. Please, just get the tweezers," I said through my clenched jaw.

"Calm down! I'm not sure I have any. I'll look, okay?"

He did have some, of course, and brought them to me, closing the door behind him. "Thank you, thank you, thank you, you are the best brother in the world." I took the precious implement from him and looked again at the beast in the mirror. Then, carefully, slowly, I closed the tweezers around the hideous hair, took a deep breath and yanked it out.

I opened the tweezers, releasing the errant strand. Jamie and I both watched it drift down until it disappeared into the little pink garbage can.

"Oh," Jamie said. No further explanation was needed, obviously. "Maybe it was just an anomaly, Sage. Maybe it was the only one you'll ever have."

"Or maybe it was the beginning of the end," I said, handing him back the tweezers.

"Sage. You are a lovely young woman. You're about to be fairly well-to-do. You're going to have to stop making yourself miserable, you know that? Now go on your date and have fun. I would even understand and forgive you if you chose to stay out all night."

"Young. I'm still young, right?"

"I just said that. Yes. You are young, beautiful and a great sister. It's time to rejoin the human race. Now get out there!"

Jamie fairly pushed me out the bathroom door, and Donny jumped up from the sofa. "Hi! I was beginning to think you'd changed your mind."

"What? No, of course not."

"I'm glad. You look great, Sage."

"Thanks. So do you." He really did. Smelled good, too.

"Are you ready?"

"Yeah! See you later, Jamie."

"Nice to see you again, James," Donny said. He reached out, shook Jamie's hand.

"It's Jamieson, actually, but yeah, it was great seeing you, too."

Donny rolled his eyes. "I knew that. God, I'm sorry. Lucy's last name. I guess I'm a little nervous." He grinned. I really liked that grin. Maybe this wouldn't be so bad after all.

In fact, the date turned out to be really fun. Donny took me to his favorite Italian restaurant and introduced me to a yummy bottle of wine he told me was a Supertuscan. I giggled, imagining rows of bottles wearing little capes. *Supertuscans to the rescue! Stronger than a spicy marinara, able to quench a thirst and create a pleasant buzz with a single bottle!*

It pleased me that Donny didn't ask what was so funny. "I know, a little cape, right?"

I nodded. "And white gloves on tiny little fists sticking out from the bottle as it flies through the air."

"Look! Up in the sky!"

"Faster than a speeding Pinot!"

We laughed together, then raised and clinked our glasses. "That's my kind of hero," I said.

We found a lot to laugh about that night, throughout dinner and afterward, walking down to the docks. It was a long walk, and I was a little grateful I hadn't brought any of my "cuter" shoes.

The lake was endlessly black, gentle as a baby's cradle. Our conversation, lively until now, stopped altogether as we watched a small boat glide into a slip, where its captain turned off the motor and tied it securely into place. Tiny waves traveled from the boat to our part of the dock, splashing finally below our feet, rocking us gently: a quiet, soothing tremor.

"Do you like living here, Donny? Do you ever think about moving?"

"I think about it once in a while. Mostly in the winter, I guess. But honestly, I don't really see myself anywhere else. This is home."

"I can see why. It's so beautiful. I always loved it here. Not just because of Grandma Lucy. I love the lake, the hills, the pretty houses. It always seemed like this was a happy place. Hopeful, I guess."

"Oh, there are plenty of hopeless people here, Sage, just like any other place. It's what you bring to a place that makes it happy. On the other hand, I don't think it hurts to look at this kind of beauty every day."

"Seattle is beautiful, too. Lots of water, and the mountains are spectacular. But it's bigger. More impersonal I suppose."

"I like the seasons we have here, too. Four distinct seasons. Snow in the winter, lots of heat in the summer. I would miss that, I think."

"We get snow once in a while. And we can always go to the mountains if we miss it."

"That's true. Sounds like you're pretty attached to the place."

"Maybe I'm more attached than I thought, actually. I don't know; I'm a little homesick, that's all. I miss my friend Chloe. I miss my cat."

"A cat person?" He sounded dubious.

"Yes, absolutely, a card-carrying member of the Society of Cat People. You have a problem with that?"

He grinned that funny little grin again. "Who me? No, not really. I am more of a dog person, no doubt about it, but cats can be cool sometimes, too. I'm really an all-around animal lover, honest."

"Okay, I guess you're all right then."

"What's your cat's name?"

"Teddy. I found him, lost or abandoned. I like to think we found each other. Anyway, my friend Chloe is taking care of him and I miss them both a lot."

"What do you miss about Teddy?"

"Well, he's always eager to see me when I get home. He loves to cuddle on the couch and watch TV. And he always knows when I don't feel good; he stays right by my side."

"Dogs are like that too, you know. And you can actually teach dogs to do things."

"Train them, you mean. Cats are trainable too. They are! People have trained cats to use toilets, play fetch, open doors even! It's harder to train them, that's true, but only because cats haven't been domesticated very long. They are the closest to their wild roots of all domesticated animals. Which means that when a cat loves you, you've really accomplished something! Dogs love everyone."

Donny laughed then. "Okay, okay, I give up! Obviously this is an educated opinion you have and I am clearly cat-deprived."

"Clearly."

He looked at me then, and I knew he wanted to kiss me. Suddenly I could feel my heart pounding. I took a long, deep breath. *Please, not a panic attack, not now.*

"Well, maybe someday I could meet Teddy." He moved closer.

"You'd like him." Another deep breath. *No, not a panic attack. Just a normal first-kiss thrill.*

"I'm sure I would." Closer.

The kiss was soft and sweet, tentative and brief. When it ended I just stood there, eyes closed, head tilted, lips ready for another kiss. But it didn't come.

I opened my eyes. Donny was staring straight at me. Then he looked down at his shoes. "I should get you back home."

"Oh. Okay." We started walking, and my mind raced. *What happened? Did I do something wrong? Is he too nice for me? Did he see another stray hair on my neck?*

We spoke a little on the way back, but it was awkward and halting. It seemed the spell was broken.

But back at the house, on Grandma Lucy's porch, he held my face in his hands so tenderly I thought my knees might buckle. "I want to see you again, Sage. Can I? Tomorrow?"

"Yes, Donny. That would be…" And there was that second kiss at last, the one that would follow me to my dreams.

~24~

Over the next several days, Jamie and I spent much of our time cataloguing the contents of Grandma Lucy's house, deciding what we wanted to keep, what to sell, what to give to charity.

My evenings were spent with Donny: dinners and walks beside the lake, a couple of movies, a moonlit boat ride. He made dinner for me at his house one night; it was delicious, and his home was amazing, floor to ceiling windows making the most of a gorgeous view of the lake.

After each date, Donny took me back to Lucy's porch, kissed me gently and said goodnight. I was in heaven.

"Heaven. I've died and gone to heaven," I announced to Jamie one evening, returning from Donny's house.

"That's fabulous, doll. Glad you're having a good time."

"He might be the one, Jamie. Really. He's sane, stable, successful, and doesn't seem to have an abusive bone in his body. And he cooks. And he's a good kisser! What else is there?"

"Do his shoes get wet?"

"What?"

"When he walks on water. Do his shoes get wet, or does he actually hover above the surface?"

"Smartass. You like him, don't you?"

"I don't know the man, Sage, and neither do you. You are *getting to know him*. You've been on, what, five dates now? And yes, I know it's intense and fun being the center of attention and all that, but be cautious, please. You can't fall in love forever and ever in under two weeks. You know that, right? And we are leaving in a week."

"I don't have to leave. I can quit my job now, with Grandma Lucy's money coming in. I don't ever have to be a social worker again."

"True, but don't you at least want to give them ample notice? Say good-bye to your clients? I know there are some you'll miss, Sage."

My shoulders drooped. He was right, of course. I hated that he was right, that I would have to return to that horrible office with its horrible phone connecting me with horrible people. But, it would only be for a short time. Two weeks would be plenty. I could do that, I supposed. And I did want to say good-bye to a few people. Ruth, definitely. And I needed to make sure that Molly's services were in place and working for her. And it would be nice to say good-bye to my co-workers, especially Rachel, and I really didn't want to let Althea down.

"Yeah, I guess I need to go. But then I can come back here. I can do whatever I want!"

"Yes, you can. Just make sure it's what *you* want, all right sugar?"

"I don't really know what I want, Jamie. Except that I want to find out if Donny is Mr. Right. What if he is? What if he's the future father of your nieces and/or nephews?"

"It could happen, I suppose. I'd just like you to take things slowly for a while. I'd hate to see you get hurt again, Sage, that's all."

"I'll be careful, little brother. I promise."

We had a yard sale the next day, a Sunday afternoon. We'd posted flyers all over town, and we got a pretty good turnout. Grandma Lucy's stuff was all much more tasteful than your usual yard sale fare, and we were able to sell almost everything. Rose came by with her daughter—the famous Norma Jean—and bought a cherry rocking chair and a few china pieces. Dozens of people wandered through, introducing themselves as Lucy's friends. Our grandmother had been well loved.

By sunset, all we had left was an old portable TV and an antique clock that had stopped working. Jamie ran those items to a nearby thrift store while I cleaned up and counted our profits: $427.75. Not bad.

Something was on Jamie's mind when he got back, but I could tell he wasn't ready to talk about it. I busied myself in the kitchen, cleaning and searching through cupboards. For some crazy reason I'd felt the need to invite Donny over for dinner, return the favor of a home cooked dinner, when I really had no cooking skills whatsoever. He had served fish in some complex sauce, and at this point I was seriously considering mac and cheese.

"You're already nervous about dinner, aren't you?" Jamie asked.

"Well? What should I serve? It should be something I can actually cook."

"Good point. What about pasta with that marinara sauce you made for me that time? That was good."

"Newman's Own."

"Oh. Well, I couldn't tell, maybe Donny Dry Shoes won't be able to either."

"Really?"

"Sure. Plus, you can sauté some mushrooms to add to it, grate some fresh Parmesan, and voila! Gourmet."

"Will you help me?"

"Of course. But it will be easy, I promise you."

We went shopping together, and still I could see Jamie's mind working on something. But I knew when to be patient; I knew that, eventually, he would work it all out and share it with me.

Jamie minced the garlic for me so my hands wouldn't smell all night. And he chopped the mushrooms because he was so much better at it. He opened the wine to let it breathe before Donny arrived, and he set the table beautifully, candles and all. Basically, Jamie ended up doing everything. But I watched. Well, at least until I heard Donny at the door, right on time as usual. I kissed him hello.

"You look beautiful," he said.

I smiled.

Jamie brought in the wine and put it on the table. He shook Donny's hand, made small talk. I really didn't pay much attention; I was much too busy studying the lines on Donny's face. But then Jamie poured the wine and handed me a glass, breaking my concentration.

We clinked glasses, sipped, oohed and aahed, and then Jamie excused himself, returning to the kitchen.

"I didn't realize Jamie was the cook in the family," Donny said.

I shrugged. "He was so sweet, he just volunteered to cook for me. Sort of. He enjoys cooking, though. Much more than I do. That's something you and he have in common."

Jamie brought out the food, steaming and smelling wonderful. "Get the bread, would you Sage?"

I did—a long French baguette, warm and crusty, from the oven that Jamie had already turned off—and laid it on the table in front of Donny, proud as if I'd made it from scratch.

We ate and chatted, the three of us. As always, I was so proud of Jamie; his ability to engage people, to show a real interest in them, ask pertinent and thoughtful questions, astounded me.

"Sage tells me you do mostly corporate law, Don. Do you enjoy it?"

"Very much. I can choose which clients to take on, so my own integrity stays intact. I wouldn't represent any company that violated what I consider to be my core values."

"Admirable. And you're still able to make a decent living?"

Donny chuckled. "Yes, actually. I think that's why I've never been tempted to go to a larger city. Small town folks just seem more in touch with the basics of life."

"Such as?" I asked.

"Decency, I suppose. Kindness. Respecting the earth and our fellow human beings. For instance, I could never be on staff at a tobacco company. To try to maintain the right of someone to sell and promote a product that causes so many illnesses and deaths? Well, maybe those attorneys tell themselves that everyone deserves fair representation, but I couldn't rationalize it that way. I would know in my soul that it was wrong. That the world would be a better place without my client's contribution. Couldn't do it."

I nearly swooned. What a wonderful, moral man. I gazed at him, studying his face as he touched his napkin to the corner of his mouth. He sat, straight as a pin, and as I watched, his eyes darted to mine. He smiled. I felt another swoon coming on.

"Did you go to college around here, Don?"

"No, I went to the University of Arizona. Liked the warm weather, but I really missed the water. Don't think I could live down there, but it was fun for a while. How about you, Jamie? Are you a Husky?"

"No. I decided on a career pretty early on, and the University of Washington wasn't going to get me there. But I had some friends who went there and I hung out on campus a bit. Sage got her BSW there."

"So what did you go into?" Don asked.

Oddly, Jamie seemed to be considering how to answer the question. He hesitated.

"I'm a hair stylist," he said evenly.

"He's a hair *designer*," I said. *Maybe he doesn't want to brag,* I thought. *That's okay. I'll do it for him.* "Jamie works for *the* premier salon in Seattle, and he is their top designer. He charges $120 for a haircut! Of course I get them for free, aren't I lucky?"

Gushing and babbling along as I was, I didn't notice at first that something was happening between Jamie and Donny. They hadn't broken eye contact since Jamie had revealed his occupation. No one was smiling. No one was eating, for that matter. What was going on?

And it hit me just as Donny asked his next question. "You ever been married, Jamieson?"

No. Please, this can't be happening.

"No, Don, I haven't. You?"

"No. Guess I haven't met the right woman. What's your reason, Jamieson?"

"I don't know, Don. I suppose I haven't met the right man. But at least our state is one of the few places where I would have the right to marry the man I love. You know, Don, not all hairstylists are gay. But I, for one, fit the stereotype. Sorry to disappoint you."

I looked from one to the other, voices screaming in my head. Donny dropped his fork onto his plate, loudly. Yet his voice remained low, controlled. "You're a…homosexual?" He finally looked at me. "Your brother's a…"

"Yes, my brother is gay, Donny. You—you have a problem with that." It wasn't a question.

"Sage, I'm sorry. I have to leave."

"What?"

"I was going to ask you tonight if you've accepted Jesus Christ as your personal savior. Clearly you haven't, if you think nothing's wrong with your brother's lifestyle. Obviously we don't have a future together if we have such fundamentally different beliefs, so it's better if I leave right now."

"What?"

"Unless you're ready to denounce the homosexual lifestyle right now, we have no future."

"Is this a joke?"

"Good-bye, Sage. Jamie, I'll pray for your soul. For both of your souls."

And he was gone, out the door, down the stairs of the porch and off into the darkness.

Jamie and I sat there, staring at each other. One word glowed red in my mind.

How?

How could I have not known, not picked up on the homophobic vibes from Donny that must have been screamingly obvious?

How did they slip past me, when usually I was so poised to pounce?

"How did he fool me?" I finally asked out loud.

Jamie shrugged. "I'm sure there were signs. You were too happy to notice."

"You noticed, didn't you? Come on, what were the signs?"

He sighed. "There was only one, really. Literally, a sign. When I went to the thrift store today, I saw it on the bulletin board there."

"Something about Donny?"

"Yes. He's heading a committee that pushes anti-gay rights initiatives, spreads anti-gay marriage propaganda. That sort of thing. There it was, bold as brass: Contact Don Weston, Chairman. The committee also believes that it is a sin for mothers to work outside the home. Oh, and they seem to think it would be okay to round up non-Christians and shoot them."

"Wow."

"I actually just assumed that last part."

"That's why you were so quiet. That's why you were acting so weird. And yet you still made dinner! You were still nice to him!"

"I just thought it would all come out in the wash. I'm a coward, really. I didn't want to be the one to tell you. I'm sorry he wasn't Prince Charming, doll."

"It should be illegal for freakazoids like that to pose as nice, normal people."

"I'm sure he's saying the same thing about us right now, Sage. Funny, I know a lot of gay people who consider themselves good Christians. I wonder what Donny would say to them. I think it's sad that he believes only in his particular brand of spirituality. Feel sorry for the man. I do."

"That's because you really are nice."

"Thank you. Same to you. Let's eat this dinner, what do you say?"

"I say, pour me some more wine please! Here's to the real Prince Charming, wherever he may be."

"And in the meantime, may you find a slightly-less-charming-but-still-perfectly-fine frog to spend some time with."

"Nice thought."

~25~

In the days before the yard sale, as Jamie and I painstakingly sorted through Grandma Lucy's belongings, we'd filled a box with items too personal, too old or too sentimental to sell. Now, a few days before our departure, we sat on the floor and went through the box, examining each treasure one by one.

There were toys, reserved for our long-ago visits: a stuffed elephant covered in rainbow polka dots, an Etch-A-Sketch, a Candy Land game, a box of crayons. There were a few letters from Jamie and me: Dear Grandma Lucy, How are you? I am fine. I hope I will see you this summer, Love, Sage.

And, Dear Grandma Lucy, I want a puppy for Christmas. Would you get me one? Love, Jamie (your grandson).

Hazy memories flashed: Jamie and me sitting at our kitchen table with Mom as she instructed us on the art of letter writing. "These letters will mean so much to Grandma, you'll see."

Apparently, Mom was right about that.

More letters: a postcard Rose had sent from the Grand Ole Opry. Many letters from people we didn't know.

There were envelopes with postmarks so faded we couldn't read the dates.

"Jamie, this one's from Grandpa!"

Our maternal grandfather, Noah Jamieson, had died around the time of Jamie's second birthday. I had one fuzzy memory of him; I was peeking at him from behind his favorite chair. "Grandpa," I called, giggling, then ducked back behind him. He looked one way, then the other. "Where is that little girl?" he asked. "Where oh where is my little Sage, my pretty girl?" Then I let myself get closer and closer until he finally caught me. "Here I am," I yelled, and he grabbed me in a bear hug that smelled of pipe tobacco and Old Spice.

"What does it say?" Jamie asked.

I pulled a single folded page out of the envelope and smoothed it out.

"It's dated January 5, 1945. He must not have been home from the war yet.

" 'Dearest Lucy, I received your letter today. A month passed before it found me, and so as I write this I am now the father of a month old baby girl. It is at times like these that I realize how cruel a thing war is. I know you must have been very brave, Lucy my love, as you always are. I'm very glad to hear that all is well with both my girls. I love her name: Georgia. It's beautiful. I know that her middle name, Rae, is in honor of my father. Thank you, my love. Pray for my safe return, sweetheart, and with God's help I know we'll be together again soon. All my love to you and our daughter, always. Yours, Noah.' Wow. People really knew how to write love letters back then."

"Pretty impressive, all right. So Great Grandpa's name must have been Ray, I guess?" Jamie said. "Did you know that?"

Another flash: "Oh my god, I just remembered Mom telling me that she was named after her grandfather! I wonder how many other memories are lurking in my head somewhere."

We continued looking through our grandmother's keepsakes. When we were finished, I realized I was disappointed.

"What's wrong, Sage?"

"I don't know. I think I was hoping for some answers."

"About Mom?"

I nodded. "I mean, we don't really know anything about how she died. How bad was her drug addiction? What were her drugs of choice? We don't know anything! Why didn't I ever ask Grandma Lucy about it?"

"I don't know. I always meant to, but I just kept putting it off. I didn't want to make her feel bad. I suppose I felt it probably didn't really matter. It was all over."

"Yeah, I had those same thoughts. But now I really wish I'd asked."

"I wish I knew the answers to all those questions too, Sage. I wish I could remember her, even just a little. I envy you that."

I nodded. My memories of our mother were precious to me, and I too wished Jamie could have a few of them.

Jamie rose and held out his hand to help me up. "Come on, Sagey. Tell me what you remember about Mom and I'll buy you an ice cream cone."

"Deal." I hugged him tight, took a deep breath and started talking even before we walked out the front door.

~26~

It was my mother who visited my dreams that night. I saw her as she had been the day she left us: her beautiful face at eye level with mine as she crouched down to make her doomed promises. Then, suddenly years later, I saw her standing at the front door, begging me to recognize her, to let her in so she could save us all. She looked pale, thin and tired through the glass in the door. She was crying. Even though I suddenly knew everything about her, I still wouldn't open the door. Knowing who she was and what was in store for her and for us, I stood frozen, unable or unwilling to move.

When I woke up, I lay in bed for a long time. I thought about my mother's sad life. She must have loved my father in the beginning. When had he become a monster? When had the drugs become a problem? When had they taken over?

I wondered about my father: his anger, his vicious nature. Had he ever cared about us? How could he lie to us, tell us our mother didn't love us? Even if it were true, if she truly had no love in her heart for us, how could anyone say that to a child?

My eyes hurt, so I closed them again. This time it was Colin's face I saw.

I sat bolt upright, eyes wide open. How had I allowed Colin into my life? One red flag should have been enough for me to toss him out my door for good. Had his abuse actually felt "normal" to me?

Yes, it had. Even worse, it had seemed… inevitable.

Now, I retraced the steps through my own life. I had succeeded in surviving my father and protecting Jamie. Then, finally and forever, we escaped. Moving in with Mary and Chloe was the first good fortune we had ever known, and yet I still wasn't happy. Not really. I was sullen and sad. I couldn't have been easy to have around. That's why Mary sent us to Coeur d'Alene that summer. The summer of Donny Weston. But Mary must have known what she was doing, because that summer changed me, at least temporarily. I think I realized there was nothing left to rebel against. No one left to fight. I felt better for a while. Until Jamie started high school, and then I had to protect him all over again. I had to, but it was so difficult, trying to protect him against the whole world instead of just our father. High school…so many dark memories. I dropped out before I graduated. The reasons were hazy now, but Mary was so supportive, and so proud when I earned my GED.

During college I started dating fairly regularly. I worked hard to blend in, to pretend I was normal. Now, thinking about that time, I caught my breath. I could count three decent guys I had pushed away, and several more louts I fell for, hard. I had my first taste of abuse and I never looked back. It seemed so obvious now! Each boyfriend, slightly more abusive than the last, had systematically trained me, prepared me for the moment I would meet my ideal abuser.

Somehow, I always knew he would come. And he did, dressed in Italian suits and oozing charm.

I shuddered. So much time wasted. Closing my eyes, one word floated through my mind: Damaged. *I am soiled. I am unlovable.* I shook my head. "No!" I shouted out loud. *It's not true,* I told myself. *Or, it doesn't have to be true. Does it?*

Then I thought about time, about a single life: a beginning, decades of possibilities and choices, and an end. People can be damaged by the choices they make. People sometimes die unfulfilled, unenlightened, unloved. It happens every day. Maybe I would be one of them. Maybe I was simply not special enough to overcome the mess I had made of my life.

Again, I tried to shake off these terrible thoughts. Time to count my blessings. I had a few good friends who really cared about me: Chloe, Mary, Sam and of course Teddy. There were some acquaintances that could become friends with a little effort. I had Jamie, thank the gods and goddesses, fate, kismet, or whatever force had brought him to me. I no longer had Grandma Lucy, but she had bequeathed a new kind of freedom to me, which I had yet to explore. There was much to be grateful for.

Grateful. Yes, I was grateful for the kind, generous, moral people who, somewhat inexplicably, loved me. How did I get so lucky, when the world seemed to be filled with people who were light-years from any of those things?

People were, for the most part, a total mystery to me. How does someone like Donald Weston, for example, come to the conclusion that Jamie is somehow tainted, immoral, unworthy?

Closing my eyes once more, I pictured the scene that always brought me peace: the view from my balcony at home. The trees and grass, and all the air traffic: birds and insects buzzing through, pausing here and there for food. It occurred to me that maybe people's mindsets are like those constant travelers. We start out with a set of beliefs, given to us by our parents and early experiences. Then off we go, traveling along in our wavy little lines, our ideas floating around us. We are sure of their veracity, confident in their correctness. Then one day we collide with someone else, mix our ideas with theirs.

Maybe now some of our ideas don't fit so well. So, we adopt a few from the other person, discard some of our own and continue on until our next collision, as does the person we just encountered.

Maybe in the end we all become a collection of beliefs, opinions, preferences, even tastes we've gathered from a lifetime of accidental encounters.

But maybe none of it is accidental at all. Are we meant to stumble upon these exact people at those precise moments? To evolve into the people we become?

When people are terrified of new concepts and discoveries, clinging desperately to their own version of truth, are they denying their destinies? Do they become something other than their true selves? Could it be that such a person becomes so convinced he is right about everything, so sure that everyone else is wrong, that he even believes he has the right to force others to his will? Is that how someone becomes abusive?

I wasn't sure why such profound existential questions had occurred to me so early in the morning, but now I wanted to share some of my musings with Jamie.

My stomach rumbled, and I needed coffee badly. I looked over at Jamie's bed, perfectly made and seemingly empty for hours. He'd probably gone jogging already. I started to feel slovenly and guilty—not a good combination—and then I heard the front door open and close.

"Sage, aren't you up yet? Come on! I've got breakfast!"

"Coming!"

I pulled some socks on and shuffled into the dining room. "Is there coffee?"

"Yes, I brought your coffee. Here."

He handed me my latté, then picked up his own cup, a teabag string hanging down the side. "Cheers," he said, touching his cup to mine. "I brought a huckleberry muffin, a huckleberry scone and a fruit salad, featuring huckleberries."

"Isn't it a little early for huckleberry season?"

"I think they were frozen. They're still good, though. Help yourself. Muffin or scone?"

"Muffin. Thanks. Did you go for a run?"

"No, I rented a kayak. I've been on the lake since just before dawn. It was so beautiful out there. I saw a group of deer at the edge of the water! It was ridiculously gorgeous!"

"Oh. I'm sorry I missed that."

"I decided you were right, Sage. I needed a break from work and I have to take advantage of being here. I honestly don't know why I was so resistant to coming back. This place is really recharging my batteries. Clarifying a few things. So, on my way to get the food, I called Sam."

I grinned. "How is he?"

"Fabulous, of course. I miss him, damn it. More than I wanted to. More than I thought I would."

"Oh, how sweet!"

"It'll be good to see him. We've made plans for Saturday night."

"That's the day we get home. Wow, you are in a hurry! I guess I was right about Sam all along."

Jamie rolled his eyes. "Yes, Sage. You were right about him, Sage. Anything else you want me to say, Sage? Or is that enough for now?"

"That's a good start."

"So have you thought about what realty company to sell the house through?"

"I've seen a few signs around town. I'm sure Rose knows someone."

Jamie sighed. "It's going to be hard to say good-bye to this place."

"I know. But I don't think either of us wants to live here, do we?"

"No. You're right. I guess we're just going to have to connect with a realtor and come back a few times to get it ready to sell. In the meantime, I'm a bit nervous about it just sitting empty."

"What if we asked Rose to keep an eye on it?"

Jamie smiled. "I'm sure she'd be happy to help out. Great idea!"

"Thanks. I suppose I have one every now and then."

He kissed my temple. "You're brilliant. You know, I've been thinking about the Mom mystery."

"What about it?"

"It dawned on me that we should talk to Mary. I'll bet she knows a lot. In fact, I'm wondering why we haven't thought of it before now."

"Well, I have thought about it. I've thought of asking her a thousand times, but something always stopped me. I always thought it was kind of odd that she never volunteered any information. At least once we'd grown up."

"Yeah, that does seem strange. I've also been thinking about Dad. Clearly he was upset by Mom's death. Maybe he truly loved her. Never got over her. Maybe he felt guilty for abusing her and driving her away. Maybe that guilt fed into his anger. It must have been hard to live with that much pain."

"You're feeling sorry for him? Again?"

"Sure. Of course. How would you like to live in his skin? No wonder he drank so much!"

I'm not exactly sure what happened next. I thought about my mother, remembered her being hit by my father. Then I saw Colin's face, snarling and angry, and it felt as if something hit me, physically hit me in the stomach. There was a sensation of being under water; I gasped for each breath, and then everything around me, everything in the world, faded to white.

When I became aware again, Jamie's face was there, looking concerned. He was speaking, but at first I couldn't hear his voice. His lips were easy to read, though. He was saying my name, over and over. Then, as though someone was slowly turning up the volume on a TV, I heard him say, "Come back to me, Sage. Are you all right? Look at me, doll."

I obeyed, looked directly into his eyes.

"Can you hear me, Sage?"

"Yes."

"Here." He put a paper bag over my mouth. "Breathe into this honey, just breathe, nice and slow."

Looking around, I found that I was sitting on the floor against a wall. Jamie was squatting beside me. "What happened?" I asked inside my paper bag.

"You tell me, sugar. Your breathing went crazy. It was like an asthma attack. You looked scared to death. Then you just went limp. Your eyes stayed open, but you weren't there. I caught you and eased you down to the floor. What's the last thing you remember?"

"You were feeling sorry for Dad. And I—I remembered him beating Mom. I remembered Colin beating me. It was like I could feel it, Jamie." Tears came then, fast and unstoppable. "I can't feel sorry for

Dad. He made her feel that way. Worthless. Like she deserved to be hit. I'll never be as good a person as you, I know, but I'll hate him till the day I die."

Jamie held me close and let me sob. "I understand, doll, I do. The truth is, I don't hate him and I don't love him. I wouldn't want to be him in a million years. I can feel bad for him objectively, you know, like I would for a stranger who had made so many awful mistakes. Honestly, I don't believe he's worthy of your rage."

"What do you mean?"

"This is what I tried to explain yesterday. Anger is a passionate emotion, Sage. It takes a lot of energy. Good God, girl. You just lost consciousness! He's not worth it."

"Aren't you worth my anger? Wasn't our mother?"

"It won't bring her back. And it might make you sick. She wouldn't want that. And neither do I, obviously." He stood up and fetched me a tissue from the bathroom.

"Thanks. Sorry I checked out on you."

"It's okay. But don't do it again, all right?"

"Guess this means I'm looking for a shrink right away, huh?"

"That was the agreement. But considering we're leaving tomorrow, I suppose it can wait until you get home. I'll be watching, though. Watching and nagging."

"I guess I should really try cutting down on caffeine again, too."

"Gee, you think so?"

"Okay, okay. I just have to take it very slowly."

"Good girl, Sagey."

We called on Rose one last time that afternoon. She was thrilled to hear our request. "Oh, it's no trouble at all. I'll keep a good eye on the house, even air it out now and then if you like. There are a few real good real estate agents in town. I'll talk to a few of them about the house."

"Well thank you, Rose. We'd really appreciate that. Just give us a call if you have any concerns, and we'll be in touch to let you know when we'll be back," Jamie said, offering his hand to her. She brushed it aside and hugged him tight.

"Thank you, Rose," I said, and she broke away from Jamie, turning to me.

"Don't even mention it, honey. I'm so sorry about my—well, my error in judgment, so to speak. I hope you've forgiven me. I had no business sticking my nose in yours."

"Ancient history, Rose. Please, don't give it another thought. I'm just glad you could forgive *me*. You didn't deserve that blast from me."

"Oh, you sweet thing, come here!"

I did, and Rose clung to me for several seconds. "You take care of yourself, honey."

"You too, Rose."

Jamie handed her one of the house keys she had given to us our first day there and we said good-bye, but somehow I knew Rose would have the last word. Sure enough, as we walked down the steps of her front porch she called through the screen door, "Don't you worry about your grandma's house, not even for a minute. I'll take care of it like it's my own, I swear I will! Come back soon, you two!"

We ordered pizza that night and opened a bottle of wine Jamie had stashed away somewhere. "I saved it for our last night," he said.

"Well done!"

We nibbled and sipped between packing and cleaning, carefully steering our conversation around any emotionally loaded topics, content to be occupied with mindless tasks.

At Jamie's urging, we finally took a breather and savored the last of the wine.

"Wasn't Rose sweet?" I said. "I can't believe how eager she is to help us."

"Yeah, she was great. Maybe you should scream at everyone you meet, Sage."

"Somehow I don't think it would affect everyone the same way. Besides, not everyone gives me a reason to scream at them so early in a relationship."

"True enough, I suppose. But you could develop some sort of Screaming Friendship Test. I can hear the commercial now: Wondering who your real friends are? Wonder no more. Quick and inexpensive, Sage's Screaming Friendship Test tells you instantly who will put up with your worst moods! But wait! There's more! If you sign up today, you'll also receive the Foul Language Tolerance Quiz."

Giggling, we clinked glasses. I was about to throw in a set of Ginsu knives when there was a knock at the door.

"It's probably Rose, wanting to give us a copy of her house-checking schedule," Jamie said.

"Maybe I'd better yell at her one more time, just to seal the deal," I said, opening the door with a Vanna White flourish.

"Hello, Sage."

"Donny. Well, I didn't expect to see you again."

"I know. Listen, I'm really sorry about…"

"Save it. Now I suppose you're going to tell me that it really doesn't matter to you that my brother is going to burn in hell. As long as I'm on the straight and narrow you're willing to overlook my tainted family? Well *you* can go straight to hell, which is of course where you will go if it exists and there is any justice in the universe at all."

"Sage, please."

Donny handed me an envelope. "I'm apologizing because I forgot to give this to you earlier. Lucy asked me to keep it for her and give it to you and your brother upon her death. I'm sorry I forgot about it— I'd put it in a separate place, not in her main file. I'm very sorry for the delay. Here."

I opened the screen door and took the envelope from him. "What is it?" I asked.

"I have no idea. She never told me. Again, I'm really sorry, Sage. Hope you have a good trip back to Seattle. I'll be in touch about finalizing the transfer of your trusts."

I watched him turn and walk down the steps, down the front walk, down the sidewalk to his car. He hesitated, just for a moment, then opened the driver's door. He didn't look back. Curious, I closed the door and turned back toward Jamie. The envelope in my hand was addressed simply: *Sage and Jamieson*, in Grandma Lucy's writing.

Her writing, same as it was in all the little notes, birthday and Christmas cards she'd sent so faithfully. I touched the ink. How long ago had she written our names? How long before her heart beat for the last time had she sat down, pen in hand, and scrawled some kind of message to us?

I tore open the envelope and pulled out three sheets of Grandma Lucy's stationary with the big L at the top of each page. Her small, neat handwriting filled each sheet. "Want me to read it to you?" I asked. Jamie nodded.

"*'My Dear Grandchildren,*

As I write this, I am sitting in my kitchen enjoying a glorious spring day. My daffodils are in bloom, and the tulips will soon follow. My doctor tells me I will not live to see my roses this year.

It's a strange feeling, knowing that death is so near. A time to take inventory, I suppose. To count your blessings and your regrets.

I wish the three of us had seen more of each other, but I'm not one to intrude. I could have moved to Seattle years ago, or made you feel guilty enough to come out here more often, but I just couldn't bring myself to do either. I know what life is like for young people these days. It's busy. You two have your careers, your friends, and you have each other. That's enough to keep up on. You didn't need any more obligations.

Truth is, you don't owe me anything at all. I have failed you in so many ways. I didn't prevent your mother's death, and it's possible I could have. I didn't take you away from your father. It's hard, knowing how big my mistakes have been. I've always told myself that I did the best I could, but now I don't know if that's strictly true.

One thing I am proud of is that once Mary Delaney told me how bad things were with your father, I told her to take you kids and keep you with her. She was about to do just that when you two appeared at her door on your own. When Mary told me you were there, I went to see your father. I told that man to let you go, that he had no reason to keep you any longer. I told him to finally do one decent thing and give you children a chance at a good life. Then I told him that if he had any more contact with you or Mary that I would get myself a gun and shoot him in the head. Fortunately, he was sober at the time and he could tell I meant it. He agreed to move away and leave you all alone.

I don't know when Craig started beating your mother. She used to make excuses for him. She said it was because of her drug addiction. But if Georgia hadn't had drug problems he would have found another reason. In fact, he did find other reasons when she'd been clean and sober for years. If she stayed out late with her friends or if she disagreed with him at the wrong time, he just went crazy. Once he started drinking, anything good in him was just lost forever, I suppose.

In the beginning, your mother truly seemed to love him. But they never should have been together. I'm grateful they had you kids, but their marriage was wrong for both of them.

I'm not sure exactly when your mother started taking drugs. Was it your father who introduced her to them? I don't know. I know they did some together. For a while, she thought drugs were the path to enlightenment. I remember her saying that. Somewhere along the way, they seemed to take over her life. But she was clean before she became pregnant with you, Sage, and she was clean until she left your father. That's what she told me and I know in my heart it's true.

When she left him, she told me that it was to find herself. She was such a talented artist, and I know she tried to follow her dreams. I know that it never occurred to her that Craig would abuse you children. She thought he would be a better father once she was gone.

The last time I heard from her she sounded happy. She had sold a few paintings and was living in some kind of "artistic community." She said she finally felt appreciated. She asked about you two and I had to tell her that Craig was treating you badly, that Mary had called me not knowing what to do. Your mother was upset by the news, she really was, but she felt powerless to help.

The next thing I heard was that she had died of an overdose. I will never know whether or not her death was intentional. Now I feel I should have tracked her down. I should have seen for myself what she was up to. I should have tried. Your mother—and the both of you— deserved that.

I asked you to come see me this summer, but now it doesn't look like that will happen. I'd so hoped for one more visit with you, my beautiful grandchildren.

Know that I love you with all my heart, that I'm sorry for all the ways I failed you, and that I'm just as proud as I can be of both of you, exactly as you are.

All my love, always,
Grandma'"

Grandma Lucy had described our father's abuse of our mother, but she could just as easily have been talking about Colin. "So Mary wasn't the only one who threatened to kill Dad!"

"What a great old dame," Jamie said softly.

"I wish I'd been there to see it happen," I said.

"He could have snapped her in two."

"But he didn't. He actually listened to her. Why then? Why did he care what she wanted? Why did her threats mean anything to him at all? This was a man who beat his wife, then his kids. He committed atrocities. He probably drove our mother to suicide! He was…"

"I know, Sage. He was a monster. But people do change."

"Do they? Do they really?"

"Sometimes it takes something big. I've known a lot of people whose imminent death really motivated them to change."

"But if someone is a bad person, can they become good? Kind, moral, decent to their core? *Are* there evil people, or is it just that their behavior is bad and so they can choose to change it?"

"I think there may be truly evil people. People who are born without a conscience and take pleasure from inflicting pain on others. Maybe it's a mental illness. Maybe it's a birth defect. I don't know. But if someone doesn't fall into that category and does terrible things for whatever reason, I do believe they can turn their lives around and become a good person."

"So you really believe that our father may have hit bottom, seen the light, made a decision to change and become a brand new person?"

"Not brand new. The person he was meant to become. The person he was always capable of being. Not particularly someone I want to hang with, but someone who is decent and kind at least. Someone who'll be good to his wife, contribute to his community…"

"Give a percentage of his earnings to charity, pet puppies and kiss babies."

"Maybe."

"Wow. You really are an eternal optimist, aren't you?"

"I'd rather be hopeful than cynical, that's all."

"That's what I've become, isn't it? I'm a snide little cynic, aren't I?"

"Oh, Sage. You're not cynical, try as you might. You never would have pushed Sam and me together if you were. You still believe in happy endings."

"I believe in a happy ending for *you*."

"You'll have one too, doll. I swear you will."

We were quiet as we headed for home. Finally, Jamie brought up the money from Grandma Lucy's estate.

"So I guess we need to figure out what to spend and what to invest, right?"

"Absolutely."

"You're going to buy yourself a new career, doll! A new life! Maybe you'll fall in love and have my nieces and nephews."

"Yeah? I'm going to buy myself a man?"

"No, you're going to buy yourself a new life. The man will come later."

"I love you, little brother."

"I love you, big sister, my savior, my champion. Love you heart and soul. You just need to figure out what you want to be when you grow up."

I groaned. "How?"

"Well, what are you good at? What fills you with joy, energizes you?"

"Nothing."

"Think, Sage."

"I don't know! I love cats! I'm good with animals, I suppose."

"There you go! You could be a vet or a zoologist or a horse trainer. You could go to Africa and study hyenas, or be a marine biologist and monitor whale migrations. The sky's the limit, doll!"

"I don't want to leave Teddy to go study wild animals."

"Then be a veterinarian and take care of sick kitties."

"I don't think I could handle that."

"Sage! There has to be some way for you to make a living and be happy, too." I watched him think, his brows furrowed, his fingers drumming on the steering wheel. "Wait! I think I might have it," he said, wide-eyed. "I know what you love doing. I know something you're so good at you make it look effortless. You are a genius at it, actually." He smiled with his whole face. "Sage, you are going into business for yourself. Oh, this is perfect! It's so obvious!"

I had no idea what he was talking about.

Knowing that my days as a social worker were numbered made it a little easier to get out of bed each morning. I hadn't even given my notice yet, there was too much to catch up on first, but even so I was a little more enthusiastic about everything. Even the idea of dealing with Elma Crow didn't bother me quite as much.

Besides, I had reason to hope that Elma would be happy with her latest assistant. Michelle was, after all, pretty close to perfect. Even some of the more difficult clients had been tamed by Michelle's soothing voice, her strong work ethic, her desire to please. No one, however, was quite as difficult as Elma Crow.

And so I was disappointed, but nowhere near shocked, when the phone brought Elma abruptly back into my life. "I want her gone," Elma's raspy voice said, once again interrupting my Cheerful Greeting.

And once again, hearing her voice hit me viscerally. It was a sickening feeling, a dread in the pit of my stomach. I said nothing.

"Are you there? I want her gone, I said. Little Miss Goody Two Shoes. I don't want her in my house. She thinks she's better than me. She thinks just because she's pretty and she can get a man to buy her a fancy ring…I don't want her coming back."

Still, I said nothing.

"DO YOU HEAR ME? CALL HER AND TELL HER NOT TO COME BACK!"

I took a deep breath, then one more. "Mrs. Crow. I assume you are talking about Michelle. Mona is her supervisor, not me. I suggest you call Mona if you are unhappy with Michelle."

"YOU CALL HER! I'VE HAD IT WITH ALL OF YOU!"

There was a click, then silence.

My face was hot. My hand, still holding the receiver, felt moist. I breathed deeply, trying to slow my heart.

"You okay?" I looked up and saw Rachel's face above my cubicle wall.

"Yeah. Honestly, I don't know what's wrong with me! She's just a mean old lady! Why do I let her get to me like this?"

"Want a coffee break?"

"No, thanks. Maybe later. I have to call Mona."

Mona answered on the first ring.

"Hi. It's Sage."

"Uh oh. I know that voice. She called?"

"Yes, and she's decided she hates Michelle and doesn't want her to come back."

"You must be joking. Michelle is going there today! Let me look at the schedule. Yes! She's due there in an hour! I can't believe that woman. Thanks, Sage. I'm going to try to track Michelle down before she walks into the lion's den. I'll call you later."

An hour later, the phone rang again. Expecting to hear Mona's voice, I picked it up.

"YOU STUPID, WORTHLESS BITCH! I TOLD YOU I DIDN'T WANT THIS GIRL BACK AND YOU SENT HER ANYWAY! I'll bet you're ENJOYING this, AREN'T YOU?"

"Mrs. Crow, I will not allow you to speak to me this way. I'm going to hang up now."

She snickered. I didn't hang up. Waiting for her to speak again was a little like turning my head to look at an accident on the highway. I didn't want to, but I couldn't quite keep from it.

Her voice got very low. "You low-life piece of shit. Your parents must be so ashamed of you."

I hung up.

Later, I would not remember starting to cry. I wasn't really aware of anything for a while. When I tuned back in, I realized I was on the floor in my cubicle, rocking and sobbing. Rachel was beside me, speaking softly to me, and several others had gathered to watch.

"Sage? What happened?" It was Althea.

I tried to speak, tried to explain. I couldn't come up with a single word.

"She's had a really rough day," Rachel said. "Sage, honey, come with me, okay? Can you stand up?"

Rachel pulled me up and practically carried me to the rest room. Looking in the mirror, I was shocked. My face was a mess: red and blotchy, wet with tears and snot, mascara running down my cheeks. "What the hell is wrong with me?"

Rachel wet a paper towel and started cleaning me up. "Sweetie, I know Mrs. Crow is not a pleasant person. But you seem to be terrified of her. Dealing with her just devastates you. Why do you think that is?"

"I don't know. She's the devil! No, really! She seems to know exactly how to hurt me, exactly what words to use. How does she know? And why does she hate me so much?"

"She's an angry and miserable woman who is bitter about the direction her life has taken. She wanted more, she expected more, and instead she just got less and less. She's old and sick and alone, living in a trailer. She spends her days trying to make other people as miserable as she is. That's all. I just have to wonder, what happened to her? How did she get to this awful place? She is to be pitied, Sage. You have nothing to fear from her."

"She called me worthless. She called me a piece of shit."

"So? Hang up when she raises her voice. Hang up when she swears at you. Teach her to treat you better."

And then I remembered the punch line. "She told me my parents must be ashamed of me." I choked them out, those bitter words.

"Oh, Sage. Your parents aren't ashamed of you. If your mom were here, she'd be so proud. She would see a beautiful, intelligent and courageous woman. Trust me on this, honey." She threw away the paper towel and hugged me.

"You must be a really great mom, Rachel."

She laughed. "I hope so. I work at it. I'm not your mom, though. But I'd love to be your friend."

"You already are." I looked back at the mirror. I was presentable. Barely. Rachel took me back to my desk, then brought me coffee, bless her. When my phone rang again, she ran back over to coach me through the call.

"This is Sage."

"Sage, it's Mona." I began to breathe again, and signaled to Rachel that it was okay; she could go back to her own work.

"Hey, Mona. I guess you weren't able to reach Michelle in time?"

"Oh, God. Elma called again, huh?"

"Yep. There was fire and brimstone and lots of other nastiness."

"Sorry. You okay?"

"I'm fine. How is Michelle?"

"Poor thing. She called me in tears! She said she just didn't understand what the problem was. She'd worked just as hard for Mrs. Crow as she did for everyone else. Harder even! She said Mrs. Crow had actually seemed to be coming around a bit, asking questions about Michelle's wedding plans: colors, flowers, what her gown looks like. Now this, just out of the blue. What did Elma say to you?"

I repeated everything Mrs. Crow had said about Michelle. "You know what, Mona? Elma sounds pea-green jealous! She was interested in wedding details, then suddenly got angry and pushed Michelle away. It makes sense! Elma's been alone a long time. Now she's saying things like 'just because she's pretty she can get a man to buy her a ring.' She is jealous of Michelle's engagement!"

"I think you're right. But it doesn't really matter. Now I have to send her someone else. Again. This is ridiculous!"

"I know. I think we should let her go a week or two without help. Maybe she'll be more willing to be nice to the next one. No, scratch that. Maybe she'll be tolerant next time. Civil, maybe?"

"I'd settle for silent. Let me know when you hear from her again."

"You do the same."

By the end of the day I was weary to my bones. Literally, my bones ached. I spoke briefly to Jamie, then gathered my belongings and headed for the door.

"Sage?"

It was Althea, standing in the doorway of her office. She must have been waiting for me.

"Please come in for a minute, I'd like to talk to you."

"Sure." She sat in the chair behind her desk, and I sat facing her.

"Sage, I'm concerned about you. What was that scene about today?"

"I was just dealing with a really difficult client."

"Elma Crow?"

"Yes. She was really angry, and…"

"She's always angry."

"I know, but she…"

"Sage, listen to me. Clients are always going to be angry and they're always going to try to get under your skin. If you allow them to, you will not be able to do this job. We all have sore spots, Sage. Scars. Elma Crow is not a significant person in your life. If she can tear open those old wounds, well…I suggest you find a better bandage. Or a different line of work. Either way, I don't want to see you fall apart like that again. It's disruptive, it's bad for morale and most of all it's unhealthy for you! Get healthy, Sage. That's my advice. It's also an order. I love you, sweetheart, but I'm not going to let you become a problem around here. Understand?"

"Yes. I'm sorry, Althea."

"I know you are, honey. So am I."

The phone was ringing when I got home, and I came very close to not answering it. "Leave me alone," I groaned at it. But something made me pick it up at the last minute.

"Hello?"

Silence.

"Hello?"

Then, a whisper: "Sage?"

"Yes? Hello?"

"Sage, oh God, Sage. Please come over."

"Chloe? What is it? Are you all right?"

"She's pregnant, Sage. Nicki is pregnant."

~28~

Risking life and limb and a hefty speeding ticket, I raced over to Chloe's apartment. She buzzed me in without a word.

Her face, both pale and blotchy, seemed years older. She looked at me with eyes full of despair, confusion, disbelief. "Oh, honey," was all I could manage. I opened my arms and she fell into them, clinging desperately.

"He called," she whispered. "He said he didn't want me to hear the news from anyone else. He said it wasn't planned but that he'd never been happier. That he would never have imagined how happy he could be. He said that this must seem so unfair to me, that he must seem like the ultimate hypocrite…"

"He is a hypocrite, Chloe. The worst kind."

She nodded. "He said that Nicki is simply the right woman for him and now they've created this miraculous child that is already transforming him. He said that he now understood my yearning to have a child, but that it was really for the best we never did. Surely I could see that, he said."

"What did *you* say?"

"I—I don't know, really. I couldn't breathe. I think I called him a fucking bastard. Twice."

"Good for you." We sank to her sofa and I kept my arm around her. She leaned against me and we rocked for a while.

"The issue was never that he didn't want a child, Sage. He didn't want one with me. He took all those years from me and now it's probably too late. I'll probably never have a baby, and he has one on the way. Paul! A father! Sage, do I deserve this? Was I just never meant to be a mother? To be happy?"

"You listen to me, Chloe. You do not deserve any of this. Haven't I always said you'd make a fabulous mom? And you will! You still have plenty of time! Some lucky guy is going to come along and fall madly in love with you! But you don't even have to wait for that. Maybe you'll just choose to have a child on your own. You can do whatever you want."

Chloe got very quiet then. She leaned back against the sofa and stared straight ahead. She sniffled a bit, and I reached for a box of tissues. She took a couple of them and held them to her face, breathing in deeply.

"You're right! I don't have to wait for a relationship to be a mother. I can have a child on my own. Mom will help and so will you. And dating won't be so tough as a single mom. I'll have a living, breathing test of character! This is brilliant! My child would have to love any man I could ever be serious about, and I would see immediately how my dates interacted with my baby. And Jamie would be a great father-figure…" Her voice trailed off.

When she turned to face me, I knew exactly what she was thinking. "Sage, do you think…"

I shrugged. "He might. Ask him." I grinned. "Maybe you'll have one of those beautiful babies after all!"

"And you really would be his or her Aunt Sage!"

"I would be anyway, honey. You are my sister by choice."

"I love you, Sage."

"I love you too, Chloe. Always and forever."

By the time I got home, I was so profoundly exhausted that I could barely move. I crawled into bed and slept soundly all night, visions of blue-eyed babies dancing in my head.

In the morning, Rachel greeted me at the door of the office with coffee, concern all over her face. "So, have you thought any more about that therapist I told you about?"

It was time to keep my promise. "Yeah, I think I'll give her a call."

Rachel seemed thrilled—and prepared. "Her name is Bridget McCorquodale. Here's her address and phone number. She's really wonderful, Sage. I'm so glad you've decided to give her a try!" she said.

"McCorquodale?"

"Yeah, isn't that a great name? Anyway, she's really kind and I just know she'll be a good match for you. But if not, don't feel obligated, okay? You've got to find someone you feel comfortable with."

"Okay. Thanks, Rachel."

But now that I had the number I didn't call right away. I dove straight into work and was frantically busy all day. Before I knew it, it was time for Jamie's daily phone call.

"How's life today?" he asked.

"Not too bad, actually. Busy."

"Good. Have you called a therapist yet?" This question had become part of our daily ritual.

"No, but I got a phone number today. I have the information right here in my hand. I'm going to call as soon as we hang up. How's that?"

"Good girl! I'm impressed. Call me after you've made the appointment. Oh, and before I forget, I've signed us up for an accounting class. It's an introductory class, aimed at small business owners, and it meets four times, all evenings. It starts at the end of the month."

"Sounds perfect! Hey—what are you doing this Sunday?"

"That's the other thing I need to tell you. I've arranged for another appraisal on Grandma's house since the other one was done several months ago, so I'm taking Saturday off and Sam and I are heading over there for the weekend. Want to come with us?"

"You and Sam are going away for the weekend?"

"Don't overreact, Sage. I just wanted to show him the house and the lake, and I have appointments with a couple of realtors. And Sam has never been there—it will be fun to show him around."

"You know, I'm looking forward to spending the weekend at home with Ted. You two go ahead."

"You're sure?"

"Absolutely. Have a great time. Give Sam a hug for me. Oh, and remember we need to plan a visit with Mary when you get back."

We said our good-byes, and as my fellow clock-watchers hurried out the door at 4:30, I picked up the slip of paper Rachel had given me, took a deep breath and called Bridget McCorquodale.

You've reached the office of Bridget McCorquodale. Please leave a message and I will return your call within twenty-four hours. If you are an existing client and this is an emergency, please press the

*pound sign after your message for delivery options and instructions on
how to page me. Thank you!*

Beep. "Uh, hello. Uh, Bridget this is Sage Whitaker. I got your
name from Rachel Simon. I'm wondering about setting up an
appointment? I mean, if you're taking new clients. Please call me when
you get a chance. Thanks."

I hung up the phone and exhaled deeply. Then I realized I had of
course forgotten to leave my number. "Shit! Shit, shit!" I called back,
apologized, and left my home number. "Oh! This is Sage Whitaker!" I
added as an afterthought. *God, I sound like a lunatic. She's going to
think I actually need to see her.*

Well, I knew better, didn't I?

There was already a message from Bridget McCorquodale on my
voice mail when I got home. I had neglected to leave my cell phone
number, but I hadn't expected to hear from her so soon.

"Hi Sage. This is Bridget McCorquodale, returning your call. I
have a couple of openings tomorrow: one at three and one at 4:30. My
next opening after that is on Tuesday afternoon. Let me know what
works best for you." She left a different number, one that she would be
at for the rest of the evening.

I was surprised by her voice. Her office recording sounded
different, smooth and professional. But in this message her voice
sounded kind of... well, chirpy. Singsongy, like a younger version of
Rose's. I wasn't sure I could sit still and listen to this leprechaun give
me advice, but I'd promised Jamie. So, I picked up the phone and dialed
the number she'd left.

"This is Bridget," the fairy-voice said.

Deep breath. "Hi, Bridget, this is Sage Whitaker."

"Hi, Sage! I'm so glad you called back. Do you know when
you'd like to come in?"

"I think I could manage the 4:30 appointment tomorrow, if that's
still available."

"Of course. Four-thirty it is. Is there anything you'd like to tell
me ahead of time? Anything in particular going on for you?"

"Uh, there have been a few things lately, but I'll just tell you
about it tomorrow if that's okay."

"Absolutely. The first visit is on a trial basis. We spend a half
hour together no matter what. If we decide we're not a good fit for

whatever reason, I won't charge you and you can be on your way. Otherwise, we'll continue for the full fifty minutes. Fair enough?"

"Sure. Uh, where is your office?"

"Oh! Yeah, that would help, wouldn't it? Well, you said you know Rachel, right? Do you know where she works?"

"I work with her."

"Really? Well, I'm right down the block from you. You know the little coffee shop on the corner?" (Silly question.) "I'm in that building, up one floor. You'll see my sign when you get off the elevator. Do you get off work at 4:30?"

"Yeah, but I can skip a break or something and leave a little early."

"Don't do that. I'll just expect you shortly after 4:30. See you tomorrow, Sage. Oh, I have to tell you, I just love your name."

"Thanks. I think yours is pretty cool, too."

She giggled, and I envisioned her wearing a sparkly gown, holding a scepter and talking to munchkins.

We said good-bye and I sat with Teddy, thinking. "All I have to do is see her this one time," I told him. "Just once, and we'll both see that I'm fine, and Jamie will be satisfied. One little appointment, no big deal."

I could handle it. For Jamie and for Mary. But I dreaded it.

~29~

The next day, for the first time I could remember, I did not look forward to 4:30. But it arrived, much faster than usual or so it seemed. Bridget had told me not to hurry, so of course I stopped at the coffee shop for a latté before going upstairs to her office. *I will start cutting down on coffee tomorrow,* I told myself.

When the elevator door opened, there was Bridget's name as promised, big and bold, with the office number, 201, and an arrow right beside it, pointing left. *Follow the yellow brick road,* I thought.

She opened the door just before I reached for the knob. "Hi, Sage," she sang, "it's so nice to meet you."

I'd been right the first time: she *was* a leprechaun. Bridget McCorquodale was a tiny person, maybe five feet even, and I doubted her weight was in the triple digits. Her hair was an even brighter red than Chloe's, but short and sticking straight up, pointing in every direction. Her face was covered with light brown freckles, and, as she stuck her hand out to shake mine, she grinned, beaming. There was nothing in my head besides the word *elf*, but her handshake was firm and warm. Her eyes, so dark they were almost black, stared right into mine. She didn't even blink.

"Please, come right in." She motioned me through a door into a hallway, then through another door, which she followed me through, then closed. The room looked like someone's living room: a big sofa with pillows stood against one wall, an overstuffed chair facing it. Framed prints nearly covered the walls, and a colorful mobile hung in one corner. I sat on the sofa and watched the mobile: green, yellow and orange dragonflies spinning slowly, around and around each other. "Would you like a glass of water?"

"No thanks, I'm fine with my coffee." A small desk sat in one corner, and now Bridget took a yellow legal pad from one of its drawers and sat in the chair, facing me.

"Okay. You said that a few things had happened recently. Tell me about what's been going on."

Bridget tucked her legs underneath her and looked like that huge chair was about to swallow her. She tapped her pencil absently on the pad of paper.

Breathe, I told myself. *Just one appointment.* "Well," I began, "my grandmother just died."

"I'm so sorry, Sage. Were you close to your grandmother?"

"I loved her very much. But, um, my father was the one who gave me the news. I hadn't seen him in years. But the real reason I'm here is because I've had a few panic attacks lately. So my brother is worried about me."

"Does your brother worry about you a lot?"

"I suppose. I worry about him, too. We look out for each other."

"It sounds as if maybe you've had to. Why don't you see your father?"

"Because he's an abusive bastard who made our lives a living hell until we moved out of his house. I'm sorry to be blunt, there's just a lot of background information to get through before you understand the panic attacks."

"Do you understand them?"

"I think so. My father showed up out of the blue, after almost thirty years, to tell me that my grandmother was dead— my *mother's* mother, by the way. Then I had to tell my brother, Jamie, the bad news because my father can't seem to bring himself to talk to his gay son. Then I had a client from hell scream at me that I'm part of an ungrateful generation that doesn't appreciate all the sacrifices our parents made for us, that basically that I should be kissing my parents' feet to thank them for my existence. She sounded a lot like my father during one of his many tirades. That was when I had my first panic attack. I thought I was dying. I had to run away."

"Oh, Sage, how awful. Let's back up a bit. What did your father say when he came to see you?"

"He said Grandma Lucy had died and that her neighbor had contacted him. He told me that Jamie and I were the only beneficiaries and that we were going to have to go to Coeur d'Alene, where she lived, to take care of everything. Then he told me that he's sober now and everything's perfect in his life. He apologized for the abuse. He invited me to his fucking wedding and he left me all his phone numbers."

Suddenly I was crying, crying in front of this teensy little stranger! How could this be happening? I had to stop this nonsense, now. "So then I had a few panic attacks. But it's been a couple of weeks now, and I'm fine."

Yeah. Fine.

"There's a box of tissues on the table to your right. Let me just make sure I'm hearing you correctly. Your father was abusive. Physically?"

I nodded, reaching for the tissues.

"And verbally, obviously. So he beat you up, in every possible way he could. You and your brother. Finally you escaped, had no contact with him for a long time. Then suddenly he showed up and wanted forgiveness. He acted as if he were a kind and gentle human being and expected your acceptance of him as such. Is that right?"

"Yes! Exactly!" I said, dabbing my eyes.

"Your last memory of him was very different from the man you saw recently. Correct?"

"As different as it possibly could be. I knew he'd kept in touch sporadically with my grandmother as we were growing up, but she made sure he stayed away from us. She never encouraged us to see him, to forgive him, even to talk to him. I do remember her saying once that he was sober the last few times he'd called. And that he didn't seem as angry."

"Why did he call her?"

"I don't know."

"What did they talk about?"

"I don't know."

"Do you think it's possible that he called to ask about you and your brother?"

"No. I... no."

"To find out where you were?"

"No, he knew where we were."

"He knew, but he didn't try to get you back?"

"No, I told you. Grandma Lucy made him stay away from us."

"How?"

"She threatened to kill him."

"Wow. What a fierce woman she must have been."

"She was one of the kindest, sweetest, most selfless people I've ever known."

Bridget smiled. "You were fortunate to have her in your life. Is that who you lived with when you left your father?"

"No, we moved in with my best friend's mother, here in Seattle. Grandma Lucy didn't want to separate me from my friend Chloe, or take us to a different school."

"Your best friend's mother. A single mom?"

"Yes."

"And were you happy with Chloe and her mom?"

"We loved it there. Yes, we were happy."

"So Chloe's mom became a mom to you. Where was your real mother?"

"She'd moved out already. She was dead by the time we moved in with Mary."

"I'm so sorry. She moved out and left you alone with your father. When she died you must have felt you'd lost her all over again. How old were you when you went to live with Mary?"

"I was eleven, Jamie was eight."

"I'm betting you were a pretty grown-up eleven."

"Yeah, I guess. I didn't get to be a kid very long. My father hated both of us, but he hated Jamie more. I had to protect him. I believe my father would have killed Jamie if we'd stayed with him much longer."

"You put yourself in harm's way? So you would be the one he'd hurt instead of Jamie?"

"Of course. Jamie was smaller. I had to protect him."

Bridget shifted in her chair. "Why did your father hate him so much? He was only eight years old when you left. He was just a little boy."

"He knew Jamie was different. We all did."

"If someone had asked you then, when you were a child, why your father hated Jamie, what would you have said?" Bridget asked.

I thought about all the names our father had called Jamie: Mama's boy, pussy, sissy, girl. Even then, I wondered how being a girl could ever be okay if it was an insult for a boy to be called one. I'd been called a tomboy occasionally, and I knew that meant I was tough, that I could climb trees. Being adventurous and strong was like being a boy, whereas my brother was seen as weak and inferior for being feminine. I understood clearly which gender was held in higher regard.

"When he was five years old my brother wanted to style hair and wear pretty clothes. He had crushes on men. He has never really been in the closet. He never thought about being something other than what he really was. It would have been too hard for him to hide it. I don't think my father ever doubted Jamie's orientation."

"I'm sure he feared it. Maybe he thought he could toughen Jamie up by picking on him. Change him."

"Maybe."

"What was school like for Jamie?"

"Well, he always had a lot of female friends. In the lower grades he had some male friends too, but by high school Jamie had started using the word gay, and they all distanced themselves from him. A few of them started bullying Jamie, pushing him around in the hallways. Once he got beaten up pretty bad. One of the football players said Jamie had been watching him in gym class or something, so he got a few of his buddies together and cornered Jamie after school. Mary went to the principal, but she got a 'boys will be boys' lecture and that was the end of it."

"How badly was he hurt?" Bridget asked, shaking her head.

I closed my eyes, remembering. "Two black eyes, a couple of cracked ribs, split lip, mild concussion."

"Oh, Sage. You must have been terrified, seeing him like that."

"Yeah, it was awful. I couldn't exactly take on a whole football team. Dad was a piece of cake by comparison."

"So you felt helpless?"

"Furious. I thought the worst was behind us when we left our father. Suddenly the world was unsafe again and Mary couldn't do anything about it. I was so angry! I knew who those boys were. Most of them were in my grade."

"You were in the same school? So you were a senior when this happened?"

I nodded.

"What did you do? Did you confront the boys?"

Cold fear shot through my veins. "I can't... I can't." And I couldn't: couldn't speak beyond those words, couldn't move, couldn't think.

"Sage? Did something happen? Did those boys hurt you, too?"

And that old slideshow began to play once more. The one I'd pushed out of my mind after Colin's last assault. Loud, taunting voices, a green field. Graffiti, orange and blue on a crumbling concrete wall. *No, I can't say it, think it, no, no, no, please don't make me think about this*... I was curled into the corner of the sofa with a cushion on my lap and vaguely aware that I was rocking. Rocking and crying. "No, no, no, please no."

"Sage?"

"I can't," I managed to whisper.

"What are you remembering, Sage? What did those boys do?"

"I said no to them. Kept saying it. No, no, please, no."

"What was the first thing you said to them?"

I took a deep breath, grateful for something to focus on. And the memory came. "I yelled at them to stop hurting my brother. I said, 'Is that how you prove how tough you are? By ganging up on one small guy? Takes a real man to need a crowd to beat someone up, doesn't it? You're just a bunch of cowards.' Then one of them said, 'Oh, look! It's the faggot's big sister coming to defend him. Figures a faggot would ask his *sister* to help him.'

"They followed me, dancing around me, yelling in my ear. Then they started pushing me—first in one direction, then another until they were in complete control of where I was going. They took me into an overgrown field, dragging me at the end, covering my mouth and eyes with their big smelly hands. I tried to scream, tried to bite them, gouge them with my fingernails. When I could see again we were in some kind of shelter, with a high wall on one side, a slab of cement on the ground."

"What happened then?" Bridget asked softly.

"Oh, God." I swallowed. Took a deep breath and wiped my face with my hands. "They raped me, one by one. I could see peeling paint and graffiti, the sweat on their foreheads, the sneers on their faces. Finally, something scared them and they started running away, but one of them, the first one, kicked me in the side before he left."

"What did you do?"

"I curled up and lay there for a long time. No cell phones back then. I had to get myself together enough to walk home. Mary called the police. I went to the hospital, went through a rape exam. I answered all the questions. I gave the police all the boys' names. Everyone was very kind and gentle.

"And then the police officer who'd taken my statement came back to the exam room. He was angry. He said, 'Are you sure you want to stick to your story?' I said, 'Yes, it's the truth.' Then he told me that the boys in question had all been at practice during the alleged attack. The coach corroborated that they were at practice from thirty minutes prior to my attack until one hour afterward. An airtight alibi. Then the cop accused me of setting them up, of having sex with my boyfriend or something and blaming those boys because they'd had an altercation with my brother. 'I don't have a boyfriend,' I said. He smiled and said, 'Oh, then you *really* needed a good excuse, didn't you?' I knew it was all over then. They'd won.

"Mary took me home and helped me take a bath. She dried me, dressed me, covered me with a blanket and held me on her lap like a baby. 'None of this was your fault, honey,' she said."

"What did you say?" Bridget asked.

"That it didn't matter. That it might as well have been my fault. Now the police thought I was a liar and a slut. Those boys would never pay for what they'd done to me or to Jamie, and worse, they would know they'd gotten away with it. They would know they could do it again. And they probably would. No one could protect their victims. I couldn't protect Jamie or myself. I said that basically there was nothing good in the world, nothing to care about, nothing to hope for, no reason to live."

"How did Mary respond?"

"She held me even tighter. She said, 'Sagey, I know life feels bleak right now, but it won't forever. I promise you that. I am so sorry that you've been hurt this badly and I know that you feel this pain will eat you alive but it won't. You will not only survive, honey, you will thrive. You are much stronger than you know. These are low life, trailer trash, pond scum, Sage. High school is the apex of their lives; for them it's all downhill from here. You on the other hand are bound for great heights. Trust me.' But I didn't believe her. Not for a minute."

There I sat, on Bridget's sofa, tears all over my face. I blew my nose. I had just recounted one of the most painful events of my life, something I hadn't talked about—thought about—since high school. Why? How did this happen? I had pushed those memories down so far, and yet they had come to me in hideously sharp focus.

"How are you doing, Sage? Would you like a blanket?"

I couldn't imagine why she would ask me that, but then I realized I was shivering. "Uh, no, that's okay." I picked up my coffee, which I'd traded for the tissues; it was still warm and it felt good in my hands.

"How do you feel about what Mary said to you now?"

I shrugged. "I think she did her best to make me feel better."

"How do you think the rapes have impacted your life?"

Colin's name flashed like neon, almost blinding me. "I haven't exactly had a lot of luck with men. I've been drawn to abusers. A couple just called me names and told me I was stupid. One slapped me once. The last one was the real deal. He broke bones; he even raped me."

"Oh, Sage. Did you report his abuse?"

"No."

"The rape?"

"No."

I was astonished to see there were tears in Bridget's eyes as she nodded. "You'd learned that lesson well, hadn't you? That no one could protect you. That no one would even believe you?"

"I knew what I was up against. He's a pretty prominent attorney."

"I'm so sorry. And now? Are you in a relationship?"

"No. I dated someone very briefly while I was in Coeur d'Alene, someone I knew as a teenager, actually, but it didn't last long."

"Why not?"

"Homophobe. You know, Jamie's going to hell and so am I because I believe being gay is all right."

She wrinkled her nose. "Oh. One of those. Hmm. Tell me about the healthiest relationship you've ever had."

I thought hard. "I can't think of one. I mean, I've dated quite a bit, you know, over the years, and there have been a few guys I liked that treated me well, but they only seemed to last a few dates and suddenly they just didn't call anymore. Or there was no spark, no fire between us, so it would just fizzle."

"So you've never had an adult, long term relationship with someone who didn't abuse you. Is that right?"

I hadn't thought of it quite like that before. "I guess that's right. Wow."

"The last man who abused you: what was his name?"

"Colin." I shuddered.

"Do you know where he is now?"

"Not for sure. I haven't heard from him for a few months."

"What happened a few months ago?"

"Nothing. He'd been calling for a while, begging me to take him back, promising the moon. Then he called a few more times to tell me how worthless I was and how no one else would ever want me. One day he left flowers at my door, but that was the last I heard from him."

"Huh. It's odd that he would give up so easily. Abusers don't like to let their targets slip away like that. What are you doing to protect yourself, Sage?"

"I keep a baseball bat by the door. Oh, and the maintenance guy let me know once that he knew the real story and that Colin would have to get through him before he'd ever hurt me again. And Marty is the kind of guy that would scare Colin. You know, big, strong, protective..."

"A non-abuser."

"Yeah, that too."

"Sounds like a nice man."

I pictured Marty's face the day he made me blush. My face felt hot again. "Yes. He seems very nice."

Bridget made a sound, just a little sound in the back of her throat. I wondered what she was thinking, but I said nothing.

She cleared her throat. "We have a few minutes left. Is there anything else you want to discuss today?"

Considering I had already discussed a whole lot I hadn't wanted to at all, I was a little afraid of opening my mouth again. "No, not really," I managed.

"Thank you for trusting me with what happened to you. I can tell you that it won't always hurt that bad to talk about it. It gets easier. Not easy, just easier. It's hard to understand why anyone would want to hurt us so badly and it's easy to blame ourselves. But it wasn't your fault. And most people aren't like that, Sage. I know your experiences make it hard for you to believe that."

"Not really. I get it, that I somehow attract abusers. They zero in on something and pursue me."

"Yes. It's your vulnerability. They sense that they could groom you into the victim they need. You were hurt so early in life, Sage, that you already believed you were unworthy of love. And so when something happened to support that belief—Colin's abuse—you subconsciously accepted it. It felt like the truth, so you allowed it to continue." Bridget leaned forward in her chair. "But look at you. You've survived! You ended your relationship with Colin. You refuse to accept your father's apology because it feels shallow to you. And, you're here! You're searching for a better way to live your life. You're trying to fight the old messages, the training your father put you through. I can see that you are very strong. It won't be easy, but I know you can create a new life for yourself. I think I can help you with that. What do you think?"

Suddenly, not seeing Bridget McCorquodale again was no longer an option. Leprechaun or not, she was my brand new lifeline.

~30~

Driving home from my first session with Bridget, I felt utterly exhausted and a little shell-shocked. We'd hardly talked about the panic attacks! Why had I revealed so much to her, so much that I'd kept hidden even from myself?

I'd always thought therapy was for sissies. I'd thought it was just whining about your problems. I could see no earthly reason why it would be helpful to dredge up all the bad stuff from the past. *It happened, I survived, I'm fine,* I'd told myself. *What possible purpose would it serve to relive it, to think about it ever again?*

Home at last, I dragged myself up the stairs to my apartment, mumbled a greeting to Teddy, tossed my purse on a chair and collapsed on the sofa. The night Chloe called about Nicki's pregnancy, I couldn't have imagined being more exhausted. But now I was so weary I could barely think! If I closed my eyes, I knew I would be asleep within minutes.

"How do you feel?" Bridget had asked before I left her office.

"Like I just ran a marathon."

"That's understandable. You just let go of a huge boulder you've been carrying around for a long time."

"Oh. Yeah. I guess so."

"And emotionally?"

This I had to think about. "Calm, actually. Almost peaceful."

"That's great, Sage. How long has it been since you felt that way?"

"I don't know. A long time."

She beamed. "Fabulous! Okay. Your shrink has some instructions for you. Go straight home. Eat a good, warm meal tonight. Maybe take a bubble bath. Do what makes you feel pampered and special. Treat yourself as you would your best friend who's going through a really rough time. Call me if you have any questions, concerns, any symptoms of anxiety or depression coming on. Anytime, day or night. I'll see you next week. This day and time works for you?"

And just like that, I had a standing, weekly appointment with a therapist.

Sleep would indeed have come very easily to me, curled up so cozy on the sofa. But... I had to feed Teddy and myself. I had to pamper myself, doctor's orders. Prying myself off the sofa would be the first step.

I was uncurling my legs toward that end when the phone rang. One more reason to get off my behind.

"Hello?"

"How did it go?"

"Hi, Jamie. That is not a question I can answer quickly. Or at all, really. She drained the life out of me."

"Must have been a good session!"

"Good? I don't know."

"No, no, I don't mean good, necessarily. I mean productive. Are you okay?"

"Yeah, I am. Really, quite fine. Totally spent, but okay."

"Good for you, big sister. Please tell me you're seeing her again."

"Yes, Jamieson. I'm seeing her again. Same time next week."

"Sage, I'm so proud of you. I thought you'd just blow it off."

"Yeah? So did I."

"What are you doing for dinner?"

"I was just trying to figure that out. I'm too tired to cook, but Bridget told me to eat well. So I guess that means take-out."

"Come out with Sam and me. It's the only chance I'll have to see you before we leave tomorrow. And Sam misses you."

"Oh, Jamie, I just want to put on my pj's and be a vegetable."

"You'll get a second wind. Splash some cold water on your face. I'll come pick you up so you don't have to drive. Come on. You'll have fun."

"If you insist."

"I do. See you in an hour."

Teddy had already dined and gone back to sleep by the time Jamie arrived. I'd washed my face and changed clothes, and I had to admit that a second wind had indeed blown a little energy through my veins. Almost like a good cup of coffee.

"Where's Sam? Are we picking him up?"

"Yeah. My turn to drive. You look good, Sagey. Really good. Must have been a great session."

I shrugged. "I don't pretend to understand the process, but I feel better. I talked about some painful stuff today and I really feel... I don't know, lighter maybe."

Jamie hugged me tight. "I'm so happy for you, doll. You so deserve to feel better. Therapy has done wonders for me."

I couldn't believe what I was hearing! "You've seen a therapist? How did I not know this?"

He shrugged. "Now you know. I was in therapy for about two years, and a little bit off and on since then. It's really helped me work through some of the childhood stuff and just some self-sabotage tendencies I've had in relationships. There was a time when I would have clung desperately to Jake and begged him not to leave me. Instead, I realized that I deserve to be treated better, that we weren't good together, and that it wasn't worth wasting any more time with the wrong person."

"You've never seemed clingy or needy to me."

"Well, doll, I have managed to keep a secret or two from you. Anyway, I'm so glad you've found someone to talk to. I think it will be so great for you."

"Well, so far so good."

"So far so fabulous, I'd say. Ready to go?"

It was great to see Sam. He grinned when he first saw me and gave me a huge hug. "Hey, sweetie. How you doin'?"

We went to a fun little restaurant, a recommendation of Sam's that Jamie and I had never tried before. The food was fabulous and the company even better. It was my first exposure to Jamie and Sam since they had officially become a couple, and it was very clear that they were extremely happy.

"Have you met Savannah yet?" I asked Jamie.

"Yeah. We had dinner together last night."

"How did it go?"

"It went okay, I think. I mean the poor kid is just getting used to the idea that her dad is gay. At that age it's got to be tough," Jamie said.

I looked at Sam. "So how did it really go?"

He shook his head. "She was a little rude at first."

"Just a little," Jamie said. "She said I was prettier than her mom."

"That's not so bad," I said.

"It was the sneer that went along with it, I think, that we interpreted as rude. Wouldn't you say, Sam?"

"Yep. That pretty much sums it up. But after a while she did lower the defenses a bit. Ultimately she couldn't resist this guy's charms. When we dropped her off she even gave Jamie a hug."

"That's huge! She must really like you, Jamieson. I'm so glad. What about Molly? Have you met her yet?"

Sam and Jamie looked at each other, and it was Sam who answered. "No, and that's my fault."

"It's okay. We'll get there," Jamie said.

"It's just that I don't want to introduce Jamie as 'my friend.' I want my mother to know how I really feel about him. So first I have to come out to her. And I haven't found the right time to do that yet."

"Right time? Yeah. Don't think that's going to happen, Sam," I said. "I understand how hard it's going to be. But every day you wait is another day you're keeping your mom and Jamie from getting to know each other."

"I know, I know. I'm just having a hard time deciding how to tell her. Should I tell her alone, or with Savannah there? Should I introduce her to Jamie and tell her at the same time? Or should I write her a letter so she can't interrupt me? Aaah! It's driving me crazy."

"Your mom is a very sharp woman. Maybe she already knows," I said.

"I doubt it."

"Think about it. Maybe *that's* why she's trying so hard to fix you up with women. Maybe she's trying to force you to tell her."

"It's an interesting theory, Sam," Jamie said.

"What is the worst possible outcome of telling her?" I asked.

"She'll disown me. She'll hate me. She'll tell my daughter I'm a sick pervert."

"Do you think she feels that way?"

"I'm pretty sure. I remember once she told me about a friend of hers who had just found out her daughter was a lesbian. She said, 'Poor Dorothy. Everyone knows! And you know they'll blame her. It's always the mother's fault.' And I told her that now there's some pretty strong evidence that homosexuality is genetic, that people are born gay. She said, 'That's just another way to blame the parents. Whatever causes it, it's certainly not *normal.*' "

I giggled. "You sounded just like her! Well, like I said, she's a very bright woman and she just needs a little education," I said. "She loves you, Sam. It's pretty hard to believe gay people are sick perverts when your beloved and perfect son is one of them. At least when you're as wonderful a parent as Molly."

"You're absolutely right. I'm going to tell her. I will call her when we get back on Sunday night and tell her I need to talk to her. Thanks, Sage. Hey. Sage, look…" Sam was sitting across the table from me, and now he motioned with his head for me to look behind me. Leaning forward, he whispered, "It's that guy we saw in Starbucks, isn't it? Wait, don't look yet. Okay now!"

I turned, just in time to see Marty catch me looking. "Sage!" he said. He pushed his chair back and almost ran to our table. "Sage!" he repeated. "It's so good to see you!"

"Hi Marty. You remember Sam."

He nodded, glancing at Sam. "Nice to see you again," he mumbled.

"And this is my brother, Jamie. I'm sure I've told you about him."

He shook Jamie's hand. "Oh! Yeah, you've mentioned him once or twice. Hey, Jamie. It's good to meet you, finally." Then he focused on me again. "So how are you, Sage?"

"I'm doing well, Marty, thanks." There it was again: that hot face thing. He knelt down beside me. "How are you?" I asked.

"I'm good, really good. I'm almost finished with school."

"That's exciting! Good for you! I know you were trying to decide what kind of business to open."

"Yeah, I still don't know. Maybe a handyman service of some kind. I'd rather not do physical labor anymore, but that's what I'm good at. I don't know. I'll figure something out." He cleared his throat. "Uh, Sage? There's something I'd like to, uh, ask you."

From the corner of my eye, I could see Jamie and Sam nudging each other.

"Oh! Uh, really?" I asked stupidly.

"Yeah. Uh. Oh, God, this is hard."

"It is?"

"It's just that I swore that I'd do this the next time I saw you. I like you, Sage. A lot. And I'd be thrilled if you'd go out to dinner with me sometime. What do you think?"

I grinned. "I think I'd like that. But why didn't you just knock on my door and ask me?"

"I tried to, about a thousand times. I wanted to ask you when I saw you at the coffee shop, but you were with your friend here, and I thought, well you know. So I made myself a promise that the next time I saw you I'd just take a chance and ask." He glanced at Sam and Jamie again. "I hope I haven't been rude."

"Not at all. Very nice to see you again, Marty," Sam said.

And Marty relaxed, smiling back at me at last. "When do you want to go out?" he asked.

"I'm free next Friday."

"Great! I'll pick you up at seven?"

"Perfect. You know where I live."

"Sure do. See you then, Sage."

"Marty? Why don't you join us now?" Jamie asked.

"Oh! Thanks, Jamie. But, no, I can't. I have a class to get to. So I'll see you Friday, Sage. Nice to meet you, Jamie. Sam, good to see you again."

All three of us watched Marty walk out of the restaurant.

"Close your mouth, Jamie," I said.

"He's cute, Sagey!"

"So I've come to realize."

"He seems familiar. Where have I seen him before?"

"He's the maintenance guy at my building, but not for long. He's getting his MBA and he wants to start his own business. I guess he's been working on it for a long time."

"Cute *and* ambitious. I've got a good feeling about him, Sage. I don't think he's a hitter," Jamie said.

"No, I don't think so either."

"Look at her face," Sam said.

"I know. She's blushing. You're blushing."

"I know! Isn't it weird?" I said.

"You've got a shrink and a date with what appears to be a nice, normal, hot guy. Things are looking up for my sis," Jamie said, raising his wine glass.

~31~

The phone on my desk was ringing as I entered my cubicle Monday morning. Early morning phone calls almost never boded well, and I was tempted to let it go to my voice mail.

Remember, this is temporary, I told myself, and picked up the phone.

"Community Support Services, this is Sage," I announced sweetly. No one interrupted mid-stream: a good sign.

"Sage, darling, so nice to hear your voice. It's Molly. I'm afraid I'm a little confused about this program you've enrolled me in. Would it be possible for you to come over and answer a few questions?"

I thought about this. I could ask a few clarifying questions. If her confusion was actually about the services being provided by the home care agency, this was really a job for Mona, the service supervisor. If, on the other hand, the questions were about the number of hours allotted, the specific services she qualified for, and of course the amount of money she had to contribute for those services, then I was the right person to ask. I could have answered all the questions on the phone, too, but it was easier to communicate in person. And even if she needed to see Mona, too, I could help her arrange that.

"I can be there in an hour. Does that work for you?"

"Of course. See you then, doll."

Doll. One of Jamie's nicknames for me. Once again I thought about Jamie and Molly, and how much they would love each other once Molly got past the whole gay son issue.

I made appointments with two other clients who lived in the same general area as Molly; might as well spend the entire morning "in the field," as we all called it.

Molly opened her door when I parked outside her house and watched me walk up. When she pulled me in for a hug, I could smell her cologne. It was expensive, I was sure of it: subtle, slightly sweet, hints of vanilla. Her dark hair was perfect, as always, collar-length and curled in layers to frame her face. Today, she wore hot-pink lipstick. When she grinned at me, I could see a little of it on her two front teeth.

"So wonderful to see you, Sage!" she exclaimed, motioning me into her kitchen. "I have coffee brewing."

"Music to my ears, Molly."

"Sit, sit. Cream and sugar?"

"Just a little cream, thanks. So, what questions can I answer for you?"

Molly stood by the coffee pot, her back to me, watching the pot fill. "Oh… this and that. You know, like why do I need so much help again?"

"Do you think you have too many hours?" I usually heard the opposite complaint, of course.

"I don't mean to complain; it's just that I find myself cleaning before she gets here, and then there's not enough for her to do."

"Well, stop pre-cleaning, and let her do it all," I said.

"Yes, I suppose I should. It's rather difficult having someone in my house, Sage."

"Do you like the person Mona is sending to you?"

"Yes, I do. She's a sweet little thing. She does a good job, too, really she does."

"When you leave her something to do?"

"Yes. And then she's a very nice companion when we go shopping or to an appointment. I enjoy that quite a lot."

"Well, good. Molly, I think that when you get to know her even better, you'll be more comfortable with the housework part of it. I think you should give it a little more time. What do you say?"

She poured the coffee into two mugs, and I went to help her carry it to the table.

"Oh, thank you, dear. The cream is in the little pitcher there."

We sat at the table together. "Would you like a cookie?"

"No, thanks. Just the coffee. Is there anything else you're wondering about?"

"Maybe just one thing. I don't know if you can help me or not."

"Well, I will if I can."

"Last night, I got a phone call from my son. He told me that he had to talk to me about something very important, and that there was someone he wanted to introduce me to. Someone named Jamie. Well, I had very mixed feelings. It seems my Sammy has finally met a woman he likes. But I had so hoped he would fall in love with you, Sage. I know you went out together at least twice."

"We're just friends, Molly. Sam and I are very good friends."

"Friends. Why is it so complicated? Friendship is a good start. Why would it be impossible for more to develop?"

I squirmed, stirring my coffee. "You're just going to have to trust me, Molly. It's not possible. I adore Sam, but we will never be more than friends."

"Okay. Since you're such good friends, he must have told you about this Jamie person. What's she like? Have you met her?"

"Molly, I really think this is something you need to discuss with Sam."

"You do know her, don't you? What's wrong? Don't you like her? I trust you, Sage, you know that. Please, you simply must tell me what you know! Is she a floozy? A gold digger? What?"

"Molly! You really need to wait and talk to Sam first. The only thing I'll say is that when it comes to Jamie you don't have anything to worry about. Jamie is a wonderful, kind, moral person who volunteers for hospice services and gives to charity every month. Jamie is…"

"…a man, isn't he?" Molly said in a voice so low I thought I might not have heard her correctly. "That's why you keep saying Jamie and person, instead of she or her." Molly looked at my face for confirmation, then down at the table. "My God. Sam is a...a homosexual, isn't he?"

Tears appeared, heavy in her eyes. I thought my heart would break for her. "Yes. But this is not a tragedy, Molly. Honest. What would be a tragedy is if Sam felt he had to continue to hide this from you. He wants you to share in his happiness. He finally feels authentically himself, and he wants you to be part of that new life."

"I read magazines. I've heard all about that stuff. To be honest, I've wondered about him. When he and Gwen broke up it was so definite, so final, and they'd seemed happy until just before they announced the divorce. They seemed to genuinely like each other. I asked myself, what could have been so horrible that it would end a marriage just like that, no question, no looking back? Sam seemed so regretful, and Gwen? Well, she was so hurt, so utterly betrayed. And Sage, it occurred to me then that Sam might be... but I told myself, no, maybe he just had an affair. A normal one, I mean. I actually hoped he had, rather than..."

"Oh, Molly. You know, chances are you've known a lot of gay people. They just didn't talk about it. Just think about all the famous ones: Truman Capote, John Gielgud, Ian McKellan, Elton John."

"John Gielgud?"

"Yes. And Lily Tomlin, Rosie O'Donnell, Ellen DeGeneres."

"Well, everyone knows about Ellen. She's funny, though."

"Liberace. Nathan Lane."

"Entertainers tend to be eccentric anyway."

"This is not an eccentricity. Molly, I truly believe people are born gay or straight or somewhere in between. It's not something they can choose or talk themselves into or out of. It's just part of who they are. You are attracted to men, you loved Sam's father; it would never have occurred to you to be any other way. Now Sam, he could pretend, and he has, but he will never truly love and feel that connected to a woman. He can only feel that way about a man."

"And this man, Jamie, he's okay? He's a good man?" Molly was upset and crying, but, good mother that she was, she was still hoping for a happy ending for her son.

"Yes. He's the best, Molly. And guess what? He's my brother."

She gasped. Literally gasped. I spotted a box of tissues on top of her fridge and grabbed it for her. "Jamie is wonderful. And he can't wait to meet you."

"Really? Honestly?"

"Absolutely."

"I'm sorry for all this blubbering, doll. I'll be all right. I just want the best for Sam, you know? And I know there are people who would hurt him for this. Kill him even. And I was always taught that homosexuality is wrong. Immoral. I simply accepted what I was told. But no one can tell me that Sam is a bad person. You say he's always been like this?"

"Yes. He tried to fight it. Tried so hard he got married and had a daughter. But in the end he had to be the person he was meant to be. It was very brave of Sam to get a divorce and be true to himself. He loves you very much, Molly, and he wants to be honest with you. It's going to be hard for him because he's afraid of hurting you or even losing you."

"Lose me! Ha! Fat chance. No, he's my son. I love him no matter what. If it means I'll have a son and a son-in-law, well…I guess that's what it means."

"I knew you'd understand, Molly." I threw my arms around her. "You know, if they do stay together, we'll be family! Won't that be great?"

"It would be wonderful." Molly dabbed at her eyes. "Listen, honey: don't tell Sam I know anything. I want to see how he's decided to tell me. But thank you for being honest with me."

"Anytime. And of course I won't tell Sam."

"If your brother is anything like you, I suppose I can understand what Sam sees in him. Hey. Don't get me wrong. It's going to take a while for me to get used to this idea. But I'm not one of those parents who could disown my child just because I don't understand something about him. No, sir. It's my job to figure it out. And I will, eventually."

"I know you will, Molly. You'll be fine."

All the way to my next appointment, I thought about Molly. I felt slightly guilty that I'd confirmed her suspicions about The Big Secret. But she'd cornered me, and, as Jamie often pointed out, I was a terrible liar. I decided it had happened for a reason.

Now I was excited. Molly knew! No more hiding, no more obstacles to Sam and Jamie being together. It felt as if a missing piece of cosmic machinery had been found and slipped back into place. Now all things would hum along as they should.

I tried to act surprised that night when Jamie called to tell me that Molly had taken the news well. According to Sam, he told me, she hadn't cried or even seemed very upset at all! And she'd insisted on meeting Jamie right away, so he was on his way over there.

"Congratulations, little brother. You're going to love her," I said.

I had a quiet evening with Teddy. Except for a brief call from Chloe, it was uninterrupted tranquility. We ate dinner and watched a little TV together, and I thought about all that had happened in the past few days: my appointment with Bridget, agreeing to a date with Marty. Yeah, quiet was good for tonight.

~32~

"Good morning, Sage. How are you?"

Rachel peeked over the top of my cubicle wall, startling me with her cheery greeting.

"Oh! Hi, Rachel!"

"Sorry, I didn't mean to startle you. I just wanted to ask how things went with Bridget."

"Well, things went pretty well. I'm seeing her again on Friday."

"That's great! And how are you feeling?"

"Actually, things are pretty darn fine right now. My brother has a new boyfriend, Sam, that I really think might be the one. Sam has just come out, really. He was even married for a while and has a daughter. So maybe I could be an aunt!"

"Sam? Good name. That's my husband's name."

"Really? Well maybe all Sams are cool. This poor guy really tried hard to be straight for a long time. Didn't work, of course. But he's crazy about his daughter, Savannah."

"That's a pretty name. I'm glad you're so excited about your brother's happiness, Sage. But what about you? Anything on your horizon that's looking bright?"

I grinned. "Maybe. Maybe a few things, actually."

She flashed that gorgeous smile back at me. "Good for you. Hey. I'm stuck here all day doing paperwork. Want to have lunch together?"

"Sure. That would be nice."

June in Seattle can be damp and chilly. But along with those drizzly days, there are usually a few gloriously clear and warm ones as well; today was one of those summer previews, so Rachel and I walked to a nearby park to eat our lunches at a picnic table. The trees were in full bloom, and birdsong surrounded us. As we sat down opposite each other, a squirrel ran up a nearby tree, chattering his disapproval at our presence.

"What a gorgeous day," Rachel said, unwrapping her sandwich.

I bit into my own, nodding my agreement. "Fabulous," I said, my mouth full. And then, "Sorry," again with a mouth full of food.

We laughed and chatted, enjoying the sunshine. During a lull in the conversation, I looked at Rachel's face. She was looking away, off into the trees. Pensive like that, with the sun streaking her hair, I thought of the phrase "impossibly beautiful." Rachel could easily be a movie star, a TV journalist, a model. It struck me that, other than Jamie, I'd never actually known such a pretty person.

"Rachel? What's it like to be so beautiful?"

"What?"

"I mean, what's it really like? People treat you differently, I know. Do they make assumptions about your intellect? Do people automatically love you or hate you, or both? Do you look in the mirror and see how gorgeous you are, or do you see flaws that no one else can? Are you happier than the average woman, do you think? Is life easier?"

"Whoa. Let me catch up." She took a deep breath. "Okay. The truth is that it's hard thinking of myself in those terms. I was an awkward kid growing up. I think I had adult features before they really fit on my face. So kids made fun of me; they didn't think I was pretty at all. And then I changed, I kind of grew into myself, during the summer between ninth and tenth grade. When I started school that fall, suddenly I was getting a lot of attention from boys, and the girls shied away from me, all except the most popular ones—the ones that had been considered pretty all along. Then I was accepted into their inner circle. The most popular boys wanted to date me, and the most popular girls wanted to be my friends. Inside, I hadn't changed at all, so it was very confusing. I enjoyed the attention. I enjoyed being part of the 'in-crowd.' But I didn't think I really deserved it. I thought somehow I'd tricked them into liking me.

"Then as time went on, I did start to understand that the world was responding to me a certain way because of my looks. I happen to have features that are consistent with our idea of beauty at this particular moment in time. That was just a lucky roll of the genetic dice. It doesn't say anything about who I am as a person, my character, my values. Is life easier? I suppose it is sometimes. I think people, especially men…"

"And lesbians."

"…and lesbians, I'm sure you're right, treat me with a little more reverence than they would treat someone they don't see as attractive. When I see that happening, though, I usually address it. Like: 'excuse me, but this person has been waiting longer,' or 'why were you so rude to that person when she asked the same question I did?' I do try to call people on it. And then there are people who resent me and treat me badly for no apparent reason. And yes, I think sometimes people assume that I'm stupid or even bad somehow. Evil or underhanded. Does that answer your questions?"

"Yeah. Thanks for being honest about it. I just have to think that life would be easier with looks like yours."

"You know, I was actually going to bring this up today. Sage, you are a beautiful woman. Don't you know that?"

I rolled my eyes. "So much for being honest."

Rachel stood, gathered her garbage and tossed it into a nearby trashcan. "Come with me."

She led me to a restroom in our building and told me to sit on the counter. "You want me to sit up there?" The restroom was not cleaned as often as we all would have liked.

"Yes," she said, very firmly.

I wet a couple of paper towels, wiped down a section of the counter large enough for my rear end, and lifted myself up. Swinging my legs, I tried not to look nervous.

"Don't be nervous! I promise, this won't hurt," Rachel said, rummaging through her purse. She brought out a few lipsticks, eyeliner and blush.

"You carry that much stuff around with you every day?"

"Not really. It just so happened that I needed a few things, so I stopped at the drugstore on the way to work this morning."

"My lucky day, huh?"

"That's right. Now, close your eyes."

I obeyed, but still wanted a play-by-play. "What are you doing?"

"Just adding a little liner to your lids. You have beautiful eyes, Sage. This will make them stand out a little more."

Next, she told me to look up. I could feel the liner going on under my eyes; when she was done, I started to look over my shoulder at the mirror. "No!" Rachel said. "Don't look yet."

"Okay." Eyes closed again, I felt a brush on first one cheek, then the other. Then came what I knew had to be lip liner, followed by lipstick.

"Wow. Now, get down, turn around and look at yourself. Really look."

I obeyed. Turning around to face the mirror, I was actually surprised by what I saw.

I didn't look half bad. I'd already been wearing mascara, but the liner truly made my eyes look bigger. And a little color on my face made my cheekbones stand out more. The shade of lipstick was good for me, a raspberry pink. Rachel had done nothing drastic or garish, just given me a little more color, and I had to admit it made a big difference.

"See? You're like me, Sage, you have that lovely alabaster skin that used to be so prized and sought after. Now of course everyone wants an olive complexion. People pay to look darker. Fashion is so fickle. So you and I, we may have to work a little harder than some, but I won't have you saying that you're not pretty because you really are! Do you see that now?"

"Please—you do not have to work at being pretty. We're not the same."

"We all have our flaws, Sage. I have splotchy skin and dark circles under my eyes, especially since I had my sons. I wear makeup every day now."

"I guess I've never really been into makeup."

"Why not?"

"Well, my mother left before I was old enough to start using it, and Mary—the woman who raised me after that—she's kind of a hippy. You know, the natural look. She still doesn't wear makeup at all."

"Brave soul."

"No, it's just right for her. I can't imagine her *with* it, actually. But, she is one of those olive-skinned beauties you mentioned. If she gets any sun at all she's instantly brown. Her daughter, though, Chloe, is a pale redhead. She wears makeup when she goes out, but she didn't really start until college."

"So no one ever taught you how to use it properly."

"I suppose not."

"And no one ever told you how pretty you are."

"Mary said those things, but I've never believed it, not really. Jamie is the pretty one."

"Oh, Sage. Both of you can be beautiful. It won't take away from Jamie if you see yourself that way."

"I know."

"I hope so."

"We should get back to work."

"Well thanks for spending your lunch with me. I really enjoyed it, Sage."

"Thanks. So did I. Thanks for the beauty tips."

"Anytime. Keep the makeup, okay?" Rachel hugged me, then, really hugged me. To my surprise, I didn't feel myself stiffening the way I usually did in a virtual stranger's embrace. It was a good hug.

Later, sitting at my desk, it dawned on me that I'd never seen Rachel wearing that shade of lipstick before. Nothing even close, in fact. I suddenly knew without a doubt that she had bought the cosmetics specifically for me. That's why she'd asked me to lunch. She'd had my little makeover in mind the whole time. Standing up, I looked over the top of my cubicle and caught her eye. I was going to say something, to expose her scheme, but she just grinned at me before answering her phone.

~33~

My second session with Bridget was rather unremarkable, especially in contrast with the drama of the first one. We talked about my panic attacks and the meltdown I'd experienced at work. I told her I couldn't understand why Mrs. Crow had such a powerful effect on me.

"It makes sense, really," she said. "She sounds like someone who is desperately unhappy. She's latched onto a few reasons her life didn't go as planned, a few groups of people to blame. To her, you represent one of those people she's decided to hate. She sees you as young and successful, since you're in a power position in terms of the services she gets. She probably sees endless potential for you. Well, once upon a time she saw herself that way, but for whatever reason things just didn't materialize for her. Then one day she realized she was old. The best of her life was over, and it hadn't been so great. People can become very bitter when that happens.

"But she knows that she gets to you, Sage. I'm sure she realizes that most people let her venom just roll off their backs. They ignore her. But she can shake you up. It must thrill her no end, so she keeps doing it. And she gets to you, Sage, because she attacks you without cause, without justification. She abuses you, calls you names, uses profanity. Except for the physical abuse, she is much like your dad must have been at his worst. Do you think that's true?"

"Yeah, I do. But I already knew that. Why do I still let her get to me?"

"Oh, Sage. When really bad things happen to us at such a young age, those memories are in our bones. When something happens to make them resurface, it's hard to reason them away. As you become more adept at recognizing what's happening, you'll be better at dealing with those triggers. But I do have to tell you, I'm not sure this job is a good fit for you. I think this is an abusive job for you."

"Jobs can be abusive?"

"Yes! You have to deal with abusive people, and you never know when they're going to surface. So that tension is there all the time. Then the phone rings and suddenly you're being screamed at and called names. Other people who don't have your issues would be able to deal with all that, but not you. I think you have to give some serious thought to a career change. What do you think about that?"

"Funny you should ask. I am thinking about it. I've had a few ideas, but my inheritance from Grandma Lucy will cover any kind of career I decide to pursue. Jamie thinks I should start a business of my own. He's planning on opening his own salon. We've started taking an accounting class. So I'm working on it."

"Good! I'm proud of you for embracing change. And for taking a risk. A lot of people avoid that at all costs and it ruins their lives. I would bet money that Mrs. Crow is one of them. What kind of business would you go into?"

"Well, Jamie thinks I should open a flower shop. He says I'm a genius with flowers."

"Wow! Are you?"

"I don't know if I'd use the word genius, but yeah, I'm good at arranging flowers. I seem to be able to put them together in unique ways. I can picture how they'll look when I'm finished. And I can do it really fast. I've never thought of it as a skill, though. It's always been so easy for me. I used to think everyone could do it."

"Well, not everyone can. Trust me on that."

"Yeah, I'm coming to realize that. Hey. There's another change I may be embracing."

"Really?"

I told Bridget that I had a date with Marty later that night. She wasn't surprised at all.

I was nervous, getting ready for the date. But I'd been using Rachel's make-up tips and felt, well, kind of pretty. After looking for strange hairs growing from my neck and chin, I was ready to go with minutes to spare. Marty was right on time.

We went to dinner, and he was so sweet and attentive, leaping in front of me to open doors. When he asked a question he really listened to the answer. He stared into my eyes in a way that made me a little nervous; he seemed to hang on my every word.

And the questions! *What do you like to do in your spare time? Have you ever gone hiking in the Cascades? On Rainier? Ever skied? Snow shoed? Skydived? What's your favorite color? Food? Animal? What was your favorite subject in school? Who was your favorite teacher and why?*

"What about you?" I asked. "Any hobbies? Do you play sports?"

"Not really, not as regularly as I'd like. I used to play softball sometimes on a friend's team. Mostly I just love getting outside, into the mountains, down by the water. We live in such a beautiful place, I think it's important to appreciate it. I love to do touristy things, too."

"Like what?"

"Oh, like spending a day at the Seattle waterfront. Walking through Pike Place Market, going to the aquarium, going to Seattle Center. Eating dinner at the Space Needle."

"That sounds like fun! It's been years since I've done any of that."

"See? We locals forget about all that fun stuff."

"You're right! I just hadn't thought about it like that."

We chatted easily, effortlessly. He asked even more questions about me and listened to every word of my answers.

Finally, he asked about Colin. "Have you heard from The Wall?"

"Not for a long time. I mentioned before that he'd left flowers at my door once, remember? I knew they were from him because they were yellow roses—his favorite, not mine. But I've never heard anything from him since then. It surprised me, too, because usually he would want the credit for doing something nice."

"Well, I have a confession to make. I was there that day. I saw his car pull in, so I went over to see what he was up to. I watched him walk to your door. He put the flowers down and started writing something, like he was leaving you a note. So I went up to him and asked him what he was doing."

"Really? What did he say?"

"He said, 'I'm writing a note to my girlfriend—what's it to you?' I said, 'I don't much care for how you treat your girlfriends. Sage is a friend of mine. I've seen the damage you've done, and I'm not going to let you hurt her again.' He started to tell me to mind my own business or something like that, so I, well I guess I taught him a lesson."

"Marty, what did you do?"

"He's a bully, Sage. Bullies only understand bullying. So I shoved him around a little, pushed him against a wall and told him that if I ever saw him near you again, he would finally get what he deserved. I told him to take his note and leave. And he did."

Bullies. Why were there so many of them? And why did I seem to be the only person who didn't understand them? I shook my head. "And he never came back. That's amazing. All the times I told him to go away, leave me alone, never call again, and he just ignored me. It only took one threat from you and he evaporated."

"He didn't evaporate, Sage. He's out there, probably hurting other women. Men like that don't change. I'm just sorry you were one of his targets. I can't protect everyone, I guess, but I could do something for you, so I had to."

"Sounds like you've met guys like Colin before."

He nodded. "My parents got divorced when I was about ten. Mom went through a string of losers. The last one beat her, over and over, and she kept taking him back. She'd tell me, 'He didn't mean it, Martin. I drove him to it.' Or, 'He was drunk, he didn't know what he was doing.' I heard all the excuses. He went after her one night when I was seventeen. I stood between them, but he kept coming. I hit him, hard, and my mother kicked me out of the house."

"She kicked *you* out?"

"Yep. Told me she never wanted to see me again. She said I was trying to ruin things with the man she loved."

"She didn't mean it, Marty, she was out of her mind. What happened? Did she come around eventually?"

Marty put his fork down and cleared his throat. He took a deep breath. "He killed her, Sage. She died two weeks after I left the house. He beat her to death. She was in a coma for half a day, but she never regained consciousness."

He spoke in low tones, staring at the table.

"Oh my God, Marty, I'm so sorry. What happened to the guy?"

"He was convicted of second degree murder. I testified that I'd witnessed previous beatings."

"What happened then?"

"Well, I'd moved in with my dad when Mom kicked me out. After she died he told me that my mom had been pretty self-destructive for a long time: drugs and alcohol, affairs with drug dealers or anyone else who'd get her high. She'd been in rehab—they'd told me she'd gone to visit a friend—but nothing worked. My dad sued for custody when they split up, but that was back in the days when fathers almost never won those cases. I'd been seeing my dad as often as I could, but my mom apparently used me to blackmail him for more money; sometimes she wouldn't let him see me unless he gave her more for child support. But she told me he was too busy to see me. Of course that money never went for my support at all."

"How awful."

"Hey, listen. I don't know how we got into this, but this is not what I wanted to talk about tonight. My mother died twenty years ago. It was rough, but it helped me become the person I am now."

"How's your dad doing?"

"Ah, now there's a happy subject. My dad is really doing well. He's remarried, very happily, and we see each other a lot. His wife, Brenda, is a real sweetie. She teaches third grade. My dad just retired from Boeing last year. They have a nice little place in Wallingford. Seeing them together is a joy, it really is. Gives me hope."

"That's what my brother does for me. Just knowing he exists makes me love the world a little more."

"I always wanted a brother or sister. No, actually that's not true. I really wanted a brother." He laughed. "But, maybe I'll have a brother-in-law someday. And when I have kids, I definitely want more than one. What about you?"

"Yeah, I don't know if the whole kid thing is going to work out for me. I'm thirty-seven. That biological clock is ticking mighty loudly these days. I've thought about becoming a single mom, but the truth is I don't think I want to do it alone. I think the reason it takes two people to make a baby is that it's hard work to raise one! I really don't think one person should have to contend with late night feedings, chicken pox, playground bullies and proms all alone. It's fine for other people, but I just don't think I have the energy to do it all. But, Jamie's new boyfriend has a daughter, so maybe I'll be Auntie Sage soon." I thought about mentioning Chloe's plan, but decided to wait for more developments on that front.

"Is Sam Jamie's new boyfriend?"

"Yep. And I introduced them! I'm so excited about them. I think Sam is great. So the aunt scenario is becoming much more likely for me than the whole motherhood thing."

"But you could still fall in love, get married and live happily ever after."

"Maybe. But I'm not holding my breath."

"I'm thirty-seven too, Sage. I'm still hoping."

"Well here's to hope," I said, lifting my glass of wine.

"And new beginnings," Marty added, staring again into my eyes in that unsettling way of his. Strangely, this time I wasn't unsettled at all.

"Marty?"

"Yeah?"

"Thanks for protecting me. Thanks for not believing I walked into a wall."

"Thanks for surviving, Sage."

The date ended at my front door; I was ready, willing and able to kiss him goodnight, but Marty just leaned down and gave me a soft little peck on my cheek.

"Are you busy tomorrow, Sage?"

I grinned. "I believe I'm free, as a matter of fact."

"Great! I have something in mind. But it'll have to be early, okay? I'll pick you up about seven."

"Seven AM? Sure, okay. What are we going to do?"

"You'll see tomorrow."

From inside my apartment I could hear Teddy: "Prrt?"

"I'll be right there, Ted! Hmm. A surprise?"

"A good one. You'll see. I'd better let you tend to your buddy in there."

"You want to come in for coffee?" I regretted the offer immediately. Would he think I was inviting him in for more than coffee? Would he think I was easy? Would I be able to resist the temptation of going further if he really kissed me? Would that mean I really *was* easy?

But Marty saved me from my confusion. "No, thanks. I've got some studying to do tonight, and I want to get a good night's sleep. I'll see you in the morning. Dress comfortably, okay?" There was that smoldering smile again.

"Okay. Good-night." He turned to leave. "I had a really great time tonight, Marty. Thank you."

He turned one more time and waved. "Wear a swimsuit under your clothes tomorrow!" he called, still smiling.

A swimsuit? Well, okay. I had one that didn't look hideous. But it was only June. The lakes wouldn't really feel warm until late summer. We had to be going to a heated, preferably indoor pool somewhere. So why did it have to be so early? Oh well; I told myself I'd find out soon enough.

Inside, I danced with Teddy and he tolerated it with only a couple of indignant squeaks. *Marty, Marty, Marty,* my brain sang. I had had a nice, normal date with a wonderfully normal—no, scratch that, better than normal guy who seemed genuinely fond of me. "Woo hoo, Teddy! Life is good."

To prove it to him, I gave him a few extra kitty treats after his dinner.

Suddenly I was impatient to share the news of my good fortune. I wondered if Chloe would still be awake. But when I picked up the phone, that Morse code tone told me I had a message.

I was mildly curious. Everyone knew I had a date tonight. Who would have called? So I dialed not Chloe's number, but the number to retrieve my messages.

Hello. My name is Amy Nelson. I am an attorney representing a woman who has filed charges against Colin Prescott. I am looking for Sage Whitaker. It is my understanding that you have information that may be helpful to this case. Please contact me at..."

My heart was pounding in my ears and I was shaking so badly that I had to listen to the message three times before I could record the number accurately. Then I sat on the sofa, number in hand, letting the message actually sink in.

Someone was pressing charges against Colin. Someone much braver than I. How badly had she been hurt? How many times had he beaten her?

Had he raped her, too?

How had they found me?

What should/could/would I do? I'd felt powerless against him. What if, with my help, this new victim might become powerful enough to make him pay? How could I not try?

But what if my help wasn't enough? If he wasn't stopped, how many more victims would there be?

And then a new question, a horrifying question.

How many have there been? How many calls had that lawyer made tonight?

The message had been left at 8 P.M., three hours earlier. Maybe it was too late to call tonight; well, I could at least leave a message.

But Amy Nelson answered her phone on the first ring. "Yes?"

"Amy Nelson?"

"Yes."

"This is Sage Whitaker." I could hear papers shuffling.

"Yes, Sage. Thank you for calling."

"I hope it's not too late."

She paused before she answered. "No, Sage. You're not too late."

I confirmed that I had dated Colin and that he had beaten me three times. That I'd sought medical attention but did not identify him as my abuser. I even told Ms. Nelson about the rape, though I knew it was probably inadmissible or improvable or both. She advised that she had contacted several women to gather statements supporting the premise that Colin was a chronic, serial abuser. Before my phone call, she had convinced two others to come forward.

Her actual client was still in the hospital.

"I should have pressed charges. It was selfish of me not to," I said.

"I know how frightening it is to take on a batterer, Sage. Don't feel guilty. Just do what you can now. This way none of you are fighting alone."

"Safety in numbers?"

"Something like that. I'd like you to come down to my office to make a formal statement. How about Monday?"

"I get off work at 4:30. How late will you be there?"

"Can you be here by five?"

"Sure. Thanks, Ms. Nelson. I'll see you Monday at five."

"Thank you, Sage. And call me Amy."

I hung up and curled into a corner on the sofa. Colin had beaten others, one of whom had landed in the hospital. A thought formed, then, something I'd professed to know—what I should have known all along.

"It wasn't my fault," I whispered.

~34~

Date number two with Marty was even more wonderful than our first evening together. Saturday morning at seven sharp, Marty was at my door, flowers in hand. He sat on my sofa and watched as I arranged them in a vase.

"I've never seen anyone handle flowers like that," he said when I put the finished product on my kitchen table.

"Thanks! Jamie says I'm an artist with flowers."

"I agree with him."

Teddy was being shy, sticking close to me, which was pretty normal behavior, Sam notwithstanding; since Colin, Teddy wasn't so sure about human males.

"Here, Ted," Marty said, trying to coax him a little closer.

Teddy watched him intently for a moment, then turned and walked into my bedroom.

"Ouch!" Marty said.

"Oh, he'll come around. It just takes him a little while to get to know someone."

"I'll win him over, I promise."

He wanted to win over my cat! *Marty, Marty, Marty,* began the song in my head again, almost drowning out the jumbled thoughts I had about my appointment with Amy Nelson on Monday. Almost.

I'd been debating about whether to talk to Marty about this new development. But now I doubted that I could really relax today if I didn't get it out in the open. And it would be interesting to get Marty's take on the situation.

"So, I have news about The Wall."

"What? Did he show up here again?"

"No. I got a call from an attorney. Colin sent his latest girlfriend to the hospital, and she's filing charges. Her lawyer wants me to provide an official statement as evidence that he has a long history of abusing women."

"What are you going to do?"

"I'm going to her office on Monday after work. I've always felt a little guilty that I didn't press charges myself. Now I have an opportunity to help another woman he's hurt. If I'd come forward earlier, maybe she wouldn't be in the hospital now."

"You can't know that, Sage. He might have hurt you worse and gone on to his next victim anyway. Don't be so hard on yourself."

"You're right that we can't know what would have happened. Not for sure. But I'm the third woman who's agreed to make a statement. There might be more by now. And that's in addition to the one who's still in the hospital. It's scary, but I really think this is my chance to do the right thing."

"Well, I think you're really brave. Do you want me to go with you on Monday?"

"Thanks, but I don't think it's necessary. I'm just going to the attorney's office, give my little statement and come home."

"But if he knows his girlfriend is pressing charges, he probably already knows who her lawyer is. He may be hanging around her office, trying to get information. He may suspect she'll try to find his other victims. I think you should let me be your bodyguard for a while, Sage. Let's play it safe, okay?"

"Okay, but only if it doesn't interfere with your life. Don't miss any school or work over this, okay? I'll have my other bodyguards fill in when you're not available, I promise."

"Deal. But I'll go with you on Monday."

"Okay. Thank you, Marty."

"You're welcome. Now. Are you ready for your surprise?"

Marty opened the car door for me, waited and closed it behind me. Sliding into the driver's seat, he looked upward through the windshield. "Have you heard a weather forecast this morning?"

"Uh, no. I got up, drank coffee and got ready with seconds to spare." I followed his gaze. There were a few clouds in the sky, but nothing looked too ominous. "I take it this mystery activity will take place outside."

He grinned. "Correct. Ready?"

Per Marty's instructions, I was wearing a swimsuit under my comfortable sweatpants, t-shirt and hoodie. "Yep. I'm ready," I said. "But it isn't exactly the right time of year for sunbathing."

"No, you're right about that."

"So where…"

"You'll see."

Marty drove and we chatted; he laughed as I tried to guess where we were going. "Taking scuba lessons? Bathing in the fountain at Seattle Center? No? Well if we're going to some indoor pool, don't I need a towel?"

"Stop trying to guess. It's going to be fun, I promise."

"Fun, but cold?"

"Trust me," Marty said. Oddly, I found that I did.

Lake Washington was blue and still as we approached it. Soon we were in a parking lot by some kind of pier, and I was following Marty onto a dock and up to a window, behind which stood several athletic-looking people wearing shorts and t-shirts, organizing papers and water-sports equipment.

One woman grinned when she saw Marty. "Hey! How've you been? It's been a while!"

Was it my imagination, or did her smile fade a bit when she saw me?

"Hey, Tara. How are you? This is Sage. Sage, Tara."

"Hi," I said, thoroughly perplexed.

"What do you need today?" she asked, shifting into job duty demeanor.

"I'd like a double. Four hours." He grinned at me.

Next thing I knew, I was squeezing into a wetsuit, tucking my outer clothes and purse into a locker and easing into the front of a double-seated kayak.

Marty had just given me a basic paddling lesson. "I'm going to be steering, so just follow my lead, okay?" Then, he slid into the seat behind me, pushed off from the dock and we headed out, the kayak making tiny ripples in the water.

"You doing all right?" Marty asked, leaning toward me.

"Great," I said. "It's so quiet and peaceful out here. It's beautiful."

"I thought you'd like it."

We paddled along, getting into in a slow, hushed rhythm. Marty pointed out a family of Canada geese, with six fuzzy little goslings hurrying to keep up.

Across the bay we went, through the Union Bay Arboretum, a place filled with plants and birds. There, near the shore, we spied a great blue heron standing on one foot, the other lifted to form a yoga tree pose. I wondered what he could possibly be meditating about. We startled him out of his tranquility and watched as he took to the air, his powerful wings working hard—whoosh, whoosh, whoosh—to lift up his body. We stopped paddling and watched him rise higher, circling around and back toward us again. But we had invaded his little haven; he did not return. Instead, he landed high in a nearby tree, glaring at us, I was sure.

We spent our allotted four hours paddling along the shores of Lake Washington. As more people arrived in ski boats, fishing boats, canoes and other kayaks, the water got choppier, but our wetsuits stayed completely dry. The warm sun and my rumbling belly were telling me our time was nearly up when Marty said, "Time to head back."

And back we went, passing our little goose family, waving to boaters.

Back on the dock, I pulled off my wetsuit. "That was amazing! Now I know why my brother likes to do that."

"I'm glad you enjoyed it. It's fun in the evening, too. Next time we'll get you your own kayak. You're a natural!" Marty said.

In the car, I said, "So you must go there a lot?"

"No, not really, not anymore. I used to teach sea kayaking there."

"Oh!"

"Tara's the only one left that I worked with. Mostly they just hire part-time people. Students, mainly."

"Did you date her?"

He looked at me. "Yeah, a few times. How did you know?"

"Just a guess."

"We were never serious. She's a nice girl. She just wasn't the *right* girl."

"Did she know that?"

He laughed. "Well, she did after I told her. Tara's more like a kid sister to me than a girlfriend, that's all. You can't choose who you fall for, right? Or who you don't."

"True, but you can choose to walk away from someone when they're not good for you."

"But if they're not good for you, they're not right for you."

"That logic is absolutely irrefutable. Well done!"

We ate lunch downtown at a restaurant with a beautiful view of Elliott Bay. Marty nodded toward the window.

"Sometime I'll take you kayaking out there. Maybe we'll see a pod of orcas."

"Have you seen some up close?"

"Yeah, I was actually surrounded by them once. It was amazing. It was really early in the morning, a little foggy. Suddenly they were all around me. I could hear them breathing. A couple of them came so close I felt the mist from their spouts. I stopped paddling and just watched them until they finally swam away. Very surreal. I've been pretty obsessed with them ever since. From pictures I've seen, I know it was J pod that I was with that day. I saw Granny, J2, who is over a hundred years old! She did a spyhop, where they put their heads out of the water to look around, and she looked right into my eyes. What a privilege to have them seek me out, to come take a look at me. I see them from a distance fairly often, but I'd love to have another encounter like that. Occasionally I see grey whales, a humpback once in a while. What a thrill! Once I saw a huge pod of Pacific White-Sided Dolphins. But mainly I see a lot of seals and sea lions when I go out on the Sound."

"Surreal seals?"

He laughed. I made him laugh again!

"Yes, very surreal."

"You have a great hobby, Marty."

"Yeah, I think so. It's kind of taken a back seat lately, between work and school. Everything has, really. This has been the best couple of days I've had in a long time, Sage. Thank you."

"It's been pretty fabulous for me, too."

"I'm glad. Really glad." He reached across the table and touched the tip of his index finger to mine, left it there for a few seconds and moved it back. He smiled, looking down at the table. "I'd love to see you again tomorrow, but I really have to study. There's an exam coming up I'm a little concerned about."

"Of course. School comes first. But I'm sure you'll do fine. Speaking of school, last Friday you said you had a class. But then you said you were free to go out last night. Did your class end?"

"No, actually I skipped it. I'm doing really well in it, so I'm sure I'll catch up just fine. You agreed to go out with me on Friday, so I wasn't going to say I wasn't available."

"Marty, I would have understood!"

"I know. But you were my priority last night. I do have to study tomorrow, like I said, but I'll see you Monday, to take you to your appointment. Should I pick you up at work? We could grab some dinner after you see the attorney, if you'd like to."

"Yes, and yes!" I wrote the office address down for him. I'm off at 4:30, and my appointment is at five."

"I'll be there at 4:30 sharp."

"Thank you. I mean, thanks for wanting to go with me."

"I want you to be safe."

"I know. That's why I'm thanking you."

This time, when we stood in front of my door saying good-bye, I didn't have time to wonder whether Marty would give me a real kiss. I looked up and there he was, moving slowly toward me. I could smell just a trace of some musky cologne, nearly replaced now by the scent of salty air. He kissed me and my mind went quiet. Peaceful. There was no awkwardness, no teeth colliding. It was, quite possibly, a perfect kiss.

When it ended we grinned at each other. Neither of us moved for several seconds.

Finally: "I'd better go," Marty said.

"Okay. Study hard. I'll see you Monday."

He jogged down the first few steps, then turned and ran back up to me. He held me close and we kissed again. I felt it all the way down to my toes.

"Wow," I whispered.

"Yeah," he agreed. "Okay. I'll see you Monday."

"Okay." I nodded, watching his eyes.

He kissed me once more, quickly, an exclamation mark. "Monday," he said again.

"Yes. At 4:30."

"Sharp."

"Yes."

Then he leaned down a little further and whispered directly into my ear. "I'm going to be thinking about you all night, Sage."

"I'll be thinking about you, too. I've already started."

Looking at my face once more, he backed away. "Monday."

Watching him make it all the way down the stairs at last, I felt both relieved and disappointed. But it really was for the best, I told myself. No need to rush.

~35~

Monday ticked by at an agonizing pace. I told myself to get a grip and stop being so excited to see Marty. *Two dates, that's all it's been. He's nothing to me. Not yet.*

I heard him before I saw him, asking for me at the receptionist's desk.

"Who can I tell her is here?" Erin asked him.

"Tell her it's her bodyguard."

My phone rang and it seemed silly, since I had just listened to their exchange, but I picked it up and played along.

"This is Sage."

"Sage, it's Erin. There's someone here to see you. He says he's your..."

"Bodyguard, I know. I heard."

"Oh. Yeah. Should I send him back?"

"No, it's okay. I'll be right there."

I put a file away, grabbed my sweater and walked through the cubicle maze to Erin's desk. Knowing I had a rapt audience by now, I greeted Marty, then spun around. Faces disappeared quickly, but Rachel stood her ground and grinned at me. "Hi, Sage!"

"Hi. Rachel, this is Marty. Marty, Rachel."

"Hi Rachel. Nice to meet you."

"And this is our receptionist, Erin."

"Erin." He shook her hand. "Very nice to meet you. Sage? Ready to go?"

"Bye, everyone," I called.

I heard murmurs of response behind us as we started to leave. Marty put his arm around me, and the murmuring swelled a bit as we walked outside.

"How was studying?" I asked.

"Good. For some reason I found it a bit hard to concentrate, though. How was your day?"

"Long."

"Are you up for this?"

"Yeah. I think so. It is a little scary. But I really feel I have to do this."

We took Marty's car and I read the directions to him that Amy Nelson had given me over the phone. They led us to a small, brightly colored building on a busy street. There was a Starbucks right next door. It was a sign, I was sure of it.

We walked into the main lobby. There was a small red sofa and chair in a corner. To the right, against a teal blue wall, was a metal staircase to an upper floor. Straight ahead was a desk; the chair behind it was empty.

"Should I go look for her? It's 5 o'clock; maybe her staff is gone for the day," I said.

Suddenly, a voice from above: "Sage, is that you? Come on upstairs."

I was so grateful when Marty said, "I'll wait here." I wasn't ready for him to know all the ugly details about Colin, not yet.

I walked up the stairs, my shoes clanging. I don't know what I was expecting exactly—probably someone imposing, in a dark power suit—but Amy Nelson was not it. When I reached the top, a tiny woman walked briskly through the open door of what I guessed was her office, her hand reaching toward me.

"Sage. I'm Amy. So nice to meet you," she said, shaking my hand. "We can talk in here." She motioned toward the room she'd just been in.

She sat behind a huge desk. It occurred to me that she looked like a little girl playing at being a grownup. Playing lawyer. Her hair was pulled back into a thick ponytail; several strands had escaped and hung over her face now as she looked down at some papers on her desk.

The building housing her offices may have been ultra-modern, with unlikely angles and bold hues, but Amy Nelson herself was nearly colorless; pale skin, light eyes. Her clothes were simple: blouse, skirt, flats. All in shades of gray.

Looking up from the pages on her desk, she sighed deeply. "I really appreciate you coming in, Sage. We need all the help we can get. Please tell me about your relationship with Colin. I'm going to record your statement, if that's all right. Take your time, and tell me everything you can think of. The more details we have, the better."

Now I sighed. "Okay." And so I told the whole story. That Colin had spotted me in a swanky lounge where I'd met Chloe for a drink after work. He sent us a bottle of Cristal, so we asked him to join us for a glass. At first I'd thought he was pursuing Chloe, but it soon became clear he had eyes only for me.

I was flattered. Thrilled, really. Colin was good-looking in a GQ kind of way: well dressed, well tended. He was charming and successful. All of this was very attractive, to me at least. Chloe never liked him, from the first moment.

He started sending flowers to me at work, with cute notes about why I should go out with him. I resisted at first, I really did. Something about him screamed Too Good To Be True!!!! But I relented, and it wasn't long before we were seeing each other almost every day.

Very soon, I noticed that he had a strong need to be in control. One of the first times he took me to dinner, he asked which entrée I was considering. "Oh, maybe the penne pesto," I mused, still looking at the menu. But when the waiter appeared, Colin spoke over me. "She'll have the *puttanesca*." Seeing my expression, he said, "It's so much healthier than pesto, Sage. So many fewer fat grams. You don't need all that fat, sweetheart."

He began to buy clothes for me. At first he'd say, "This will look so good on you!" But soon he was saying things like: "This will make you look less like a whore."

He would get angry, so angry, over tiny things. If I'd forgotten to wear a piece of jewelry he'd given me, he would rant about my lack of gratitude, my inability to appreciate his generosity. If I was five minutes late for a date, he'd rage about how selfish and inconsiderate I was. He would be late pretty habitually, thirty, forty minutes. Even an hour. But that was because of his important career. My job was no excuse. My job didn't merit such devotion. I needed to be there for *him*.

My friends were never good enough for him. He constantly tried to undermine my relationships with Chloe, Mary, even Jamie, by pointing out the many ways they failed me. Colin was always jealous of any time I spent with anyone else, always angry that someone had lured me away from him for an afternoon, a couple of hours, and finally even for a half hour chat over coffee.

One night when he got really abusive, verbally, I told him I was breaking up with him. He began to cry and beg for my forgiveness. It was the case he was working on, he said. It was the pressure. He would never hurt me intentionally, he said. He was so very sorry. It would never happen again.

About a month later, he beat me for the first time.

I told Amy Nelson everything. She nodded, asking questions here and there: "Which hospital did you go to? What did you tell the doctor? What tests did they run? Did anyone at work notice your bruises?" And of course, everyone had noticed my bruises. I gave them my explanations and no further questions had been asked. But Marty knew the truth and so did Jamie, although not quite the whole truth. Only Chloe knew the full extent of Colin's abuse. Until now.

When I was finished, Amy turned off the tape recorder. She thanked me again. I started to stand up, but she stopped me.

"Sage? There's one more thing. The woman who's pressing charges against Colin?"

"The one in the hospital?"

"Yes. Her name is Anna Curran. She would like to see you, if you are willing. It's entirely up to you. I can't officially advise you to have any contact with her. You understand? It could possibly hurt the case if anyone ever found out you two had spoken."

I nodded, and she handed me a slip of paper with Anna's information on it. The hospital, the room number, her cell phone number. "Then why are you giving me this?"

"It seemed really important to her. I promised her I'd pass along the information."

Amy pushed her chair back from the monstrous desk. "Thanks again for coming. I'll walk you to the stairs."

At the top of the staircase, Amy offered me her tiny hand once more. "This is a very brave thing you're doing, Sage. Colin needs to know that he cannot treat women this way and get away with it. He thinks he'll win this case; he's sure of it, in fact, sure that his money and power will keep him out of reach. But he's not untouchable, Sage. We will make him pay."

"Does he know that... that other people have come forward?"

"I don't think so, not yet. But he will soon, because I'll have to share all the information I have with his attorney before we go to trial. I'll protect you as far as I can, Sage, but he knows what he did to you. Even if he doesn't have your name, he'll know who you are from your statement, won't he?"

"Yes," I whispered.

"Do you have a restraining order in place?"

"No."

"I can help you get one. Help explain the circumstances."

"I guess that might be a good idea."

"Okay. Call me tomorrow and we'll get moving on it."

"Amy? Why does Anna want to see me?"

Amy shrugged. "I really don't know. She didn't tell me, and I certainly didn't ask."

"Plausible deniability?"

She smiled, saying nothing.

I nodded. "I'll call you tomorrow about the restraining order. One more question: how did you get my name?"

"From Anna. Colin had mentioned you and other ex-girlfriends several times while they were dating. When she'd recovered enough to contact me about pressing charges, she gave me all the names she could remember. Once I had your name, well, it's not so hard to find someone these days. Anna knows enough about abusers to know that they abuse habitually. She knew there had to be other victims, and she really wants him to pay for everything he's done."

I could barely speak, my throat was suddenly so dry. "She's so brave," I managed.

"You're brave, too, Sage," Amy said. "Don't sell yourself short. And don't worry. Colin will be punished for what he's done to all of you."

Amy Nelson no longer looked like a little girl to me. She seemed to be made of steel.

~36~

The workweek had flown by. I'd called Amy on Tuesday as promised, and she petitioned the court on my behalf for a temporary restraining order against Colin. I missed half a day of work so that we could appear before the judge on Wednesday. Amy convinced him that even though Colin and I had not had any contact for some time, the upcoming legal proceedings against him could possibly result in a new danger for all of his past victims.

As we left the courthouse, Amy said, "This means that if he comes near you, if he calls you, if he initiates any contact at all, he is in violation of the order and will be arrested. All you have to do is call 911 and say I have a restraining order against someone who is now approaching me or on my premises and the police will be there, lickety split. We hope."

"Yeah. We hope. So now what?"

"I have two more statements to get, and the meetings are set up for this week. Then I'll turn over all the material I've collected to Colin's team of attorneys. Then we'll wait for their response. I should know something by the end of next week. In the meantime, if anything happens, please let me know."

"I will. Thank you, Amy."

"You're welcome." She lowered her voice. "Are you planning on visiting Anna?"

"I'm not sure yet."

"I spoke with her this morning. She's developed an infection with a pretty high fever, so she'll be in the hospital a while longer. She's not feeling great right now, so give her a couple of days."

"Yeah, okay."

I still couldn't decide whether to go meet Anna Curran, this stranger with whom I shared something so horrible. Honestly, what more did she want from me? Did she want to form a club or something?

On my way back to work I decided not to decide yet. I would wait until after my Friday appointment with Bridget. Maybe she would have some insight about it.

So much had happened since my last appointment with Bridget, in fact, that I could hardly wait for the next one. Two days later, I didn't even stop for a latté before I bounded up the stairs to her office.

"Big news," I said as I sat on Bridget's sofa. I told her about the phone call from Amy Nelson and my appointment with her.

"What a brave thing to do, Sage. You're exposing Colin as the monster he is. You're doing what you can to make sure he stops hurting women."

"I really didn't feel I had a choice. But get this: the woman who is pressing charges against him wants me to go see her in the hospital."

"She wants to meet you? Do you think you'll go?"

"I don't know. It would feel strange. What do you think?"

"It might be awkward, but if this is her request she must have something in mind to talk about. You could just go and hear what she has to say."

"I am curious about what she wants."

"Maybe she just wants to thank you. Maybe it's that simple. Of course it's completely up to you. So what happens next on the case?"

"The lawyer is collecting statements from as many of Colin's victims as she can track down. She'll be presenting all of the information to Colin's attorney. Then we go to trial."

"If he doesn't settle, I suppose."

"I guess."

"Well, that is big news. Is there anything else going on?"

"Yes, actually. Things are quite wonderful right now."

"Really? Does it have something to do with your date last Friday?"

"Yes, it does. That date went so well we saw each other again on Saturday."

She smiled. "That's great! How is your radar working? Any red flags?"

"I don't know about my radar, but Jamie's has always been accurate and he approves."

"Jamie knows Marty?"

"Well, they met a week ago. After my session with you, Jamie talked me into going out and we ran into Marty. That's when he asked me out. He said he'd been wanting to for a long time. He was so sweet, even a little shy. He's this big, strong, macho kind of guy who's shy!"

"He sounds great, Sage. So you're going to see him again?"

"I already have. He insisted on coming with me to the lawyer's office on Monday. He was concerned that Colin might be staking out the office, watching for his past victims. Well, there was no sign of Colin, but it was nice having such a charming bodyguard. Then we went out for dinner afterward."

"So things are progressing quickly?"

"No, not really. Not sexually. We're taking things slowly. But we're having a lot of fun together. I really like him. So we'll see where it goes."

"I think that's a good approach. Now, how have you been feeling this week otherwise? Have any issues come up at all? Anything negative you've been thinking about?"

"Not really. No."

Bridget smiled. "I'm so glad you had a good week, Sage. I'd like to talk to you a little bit about your father, if that's okay."

"I suppose."

"You said he showed up that night and told you that your grandmother had died. And that he'd turned his life around, stopped drinking, stopped abusing."

"Yes. And that he was getting married, and wanted me to come to the wedding."

"That must have been a lot to digest. I'm surprised you let him inside at all."

"I wasn't going to. But he said he had something important to tell me, so I picked up my baseball bat and followed him to my kitchen table. I held the bat the whole time he was there."

"Did he acknowledge the bat?"

"He said he understood why I couldn't trust him."

"And then he left you his phone numbers and said that any further contact would be up to you?"

"Yes. And at first I was angry that he never mentioned Jamie, didn't ask about him, nothing. But then the next day his fiancée went to Jamie's salon. She asked for him, as a customer, and he cut her hair. She revealed who she was when she was in the chair. Wendy."

"What was she like?"

"Like a cardboard cutout stock southern conservative Christian fundamentalist character from a bad movie. She told Jamie, 'We love the sinner, sweetheart, we just hate the sin,' meaning homosexuality of course. She said she had it all figured out, the reason that Jamie is gay. He felt rejected by his father, and so he set out to find a man who would love him, or some such nonsense. I understand those people are convinced of what they say, mindless as it is. But she wasn't there when we were growing up. My father hated Jamie almost from the day he was born. Jamie was always different. Always. My father was looking for a rough and tough football player I guess, and Jamie was never going to be that. He played with my dolls. He pretended to be a mommy. He just was who he was, and my father tried to scream it out of him, beat it out of him, shame him into changing. That's what ignorance does, and I have no patience for it."

"You protected Jamie."

"As much as I could. I distracted Dad, pushed him to hit me instead. There were a couple of times I thought I'd gone too far. I thought he might kill me, and that would mean I'd be leaving Jamie behind, all alone."

"That must have been so frightening. How badly did he hurt you?"

"Well, I know he broke some ribs a couple of times. He blackened my eyes fairly often. Once he kicked me in the kidney area really hard and there was blood in my urine for a couple of days. He beat me unconscious a few times. But it was worse when I couldn't protect Jamie. When my father threw me aside and started hitting my brother..." I stopped for a moment, fighting back tears.

"What did he do?"

I took a deep breath. "Usually he pulled Jamie's shirt off, sometimes his pants too. Then he would take off his own belt, double it up and start whipping Jamie with it. Over and over that belt would hit Jamie's skin. The welts became cuts and the cuts bled and bled and still our father kept swinging that belt. Oh God, the sound of the belt making contact. Horrible." I shook my head, hearing that sound. "Anyway, I would jump on my father's back, I would scream for him to stop, I would bite him, scratch him, anything I could think of. Finally, finally, he would stop and sneer at us both, hurl some awful names at us and go downstairs to his dinner, his beer, his TV. And I would wet a towel and clean Jamie's wounds. He always cried really softly so that Dad wouldn't come back upstairs. He was so careful that way. Then I would hold Jamie and rock him until he fell asleep. When he did, I'd just stare at him. He was so beautiful. How could anything be wrong with Jamie? He was a pure soul. He's still perfect. He has scars on his back, but they didn't change him."

"The scars didn't mark his soul."

"Never."

"What about your scars, Sage? Did they change you?"

"Yes, I think they did. We already talked about how abusers know I'm an easy target. They can just tell, right? So they see something about me, something that wouldn't be there if all that crap hadn't happened to me. Doesn't that mean I've been changed?"

"Absolutely. You are different than you would have been without those experiences. But..." She leaned forward, making sure I was looking at her.

"But?"

"But you don't have to be a victim, ever again. You can choose to be strong. To demand gentleness. You can decide never to tolerate abuse again. There is a catch, though."

"What catch?"

"You have to believe that you deserve to be treated well. I mean really, truly believe it."

Tears filled my eyes again; I couldn't stop them this time. It was ridiculous, what she was saying. I tried to tell her so. "I do believe it! Of course I do! I don't deserve to be knocked around like that."

"No, you don't," Bridget said quietly.

"I don't! How could you think I—that I... ?"

"That you what, Sage?"

"That I asked for it? That I'm not worthy of being loved? That it was all my fault?" I gasped, suddenly unable to breathe. My heart pounded; my chest hurt.

Bridget's eyes appeared directly in front of me, staring straight into mine. "Sage? Are you all right? Listen to me: take one deep breath in. Now let it go slowly. Good. Again. In through your nose—and out through your mouth, very slowly. Good. One more time."

Her voice was so soothing, listening to it was easy. Three deep breaths and I was breathing almost normally again. "Thank you," I managed.

"Don't talk yet, just concentrate on your breathing. You were hyperventilating, Sage, but you're okay now. Another deep breath. And out. Good. Now. Can you tell me what you were thinking about?"

"I was angry."

"Angry with me?"

"Yes. For assuming that I thought I deserved... everything."

"Why did you cry?"

"I don't know. It snuck up on me."

"Do you remember what you were saying?"

I thought about it; looking at the floor, I nodded.

Bridget continued. "I never suggested you weren't worthy, nor that you asked for the abuse in any way. None of it was your fault, Sage. Not your father's beatings, not the rapes in high school, not Colin. Yes, your early experiences made you vulnerable, but everyone who has treated you badly is at fault, not you."

Still staring at the carpet, I nodded. "I know. I do! It hit me when I found out about Colin's other victims."

"I'm not so sure. I'm sure the thought occurred to you, and it probably felt like a profound realization. But knowing it in your head is very different from feeling it in your gut. I don't think you're there yet. But you will be, eventually," Bridget said.

We shifted into small talk; Bridget asked what I wore on my first date with Marty. I knew she just wanted me to leave on a positive note.

But as we said good-bye at the door, Bridget stopped me. "One thing, Sage. I know you trust Jamie's judgment, but if you feel unsafe or uncomfortable in any way, with Marty or anyone else, please just get out of the situation. Be very careful. You have every right to protect yourself."

"I promise I'll be careful."

"Good. See you next Friday. But call any time if you need to."

I walked slowly down the stairs. I'd felt so great when I arrived; now I wasn't sure what I felt. I began to doubt everything. Maybe Marty wasn't such a safe bet. Maybe Sam wasn't Jamie's Mr. Right. Maybe life wasn't so wonderful after all.

And maybe I should just go find out what Anna Curran had to say.

37

Everyone hates hospitals. With the obvious exception of the birth of a baby, a hospital is a place of sad stories, of pain and loss and endings.

And why is it that whoever I see in a hospital, whatever the circumstances, that person always seems to be in the absolute farthest end of the farthest wing? So it was with Anna Curran, whom I did not know but who had summoned me to this endless, shiny corridor.

Her room was the last in the hallway, of course. I tapped on the door and peeked in.

"Are you Sage?" a tired voice asked from the far end of the room.

"Yes. Are you Anna?" Stupid question.

"Come in," she said.

I walked toward the voice. "Over here. The curtain is partly closed." I saw a hand motioning.

I had known that Anna's condition was fairly serious, but I really wasn't prepared for the way she looked. I walked through the curtain and saw a ghost.

She was so pale. Now I knew what the word ashen meant; she was nearly gray. Her eyes had been blackened. I recognized the shade of yellow that ringed them now. Her whole face was bruised, in fact. And her face looked so thin, I was reminded of Jamie's friend Bobby, whose eyes had peered out at me from the edge of death.

"Hello, Anna," I said.

"Please sit down." She nodded toward a chair beside the bed. "I'm glad you called. Thank you for coming."

"Of course."

"Thank you for meeting with Amy."

"It seemed like the right thing to do."

"It was. It was the right thing to do, Sage. Do you know what he did to me?"

"I…"

"He broke my nose and one cheek bone. He broke a rib, punctured a lung and ruptured my spleen. My spleen had to be removed and now I will always be more vulnerable to infection. After all that, he knocked me down a flight of stairs. That fall broke my leg. I lay there, at the foot of the stairs. I couldn't breathe, I was in absolute agony, and he walked up to me, called me a whore and kicked me one more time before he just left me there to die. I probably would have died if my mother hadn't happened to drop by. If she hadn't found me when she did…well, things would have been very different."

Maybe she just wants to thank you, Bridget had said. I shivered. Somehow, I did not believe that was what Anna had in mind.

"I'm so sorry," I whispered.

"How many times did he hit you?"

I cleared my throat. "There were three different…incidents."

"Three? You allowed him to beat you twice after the first time?"

"Yes, but…"

"And you didn't press charges. You could have stopped him and you didn't. This is your fault too, you know that? You are part of the reason I almost died and that I am still in here fighting for my life. Do you know that? Do you think about it?"

"I was afraid of him."

"Oh, I see. 'I didn't turn him in because I was a coward.' That explains everything. How dare you? Do you think that you are the only person that matters in this world? Do you think your life is worth more than mine? How many more people had to become his victims because you were too afraid to come forward? Did you think he'd never beat another woman?"

Anna Curran's voice had risen as she spoke and now she was screaming at me. She was screaming in my face, and I deserved it.

"I'm sorry! I do think about it. It weighs on me, it really does. But I can't change the past now. All I can do is move forward and do everything I can now to put him away. And honestly, Anna, there was a part of me that did believe he wouldn't hurt anyone else!"

"How could you possibly think that?"

"Because I thought it was my fault! I thought he could see inside me and just knew that I…"

"That you what?" Anna asked, her voice softer now.

"That I would accept it. That I felt inherently inferior and I knew I would be beaten. That a part of me expected it. Normalized it. Understood it. And that when he apologized and showered me with gifts, he knew I would feel it was more than I deserved. He knew that I would allow him to come back and do it again."

"This had happened to you before."

"Yes."

"Another boyfriend?"

"No, not to this extent. No, I had very early training for this."

"Your parents?"

"My father." I looked out the window. I could see trees in the parking lot trembling in the wind. Pink blossoms blowing away, petal by petal.

"I'm sorry, Sage. My father taught me how to defend myself. He told me never to allow anyone to touch me in any way that didn't feel right. I was his precious little girl. I still am. I can't imagine him hurting me, ever."

"I can't imagine having a father like that. It would be wonderful, I'm sure. I'm surprised Colin zeroed in on you. You are not a classic victim. Me, I'm textbook. I'm very sorry for everything. For not coming forward. For all of the pain you're going through. I'm sorry that Colin exists. You can blame me for all of it if you want. I did what I did to try to protect myself. Protecting myself is just something I'm not very good at. I hope you recover quickly, Anna."

I was almost out the door when I heard her response: "I hope you do, too, Sage."

Three days later, Amy Nelson called. Anna Curran had died suddenly the night before. Another infection had set in and she just wasn't strong enough to fight it off. Her fever was too high, her body too weak.

Important news: that was how Amy had prefaced our conversation. Important because Anna was a human being whose life had been cruelly cut short. Important because her family would mourn her forever. Her father, who had taught her to protect herself, would have to learn to live without his little girl.

Yes, this news was important for all those reasons. And, too, because Colin was now a murderer. Amy's case had fundamentally changed. She was pursuing a killer.

"Sage, a friend of Anna's has come forward to say that she witnessed Colin pushing Anna and screaming at her the night she was beaten. I think we have him cold for Anna's death. Is there anyone at all who witnessed any of Colin's violent behavior toward you? Think about it. Ask your friends. It would be great if I could get a statement to that effect."

"Well, Jamie saw him yell at me a couple of times. So did Chloe. But he was pretty careful to avoid witnesses. I see that now. He always beat me behind closed doors."

"I'd love to talk to both Jamie and Chloe."

"Okay. I know they'll be happy to help."

When I called Jamie and Chloe, they both promised to call Amy that very day. I hoped their input would help.

I don't really know what made me mention all this to Rachel that day. I suppose I was just feeling a little lost, thinking about Anna, thinking that it so easily could have been me who had died.

"It's just so ironic," I told her during a coffee break. "She seemed so strong and self-assured, and yet somehow she got involved with the wrong guy. He beat her up once and she was pressing charges! And the beating killed her. Rachel, he beat me really badly three times, and here I am, healthy as can be! It's not fair."

"Well, I'm glad you're still here, Sage. I'm really sorry that he killed that poor woman, and you're right, it's not fair. But it wouldn't have been fair if you'd died, either."

"I suppose. Anyway, now my brother and a friend of mine are providing statements that they witnessed Colin yelling at me and just generally treating me badly. The lawyer thinks that may help."

"Sage, I have something that might help too."

"You do?"

"Be right back."

Rachel dashed out of the coffee room and just as quickly dashed back in. She was holding a couple of calendars, and she flipped them open now. On certain dates, she'd written notes: *Sage/black eye, bruise on cheek, limping. Flowers from boyfriend, Colin. Sage/two black eyes, finger-shaped bruises on arm. Dozens of phone calls from boyfriend Colin, flowers.* And: *Sage/looks like hit by truck! When Colin called, she told him to get lost!* It was all there, everything she'd ever noticed. When I looked up from her notes, Rachel was beaming.

"Rachel! I can't believe you did this!"

"Sage, no one believed you'd fallen down stairs or bumped into walls. No one is that clumsy. And you sure got a lot more graceful after you dumped that bastard! I kept track, just in case. Remember, my husband is an attorney. I thought this might come in handy someday."

Amy Nelson told me that when she presented her case to Colin's well-heeled attorneys, they were visibly shaken. Of course there was a plea deal; Colin pled guilty to voluntary manslaughter and six counts of assault and battery. Because of his previously clean record and his standing in the community, his attorneys asserted that Amy would not be able to convince a jury to punish him more severely. When she considered the charisma factor and the television cameras he would no doubt dominate during a trial, Amy reluctantly agreed.

Colin was sentenced to seven years in a minimum-security prison. Seven years, for the beatings of four women, one of which resulted in a death. And, because of all those wonderful qualities his lawyers described *ad nauseum*, Colin was not taken into immediate custody but was given a two-week period to "get his affairs in order." Amy argued that he was a danger to that very community in which he enjoyed such an impressive reputation; the judge sternly warned Colin to stay away from women—especially those who held restraining orders against him—and to watch his anger as he prepared for his incarceration.

I was not identified by name in the complaint against Colin, so I wasn't there during his sentencing hearing. I was relieved not to have to face him. Amy called the moment it was over and described it all in detail.

But it wasn't over at all, not really. Colin would be free for two more weeks, and then gone for only seven years. What would have happened if Anna hadn't died?

At that point I knew I should be careful. I was sure that Colin knew I was among the victims listed in the complaint. I knew he would be very angry now. But there were others who knew all this, too.

Jamie, Sam, Chloe and Marty all volunteered immediately to stay glued to my side for the next two weeks. Jamie drove me to work, Sam picked me up and drove me home. I spent the weekend with Chloe at her place. And weeknights, Marty was waiting at my apartment when Sam and I pulled up. We'd eat dinner at home or go out with Sam and meet up with Jamie at a restaurant. Marty slept on my sofa those nights after long talks, and lots of handholding and kissing. He managed to bond with Teddy during that time, and I was falling fast for him, too.

It was day eleven, a Monday, at nine o'clock at night when Colin appeared at my door. Marty looked through the peephole and nodded to me. "Get the hell out of here," Marty yelled through the door.

"Listen, man, I just want to talk to Sage. I'm…I have to go away, and I just want to say good-bye. Sage? I just want to say I'm sorry for everything."

Most people wouldn't have picked up on it, but I heard the slight slur, the subtle running together of his words. Colin was drunk. Really drunk. Colin didn't have to be drunk to be dangerous, but it sure helped.

"Go away, Colin. I mean it," I said.

Then—a gunshot. Then another and another. Marty was moving fast, grabbing my baseball bat and backing away from the door, blocking me with his body. I turned and ran to the phone and pushed 9-1-1 as fast as I could and then the door was open and Colin was inside. He pointed a gun at Marty's face, but he was looking at me.

"Put the phone down, Sage."

Slowly, I did as I was told.

"Drop the bat," he said to Marty, walking toward him. Marty let the bat drop to the floor and Colin kicked it back toward the door.

Colin laughed. "You think you can ruin my life? You think you can have any power over me at all? You're nothing, you understand? You stupid cunt! You are the dirt under my shoes."

Marty held his hands up, palms toward Colin. "Hey. I know you're angry, but this is not the way, Colin." He spoke so calmly. "This won't solve anything. This will only make things worse."

"Yeah? Worse than my career ending? Worse than spending seven years of my life locked up? For what? For having really bad luck with women? Do you call that justice? I didn't mean to kill Anna, it was an accident. And you..." He looked at me. "I loved you, Sage. We could have been happy. You would have had a better life with me than you ever could have imagined. Yes, I had some problems with my anger, but that was partly your fault, too, and you know it. So you thought you were better off without me. Okay, that's fine. But then to betray me, to talk to a lawyer, get a restraining order when I had no intention of coming near you ever again? Because of you my life is over. How could you do that to someone you once loved, Sage?"

His face was as twisted as his logic. There was no possible way to argue with him in that state, no way to make him see how wrong he was, but still I tried. "Because of you Anna's life is over, Colin. Really over."

"I told you that was an accident, you bitch."

"Yeah, you accidentally hurt her too badly while you were beating her. And what about the others, Colin? Are you going to kill all the women who came forward? I'm sure they were all partly at fault when you were beating them up, too."

"Shut up!"

Colin started coming toward me with that familiar sneer on his face. But he stopped and looked at Marty. "I've seen you before, haven't I? Yeah, I remember. You were a big man shoving me around that day, weren't you? Funny how small you seem now, at the other end of a gun. Wait a minute! This is perfect. They'll say poor Sage just chose another abusive man, and this one killed her. Sadly, he felt so guilty he turned the gun on himself. Tragic story, but all too common. Get over there, right there, beside her."

Colin looked back at me, just for a split second, and Marty slammed into him. The gun flew into the air as Colin hit the ground hard. Marty sat on him and pounded his fist into Colin's face and I watched the gun land, ran to it and picked it up. In movies, people always let the bad guy get the gun a second time. I was not going to let that happen.

It felt warm and it fit in my palm and I wrapped my finger around the trigger and lifted it up. "Get the fuck out of here, Colin!" I screamed, but Marty was still on him, still pounding and screaming in his face. Colin was moaning and begging him to stop.

But Marty didn't stop. He kept pounding, every punch punctuating his words: "You think you can just do whatever you want? You think you can beat women, kill them, because they displease you? Because you own them, that's what you think, don't you, you sick bastard."

"Marty, stop! You'll kill him!"

Marty backed away from Colin and stood beside me, still watching him. "Someone needs to stop him, Sage. He'll kill again, you know he will! It might be you next time."

Colin moaned. We watched him roll over and start to get on his feet. Swooning a little, he turned to face us. Now it was his turn to hold up his hands in surrender.

"No," Marty said. "Never again." And then, in one swift, fluid motion, Marty turned, took the gun from me, swung it toward Colin, cocked it and fired once. The sound was a deafening, echoing bang. Then, for a moment, there was no sound at all.

I saw Colin fall. His face was gone.

In my memory, all through the rest of the night I moved in dream-like slow motion, like wading in waist-deep water. I called 911 but was told the police were already on their way to my address. Someone had heard gunshots and reported it.

The police arrived. I was shivering, and someone wrapped a blanket around me.

I listened to Marty tell the police that Colin had brought the gun and told us he was going to kill us, that Marty had managed to get the gun away from him, had hit him repeatedly to subdue him.

Then came the lie.

"He said he'd leave and I lowered my hands, but he lunged at us again and I just raised the gun and shot. It all happened very fast."

One police officer examined the body, another took pictures and another was listening to Marty's story and taking notes. He looked at me. "Is that what happened, Ms. Whitaker?"

I swallowed, thinking a thousand thoughts in a few seconds. "Yes," I whispered. "That's exactly what happened."

What purpose would it have served for Marty to go to prison? I knew the real reason Marty had killed Colin. He was correcting a past mistake. This time, he had managed to save someone he cared about.

When Colin's body had been taken away, the police stayed behind to take a few more pictures. They said that because there was a restraining order in place, because it was clear that Colin had shot through the door of my apartment, and because Marty and I both witnessed the events, they would be closing the case after they filed their reports. It was all over, they said. They said goodnight and left.

Marty called a locksmith friend of his to come replace the locks that Colin had shot through on my door. Then Marty scrubbed the carpet and walls clean while I sat on the sofa wrapped in my blanket, numb, just watching him. Looking down, I realized that Teddy had come out of hiding, crawled onto my lap and started purring. I hadn't even noticed.

When his task was done, Marty sat beside me.

"Thank you for cleaning," I said, staring at the huge wet spot on the carpet.

"Thanks for…"

"No. Please don't say it."

"Okay. Do you want me to stay?"

I shrugged. "It's late. You might as well stay until morning."

I climbed into my bed and tried to sleep, but Colin's faceless body was all I could see when I closed my eyes.

I didn't hear him leave, but Marty was gone when I got up.

38

That morning I sat on my sofa. Just sat. I looked at the remote control but simply didn't have the strength to turn on the TV. Very few thoughts entered my mind at all, but it did occur to me that I needed to explain my absence at work. So I picked up the phone and called Althea.

When she answered I had no idea what to say.

"Hello?" she said for the third time.

"Uh, it's Sage."

"Sage? What's wrong? Are you sick?"

"Uh, I—no, not exactly. There was a shooting last night."

"A shooting? Where? Are you all right?"

"Yes. I'm all right. My—someone I used to know was killed last night in my apartment. The police were here very late and I didn't sleep at all. So I was wondering if I could take a sick day. I mean, I'm not really sick, I just can't..." I broke off, too exhausted to continue.

"Of course! Get some sleep. Sage? Are you sure you're okay? Is there anything I can do?"

I sighed. "No. I mean, there's nothing. Thank you."

I clicked the phone off.

There was still a spot on the carpet. And I saw Colin's body again, his blood seeping into that spot.

I picked up the phone again and was trying to decide who to call when it rang.

"Hello?"

"It's Marty. Are you okay?"

"Yeah. Are you?"

"Listen, sorry I had to leave, I just..." He stopped. I could hear him breathing.

"You couldn't stand to be here anymore, right?"

"I...well, I knew you were safe, so..."

"It's okay. Really, it's all right. I don't blame you."

"Are you sure?"

"It's okay that you left, Marty. Don't worry about that. Listen, I've got to go. I'm expecting another call."

"Okay, then. You take care of yourself, Sage."

"You too, Marty."

I called Chloe. Before she could even say hello, I found myself screaming into the phone. "COME GET ME, PLEASE, YOU HAVE

TO COME GET ME NOW, I HAVE TO GET OUT OF HERE,
PLEASE CHLOE!"

She asked no questions. "I'm on my way."

I packed a bag, put Teddy in his carrier, locked the apartment
and met Chloe in the parking lot. I was still wearing my pajamas.

I never saw the inside of that apartment again.

Jamie left work as soon as Chloe called. He spent the afternoon
with us and listened to my story. "Marty didn't have to kill Colin,
Jamie. It was a choice he made. Colin was helpless. And I covered for
Marty. I lied for him. I had to make a decision, right then and there. So I
did. And now I have to live with it."

"Sage, listen to me. Sooner or later Colin would have hurt
someone else. Maybe he would have killed again. I know that you
probably wouldn't have killed him under those circumstances. But it
happened. Marty isn't the bad guy here. Maybe what he did was wrong,
but he's not evil. And he knew that Colin was evil. Colin intended on
killing you both. Maybe he would have kept coming after you, you don't
know. I feel bad for Marty. Colin was a horrible man, but poor Marty
has to live with the knowledge that he took a life. You, Sage, you're
blameless here. You protected the guy who saved your life. I know it all
must have been a terrible trauma to go through, but we're here for you.
And we always will be. You're going to be fine."

"I know."

"When will you see your shrink again?"

"Friday. I already called." I had cancelled two sessions with
Bridget while I was being chaperoned 24/7. Once I knew Jamie was on
his way to Chloe's, I decided it would be a good time to confirm my
next appointment.

"Good girl," Jamie said.

Sam joined us later, and the four of us went to Mary's for dinner.
It had taken a while, and some extreme circumstances, but we'd all
finally made it over there together.

Mary encircled her three kids with her arms, just folded us right
in. "My darlings. Well of course Chloe filled me in, but Sage tell me, are
you really all right?"

"I'm okay. I'm exhausted. Numb. Sometimes it feels like it was
just a nightmare I had a long time ago. And sometimes, it feels as if it's
happening right now, and over and over again."

"You are in shock, sweetheart. And you are traumatized. But you are going to be just fine. You know the old saying, 'What doesn't kill you makes you stronger'? Well, it's true. But it really should be 'What doesn't kill you makes you stronger, but first it really beats the crap out of you.' Right?

"Now, Jamie, how are you, my beautiful boy? And, it's Sam, right? I believe we met at Chloe's party."

"That's right. Nice to see you again, Mary."

We had a wonderful dinner, the five of us. As we were finishing up, I looked from one face to the other and tears just filled my eyes.

"Sage?" Chloe said. "Honey? You okay?"

"I just love you all so much," I whispered. "You're my family and I love you."

"To family," Mary said, raising her glass.

"Family," everyone said, clinking their glasses together.

When the dishes had been cleared, we gathered in the living room to chat some more. I'd been hoping to find a chance to ask Mary some questions about Mom. I opened my mouth to begin, when I noticed Chloe fidgeting and blushing.

Chloe had always blushed easily, one of her traits that I appreciated and she detested. She could never hide that she had something on her mind.

"Chloe? What is it?" I asked now.

"Um, I have something to discuss with Jamie. I've been wanting to for a while, but well, a couple of glasses of wine and having you all here has given me a little courage."

"I'm intrigued! Please, Chloe, we're all ears," Mary said.

And it hit me. Chloe was going to ask Jamie to father her child! Right then! I held my breath.

"Jamie, you know I love you like a brother. But you're not really my brother. I mean, we're not related by blood. But like Sage said earlier, we are still family."

"Of course we are, sweetheart."

"Yes. So, as family, it would seem natural if this should happen. At least to me. Oh, God, this is much harder than I thought it would be."

I sat there, agonized by Chloe's discomfort. I pictured the beautiful baby the two of them would create. My little niece or nephew! "You can do this, Chloe. It's Jamie! It's okay," I blurted out.

"You know about this?" Jamie asked me.

"Yes. Well, it's come up. At least if it's what I think it is. Never mind. Just go ahead, Chloe!"

She cleared her throat. "Okay. Here goes. Jamie, I am pushing forty and I really want to have a baby. I understand now that if it's going to happen, I have to make it happen on my own. And I can't think of another person's sperm I'd rather use than yours. Would you consider having a baby with me?"

Jamie sat back in his chair. "Oh. Wow! Chloe, I am so incredibly flattered!" He stopped then, and looked at Sam, who was looking at the floor. "Listen, this is a lot to take in. I really need to think about this, is that okay?"

"Of course! I wouldn't expect an answer tonight! Take all the time you need!"

Suddenly none of us knew what to say.

"Coffee, anyone?" Mary asked.

"I'll help you, Mom," Chloe said, leaping up to follow Mary into the kitchen.

"Why didn't you give me some warning on this?" Jamie said when they were gone.

"I didn't know she was going to ask tonight! I just figured out what it was about after she started talking!"

"But why didn't you tell me after she talked about it before?"

"I…I don't know! I've been a little preoccupied!"

"You're right. I'm sorry. I'm just feeling a little blindsided! This is a huge responsibility!"

"It doesn't have to be," Chloe said softly. She was standing in the doorway. "You could just be a donor. I would be a single parent. There would be no obligation."

"Sweetheart," Jamie said, getting out of the chair and walking to her. "I just don't think I could do it that way. If I had a child I would want to be a real father. We would have to work out a joint custody arrangement. I would want to be in his or her life. I'd want my child to have good dad."

"And you would be! I was hoping you'd feel that way! I'd want us to raise the child together."

"But you see, Chloe, we'd never really be together, would we? It would always be your place or mine, your turn or mine."

"Lots of parents do it that way."

"Yes. But it's not ideal. People do it, and some do it very well, Sam for example. But it's a compromise for everyone involved. Honey, I really think an anonymous donor is the way to go if you have your heart set on being a single mom. But think about it carefully, okay? It's a really tough job."

"So your answer is no?"

Jamie held Chloe's hand in both of his. "I'm afraid so. I love you, Chloe, and if I were ever to do this with someone I know, it would be you. I just can't. If I were ever to have a child, I would want it to be with my partner. My husband. I'd want a family to come home to every day. And I think that's really what you want too."

"Of course that's what I want! It's just never going to happen! Paul made sure of that." Chloe collapsed in a heap on the floor. I rushed to her.

"Why, Sage?" she asked, crying hard now. "Why did I stay with him? Why did I allow him to manipulate me? He controlled my life and I was *grateful*. I'm such a complete fool. And now I've failed at the best chance I had to have a baby."

"This is not a failure, Chloe," Jamie said. "You asked. And I really am incredibly touched that you did. This is just not right for me. But I know a lot of great guys who would make wonderful donors, if you choose to go that direction. Just let me know. All right?"

"Are you okay?" I asked her.

She nodded, sniffling. "Mom just said you'd turn me down. She said it would be too important to you to be a good father."

As if on cue, Mary appeared. "Coffee's ready in the kitchen, everyone. Is everything okay?"

"Yes, everything is fine," Chloe said. She stood up. "But I could use a tissue."

Chloe spent the night at Mary's. I was invited, too, but Jamie asked me to come home with him, and I thought maybe Chloe needed some time alone with her mom.

In the car with Jamie and Sam, I suddenly realized how quiet Sam had been since Chloe's meltdown. "Hey," I said, tapping him on the shoulder from the backseat. "How are you doing?"

"I'm good. Relieved, actually."

"Relieved? About my answer to Chloe?" Jamie asked.

"Yeah. I really liked what you said about wanting a family. I can tell you first hand, you're right about it being hard to share a child. It's hard for all three of you, even when the parents like each other. And of course I'm glad that you don't want to be just a donor. I don't think I could ever do that, either. I would want to know my child."

"I just feel really bad for Chloe. She has always wanted to have a baby. But she really doesn't want to have one alone. She just thinks she has no choice. But she thought this would be a good compromise," I said.

"Sage, was this your idea?"

"No!"

"Sage?"

"No, really! Chloe came up with this all by herself. The very night she found out that Nicki is pregnant. Oh! I don't think you knew that."

"Nicki? As in Paul's new squeeze? Oh my God. No wonder Chloe's such a mess! The poor thing!"

"Paul's her ex?" Sam asked.

"Yeah. Paul's her ex who never wanted to have kids. Ever. Wouldn't even consider it," Jamie said.

"Oh. And now he's…"

"Yeah," Jamie and I both said.

"Oh, shit. Poor Chloe."

I sat there, feeling sorry for Chloe…and for myself, too. "You know, Jamie, you and Chloe would have made a really beautiful baby. I would have been Auntie Sage at last."

"Well, doll, you and George Clooney would make a pretty baby too. Doesn't mean it's going to happen."

"Good point."

"Speaking of Auntie Sage, however, I was wondering if you could do me a favor?" Sam said.

"Sure, what is it?"

"Would you be willing to spend a day with Savannah? This Saturday? I have to work, and Gwen is going out of town. Jamie's working, of course. I could let her spend the day with one of her friends, but I really want you two to get to know each other better. What do you think?"

"Sure, I'd be happy to. How is she doing with the whole gay dad thing?"

"Well, Gwen has been really great, giving her things to read to help explain everything. And just her acceptance has been really helpful.

Of course Savannah hears all sorts of anti-gay rhetoric at school. That must be really hard for her. But she loves your brother, and I think that's helping too."

"Who wouldn't love Jamie? I knew she'd come around. Any suggestions on what we could do on Saturday? I want her to love me, too."

"Well, she's been wanting me to take her to the zoo for a while now, and I haven't found the time. She loves animals. She's even talking about becoming a vet."

"Girl after my own heart. The zoo it is."

"Thanks, Sage."

"My pleasure, Sam." I knew I sounded confident and comfortable, but I was already nervous about being alone with a teenage girl for an entire day. At least it would keep me busy. Keeping my mind occupied seemed like a great idea.

Suddenly, a revelation: "Jamie! We completely forgot about asking Mary about Mom and everything!"

"I know, Sage. That's okay. I think the evening was eventful enough. Besides, I think I'm really okay with what I already know. There might be a puzzle piece or two missing, but I have a full enough picture. Don't you?"

I was going to say, *How can I know whether what I don't know is important, unless I find out what I don't know?* But at that moment I was too utterly exhausted even to say the words out loud.

We stopped at Chloe's long enough to feed and pet Teddy. Chloe had kindly shut Luna away in her room so that we wouldn't risk any carnage between the two. Teddy had gotten used to the change of scenery fairly quickly, for a cat, so I expected to find him curled up on the sofa or some other comfortable spot. But when I unlocked the door and walked in, I found him at the bedroom door. Luna's paw was reaching out from inside the room, and Teddy was sniffing at it. He looked at me as I approached, but went right back to his new friend.

"You always want what you can't have, huh, Ted? I know the feeling." I emptied a can of food into his dish, then squeezed passed him to check on Luna. I had to block both cats to close the door between them. Finally, I said good-bye and left them to their unrequited love.

39

As promised, I spent that Saturday with Savannah at the zoo. Of course we stopped at Starbucks. She sat at the table across from me and sipped her hot chocolate while I desperately tried to make conversation.

"So, how's school, Savannah?"

She shrugged. "It's school."

"What's your favorite subject?"

Another shrug. "Science, I guess."

"That's great! You can do anything if you're good at math and science. Do you like math too?"

Yet another shrug. "It's okay."

"Is your hot chocolate good?"

"Yeah."

Silence. But at least she didn't shrug that time. I decided to stop being so desperate and just wait for her to speak again.

We were in the car, almost to the zoo, when she finally spoke. "Sorry you got stuck with me today."

"I didn't get stuck with you, Savannah. I heard you wanted to go to the zoo, and I love the zoo! I wanted to get to know you better, so I thought this was a great opportunity. That's all. Sorry you got stuck with me. That's more accurate."

"It's okay."

Then, not another word until I paid at the gate and we walked in. I was very hopeful when she turned and touched my arm. "Uh, Sage?"

"Yes?"

"I need to use the rest room."

I waited for her outside. She walked out at last and approached, somehow not looking at me at all.

"Where would you like to start?" I asked.

Finally, an opinion: "The rainforest. I want to see the jaguar."

The jaguar enclosure had been greatly improved in recent years; now there were trees to claw, rocks to climb, even a stream. I was pleased with Savannah's interest in this magnificent creature. When he was in his cave-like resting area, like now, you could see him from mere inches away. I stared at his huge face. He squinted, panting open-mouthed.

"Isn't he beautiful?" I said, mostly to myself.

"He's amazing," Savannah answered, startling me. I looked down at her. She was enthralled. I crouched down, putting my face close to the jaguar's.

Savannah joined me. "Look at his paws," she whispered.

"He's a huge, powerful animal. Look at his teeth. They're made for ripping and tearing meat. I have mixed feelings about animals in zoos. What about you?"

She nodded. "In the wild, they have to kill prey animals to survive. Nature is rough. But that's really where they belong." Her eyes never left the jaguar. It seemed she had come to terms with necessary destruction.

We sat and stared at the big cat for a long time. Other people passed by quickly, barely acknowledging this incredible creature that had us mesmerized.

Finally, Savannah touched my arm. "Do you want to go see the ocelots?" she asked.

"Of course!" I said. We both looked back at the jaguar, saying our silent good-byes.

The ocelots, we knew, were just inside from the jaguar's enclosure, in the building dedicated to the other rainforest creatures. These cats were much smaller and shyer than their enormous cousins. There was only one on display today and Savannah and I looked for a long time before we finally saw her. She was in the far back, lying on a tree branch. Her eyes shone in the low lights.

"She's so beautiful," Savannah murmured.

"I'm guessing you're a cat lover," I said.

"I love all animals, but cats are my favorite."

"Do you have a cat?"

"I have one at my mom's. It's hard because I'm only there part of the time. I really miss her when I'm at Dad's, but I know it would be hard on her to go back and forth with me. Plus my mom is really attached to her."

"Cats do hate change. What's her name?"

"It's Lucy. Mom says she's a red tabby, but her fur is orange. It's like when people have red hair, it really looks more orangey sometimes. Anyway, Mom said she looked like Lucille Ball, because of her wild looking red hair."

I smiled. "Lucy is a great name. I have a red tabby, too."

"Really?"

"Yep. I thought he looked like a tiny little teddy bear when he was a kitten, so I named him Teddy. You know, if you get homesick for Lucy when you're with your dad, you can always come over to my place and spend time with Teddy. He'd love you, I know he would. I'm staying with a friend right now, but as soon as I have my own place again, I'll have you over to meet him."

Savannah looked at me for a long moment. Then she looked back toward the ocelot, who had jumped down from the branch and started pacing. "Thanks, Sage. I'd like that."

The two of us were very good zoo partners. We loved to linger at each enclosure, watching the animals for a good long time. Suddenly we realized we'd been there for five hours, and we were both famished.

I took Savannah to a nearby café for a late lunch. We both ordered ginger ales and studied the menu.

Savannah continued to look at the menu with great concentration after I'd already decided. "Sage?" she asked. I was sure she was about to ask which dish to order and was getting ready to recommend one, so I wasn't quite sure I'd heard correctly when she asked her question. "Why do you think my dad's gay?"

The chicken Caesar is really good, I still wanted to answer.

Deep breath. "Well, I think people are usually born gay or straight. It's just part of who they are, like having blue or brown eyes, being tall or short or having light or dark skin. Sometimes people realize it very early, and sometimes it takes a while to figure it out. Sometimes people know but they hide it from everyone else because there are other people who think there's something wrong with being gay."

"Like Dad."

"Yes. Your dad is gay. But he tried really hard not to be for a very long time. He tried to be and do what other people wanted, instead of living his life as he truly is. Telling you he is gay was a very difficult thing for him to do, Savannah. But he was trusting you to love him anyway. He's still your dad, still the same great guy he's always been. What does it matter who he dates or falls in love with?"

"Jamie's cool. But it's hard for me. Everyone at school would hate me if they knew."

"Know what? I'll bet that's not true. And you know what else? The people who are loudest about being anti-gay? Sometimes those are the people who are starting to realize it about themselves."

"You think so?"

"I do. I feel really bad for people who were raised to believe that being gay is a horrible thing. Because when one of them turns out to be gay, you know they've had to somehow come to terms with all those awful things they've heard their whole lives. Sometimes their families disown them. The people they love most tell them, 'I will no longer love you if you are gay.' Wouldn't that be terrible?"

"What was it like for Jamie?"

"It was bad. We didn't have a good father. He was pretty mean to us. Especially Jamie."

"I'm glad I have a good dad."

"You've got a great dad. You're really lucky."

"I guess so. I wasn't very nice about the gay thing at first, but I'd never stop loving my dad."

"You were surprised. You didn't know what to think. But your dad knows you love him."

"Yeah. Thanks, Sage."

"You're welcome. Hey, the chicken Caesar is really good."

When I took Savannah home to Sam's place, she hugged him before saying good-bye to me and running off to her room.

"What the…?" Sam said, grinning.

"We had a good day," I said. "She's a fabulous zoo companion, I'll tell you that. She knows her animals. Um, Sam? Ever thought about getting a cat? Then she'd have a cat in both of her homes, and she really loves cats."

Still grinning, he leaned toward me. "I'm already planning on it for her birthday."

Now I was grinning. "I love you!" I hugged him tight.

Time flew by over the next few weeks. I saw Bridget as scheduled on the first Friday after Colin's death—the day before my zoo date with Savannah—then started seeing her twice a week for a while. Jamie and Sam volunteered to clear out my apartment and turn in my notice to vacate when I realized I could not face going back. They piled my furniture into a rented storage unit. Jamie even hired someone to clean the carpet. Chloe helped me look for a new place to live. I went back to work, and Jamie and I worked hard at our accounting class. Life was busy.

Then, we got our money from Grandma Lucy's estate. Suddenly it was all real. Instead of a new apartment, I started looking for a house. And finally, finally, I turned in my two weeks' notice at work.

When Jamie had first come up with his brilliant idea for my new career, back in Idaho, I had dismissed it. The responsibility—and risk—of owning and operating a business seemed overwhelming at first. And this talent for flowers that Jamie said I had was just a hobby for me, nothing serious. But he insisted I was really good. That it was a true gift as well as something I loved. His argument was pretty compelling, and eventually Jamie's Big Idea was starting to feel as if it were my goal all along.

So I'd been diving into our accounting class with all my energy, and found that I was pretty good at that, too.

With Bridget's help, I was learning to live with the trauma of Colin's death, and my complicity in Marty's actions. Colin's faceless body was beginning to haunt me less often. I was starting to sleep again.

Now, I was wrapping things up on my last day as a social worker. It was a busy day; I wanted to leave my caseload as under control as possible for whoever would take my place. So at first I ignored my cell phone when it rang from within the depths of my purse. Then it rang again. And stopped, and rang again. Whoever was calling really wanted to talk. So I dug out the phone from my bag and looked at the number of the incoming call.

It was Marty. It hadn't even occurred to me until this very moment that he hadn't called since the morning after Colin's death. It had been almost seven weeks since then, and he hadn't been in touch at all. But then, I hadn't tried to call him, either.

"Hello? Marty?"

"Hey, Sage. Thanks for picking up. Are you at work?"

"Yeah, I'm still here. It's my last day, actually."

"Really? Good for you. I know you didn't like it much. What's next?"

"I'm starting a business. I've got a lease on a place that takes effect the first of the month. So what's next is I'll be working my butt off. But it's pretty exciting."

"What's the business?"

"A flower shop. I'm calling it Wisebuds. What do you think?"

"Very clever. Well, good luck. I'm sure you'll do well."

"What about you?"

"Oh, I'm considering a few different options. I'm not quite sure yet. I just, well, I've missed you, Sage. And I was wondering…if you're okay."

"I am. I really am. Things seem to be coming together for me. I'm...I'm moving on, I guess."

I was pretty sure we both knew what that meant.

The truth was, since that horrible night, I simply couldn't think of Marty the same way. I could vaguely remember feeling excited about our budding relationship, thinking I may have been falling in love with him. Now all those feelings seemed completely foreign, like they'd happened to someone else. Someone I barely knew.

"I'm glad things are going well for you, Sage. That's all I really wanted to know. You take care of yourself, okay?"

"You too, Marty."

"Sage? I'm sorry things turned out...well, I'm sorry things couldn't be different."

Yeah, I supposed I was sorry too, in a way. Marty was apparently not my Prince Charming after all, and I'd really had high hopes that he might be. But now, I wasn't surprised, I wasn't even disappointed, really. I felt a whole lot of nothing.

But when I started to say good-bye, a memory popped into my head. Something Marty had once said to me, something I had forgotten until just that moment. When he had first told me about confronting Colin at my apartment—the yellow rose incident—Marty had said that if Colin ever returned, he would finally get what he deserved. Well, he had returned. And Marty had followed through on that promise. Had Colin truly deserved to die the way he did?

Marty was asking, "Sage? Are you still there?"

"I'm here, Marty. Uh, listen, I need to ask you something."

"Sure, Sage. Anything."

"Are you really okay with what happened? I mean, does it bother you? Do you have trouble sleeping at night or anything?"

Marty was very quiet for a while.

"It's okay if you don't want to talk about it," I said finally.

"No, it's not that. I'm just trying to get my thoughts together. I want to say what I'm really feeling, and I'm not very good at that. The truth is, in my head I tell myself I did nothing wrong. He was a really bad guy and he was going to spend his entire life hurting people. He'd already killed one woman. How many others would there have been? But at the moment I pulled the trigger he was pretty helpless. I do see that whole scene at night, just the way it happened, over and over. It does keep me awake sometimes. And I have moments where I think, 'I really did this. I took a life. Was I justified? Did I have the right to make that decision? I just don't know. But there are fewer sleepless nights now, and those thoughts are starting to fade. I know I'll be okay. One thing I know for sure—the world is better off without him."

"I can't argue with that."

"Are *you* really okay, Sage?"

"I think so. I will be, anyway. I'm sorry this happened, though. I'm sorry that either of us ever crossed Colin's path. You were put in that position because of me, and I'm really sorry about that."

"Sage, don't ever blame yourself for anything that happened. Please promise me that you won't do that. I'm nowhere near sorry that I got to spend some time with you. That was all good, okay? No regrets."

"Still, I …"

"Please, Sage. I'm really fine. Don't ever think you were bad for me, in any way. And call me okay? Any time, day or night. If you need to talk, or if you, well, if you change your mind about anything, I'll be there. You have my number, but let me give you one more. If something happens, if I change my phone number, you can always call this number. It's Dad and Brenda's home number. Write this one down, okay?"

I thought about just pretending to write it down, but it seemed I just couldn't do that to Marty. "Let me grab a pen," I said, and I took down the number. I even wrote 'Marty's Parents' beside it. "Got it. Thanks."

We said good-bye and still I didn't know what to feel. I did think Marty would have been better off if he had never known me. And I believed that, ultimately, Colin had ruined what could have been my last big romance. Even so, it wasn't sadness I felt exactly. No, it was more like a gaping hole had appeared inside me where all my emotions used to be.

Chloe, too, seemed fairly zombie-like since the night at Mary's. She was pleasant, a perfect roommate in fact, as I continued the search for my new home. But something was a little off. She was just a bit distant.

I tried to talk to her about it. "What's wrong?"

"Huh? Nothing, why?"

"Well, you had a big disappointment, and you seem to be feeling a little down. Are you?"

"No, not at all. I'm concerned about finding a teaching job, that's all. I should have more experience by now, and I don't because I pissed away fourteen years. But otherwise I'm right as rain. Really. Stop worrying about me."

"I'll try."

And I did try, but a tiny voice told me to keep an eye on my friend.

That weekend I found my house. It was a brand new rambler, just finished, but in an older neighborhood on an oversized lot. I was thrilled not to be inheriting anyone else's mistakes, or old plumbing or electrical nightmares. Best of all, I could see the waters of Puget Sound from most of my windows, especially if I stood on my toes.

It was the last open house Chloe and I went through that Sunday. I knew it was mine the moment we walked in. To the right, I saw a gas fireplace with a stone mantle in the living room. Beyond the living room was a small dining room, and beyond that was a huge kitchen and family room area. The bedrooms were down the hall; two were fairly small, but the master bedroom was enormous, with its own spa-like bathroom, complete with stone floor. It wasn't a huge house, but it was huge for me, and its back yard was adorable, with a little stone patio and a flowerbed already planted with bulbs. Tall red cannas stood tall and proud against the fence.

And the price was low enough that I could pay cash and have no mortgage payment at all, thanks to Grandma Lucy.

The only downside that day was Chloe's lack of enthusiasm. "Don't you like it?" I asked.

"Yeah, I like it," she said. "It's nice."

"You should get a house, too, Chloe. You can afford it, with Paul's payoff, right?"

"Yeah, I guess. I don't know if I want a house, though. Too much work." She sighed.

"Well, this one will be like a second home to you. You can be here as much as you want! It's going to be great!"

"Yeah." She smiled a little. "I'm happy for you, Sage." She turned and walked away from me a few steps.

"Uh huh. You're thrilled, I can tell."

She spun around. "Give me a break, Sage! I'm just a little depressed. I've come to realize that none of my hopes or dreams for my life have or ever will come to pass. Ever! Nothing turned out the way I wanted it to. I think I'm entitled to a little depression, don't you?"

"Yes, I suppose it makes sense that you are depressed. But that doesn't mean it's healthy. Maybe you should see someone. Maybe you need medication. You should find out."

"None of this is going to change. I know what a therapist would say. I have to accept all this and move on. Make lemonade out of lemons, blah, blah, blah."

"I think if you just get on with your life, things will feel different very quickly. You're going to teach! You've always wanted to do that. You'll meet new people, try new things. It's going to get better. Trust me."

"Trust you, Sage? Trust that you know how to handle tough times? You can't even decide on a career, and you're thirty-seven! You worry about Jamie, you worry about me, you interfere in our lives, and then merrily go about finding the most abusive boyfriend you can find. You think your life is coming together now that you can finally afford to buy a house for the first time, and it's because your grandmother died and left you the money! Which, by the way is kind of a slap in my mother's face. Why didn't your beloved Grandma Lucy bother leaving anything to Mom? Mom took you and Jamie in and made huge sacrifices in the process. Did you ever think of that? She never saw a dime from anyone for your support. Now overnight you have all the money in the world? Maybe you should think about having a little gratitude for what's been done for you! Trust you? I don't even like you half the time!"

I was stunned. Chloe had never spoken to me like that before; I couldn't even remember her getting angry with me. "How long have you felt this way? How long have you been hating me in silence?"

"I don't hate you, Sage, I just…"

"You just don't like me, respect me, or trust me. Sounds an awful lot like hate to me!" More people were milling through the house now, trying to ignore our conversation. "Look, let's just go. I'll talk to the real estate agent and then we'll go get my stuff. I'll stay at Jamie's until I can move into the house."

"Sage, I'm sorry…"

I went to the agent and told her I wanted to put in a cash offer on the house. We made an appointment for the following day, then Chloe and I drove to her apartment in silence. I collected my belongings and my cat and showed up at Jamie's unannounced.

~40~

Things went well over the next few weeks. My offer on the house was accepted and because it was brand new and vacant, I took possession almost immediately; I started moving in within a week. I went shopping for a few odds and ends; I even bought myself a new queen-sized bed and put the old twin in my brand new guest room.

It was hard not to think of Chloe when I looked in that room.

It was hard, in fact, not to think of Chloe, period.

Bridget and I still met each Friday—I was back to just one session per week. She was concerned about my lack of emotion around Colin's death, the end of my relationship with Marty and my falling out with Chloe.

"Well, I don't know what to tell you. Life is good! I'm living in my own house for the first time in my life. I'm about to start a brand new career and I'll be my own boss. I'm taking control! I'm in charge! Why should I mope around about the bad things that have happened? Why shouldn't I celebrate the good?"

"Yes, that's true. You've accomplished some wonderful things, Sage. Things you should be proud of. But I don't exactly see you turning cartwheels. I don't see you displaying much emotion of any kind. So you tell me, what exactly are you feeling?"

"I, uh, well…Yeah, okay, I'm feeling really happy for Jamie. He and Sam are going strong. Sam's daughter loves Jamie and she seems to like me as well. Jamie has a brand new family, and he's really happy! I'm thrilled with my house. I have a view of the water, did I tell you that?"

"Yes, you mentioned it once or twice."

"Yeah, well, it's beautiful! I love it! I've bought some new art and I have a really comfortable new bed. Teddy has adjusted well."

"Those are all reasons to be happy."

"Yes, they are! And I am happy! Sure, it would be nice if the person I thought was my best friend actually was my best friend. Sure, it would be great if she could share all this with me. It would be tremendous if she actually cared about me at all. But no, it seems that was all a big fat lie and she's just been putting up with me all these years because she felt obligated! Or sorry for me! And now she thinks I don't even deserve the money my grandmother left me!"

"Before this happened, you mentioned that you thought Chloe was depressed. Maybe she simply took some things out on you. Maybe she has had some frustrations with you over the years. But that doesn't mean she doesn't love you. It must have been very hard for her to watch you in unhealthy relationships. She must have been terrified for you."

And I saw it, suddenly. I saw everything from Chloe's perspective. All she ever heard from me was negative crap about Paul, or about my many worries about Jamie. How ridiculous I must have seemed, spouting off about their problems while I sat there with bruises on my face. How many times had she wanted to shake some sense into me? How had she held herself back?

And she was right about something else, too. I owed everything to Mary. She had taken us in without any expectations or conditions. She had truly cared for us simply out of kindness. I should have thought to offer her some of Grandma Lucy's money. Why hadn't it occurred to me?

Once again it seemed that Bridget had read my mind. "As far as the money is concerned, perhaps Chloe was really feeling a little guilty about taking Paul's money, and she took it out on you."

"Why should she feel guilty about that? He forced her to abandon her career!"

"I know, I know. But she sounds like someone who wants to be self-reliant. Accepting help from someone would not be her first choice. She felt she had no other recourse. You said she could have gotten a lot more from him if she'd pushed for it. She didn't. That tells me she really would have preferred not to take anything at all."

It was true, I could feel it. I nodded. "She would have loved to be able to tell him that she didn't need his help."

"And it's not like teachers make a fortune. She's looking at a tough time ahead of her. She feels betrayed, used and tossed aside. And you, who she watched making bad choices and floundering all that time, now seem to have it made financially. Of course she would feel a pang of envy, even resentment. But instead of keeping her mouth shut until it passed, she felt so miserable that she lashed out at one of the people she loves most."

"I think you're right," I whispered. Tears filled my eyes, blinding me for a moment. "I hope she can forgive me."

"Oh, Sage. Of course she'll forgive you. I'm sure she already has. You should find out."

Once the tears started, though, they just didn't stop. It wasn't just for Chloe, now. I was mourning the death of my embryonic love for Marty. Colin's faceless body was falling before my eyes again, and Marty was holding the gun that had killed him. That gun had killed our budding romance at the same time. Had it killed a part of Marty's soul, too? I mourned it all, wept for it all.

Would Colin have eventually killed me? Everyone in my life seemed to think it was a real possibility. I thought of him at my door, threatening Marty and me. *It all could have ended so differently.* I shuddered, thinking of what might have happened. Colin could have killed Marty. I would have done everything in my power to prevent that outcome. The thought of Marty's life ending that way—trying to protect me—that just felt so incredibly wrong. Yet he had put himself between Colin and me. He had risked his life for me.

And then it hit me.

I knew that I would have done the same for Marty. I would have leaped in front of him, taken a bullet meant for him, if it had come to that. I would have killed Colin to protect Marty. I would have killed Colin trying to protect myself.

And what if Marty had made a different decision? If Colin had lived, would he have left me alone? Or would he have come after me, again and again?

Had Marty actually saved my life? And the lives of other women? It was impossible to know. All I did know was that he had made a decision he would have to live with forever. He had done that for me. In effect, he had taken a bullet to protect me.

I let out a long breath and wiped my tears away.

"Sage? What is it?" Bridget asked.

"I have to forgive Marty."

"Forgive Marty. For killing Colin?"

"Yes. But also for putting it all on the line for me. I think it scared me that he was willing to risk everything for me."

"And now?"

"Now I know I would have done the same for him. And I understand that Marty looked beyond the circumstances of the moment. He knew who Colin really was. We'll never know how many people Marty saved when he killed Colin. But we know that Colin was a chronic abuser. Seven years in country club prison probably wouldn't have changed his character. It might have made him even more dangerous. I know that's all speculation, but I also know that Marty was not the bad guy in all this."

"I think these are all really good observations, Sage. I think you're seeing things more objectively now. Marty made a choice that most of us will never be faced with, thank goodness."

"Yes. And I very easily could have been the one to make that choice. And I don't think it would have taken Marty so long to forgive me."

Suddenly there were a lot of people I needed to see. Chloe was first on the list. She sounded so relieved when I rang her buzzer. She ran down the stairs to meet me, grabbed me and hugged me tight.

"Oh, Sagey. I've picked up the phone to call you a thousand times. I feel so bad about all those awful things I said. Please forgive me?"

"I'm sorry, too, Chloe. I should have been more understanding. And I shouldn't have been such an idiot all these years."

"You're not an idiot. You're a survivor. I was just feeling sorry for myself and I got so mean! You have nothing to be sorry about. You tried to tell me time and again that Paul was a jerk. Maybe he wasn't abusive physically, but I allowed him to control my life. You were right about him. He wasn't so different from Colin."

We had dinner together that night at my new house. We shared a bottle of wine and got caught up on each other's news. She stayed overnight, the first person to sleep in my guest room after all.

The next day I made arrangements to meet Mary and Jamie for lunch. I wanted to express my gratitude for all she had done for us, and I thought we would ask some long overdue questions at the same time.

"Mary, you know we love you, right?" I asked when we were seated.

"Of course, honey. I love you both, too. Like you're my own."

"But we want you to know that we understand everything you've done for us. All the sacrifices you made, all the support you've given us. And I think that Grandma Lucy should have left you something out of her estate for all that you've provided for us. Jamie and I have talked about it and we think that you should get the proceeds from the sale of Lucy's house."

Mary stared at our faces, one at a time. "You're serious. My goodness." She smiled then, shaking her head. "Okay, listen up. I'm only going to say this once. Lucy offered me money and I told her the same thing. I will never take a penny for doing what was simply the right thing to do. You were children. Precious, wonderful children, who needed to be protected and loved. The truth is, I should have stepped in long before I did. If I had, you would have been spared a lot of suffering. I have to live with that knowledge, and it's not easy sometimes. If I did a decent job of taking care of you once you came to live with us, then that is my compensation right there. Knowing that I did, ultimately, do the right thing. Yes, money was tight then; it's not now. I'm doing quite well for myself, and I think that may be, in part, a tiny bit of good karma. Oh, my darlings. Don't ever think you owe me anything. Promise me?"

She reached across the table and the three of us held tight to each other's hands.

Soon we were munching on salads and laughing over shared memories. We were having such a good time that I wasn't sure I wanted to ask about anything unhappy. So Jamie, after all, was the one to venture forth.

"Mary, what exactly happened with our parents? How did our father become such a monster, and why did our mother die the way she did?"

Mary's smile disappeared. She took a deep breath and put her fork down. "Well, I was honestly beginning to think you'd never ask. Brace yourselves, my darlings. This may not be the story you're expecting."

Jamie and I looked at each other, then back to Mary as she began to tell us what we'd waited so long to hear.

"When your parents moved in down the block, I was thrilled. We clicked immediately, the three of us. We were over at each other's houses all the time. Your mother—Georgia." Mary stopped and smiled at the name. "She was stunning. And brilliant! She was good at whatever she tried. We were both trying to find our voices as artists, but while I struggled in fits and starts along the way, everything came so easily to Georgia. But she became bored easily. She just couldn't seem to stay with any one thing very long.

"It was a crazy time back then. We experimented with drugs, like a lot of people, but your father was always the one I thought might have a problem, not Georgia. He always wanted to push the limits on everything. Whatever the drug of choice was for the evening, he would take more, mix it with other things, or drink to excess. He could be counted on either to pass out at eight o'clock or to stay up all night long with an energy so frenetic it frightened us.

"Eventually, Georgia and I both decided we'd had enough of that kind of life. We both said we wanted to grow up, to move on. I was seeing Chloe's dad at the time, and Georgia and I found out we were pregnant at about the same time. We were going to be mothers together! We were so happy, shopping for baby clothes and furniture.

"Then Chloe's dad left. He decided he just wasn't ready to be a father. I almost lost Chloe during that time, I was so distraught. Georgia was there for me, day and night. Georgia was the best friend I'd ever had. She helped me start my business. It was because of her that I had the courage to trust my own talent, my own ability to provide for my child. When our babies were born—you and Chloe, Sage, best friends from the day you first saw each other—Georgia and I grew even closer.

"Before long, Georgia grew restless again. She was always seeking out excitement, something new. She would read a book and adopt its philosophy completely, without question. Until the next book came along with a completely different point of view. Then she would wholeheartedly believe that was the ultimate truth. And then something else would come along and she would change her mind again, completely and overnight. It would be an understatement to say that she had a short attention span. She flitted from one hobby to the next, from one project to the next, from one idea to the next. Whatever she was involved with at the moment had her complete focus. Obsession, really. To the exclusion of everything else.

"When Jamie came along, she tried again to make motherhood her priority. She read every book about parenting she could find. She utterly personified the earth mother identity. You two were never out of her sight. Her patience was limitless. But only for a while. And then she crashed.

"When Georgia was feeling well, she was the best at whatever she was doing. But when she was depressed, she was…well, she just wasn't there. Literally. You could look into her eyes and see nothing. During those times, she believed in nothing. She hated herself, her life, every piece of art she'd ever created. I can't tell you how many paintings she destroyed over the years. That painting you asked me about, Sage? Field of Flowers? Your mother painted that. It was always my favorite, and I caught her one day with a knife in her hand, ready to rip it to shreds. Somehow I convinced her to let me take it. There was pottery, so many beautiful pieces smashed against a wall. Worst of all were the times when she was completely immobilized.

"When you were just a couple of years old, Jamie, Georgia started having affairs. It seemed she didn't care who she got involved with. She just wanted the attention, the thrill of a new relationship. At first she would tell me about them. There was this ongoing saga of the greatest man in the world, until he wasn't, and then she was on to the next one. Often, she would forget to pick you up at school, Sage, or she would drop you both off with me and leave for hours.

"It didn't take long for Craig to figure out what was going on. He was heartbroken at first, then angry. Really angry. That's when he started getting physical with her. At times he would come to me in tears, begging me to give him some magic formula to win her back. To transform her into the person she'd once been.

"Finally, I told Georgia I couldn't be her friend anymore. I told her I couldn't sit by and watch her ruin her own life, let alone the lives of her children. I flat out told her to make a decision, either to stay with Craig and work on their marriage, or leave and find a new life that would make her happy. I told her that if she were going to be a mother, she had to be a good one. Otherwise, I told her, she should leave you both behind because you would have a better life without her.

"I have regretted saying that so many times. I didn't really believe she could actually leave you. But that's exactly what happened. She packed her bags and left with her newest love. She came over one more time, to say goodbye to me. She told me that I was right, that she had to find a better life for herself. She wasn't cut out to be a mother, she said. She was destined for greatness. She was headed to California, to live among painters, sculptors and writers. She would grow as an artist, deepen her talent. Maybe she would pursue acting, because surely she was blessed with that face for a reason! She said she would visit her children with tales of her grand life. They would be proud of her and understand why she'd had to leave.

"I told her that she would regret this decision, but she laughed and said I just didn't understand, because I was not among the truly gifted. And then she was gone.

"After she left, your dad began to spend a lot of time with me. We would talk for hours. He wanted to go through every detail of their life together, picking it apart, analyzing every moment, hoping, I suppose, that eventually he would come upon some magical answer to explain all that had gone wrong. He so wanted to fix everything. To bring her home and make a life with her again.

"That's when he really started to drink all the time. The more he drank, the more he opened up to me. One night, your dad told me some things about his past. Horrible things."

Mary paused and took a sip of wine. She looked at each of us, slowly, directly, her eyes moist. Jamie held my hand under the table.

"How much do you know about your dad's family?" Mary asked at last.

We looked at each other. "Nothing," I said. "I remember once he said he had a brother who had died really young, but he didn't give us any details. And we met his sisters a couple of times. Both his parents were already dead when we were born. That's all I know."

Mary shook her head slowly. "No. His parents were still alive when I was your father's friend. He just had no contact with them. You see, your dad and his brother were terribly abused. Both of his parents routinely beat the boys. They called it whipping, but it was worse. He showed me scars that went the full length of his back. The girls were spared the beatings but they endured other kinds of abuse. The family was very poor, but their parents would have dinner and let the kids go hungry, telling them they didn't deserve to eat. For further punishment, they would lock the boys in a tiny closet for hours on end, then beat them for crying or having accidents. Your father often took the blame for things his younger brother had done, trying to protect him. But their parents would usually punish them both anyway."

Here Mary stopped again. She looked down at the table and cleared her throat. "When Craig was about ten, his father began to abuse him sexually. He told me it only happened a few times. The last time, Craig fought back. At school, he had traded a precious sandwich for a pocketknife and kept it hidden under his pillow, waiting for the next time his father came into his room at night. It was dark, and he couldn't see very well, but he plunged that little knife into whatever part of his father he could reach. It turned out to be his leg, but the pain and surprise stopped the bastard in his tracks. Craig ran out of his room, grabbed his brother who was already in the hallway, and the two of them ran as fast as they could to the nearest police station, because a teacher had once told him that the police could always be trusted. A kind officer took them to his own home that night. Apparently there had been a lot of rumors floating through town, and when Craig said his parents hurt them the police officer knew it was true. Craig and his brother ended up in a foster home, but their parents fought for custody and won. After only a few months, they were returned home. Craig's father never visited his room at night again, but the beatings never stopped.

"One night, Craig's little brother Charlie got caught taking food from a cupboard. Their mother began hitting him with a broom handle. Craig said she just kept screaming and swinging that broom. Charlie was on the floor and she kept hitting him and hitting him. When she stopped, Charlie wasn't moving. Craig ran to him, and he could see that Charlie wasn't breathing. He was gone. Craig said his mother was actually upset. She cried. She and their father put Charlie in the car and drove him to the hospital. They made Craig and the girls go with them, even though they didn't want to. They told the people in the emergency room that Charlie had fallen down a flight of stairs.

"Then a miracle happened. No one believed their story. They were arrested and once again Craig was placed in foster care. This time the girls went with him. He never saw his parents again. He received a letter from his father once, telling him that he had taken the blame for Charlie's death so that his mother wouldn't have to go to prison. He wanted Craig to come visit him. Of course that didn't happen.

"After he told me about his childhood, your dad became very distant. Every time I did see him he was drunk. Gradually, drinking took over his life. The more he drank, the meaner he got. Before my eyes, he seemed to be transforming into the kind of monster his own parents had been. It was horrifying. I tried to talk to him about it, to convince him that he would never be able to live with himself if he kept inflicting pain on his babies. I know, intellectually, that many abused children become abusers as adults, but in my heart I simply don't understand how that can happen. How can that precious, perfect little child end up becoming so cruel himself? It makes no sense.

"I know you wanted to know about your mother, but the real tragedy here is your father's story. I do believe your mother loved you both very much. I just think she didn't know how to be a mother. She thought it was some kind of magical ability that a person either had or didn't. The truth of it, the mundane aspects of parenthood, the routine, the monotony...that's what she couldn't handle. She thought that if being a mother didn't feel profound and mystical every minute of every day, then she was somehow failing at it.

"I also think that because she was so talented, so larger-than-life, she expected more from herself than any human being has a right to. She could never live up to her own expectations, and she punished herself endlessly. But she punished your dad, too. She knew about his past and when she was at her worst, she tormented him about it. She called him weak. She called him a...you know. A fag. She knew Craig was a victim of his father's brutality but at times the most vile things came out of her mouth. She could be so vicious sometimes."

Jamie squeezed my hand. I closed my eyes. Visions of my father came then. The usual memories of beatings, his loud angry voice, and then—something new. I saw him cowering in a corner, his face covering his eyes as he wept. "I'm so, so, sorry," he said, over and over. And I remembered. That was how I found him sometimes, when the storms were over and all was quiet in the house. I would tiptoe down to test the waters and there he would be, this regretful stranger. He would tell me to bring Jamie downstairs. My father would wipe his eyes and serve us dinner and we would pretend, for a little while, that we were a family.

Yes. Those moments happened, too.

When I opened my eyes, Jamie was watching me. Mary just stared at the table.

It was Jamie who finally spoke. "So our mother was a narcissist who tormented a survivor of unfathomable abuse. I thought she was the innocent one in all of this! And she walked away from her children because we were too boring for her? And our father started beating us, why? Because that's what he'd learned as a child, and he hated his life after our mother left? I mean, it was our fault that she left, right?"

"Your father was responsible for his own actions. She didn't cause that. The two of them, Georgia and Craig—" Mary shook her head. "They were drawn to the best in each other but in the end they nearly destroyed all those things. Ultimately, they personified their own worst fears about themselves. Georgia continued down that ugly path alone. Your father, well, it looks as if he may have turned things around for himself." She took a deep breath before continuing. "I heard from him a few days ago."

"What?" Jamie and I both said.

"He called. He asked if I'd spoken to you, if I'd heard his news. I told him I had, along with a rumor that he was now non-violent and completely sober. He assured me that was the case. He also asked if I might try to persuade you both to attend his wedding. He invited Chloe and me as well." There was another long pause. "I think I might go."

"Why?" I asked.

She shrugged. "We were friends once, good friends. I liked Craig before—well, before everything changed. Don't get me wrong, I hate everything he's done, all the pain he's inflicted. The torture he put you two through..." She shuddered. "I have a hard time forgiving anyone who hurts a child. Maybe I just need to see for myself that he's changed. Part of the reason I didn't take you away from him sooner was that I was waiting for the Craig I knew to return. I've always felt awful that your suffering was prolonged because of my poor judgment. It would help to know that he'd always had the ability to become a good person again. And it seems to mean a lot to him that you two believe that he's changed. So, if you can't bring yourselves to see him, I'm willing to see him for you. Just a thought. I haven't quite decided yet."

Jamie leaned back in his chair. "You know, I have always tried to grant my parents the benefit of the doubt. Poor Dad was an alcoholic. Poor Mom was abused by him and forced to leave. How sad that she never got to rescue her children. But she never would have! She was off on another grand adventure! She couldn't have cared less about us. That's the truth."

"Your parents were deeply flawed, Jamie. But they weren't monsters. Your father suffered horrible cruelty and sadly, became abusive himself. But now he may have turned his life around. He's reaching out to you. Maybe you need to hear what he has to say."

Neither Jamie nor I had much to say for the rest of our time together that day. I didn't know what to feel. Suddenly my mother was no longer blameless. She had left us behind, deliberately, consciously, telling herself she wasn't meant to be a mother. But she was a mother. She couldn't undo that. We had been conceived, carried in her womb and born. For a while she had wanted to be a loving, nurturing mother. For a while.

And our father. Mary had said he wasn't a monster. But after my mother left he became pretty monstrous. Why? Couldn't he love us without her there? And all those times he told me that my mother never wanted me: was that the truth?

I reflected on what an ugly thing truth can be. But my father did not seem like a monster now. He seemed...human. What he had gone through as a child...well, who couldn't sympathize with that? And yes, he had victimized innocent children. His own children. Was that in itself unforgiveable, or, if he had truly changed, did he deserve a second chance?

When I got home, I called Chloe and filled her in. "Did you know any of this? Do you remember anything?"

"No. Mom never said anything negative about Georgia. Only that she was so beautiful. And how sad it was that her talent had been wasted."

"Your mom said she might go to Dad's wedding."

"Really?"

"Yeah, and I think I understand her reasons. She said you were invited, too. Do you think you might go?"

"I don't know. I guess I might if Mom doesn't want to go alone. Would you be okay with that?"

"Of course. Your mom would only go for us, to make sure he's really changed. And I wouldn't want her to go alone. But you know what? It was strange, talking to your mom about this. I felt something I never imagined I could feel."

"Really? What?"

"Sympathy for my father. If he really has turned things around, he must feel so terrible for everything he's done. He must need us to hear him out. Maybe forgive him, if we can."

Chloe was silent for a long time. "Are you there?" I asked.

"Yeah. I never thought you'd ever be able to say anything like that. Hey, Sage?"

"Yeah?"

"You're a really great person, you know."

~42~

"How are you feeling about Mary's revelations?" Bridget asked. I had just told her the whole story.

"I don't know. I've had new memories of my dad lately. Times when he apologized for hurting us. I remembered him crying before, but now I'm remembering that he actually tried to act normal. Kind, even. He asked how our day was at school. He washed our wounds and put bandages on them. Put ice bags on our bruises. Kissed us goodnight."

"Sounds like he was actually gentle during those times."

"Yes, he was. I know in my heart he was truly sorry at times. But then it would be a new day, a bad day, and he would be filled with so much rage. He would turn back into the monster."

"So you never knew which father would appear."

"No, but I had to prepare for the worst, just in case."

"Sage, I want you to know that it's truly miraculous that you have developed any trust at all. And yet you have a really solid group of people around you. You must acknowledge what an accomplishment that is for you! You are so much braver than you know. So these new memories about your father, have they changed the way you feel about him?"

"I think so. I mean, I feel everything I've always felt about him, but now it's more complicated."

"How so?"

"Now I feel sad for him too. I am so sorry for everything he went through as a child." Chloe had complimented me for finally conjuring up some sympathy for my father. But since then, a whole new wave of rage had washed over me. Did that mean I wasn't such an admirable person after all?

I continued. "Still, in a way I'm even angrier that he allowed himself to become an abusive parent. Knowing what it's like to be beaten by someone who is supposed to love you! By the person whose job it should be to protect you! But instead of condemning what his parents did and resolving to be a good father, he became just like them! How dare he! What is that, laziness at its worst? Just do what you know? Even when it's the sadistic torture of innocent children? How can he ever look at himself in a mirror? How could he have the gall to tell me he's forgiven himself?"

Bridget leaned forward and touched my knee. "Sage, you're shouting. It's okay, but I wanted you to be aware."

I caught my breath. Not only had I been shouting, there were tears on my face. I closed my eyes. "How could he have those moments of clarity, when he felt so horrible about what he'd done, then let it happen again? Were we such terrible kids? Were we so unlovable?"

"I think it's much more likely that *he* felt unlovable."

"Yeah. Well. He was."

"And now it's possible that he may have conquered the demons that made him that way. Have you been in touch with your dad since his first appearance?"

"No, but he called Mary to invite her and Chloe to the wedding. He wanted her to talk us into going, too. She wouldn't do that, of course, but she and Chloe are thinking about going."

"Really?"

I nodded. "Mary wants to know for herself that Dad really has changed. She wants to know that she wasn't completely stupid for believing he could. And I think she wants to be able to tell Jamie and me that he really is a new man. Or the man he once was, I guess."

"And that he loves you both, I would think."

"Yes, I'm sure that's a big part of it."

"What would that mean to you?"

"I don't know. I've hated him for so long. It always felt good to me, that hatred. I never wanted to see him as anything other than the devil, you know? He was pure evil in my mind. There were no explanations for his behavior that ever would have been good enough. And the whole homophobic thing. His way of thinking was wrong, and it led him to do horrible things. Jamie has always said that just having to live with what he'd done was punishment enough for our father, but I never bought into that. As far as I was concerned, Dad could suffer disease, poverty and pestilence for the rest of his life and it still wouldn't be enough."

"And you're still angry."

"I'm angry all over again! I'd always thought that my mom was innocent in all this. That she was a victim too. But that's not true! She was self-centered and crazy! She abandoned Jamie and me! And she was so cruel to my father. She said such deliberately vicious things. She used his father's abuse against him, cutting him to the quick! Now I don't know which of my parents to hate more."

Bridget tucked her legs under her and looked down for a moment. "Sage, everything you're feeling is justified. You've been hit with a lot of new information. You've had a set of beliefs about your parents and your childhood that felt completely solid. Those beliefs formed a seemingly unshakable foundation that you've built your entire life on. Now it's all in question. Maybe your father was never a truly evil man. Maybe he was a survivor who went through a horrific time in his life and dealt with it really badly. Yes, for a time he became the worst version of himself, and you and Jamie suffered terribly as a result. But you all somehow survived. And it's possible that he found a way back to being a good person. Your mom wasn't so fortunate. We'll never know if she would have eventually gotten the help she needed. Maybe not. Maybe she was the real villain here. We just don't know. But she was your Grandma Lucy's daughter, so it's possible that there was a lot of goodness inside her somewhere."

I let out a long breath. "I don't know what to think."

"I know. Take some time. I have a suggestion. As you process all this, write down what you think and feel, especially when you're having really strong emotions. We'll go through it next week."

And so I wrote. Pages and pages of vile, ugly words expressing all the rage and hatred I could summon. I named all of my tormentors, described every revenge fantasy I could imagine. I screamed. I cried. So many tears, I was sure they were all gone. And yet there were more.

At work I barely functioned. I avoided eye contact, hid from people who might want to talk, saving my words for the journal.

When the week ended, I climbed the stairs to Bridget's office profoundly exhausted.

"Did you keep a journal this week?" she asked.

"Yes."

"How was that?"

I looked at her and tried to form an answer that would make sense. Three times, I opened my mouth to say something and just closed it again.

"Looks like it might have been a difficult process for you?" she asked.

"Yes."

"Exhausting?"

"Yes."

"Then you didn't hold back. You wrote down everything you felt?"

"Yes."

"Were you able to come to any conclusions? Any clarity?"

"I don't know. I don't feel much of anything right now."

"Are you still angry?"

"No. I…No."

"Did you bring what you wrote?"

I gave her the journal and watched as she leafed through it. She nodded a few times, even smiled once or twice.

"You did a great job, Sage. This must have been tough for you. No wonder you're so spent! Ok. We don't have to talk about this today. You need to take care of yourself over the next few days. Do whatever it will take to recharge your batteries. Then, when you start to feel more like yourself again, sit down and read this. The whole thing. Next time we meet, we'll spend the whole session on the journal. Deal?"

So I left the evil diary alone for a few days. I eyed it suspiciously from across the room a couple of times but managed to avoid it. And, slowly, my energy did return. My brain seemed not quite so addled. So when I got home on Wednesday, I sat down with a cup of tea and read all the words I'd written the week before.

My eyes scanned the ugliness I'd poured out and an odd thing happened: I became even calmer. It all seemed slightly foreign. Ancient. As though all the trauma, the rage, the endless pain had happened to someone else.

When I closed the book, I sat for a while, finishing my tea and breathing. I asked myself what I was feeling, and the answer came with brightness and clarity. Compassion. Yes, I felt the sorrow for myself, but I could also see everyone else's perspective. My father, who had gone through such suffering as a child. He'd been an innocent victim too. Sadly, it took a while for him to find his way and become whole again. Even sadder, Jamie and I became his victims before he fully recovered. And my mother: had she been mentally ill? Would there have been other possibilities for her if she'd been treated? Would she have stayed with us? Would she have survived?

I decided that, ultimately, all the pain of the past could be left behind. Maybe my father did deserve to prove himself. And maybe I could stop hating him. *And myself.* The thought just appeared in my head, a surprise at first. I nodded. It fit.

When I took all these revelations to Bridget two days later, she was not at all surprised.

"You have come a long way, Sage. So what happens next?"

"I don't know, really. Mary thinks my father really wants us to forgive him. She believes it's important to him to see his new life, his new…self, I guess. And I'm starting to hope that could happen."

Bridget cleared her throat. "Listen: I have a suggestion. You and Jamie could go to the wedding with Mary and Chloe."

"No, no, no, I'm not saying I'm ready for anything like that!"

"I know, but think about it. This would be a chance to see him safely, in a crowd. You would see him at his best, with people who know and care about him. Being there would give you a little window into who he is now. Even if you never see him again, it might help you say good-bye to him in a healthy way. Going to the wedding may help you move on."

Bridget's idea didn't seem, well, crazy to me. It seemed like a rational move.

I had options. I could go to the wedding or not. I could see my father or not. Going to the wedding could be a new beginning or a graceful end. It was all up to me.

But now something else occurred to me, and I needed one of Bridget's patented reality checks. "What would you think if I asked my father if Sam can come to the wedding too?"

"Ah. A character test?"

"Sort of. But Sam is so important to us now. He's family."

Bridget nodded. "I understand. His absence at the wedding would be a glaring omission for you, and proof that your father hasn't changed as much as he claims."

"Yes! Exactly!"

"But Sage, this is your father's wedding, not yours, not Jamie's. Your father is not obligated to invite anyone he's not comfortable with. And his estranged son's gay partner might well fall into that category."

I sighed. "So you think I shouldn't ask?"

Bridget smiled. "I wouldn't say that. Ask if you feel that strongly about it. Just maybe don't go into attack mode if he doesn't respond the way you want him to. Maybe just be prepared for him to say no, and to respect that decision. Don't make it a condition for you or Jamie to go, that's all I'm saying. Listen: if you decide to go to the wedding, you need to think carefully about your reasons. I think you're ready, but you need to feel ready. So take some time and think it through."

But I was already thinking, already wondering what Jamie would say about the idea.

"Did you hear me? Jamie?"

I'd arranged to meet Jamie and Sam for dinner that night, and now I was waiting to hear Jamie's thoughts on my newfound empathy with our father.

He stared at me. "You're actually thinking about going to the wedding?" he finally said.

"I don't know. Maybe. It made sense when Bridget suggested it."

Jamie leaned back in his chair and looked at Sam, then shook his head and leaned forward again. "I don't know what to think, Sage. All this time I've been wishing you could let go a little. Just not hate him quite so much. I was afraid the anger was toxic for you. But this seems like such a quick turnaround! I know we have more information now. We know that he was horribly abused. And I'm sorry about all of that. But he became an abuser. There is no excuse for that. He was an adult. He had choices, and he chose to beat his children. To scream at them, call them names. Yes, his parents were monsters, but he didn't have to be. And yet he was. For a long time. I still have scars, Sage. And you! You kept allowing people to abuse you. It kept getting worse until you found Colin, the worst of all. I easily could have lost you, Sage."

I took a deep breath. "I understand everything you're saying. I felt all this stuff too. But Bridget had me write everything down and that helped me, I don't know, work through it faster. I'm not saying that I think our father is the greatest guy in the world. I'm just saying he might not be the worst. And maybe he deserves a chance to prove to us that he's changed. That's all. And the wedding would be a safe place to check it out. But I don't want to go without you."

"I don't know, Sage. I don't think I could go there and smile and say congratulations when I'm actually seething inside."

"Why has it taken you so long to be angry? Why now?" I asked. He shrugged. "I honestly don't know."

"Jamieson," Sam said. "You were a little boy when your father beat you. You couldn't get angry with him then, it was too dangerous. And you just wanted your daddy to love you. So you made excuses for him. You forgave him, over and over. It's taken you this long to get pissed off because now it's safe. He can't hurt you anymore. It's almost like Sage was angry *for* you! She felt the things that you couldn't. Now she's moving on. Hey, I think it's great that you're mad at your dad. It shows you are human, after all. However," he continued, nodding toward me, "I also think it's pretty fabulous that Sage is able to feel a little compassion for the man after all this time. Isn't that what you've always wanted for her?"

Jamie looked at me. "Guess I need to be careful what I wish for, huh?"

I shook my head. "No. You were right. You told me I didn't have to carry around all that anger, and that it would be healthier for me if I could let it go. Well, I'm nowhere near all the way there yet, but this one tiny step I've taken has already made a huge difference. I feel better. I can breathe again. Life doesn't feel like such a constant struggle. Jamie, it was good advice."

Jamie looked at me for a long time. Finally, he took a deep breath and squeezed my hand. There were tears in those blue, blue eyes when he whispered, "I am so proud of you, Sage. You deserve to breathe easy.

"You know what I keep wondering?" he went on. "What if I'm damaged too? What if this generational abuse is just destined to continue? What if I have a child someday and I can't be trusted to take care of him? Could I become a monster too?"

He choked on those words. Sam put his arm around Jamie, pulling him close, and I squeezed his hand tighter. I literally could not believe what I had heard. "Jamie, that is not even a possibility," I said. "You have the purest heart of anyone I know. You are good and kind to your core. If you have children they will be so lucky to have you as a daddy. Please believe that."

We stayed in our little huddle for a while, until Jamie finally nodded and looked at our faces. "I love you both so much."

"You'll never know how grateful I am for that," I said.

~43~

I had put off the phone call long enough. It was a difficult one to make, and I wasn't even sure why. It would be a pleasant one, I told myself. I was doing something kind, something that would be good for us both.

I called Marty's cell phone first. "I'm sorry, this number is not currently in service." I tried again: same message.

Next I tried his home number. No longer in service. I sat, phone in hand, wondering what to feel. Suddenly it was clear. I did not want to lose touch with Marty, not completely. Then I remembered the third number he'd given me and rummaged through my purse to find it. His dad and stepmom's number!

"Hello?" It was a woman's voice.

"Uh, hello. Is this Brenda?"

"Yes, who's calling?"

"Hi, Brenda, my name is Sage, I'm a friend of Marty's?"

There was a long silence.

"Hello?"

"Yes, I'm here," she said. "So you're looking for Marty?"

"Yes, I'd like to talk to him. He gave me your number in case I had no other way to reach him. And I guess, well, I don't have another way to reach him."

"I've heard a lot about you, Sage. Marty told us everything. You know, normally I mind my own business, and I'm sorry if I'm being rude. I will give you Marty's number because he wanted me to. But I want you to know something. He really cares for you. It broke his heart when things didn't work out between you and he decided to leave town. So if you..."

"He left town?"

"Yes, he's in Oregon. Cannon Beach. So if you..."

"What's he doing?"

"He's teaching sea kayaking down there. He's working out of a friend's surf shop. If it goes well he's going to be a full partner in the business."

"That's wonderful. That's a perfect business for him. Something he truly loves. I'm happy for him."

"Look, all I'm saying is that if you don't think you can love Marty, then maybe you should just leave him alone. Let him get over you. I know that what happened was tough. I know it's not an easy thing to get through. So if you can't get back to where you were with Marty, that's understandable. Just don't give him any wrong impressions, that's all I'm asking."

"Brenda? Marty told me a little bit about you, too. All good things. I'm glad you're so protective of him. He deserves that."

She gave me the number and we said good-bye.

I sat there for more than an hour before I made that call.

Days later, I made yet another difficult call.

"Dad?" That word still tasted a little sour in my mouth.

"Sage? Sage, is that you?"

Barely twenty-four hours after our discussion about our father, Jamie had called to say that he would of course go to the wedding with us. "I'd never let you go through that without me, doll. Besides, maybe the bastard really has changed. I suppose I do need to see for myself," he'd said. So I told him that I would RSVP for both of us, but I'd let some time pass to make sure Jamie didn't change his mind.

Now, here I was, accepting an invitation from the devil himself.

"Yes, it's me," I said. "I was thinking…well, Jamie and I were thinking that we would come to the wedding with Mary and Chloe, if the invitation is still open."

"Of course it is! Of course, you're all welcome."

"Thank you. But I have a question."

"Ask me anything."

"I'm asking this for Jamie. But he has no idea I'm doing this."

"What is it, Sage?"

"I would like Sam to come too. Jamie's boyfriend. He is so much a part of Jamie's life that it would be a lie for him not to be there. He is part of our family now, do you understand?"

He paused, just half a beat before he answered. "No, I don't suppose I'll ever really understand completely. But I understand love, Sage, and I guess Jamie must love this man."

"Yes, very much."

"Then he is welcome at my wedding."

Now I paused. "Really?"

"Yes. Really."

"Well, okay then, would it be all right if Sam's daughter comes, too?"

"Sam has a daughter?"

"Yes, sometimes gay people have children." I immediately regretted my sarcasm.

"Yes, of course. Bring whoever you want, the whole family. Thank you, Sage. You've made me…"

His voice broke. My father was crying.

"I'm sorry, Sagey. I don't mean to…I just…I'm so very happy you're all going to be there. It means so much to me."

This voice belonged to someone I didn't know. This man did not sound evil at all.

When I spoke again my voice sounded different. Softer. "It's okay. I just need all the details, and I promise we'll be there."

~44~

A few days later, I took possession of my very own store and slowly began turning it into a flower shop. So many details to attend to. The sign above the door: **WISEBUDS**. I liked it. It had a casual, fun feel. Mary painted flowers on the windows, and a mural of vines and buds across one wall. I set up the tables and equipment I would need and ordered my inventory. In one corner of the shop, I set up a small espresso stand and a couple of tables. I wanted people to shop for their flowers comfortably. And with plenty of caffeine to keep them lively. So I was the proud owner of two businesses in one!

Mona came to work for me as an assistant—and barista! Turned out she had worked at Starbucks years earlier and really knew how to make a mean latté. I couldn't pay her much, but she agreed to a percentage of profits—if we ever made a profit. Like me, she was through with the world of social work.

We opened the shop and started putting in long hours. Business was slow, but gradually picking up. I put ads in the paper and handed out flyers everywhere I went. A friend of Jamie's designed a website for us.

Weeks passed, and I watched my little business take wing. My two favorite scents—coffee and flowers—greeted me each morning. Early on, Mona and I screamed with excitement when orders came in, but soon it wasn't such a novelty anymore. I taught Mona to arrange flowers and she taught me to steam milk.

I loved putting flowers together, trying new color combinations, using unusual trimmings for bouquets. I had never felt so creative. So talented.

When my father found out I had opened a flower shop—from Mary, I later found out—he called, offering to cancel the order for his wedding flowers and use us. But I wouldn't let him do it, even though I really needed the work.

"It's too late," I said. "Weddings are a lot of work. I couldn't do that to another florist."

"You're a very moral person, Sage. I can't claim any responsibility for that, but I'm proud of you just the same."

I'd cut down on my time with Bridget. Now I saw her just once a month. We'd had one session since Jamie and I had decided to go to the wedding.

"Good for you! Are Mary and Chloe still going?"

"Yep. And he agreed to have Sam and Savannah there, too."

"Wow! That's wonderful, Sage. You and Jamie will have a lot of support. Remember that you can always leave if you're uncomfortable."

"I know. But everything you said before really makes sense to me now. I can check out this new life of my father's, see for myself how he interacts, who his friends are. I have no expectations. It's just that if I'm ever going to see him differently, this might be the place where it can begin to happen."

"Sounds like you have a very healthy attitude about it. I'm really proud of you, Sage."

I smiled, hearing that word again: proud.

Bridget continued. "Listen: I will be on call for you the day of your father's wedding. If anything happens that you need to talk about, call. I'll make sure my service knows to put you straight through to me, okay? So don't hesitate."

I nodded. "Thanks. But I'm sure I'll be okay. See you next time."

Next time would be in another month, we agreed, barring emergencies. We were testing the waters, and I was beginning to feel pretty seaworthy.

The day of my father's wedding, I left the shop in Mona's hands. I dashed home, put on a pretty dress, tucked Bridget's number in my purse, just in case, and drove to Jamie's to carpool with him, Sam and Savannah. Mary and Chloe were there too, and followed us in Mary's car.

It was a beautiful fall day and the wedding was held at a small venue overlooking Lake Union. The ceremony itself was lovely—the bride carried apricot and white roses and wore an ivory suit. There was little fanfare, but my father seemed truly happy.

At the reception, we introduced Dad and Wendy to Sam and Savannah. Dad shook Sam's hand and didn't even flinch.

Then he turned to Savannah. "Very nice to meet you. You know, Wendy is from a beautiful city named Savannah. I've been there, and you are even lovelier than your namesake."

He was a stranger, this man before me, but he was a kind and generous stranger. He was someone I might like to know.

I looked at our little group. Chloe was truly stunning; Jamie had styled her hair at last and it hung in long, loose waves. Sam and Jamie looked so handsome in their suits, and Savannah wore a beautiful, deep purple dress purchased by Auntie Sage, which was what she now called me. And Mary, dear Mary, in her laciest skirt, had put her arms around Jamie and me just before we were seated for the wedding. "This is a very healing moment for you, my darlings. For all of us."

When my father greeted Mary, they hugged for a long time. I saw him whisper to her; he brushed a tear away when they separated at last.

I loved my family, all of them: new members and old. I didn't really count my father among them, but at that moment I could almost imagine a time when I might.

Sadly, we learned that one of my father's sisters had died in recent years, but the other, Aunt Leona, was there. She too had just reconnected with our father. She'd come all the way from Rhode Island for the wedding. "Is it really you?" she asked Jamie and me before pulling us into her arms. "I'm so sorry we didn't keep in touch over the years. I'm going to give you my number and my address, and we just have to start over, all right?"

Before we left that night, my father borrowed a camera from the photographer and personally took a picture of Jamie, Sam, Mary, Chloe, Savannah and me. He promised he would send us copies.

After the reception, Mary was tired and decided to go straight home, but before she left she walked over and kissed me on the cheek. "I'm proud of you, Sage," she whispered.

"Thanks, Mary. Hey—what did my father say to you?"

She smiled. "He thanked me for forgiving him. He thanked me for any part I may have had in convincing you and Jamie to come today. So I thanked him for turning back into a human being. I said that I always knew he had it in him somewhere." Mary touched my arm, then said goodnight to everyone else and waved to all of us as she walked through the door.

The rest of us decided to leave soon afterward. We decided not to say good-bye to the groom, since he was surrounded by a group of his friends. But my father saw us heading toward the door and sprinted across the room to say good-bye. He was glowing. "I just can't thank you enough for being here," he said. He looked from my face to Jamie's. "It meant…everything to me. Sam, Savannah, so nice to have met you. Chloe, wonderful to see you again, honey. Please, please, allow me to take you all to dinner when I get back from my honeymoon. Please," he said again, and again: "Please."

Much to my surprise, Jamie spoke first. "Well, call us when you get back. Where are you going, anyway?"

"Just over to Coeur d'Alene. Lucy's death made me remember that place. I always thought it was beautiful. So we're staying at the resort, playing a little golf. It'll be nice, I think. We'll be back in two weeks. I'll call you. But I'll send those pictures to you before we leave, I promise."

We didn't hug; he didn't even try. He just stood for a moment, looking at us, then waved a salute toward the whole group, turned and walked back to his bride.

No one wanted to say goodnight yet, so we decided to go to my house. Savannah fell asleep in the guest room and the rest of us drank wine and talked.

Chloe spoke after we'd settled in a bit. "Something happened the other day that I'd really like to tell you about. You know, I was pretty depressed for a while there. I know I've been a little difficult to be around at times. And I'm sorry, I really am."

"You don't have to apologize, Chloe," I said.

"I know. But that makes me want to more. Anyway, I've been moping around about Paul leaving me and having a child with someone else, ruining my life, stopping the world on its axis, et cetera, et cetera. Well, a few days ago, I was shopping downtown. I was passing by a shop with baby clothes in the window and I looked in. I couldn't help it—all those tiny outfits, just waiting for a brand new baby to wear them. So I was looking at all this baby stuff, on the verge of tears, and I looked up and there was Paul, inside the shop."

"Oh my god!" I said.

"Yep, and he was with Pregnant Nicki. And, get this—they were fighting. Screaming at each other! I couldn't really hear what they were saying, but I could sure read the body language! At one point, he looked away from her for just a moment, and I could see it all in his face: the panic, the regret. I'm sure he was thinking, 'What have I done?' And I realized that my life is where it is because of my choices. I could have left Paul ages ago. If it were that important to me to have a baby, I would have left him and found someone who wanted one! Instead I convinced myself I was happy enough with him to give up on that dream. And a thousand others. I did this. Paul is, as you have often said, Sage, pathetic. I feel sorry for him. But I'm not going to feel sorry for myself anymore. I'm going to figure out what I truly want and go get it."

"Good for you! Did Paul see you?"

"I don't think so. I moved on and didn't look back."

"That's what it sounds like you've done, all right," Jamie said.

"I have something to say, too," I said. "I've been in touch with Marty."

"Really?" they all said at once.

"Yeah. He moved to Oregon and started a business. He's already talking about coming back, but we're taking things slow. We're going to visit each other now and then and just see what happens. I told him that I was shell-shocked for a while and didn't know what I felt. And now, I realize I really miss him and I want to give it another try. And so does he!"

And then everyone was talking at once, hugging me, patting me on the back. "So I guess you all approve?"

Jamie smiled before he spoke. "You know, I understand the moral dilemma you have about what Marty did. It's a big one. He had a split second to make a decision, and he made it. It probably wasn't the right one, but it may have saved my sister's life. So from my point of view, I'm very selfishly happy that he did what he did. I don't believe he would ever be a dangerous guy. Someone had pointed a gun at both of you, had told you he was going to kill you. Marty took control and reacted to the situation. I think he's a good man, Sage."

"I believe that, too. I'm a little angry with myself for taking so long to come to that conclusion. Initially I wanted to call him to apologize. I felt like his whole life had been turned upside down because he just happened to meet me. This huge life-altering event happened to him just because he was seeing me. It hit me hard when I realized that and I wanted to say something, do something to let him know that I understood and I was just sorry that it all came down the way it did."

"But Sage, Marty knew before you started dating that Colin was abusive. He knew what he was getting into, better than most men would," Chloe said.

"He was probably drawn to you partly because you'd been abused. He cared about you and wanted to protect you," said Sam.

"I think that's true," I said. "He admitted that he threatened Colin that time he showed up with the roses. I still can't believe that's all it took to convince Colin to stay away."

Jamie looked away.

"Jamie?" He wouldn't look at me. "What is it?"

"Oh, all right, I don't suppose it matters now, anyway. After that night, when Colin left the roses at the door? I paid Mr. Prescott a little visit."

"You did? What did you say?"

"I told him that I knew everything that he'd done to you. That we had hospital records and that I was willing to perjure myself and swear that I'd witnessed a beating. I said that I was pretty sure I could get other 'witnesses' to volunteer as well. Basically I said that if he didn't leave you alone, I would ruin his life. His career, his money, the reputation he was so proud of, it would all be gone. Still think I have such a pure heart?"

"Wow. God, Jamie, what if he'd hurt you?" I said. "What if..."

"Sage, nothing happened to me. It's all over. But I had to do something. I knew he'd never stop coming after you. Well, he backed off for a while at least."

"You say I'm your protector, but you're the one who's been looking after me, for quite a while now. You do! You talk me down when I'm upset, you call me almost every day. Now I find out you threatened Colin. Thanks for looking out for me, little brother."

"We look out for each other, Sage. Always have, always will. As for Marty, Sam is right. Marty is definitely a rescuer. There's no reason to blame yourself for his choices. They were his to make. You know that. You've taken responsibility for your bad decisions. Colin was an abusive bastard, but you allowed him into your life. There are reasons, there are explanations that help me understand some of the choices you've made, but ultimately you are the one who made them. It's the same for Marty."

I nodded. "You know something? I'm getting a little tired of learning and growing through adversity and mistakes. Why can't I figure out how to be smart *before* I go through all this crap?"

"Yeah! Why can't we be wise along the way, when we need to be, instead of having to learn so many things the hard way?" Chloe said.

Jamie shrugged. "I don't know. But no one seems to be immune from the crap. I guess you just have to hope that you'll be smarter for the next challenge that comes along. Because there's no doubt that it will."

~45~

My fourth month as a businesswoman began with a flurry of activity. I landed my first big wedding, then my second, then a couple of funerals, all in the first week.

I was sitting at a table with a bride-to-be one morning, sipping coffee while she flipped through a catalogue, when the bell on the door rang, announcing the arrival of another customer. I looked up to smile at whoever it was.

It was Rachel, and my smile widened. "Hey!" I excused myself from my bride and ran to Rachel; she hugged me tight.

"It's so good to see you, Sage! I've missed you so much."

"I've missed you, too. I've been thinking about you a lot. I keep meaning to come to the office for a visit, but I've been so busy with the shop."

"Well, I'm here as a customer, actually. I've heard such great things about your shop. Next week is my parents' fortieth anniversary and I want to order flowers for their party."

I knew she could have gone anywhere for the flowers. "Thank you, Rachel," I said quietly. "What do you have in mind?"

Mona greeted Rachel as well, then took over with the bride so I could help Rachel. We discussed table arrangements, corsages and boutonnieres. Inevitably, we shifted into office gossip. Rachel got me caught up on all the news: dear Ruth, the cookie-maker, had become so forgetful that her son had moved her into an assisted living facility. Molly was now everyone's favorite client—no surprise there. Althea was engaged to a commercial airline pilot! "They're going on a photo safari in Kenya for their honeymoon. She's really happy."

"That's wonderful! I'll have to send her a gift," I said.

"She'd love that," Rachel said. Her smile faded a bit then. "Uh, Sage, there's something else. Something that just happened recently. Elma Crow died. Her homecare assistant found her, and the medics said that she'd been dead for days. Isn't that terrible? What a sad, lonely woman."

"Was Michelle still her assistant?" I glanced at Mona.

"Yeah. I know, I feel really bad for her, too. But she was a complete professional, as always. She called 911 and stayed until they took her away. No one could find a single phone number to call, no friends, no family. Anyway, she's going to be buried in that cemetery just a few blocks away from the office. What's it called? Green Pastures, I think, or something like that."

"Yeah, that's it."

"I don't know why, really, but I made some calls and found out there won't be any services. She's just being buried there tomorrow morning. Again, I'm not sure why, but I thought you might like to know."

I asked about more pleasant things, then: Rachel's family, her vacation plans, other co-workers. We finalized her order and hugged good-bye.

Our bride was finished looking through catalogues and ready to make some decisions. Taking a deep breath, I went over to help.

Later, as we were closing for the night, Mona said, "I think I'll send Michelle a card. That had to be a tough day for her."

"That would be nice. I'm sure she'd love to hear from you."

"Hey. Feel like a cappuccino before we go?"

"I'd love one."

Mona worked her magic and we sat together, warm frothy coffee in hand.

"Well," Mona said, "Here's to the tragic life and death of Elma Crow."

"Here's to lost souls everywhere," I replied.

I went to the shop early the next morning, two hours before we opened. Standing in front of the cooler, I took a quick inventory of the flowers in stock, then opened the door and grabbed handfuls of roses, irises and lilies. I arranged them quickly and went back for more. The bouquet grew into something I had not planned; it was enormous and colorful and complicated. Twisted twigs finished it off—the arrangement was delicate, but at the same time, bristly.

Mona arrived as I was leaving. "I'll be back in an hour," I told her.

At the cemetery, I stopped at the office to ask directions and was given a map with an X in black felt pen marking the spot. The employee thought the work on the grave was completed, but she wasn't certain.

But the burial was indeed over when I arrived. The grave was fresh, the headstone small and spare. There was a name, Elma Crow, and dates: 1931-2014. A beginning, an end.

I put the flowers down beside the marker. They dwarfed it. "Well, Elma, here we are. I'm sorry for intruding, but I have a few things to say to you. I have a lot of apologies, actually. So, here goes. I'm sorry your life was so miserable. I'm sorry you died alone and unloved. And I'm sorry I never asked for your story. What turned you into the person you were? I would truly like to know that now. I'm sorry I was so caught up in my own life and my reaction to you that I didn't think to care about any of that. Now it's too late, and I'm sorry for that, too."

Behind me, I heard a sound that seemed somehow inevitable. "Caw! Caw!" Slowly I turned, and there it was: a lone crow sitting a few feet away, head tilted, eyeing me.

"You're not really so tough, are you?" I asked. The bird spread its black wings and flapped them at me twice before catching the wind and taking flight. I watched it disappear into the distance. "Be at peace," I whispered.

I looked back at the headstone, at the stark parameters of Elma's life, and I alone cried for her.

My cell phone rang before I reached my car: Jamie. He wasn't calling every day anymore. He had opened his very own salon just a few weeks earlier—Chez J—and it was already gaining a reputation as a chic, high-end salon. We were both busy now. And happy.

"Hello, baby brother!"

"Hey, Sagey. Before you ask, Sam is fine, life is wonderful, et cetera, et cetera. But I do have some bad news. Bobby died a few days ago."

Bobby. Jamie's hospice client that I'd met on our way to Spokane. It seemed like such a long time ago now. "I'm so sorry, Jamie."

"Well, I hate clichés, but it really was for the best. He was suffering so badly at the end. I just feel for Noel. Anyway, I want to send flowers to the apartment and to the funeral home. Huge arrangements, okay?"

I smiled. So far, Jamie had sent flowers to all his friends at least once, and he'd set up reminders with the shop so that we automatically sent out bouquets on his friends' birthdays and anniversaries. I supplied fresh arrangements to the shop regularly. And I knew he was referring his clients to me as well. "Thank you, Jamieson. But I'm not at the shop right now. I'll call you back for all the details when I get there."

"Perfect. Talk to you then, doll."

Driving back to the shop, I thought about Bobby. I had met him only once, as he was slipping away from his brief life. I wondered what he had been like before he got sick. What were his dreams, his ambitions? Had any of them come to pass?

One thing was certain: he had fallen in love and remained in love with the same person until his death. That was something—something that was denied many. Maybe Bobby was not someone to be pitied at all.

Mona was giddy when I arrived at the shop. "We got another wedding, Sage! Erin, your office receptionist! Isn't that great? It's going to be a huge wedding, too, I guess they both have big families."

"That's wonderful!"

"And we have lots of time for this one—it's not until next spring."

"Fabulous!"

"I know! Hey—want a celebratory cappuccino?"

I was trying to keep my intake to three coffee drinks per day and I was already at my limit, but I was considering the offer when someone walked through the door of the shop.

I couldn't believe my eyes. It was the beautiful bully, the woman I had so admired before she publicly skewered me. Rachel had defended me so valiantly she'd actually apologized. To Rachel.

The woman glided through the shop, looking at the flowers in the cooler, the vases on the shelves. I watched her until she looked our way at last. There was no recognition in her eyes as she spoke. "I need an exceptional bouquet for a very wealthy friend. This is an extremely successful and well-known person in the area. So you see the bouquet must be something special. What would you suggest?"

My mind raced. Should I help this woman? Perhaps she would have a lot of important connections. We could win her over and become the most trusted florists in the business! Perhaps all of Seattle's elite would get their flowers only from us! I had to come up with a really great suggestion.

"Well, how about some tropical flowers? We just got some in, so they're really fresh. That would be an unusual choice, and very elegant."

She looked down on me with her cold, hard eyes. "This friend is very successful, as I mentioned. She often goes to the tropics, so you see tropical flowers would not be impressive to her at all. Do you understand?"

"Yes, I do understand. All right, what about roses—a classic choice! We have some unusual colors and I think several bright colors of roses make a spectacular bouquet. What do you think?"

"I think roses would be exceptionally mundane. Any other ideas?"

"Dendrobium orchids?"

"Dull."

"Chocolate lilies?"

"Also known as skunk lilies? No thank you. Clearly I've come to the wrong place."

My heart began to speed up. I looked at the floor and took a deep breath. "Tell me exactly what I could have said to impress you."

"Hmm?"

"What did you have in mind?"

"Oh. Well, I'm not sure. Something impressive."

"Okay. What does impressive mean to you? Big? Artistic?"

"Unusual, I suppose."

"Perfect! I think I have the answer." I'd been working on a new project—a line I called The Palette. Each bouquet was one-of-a-kind and put together in unique and interesting ways. I just happened to have one in the back room cooler, so I walked over to get it, hoping it still looked fresh. It did.

The flowers—deep red and orange roses—were arranged in three double rows: short in the front and progressively taller to the back rows. There were no trimmings, no ribbon, no greens, no baby's breath, and the vase was simple as well, just a large rectangle of green blown glass.

I watched my adversary's face carefully as I walked out with my creation. For just a brief moment, I could see that she was impressed.

"I know you said you didn't want roses, but is this the kind of thing you were thinking?"

"It's definitely closer. Yes, I think that will do."

"Great!"

I could feel her watching me as I rang her up.

"Wait a minute. We've met, haven't we?" she said.

"No, actually, we have not met. You demanded my name once and did not give me yours." I looked up at her. "We can start over, though." I looked at her credit card before I gave it back to her. "Very nice to meet you, Pamela. I'm Sage. This is my partner, Mona. I'm glad we were able to find something suitable for you."

She was trying to place me, I knew, and I didn't think it would take long before it all clicked into place.

Sure enough, I saw the recognition in her eyes before she signed the receipt. She tapped the pen against the counter.

"Sage. Yes. Well, I owe you two apologies, I suppose. One for, well, you know. And the second for not apologizing at the time it happened. I was in a bad place that day and I was overly sensitive. Apparently, I jumped to the wrong conclusion. I am a person of strong opinions and sometimes I express them before I have all the information. For that I am sorry."

I smiled. My heart was once again beating at its normal rate. I took a nice, long, deep breath. "Hey, we all have bad days. The important thing is to learn from them, right? Have you taken the bar exam yet? How did you do?"

Now Pamela smiled. "I took it last month and I passed! I was so relieved." She signed the receipt at last and handed it to me. "I am really sorry, Sage. I can see that you are a kind and gracious person. And I love your flowers. I'll see you again, I'm sure."

I held the door for her as she left. As soon as the door closed, Mona started clapping. "Yeah! Way to go, partner! I can't wait to hear this story!"

And so, before I called Jamie at last, I told the tale of Pamela—a story with a very different ending than I ever would have imagined.

~46~

It was a Saturday afternoon when Althea Markham walked into the shop. I was on the phone, and motioned to her that I would be one minute. I wrapped up as quickly as possible. "Well, the yellow roses aren't really in great shape right now. How about pink?" Usually I was pretty successful in talking people out of yellow roses. I still couldn't stand looking at them. "Great! Okay, got it. They will be delivered after 3 PM tomorrow. Thank you!"

I hung up the phone and rushed over to Althea. "Hey! It's so wonderful to see you! How are you?"

"You look fabulous, Sage! Let me take a good look at you. Yes, this new career must agree with you. And I am very well, thank you. Don't know if the grapevine has stretched out this far, but I am getting married."

"Yes, the grapevine has followed me. I heard. Congratulations! I'm thrilled for you! When is the big day?"

"December twentieth. A Christmas wedding. It's going to be in the evening, very elegant. Black, red and white. I'm thinking my bridesmaids will carry white flowers and my bouquet will be red roses. What do you think?"

"I think it will be exquisite!"

"Will you do my flowers?"

"I would be honored, Althea. Thank you!"

Althea knew exactly what she wanted, so it didn't take long to finalize the complete order for her wedding. Afterward, Mona made coffee for us and we chatted a bit.

As she was leaving, Althea stopped at the door. "Please email me your address when you get a chance, Sage. I'm hoping you can attend the wedding, too. Not as my florist, but as my friend."

"I'll be there," I said. "That means a lot to me, Althea."

"It means a lot to me, too. Congratulations on your new life, Sage. It's clear you're happy. I'm so pleased for you."

I watched her walk away. "Wow. Althea Markham is my friend. I feel like I've evolved into a higher life form."

"No, Sage. You've just found your calling, and good things will come to you now. To both of us, I'm sure of it."

"To both of us," I said, lifting my coffee cup in a toast.

The following Friday I almost forgot about my scheduled session with Bridget, but when I saw it on my calendar I looked forward to seeing her. It would be the first time since my father's wedding.

"So it went well, then," she said after I described the evening. I'm so glad. Have you been in touch with your dad since then?"

"Yeah, we've talked on the phone a couple of times. I think Jamie and I will go out to dinner with him together the first time. I'm supposed to call him when we're ready to see him."

"Dinner is a good idea. That will give you a chance just to talk. And you'll be in a public place, so you'll probably keep it fairly light. That will be a good start."

"I think so."

"And how is business?"

"It's building. We've had a really good month so far, and orders are already starting to come in for the holiday season. We've got a wedding close to Christmas, too. We're getting busy."

"Are you enjoying it?"

"I love it. I never thought I could enjoy what I do for a living so much. It's not like work to me at all. Mona and I work really well together and we just have fun at it. She is now a full partner.

"You know, at times I've thought it was kind of a frivolous career, that it wasn't important in the grand scheme of things. But Jamie helped me put things in perspective. He said it was just like cutting hair. When a client leaves his chair feeling great about how she looks, she's going to carry that with her. Maybe she'll treat people a little better, you know, respond better if someone cuts her off on the highway. Maybe it will have a ripple effect on countless people down the line. So it has to be the same for me. I'm helping people do really nice things for each other. I'm helping them say 'I love you' or 'I'm sorry' or 'Happy Anniversary.' I'm helping to make weddings memorable. Flowers even comfort someone who's grieving. I think I'm making a valuable contribution."

"I agree completely," Bridget said.

"And I'm not too worried about money. Now that we've sold my grandmother's house the pressure is off a bit. Life is good." Rose had found us a great real estate agent who helped us set a price, and the house had sold in two weeks. After the sale closed, I'd sent Rose three dozen red roses as a thank you, and she had gushed on the phone for an hour.

"We've even hired a delivery person, part-time to begin with, but we'll see," I continued. Until our new hire, Mona and I were taking turns delivering. "We found a woman whose kids are in school during the day. She just wants a little extra money. She uses her own mini-van—with a gas allowance—and she says that so far she loves the job. Everyone is so happy when flowers arrive! Anyway, she's working out really well, and now I don't have to work such long hours. So I've started something else. I'm volunteering for the hospice program that Jamie is involved with. I just go into people's homes a couple of times a month and help out. I clean for them, cook a couple of casseroles for them to freeze. Sometimes I just talk to them. I bring them flowers, too, give them something beautiful to look at."

"That sounds wonderful, Sage. I guess you weren't completely finished with social work after all."

"I suppose I wasn't. I feel like I'm really making a difference for people. Both at work and through hospice. That's all I ever wanted. I'm also thinking that at some point I'd like to volunteer at a domestic violence shelter. I'm not sure what I'd do exactly, but I really want to help women in those situations. I feel so fortunate to be alive, and I just want to encourage others to escape. To survive."

"I think that's a terrific idea, Sage. When you're ready, I have contacts I could put you in touch with."

"That would be great, Bridget. Thanks."

"So things are really coming together for you."

"Yes. That's exactly how it feels."

Bridget grinned. "It's a great feeling, isn't it? Take some time to drink it all in, Sage. You deserve it. And how are things going with Marty?"

"Slowly. We talk on the phone at least once a week. We have great conversations. Sometimes for hours. But we both agree that there's no need to rush anything, especially since we're so far apart. Sometimes he says that he should just move back, that the longer he stays down there and builds up his business, the harder it will be to pull up stakes and move again."

"That does kind of make sense. He's saying that if he's going to move back it should be sooner rather than later. He's asking you if there is a reason for him to move back. Is there?"

"Well, his family is here."

"Sage, that's not what I mean."

"I know. I do feel that there is something between us. I think it could go somewhere."

"Then maybe it's time to tell him that."

"Maybe. I just don't want him to shut down his business, move back here, and then not have things work out between us. I don't want to disrupt his life for nothing."

"That's his risk to take. His choice. There are no guarantees for either of you."

"For once I'd like to have all the answers. I'd like to know what the right choice is now, before I decide. Just for once, can't I know for sure I'm doing the right thing?"

Bridget shook her head. "Nope, sorry. You're stuck here in the muck with the rest of us. Floundering sometimes, making guesses, taking chances. Living life. That's all we can do, Sage. Learn from the past and make our best guesses about the future. Hopefully we can make smarter and healthier choices as we go. The question is: What does your gut tell you about Marty?"

"All I truly know is that I can't bear the idea of not having him in my life."

"You two need to see each other face to face. You have to tell him how you feel, Sage. So that *he* can make his best guess."

"Maybe you're right."

Bridget sat back in her giant chair and grinned at me.

"I'm so happy for you, Sage," she said. "You've come such a long way. You've really grown in the time I've been seeing you. And no more anxiety attacks?"

"No. Not since the one I had here. Whenever I feel anxious about anything, I just take a few deep breaths and I'm able to face whatever is causing it. I feel really great these days, Bridget. Thanks for all your help."

"You're the one who did the work, Sage. I just nudged you in the right direction every so often. So thank you, for trusting me."

"This is starting to feel like we're saying good-bye," I said.

"Well, that's up to you. I think you're in a really good place right now. You'll be just fine without me. If you don't feel ready to stop, we can continue, but I think you're ready."

"I think so too," I said.

"However, if anything ever comes up for you, anytime at all, call me up and we'll meet again. You'll always be my client now, Sage. I will always be here if you need me."

There was so much to feel as I walked down the stairs. I was so proud of myself! So triumphant! And yet, calm. Peaceful. And sad to leave Bridget behind. I would miss her. I was even a little scared of life without her. But as she said, she would always be there for me. If I ever needed a safety net, she would be there, waiting to hold me gently until I found my footing once more.

When I got home that night I greeted Teddy, then picked up the phone.

"Hi, Marty. It's me. Hey—I was wondering. Do you have plans for your next day off? Yeah, I'm thinking it's time for us to get together. What do you say?"

The reaction I got was…unexpected. Marty's busiest workdays were Saturday and Sunday, but because my shop was closed Sundays, he insisted on taking that Sunday off and driving up. He left in the wee hours of the morning and arrived at my door before my second cup of coffee.

We both started to say something, and then suddenly we were just clinging to each other, holding on tight.

"I'm in love with you, Sage," he whispered.

I looked at his face, his kind, gentle face. Marty had committed a terrible, violent act under terrible, violent circumstances. He had done it to protect me. To save my life, the life that now felt so precious. I'd been afraid that one moment was all I would ever see when I looked at him. Now it all seemed so far away, blurry and faded as an old photograph. "I love you, too, Marty," I said.

We spent the day catching up, snuggling on the sofa. Teddy spent much of it on Marty's lap. At one point Marty was rubbing Teddy's neck and just out of nowhere he said, "Did you know that cats are the most recently domesticated of all animals?"

I grinned at him.

Marty and I hadn't made love yet, but we both seemed to understand that there was still no need to rush. Today we just enjoyed a long, lazy, uncomplicated day together.

My Sunday evening had already been planned, and so Marty simply became part of the plan. We spent the evening having dinner at Mary's with the whole family: Chloe, Jamie, Sam and Savannah, Mary herself of course, and even Molly joined us this time, with her new gentleman friend, as she called him.

I had warned Chloe ahead of time that I was bringing Marty, but we surprised Jamie and Sam. "Marty!" Jamie yelled from across the room. "Great to see you," he said.

"You too, Jamie," Marty said, and held his hand out. Jamie brushed it aside and gave him a hug.

I introduced Marty to those he hadn't met, and then Molly cleared her throat. "Everyone, I want you to meet Leo, my gentleman friend. Leo and I met at a PFlag meeting."

"Molly! I didn't know you joined PFlag. That's great!" I said.

"PFlag?" Marty asked.

"Oh, you know, it's for people who have gay family members. We meet once a month, and it's just been so helpful," Molly said.

"It stands for Parents, Family and Friends of Lesbians and Gays," I added.

"And bisexuals and transgenders," said Sam. "Jamie's the one who recommended it to Mom."

"Yes, and I'm so glad I joined. I've learned so much! Leo's daughter is a lesbian," Molly said. "He helps to counsel people now. You know, when they first find out, some people have a hard time adjusting. Isn't that sad?"

I caught Sam winking at Jamie. Leo just smiled and patted Molly's hand.

Savannah showed me pictures of her new kitten. "He's black and white. Dad said he's a tuxedo cat. I named him Oscar. You've got to come see him, Auntie Sage!"

I grinned. "I will soon, I promise."

Sunday dinners had become a tradition over the last few months; Mary had begun to invite us each week, and I suggested we carve it in stone. Losing Grandma Lucy had taught me a valuable lesson. I was not going to take anyone I loved for granted, ever again.

The guest list varied a little from week to week, but the core group always attended: Chloe, Jamie, Sam and me, and our wonderful hostess, Mary. Now I looked from one to another, as we sat at Mary's table. How I loved these faces, this cast of characters I'd been so fortunate to collect.

Marty sat beside me and touched my hand under the table. Conversation flowed as we enjoyed Mary's delicious meal. We were all happy tonight, excited about our lives. Chloe shared stories about her first few weeks of teaching; she described moments of triumph, of inspiration. "Teaching really is what I was meant to do," she said. "I was feeling sorry for myself about not having children—well now I have thirty!"

Sam announced that Chez J had suddenly become THE salon for local celebrities. A Seattle news anchor had stopped in one day for a cut, then apparently spread the word about Jamie's talent! Now the salon was to be featured soon on Evening Magazine! They would be filming the segment the following week.

My good news—Marty's presence—spoke for itself.

"Well, I believe champagne is clearly in order," Mary said. She brought out a bottle, popped and poured—and gave Savannah ginger ale in a champagne flute. "I'd like to propose a toast," Mary said. "To the good times. May we savor them while they are here, and may they outnumber and outweigh the bad times for us all."

"To the good times," we all repeated.

Across the table, Molly nudged Jamie. "Go on, tell them!" she said.

"Okay, okay!" Jamie laughed and stood up. "I actually have one more announcement. As exciting as Evening Magazine may be, we have even more important news. Sam, Savannah and I have decided to move in together!"

I looked from Jamie to Sam. They both beamed. Sam rose, standing next to Jamie, and raised his glass. "To Sage, who knew from the beginning that Jamie and I belonged together. How wise you are, indeed."

"To Sage!" everyone said. My face hurt from grinning so wide. I raced over and hugged Jamie and Sam both at once. Savannah joined us and I cried with joy for them, for myself, for the whole wide wonderful world.

At that moment, I realized something. I knew it in my bones, with more certainty than I'd ever known anything before. I knew that my days of being abused were over. There was another way to live. Another way to think, and feel, and be. If necessary, I would protect myself as I would anyone else I loved. And I would, from that precious moment on, accept that love is by nature gentle and kind. I would hold this knowledge as sacred and unshakable. In love, even for myself, I would be wise. I deserved that, after all.

"Such wonderful news," Mary said, and for a moment I thought she was speaking of my silent epiphany. "Have you found a place yet?"

"No, but we're looking," Jamie said. "We're going to buy a house."

"That's fantastic!" I said.

"Sit down, everyone, and I'll dish up dessert," Mary said.

Chloe and I automatically followed her into the kitchen to help. I turned around at the doorway and saw Marty watching me, grinning.

Would we be making a similar announcement at a future Sunday dinner? It was too soon to know, of course. But I did have hope.

Hope. I had allowed it into my life at last. Dishing up Mary's peach cobbler, I marveled at the changes hope had made. It occurred to me that, as we strive to be wise, we must never abandon hope. Maybe hope, and having the resolve to embrace it, is itself the most important step toward wisdom we can take.

I doubted that I would ever forget this night. And yet, if I were very lucky, perhaps it would eventually blend into a multitude of other such happy evenings. As Mary, Chloe and I served the cobbler, I imagined a time years from now when this one evening had become, at last, just part of a lovely blur.

~47~

Somehow I'd forgotten all about setting up the coffee maker Sunday night, so Monday morning I rose early, threw on my thickest robe, brewed a pot, then took a cup out to the little table on my patio. Monday—a day I'd once so dreaded—was now a day off I had granted myself. I loved my new boss!

I'd recently hung a beautiful blown-glass hummingbird feeder—Mary's housewarming gift—but so far had had no takers. Mary had told me that it might take some time for the local birds to incorporate a new feeder into their daily routine. I took another sip, watching the feeder anyway.

And there he was: a male Anna's, hovering next to the feeder. I froze, and he dipped his beak into the nectar several times, his crimson neck radiant in the morning sun. Then he hovered again, watching me for a few seconds before buzzing away.

I remembered, as a child, asking Mary about the bird's name. "Who is Anna? Why is it hers?"

Anna. And of course my mind went to the only Anna it could. The Anna that Colin had killed. The Anna whose daddy had taught her to love and protect herself. The one who could not understand someone who cowered and remained silent.

"I'm so sorry, Anna," I whispered. "I wish you were here to see how well I've healed." And as irrational as it was, I promised Anna I would take care of her tiny, beautiful birds.

Marty appeared and I rose to greet him. He brushed the hair back from my face and kissed me deeply. When I opened my eyes to see him watching me, my face burned. "I wonder if you'll always be able to make me blush," I said.

He grinned. "I hope so."

We had another glorious day together and Marty left that night. He would be busy for a while, packing up and moving back, starting his business back up in a different area. Two days—and one amazing night—together made us realize that we no longer wanted to take things slowly. We wanted to be together now. It felt like a very wise move.

When he was gone, I sat with Teddy on the couch, enjoying his loud purr. On my mantel was the photograph that my father had taken at his wedding. He had sent a framed copy to each of us. It was a great picture; everyone looked so happy. My father had sent a note in the package: *An embarrassment of riches, these bright, healthy, beautiful children of mine. Let's get together soon. Love, Dad.*

Love, Dad. Two words that until recently I could never have imagined putting together.

I didn't know whether my past would ever haunt me again. But I knew that I had fundamentally changed. I knew that I would choose happiness; I would not become trapped in anger and bitterness. I would try to be a little more understanding with those who do fall into those tricky snares. I would be kinder and more forgiving—even to myself. And I would allow love into my life, in all its strange and precious forms.

Teddy rolled onto his back and I rubbed his belly. His purr revved up even more. He had always been able to soothe me. Now I seemed able to return the favor. Closing my eyes, I drank in the absolute peace and joy of this little moment.

The National Domestic Violence Hotline provides education and access to organizations helping survivors escape abusive situations. Call 1-800-799-SAFE (7233) or TTY 1-800-787-3224, or visit www.ndvh.org.

PFLAG—Parents, Families & Friends of Lesbians & Gays—is a national non-profit organization that helps to provide education about issues affecting gay, lesbian bisexual and transgender people. They also serve as a support to family members and friends of gays and lesbians. You may find more information at www.pflag.org and www.gayisnormal.com.

Made in the USA
San Bernardino, CA
28 August 2016